D0062082

ALSO BY A. B. DANIEL

Incas: The Puma's Shadow

INCAS

BOOK II
THE GOLD OF CUZCO

A. B. DANIEL

TRANSLATED BY ALEX GILLY

A TOUCHSTONE BOOK
PUBLISHED BY SIMON & SCHUSTER
New York   London   Toronto   Sydney   Singapore

TOUCHSTONE
Rockefeller Center
1230 Avenue of the Americas
New York, NY 10020

This book is a work of fiction. Names, characters, places, and incidents either are products of the author's imagination or are used fictitiously. Any resemblance to actual events or locales or persons, living or dead, is entirely coincidental.

International rights management for XO Editions: Susanna Lea Associates
Copyright © 2001 by XO Editions. All rights reserved.
English translation copyright © 2002 by Alex Gilly

All rights reserved, including the right of reproduction in whole or in part in any form.

First Touchstone edition 2002
Published by arrangement with XO S.A.
English language translation published by arrangement with
Simon & Schuster UK Ltd.
Originally published in France in 2001 as
Inca: L'Or de Cuzco by XO S.A.

TOUCHSTONE and colophon are registered trademarks of
Simon & Schuster, Inc.
For information regarding special discounts for bulk purchases,
please contact Simon & Schuster Special Sales at 1-800-456-6798 or
business@simonandschuster.com

Manufactured in the United States of America

1 3 5 7 9 10 8 6 4 2

Library of Congress Cataloging-in-Publication Data is available.

ISBN 0-7434-3275-4

INCAS

BOOK II
THE GOLD OF CUZCO

Tropic of Cancer

Atlantic
Ocean

Panama

Orinoco

Equator

Quito

Tumebama

Tumbez

Amazon

Cajamarca

Madeira

Hatun Sausa

Lima

Cuzco

Titicaca

Pacific
Ocean

Paraguay

Tupiza

Tropic of Capricorn

1,000 kilometers

Furthest extent of
the Incan empire

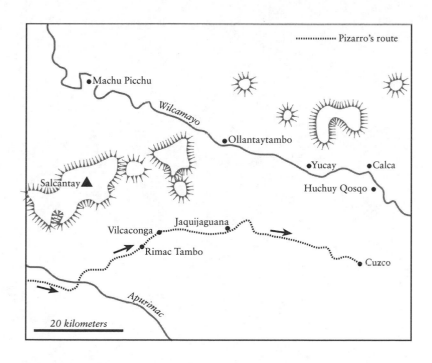

.... Pizarro's route

Machu Picchu

Wilcamayo

Ollantaytambo

Yucay ● Calca

Huchuy Qosqo ●

Salcantay ▲

Vilcaconga ● Jaquijaguana

Rimac Tambo

Cuzco

Apurimac

20 kilometers

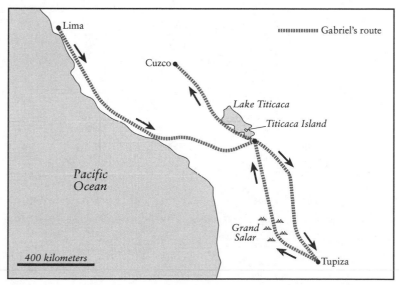

Lima

Gabriel's route

Cuzco ●

Lake Titicaca

Titicaca Island

Pacific
Ocean

Grand
Salar

Tupiza

400 kilometers

PROLOGUE

The Huaylas Cordillera, April 5, 1533

On foot, leading his horse by the bridle, and carefully choosing his step through the crumbly rocks, Gabriel pressed on. He was preceded only by two porters carting the tent canvases. The path was just wide enough so that his bay followed without shying.

They had been traveling blind along a clifftop since dawn, pressing on through a fog so thick that they hadn't been able to see either the sky above or the river grumbling angrily far below. But now the fog cleared from the bottom of the cliff as though suddenly inhaled into a giant's mouth. It stretched itself thin, gathered up in parts, and shredded itself on the sharp rocky edges. A lukewarm breath of air caressed Gabriel's face.

He blinked, put one hand on his horse's shoulder, and came to a halt. In an instant, the light became dazzling, the sky a pure blue.

And in this lucidity he realized that they were only halfway along the cliff's ledge. The path didn't lead up into a great valley as they had imagined, but rather into a breach in the mountainside, a gully so narrow that it seemed to have been cleaved open with a giant axe. A myriad of luxuriant plants and lichens clinging to the cliff face sparkled humidly under the sun. Six hundred feet below, the swirling river, fattened by the recent rains, growled like a wildcat. It was so full of earth and pebbles torn from its banks that its water was now a dark ocher color, as thick as the mud that the Incas used to cob walls. Tree trunks, branches, clumps of grass, orchids, and *cantutas* occasionally floated by.

Gabriel glanced back at the long column following some distance behind him. It looked like an immense, variegated snake against the verdurous rock. The column was headed by a hundred or so porters stooping under their loads of gold; following them were almost as many llamas, packed like donkeys; then came the Spaniards, pulling their horses along by the reins, Hernando Pizarro's blood-red feather sticking out of his silver-plated morion; and finally, the big dais of their favorite "guest," the Inca general Chalkuchimac.

Gabriel had left Cajamarca five weeks earlier to join Hernando, who had gone south in search of gold: as much gold as he could possibly get his hands on. This was the return journey, and their mission had been more than adequately accomplished.

Hernando was as crafty as he was violent. He shied from neither lying nor violence to achieve his ends, and somehow he had convinced the captured Inca Atahualpa's chief general to accompany the conquistadors. Consequently, Chalkuchimac, reputed for his ferocity, was following them in his palanquin all the way to Cajamarca, with the intention of there joining his master. He had a mere twenty warriors escorting him. Gabriel couldn't help but admire Hernando's feat, despite his contempt for him, which grew more pronounced with each passing day. Certainly, the peaceful capture of the Inca general might mitigate—perhaps—the men's constant fear. Ever since what the Spaniards had taken to calling among themselves "the Great Battle of November," not one soldier had woken in the morning without dreading an attack by Atahualpa's army. Rumor had it that it was still a large and powerful force.

"*Hola!*" grumbled Pedro the Greek behind Gabriel. "Would his Lordship deign to move forward, or must we stay planted on the spot until Christmas?"

Gabriel smiled without replying. The Greek giant had been grumpy since morning. He was tired of leading his horse instead of riding it. Or perhaps it was the absence of his usually inseparable companion, Sebastian the African, who was walking a little farther back in the column, that was the cause of his ill humor.

They set off again, though cautiously, holding the bridles close to the bit to prevent the animals from shying.

And soon enough they fell into a regular rhythm of climbing up and up, happy to at last feel the sun warm their faces. A shadow passed over Gabriel before veering off and traveling across the cliff face like a visible black gust of air.

Gabriel turned his face skyward: an enormous bird was gliding slowly, lazily, between the two sides of the canyon, not once beating its wings. It looked huge to him, despite being so high.

Gabriel measured in half-day blocks the elapsing of the time left that stood between him and Anamaya. It passed excruciatingly slowly. He would look ahead at each mountain ridge that they came to and vainly hope that it would be the last, that beyond it they would at last begin the descent toward Cajamarca.

He missed the whole of her: her voice, her mouth, the nape of her neck, her fragrance of dried grass and peppered flowers. He longed to kiss her shoulders and her belly, but his mouth tasted only the mountain's cold breath. He would wake in the night yearning for her caresses and her whispers, for the infinite blue of her eyes, eyes that he would lose himself in when they made love. He dreamed of her body that she knew how to deny him and give to him simultaneously, of her savage tenderness, of the way she would tilt her head forward and half-close her eyelids when she whispered that she loved him. He laughed at the memory of her timidity when he had taught her that word in the language of Spain.

He would awake, a bashful lover, and go outside to wait for dawn wrapped in his damp blanket. He would look for her through the fog and the rain, on the mountaintops and in the depths of the valleys. It was at those moments that Peru, that unknown country as strange as a distant star, would appear to him as magnificent: magnificent because it was hers. And sometimes, during the course of their long, long daily marches, he would look into the dark and fearful eyes of the porters and try to find something of her in her people's features.

"Oi! The dreamer there!" grumbled Pedro de Candia brusquely from behind. The Greek pointed his gloved hand and said, "Have a look at what's up ahead."

Three hundred paces farther, set above a bend in the river, a rope bridge joined the two sides of the canyon. The bridge was so long that it sagged like a necklace on a hollow chest.

Gabriel slowed the pace. The giant Greek, his cheeks pale under his bushy beard, came up beside him and muttered:

"I don't like it. And the horses are going to like it even less."

But Gabriel didn't hear him. Instead he whistled appreciatively between his teeth.

"By Santiago! How in the world did they build that thing?"

"Who gives a damn, mate? Ask yourself instead how you're going to get across it, and whether it's going to hold."

"By placing one foot before the other, I imagine," teased Gabriel. "You're not frightened, are you, Pedro?"

"I'm not frightened, mate! I just don't like it, is all."

"Well, old friend, I'm afraid that all you can do is learn to like it. But perhaps your horse shall learn to fly, a veritable Pegasus."

Pedro looked unconvinced.

They pressed on to the end of the path. There they discovered the massive pillars to which the ropes were attached. Delicately woven strand by strand, each rope was as thick as a man's thigh. The guardrails were made of a complicated system of ropes and knots. The bridge was wider than the track that they had just come up.

Gabriel stood transfixed, full of admiration. The Inca builders and architects had managed to create a structure as elegant as it was beautiful without resource to any iron tools at all: no saws, no gouges, and no planes. Three of the gigantic rope cables held up a roadway built of meticulously laid-out logs. A bed of twigs and leaves had been spread on top of the logs, making the passage less dangerous and slippery, and evening the surface.

"By the Sacred Virgin," groused Candia, "look there! Look, Gabriel, it moves! It sags. . . ."

"Yes," said Gabriel. It was indeed a heavy structure suspended over a very deep ravine, the river growling far below, and the whole thing was swaying gently in the slight breeze.

"It'll never take the weight of the horses!" insisted Pedro.

"*Hola*, Pedro! I've known you more heroic than this! But rest easy, see the size of those cables and logs. It's a solid piece of work."

A group of Indian guards appeared on the other side of the chasm. The rest of the column now arrived in straggling parcels, and now the porters hung around the start of the bridge apathetically, although curious to see how the Strangers and their horses would cross it.

Gabriel removed a long blue scarf (the same color as Anamaya's eyes and which until now had never left his neck) and began to wrap it around his bay's eyes.

"Do like me, Pedro, blindfold your horse so that he sees neither the river nor the height."

Gabriel murmured comforting words to his horse—reassuring himself as much as the animal—and with infinite caution he set off between the pillars, holding the bay's bridle high. A few steps later and he found himself above the abyss. The farther he advanced, the more violent became the rumbling of the river, like a sustained barking rising from far, far below.

Glancing back through the rope work he saw the column, the Inca general's palanquin, and the feather in Hernando's helmet reach the end of the bridge. Everyone was watching him. He roared out:

"Follow me, Pedro! All's well, she holds!"

"I'm behind you!" bellowed Candia in his stentorian voice. "Did you think that I'd let you play the hero all by yourself?"

Gabriel grinned and quickened the pace a little. The bay was doing well and appeared confident. They descended easily enough toward the lowest point of the bridge. Here the slope became even steeper. Gabriel had to throw his shoulders back to keep his balance, as though with each step the heels of his boots were sinking into sludge rather than landing on a bed of branches.

The din of the river below was now deafening. One could see whirling mud and enormous waves crashing on the rocks and producing an explosion of foam so violent that a sort of Scotch mist rose from that part of the canyon.

He heard a muted sound, a cry. His bay ran into his shoulder, snorting heavily. As he turned, Gabriel heard Pedro bawl:

"Goddamned bitch of a bridge!"

Gabriel all but laughed. The Greek had slipped and was splayed out on his backside, one boot already lost in the abyss. But his hand hadn't let go of his horse's bridle and the animal, its neck arched, its hind legs dug in, was preserving its master from a long, long fall and certain death.

Heaving himself over, Candia grabbed a rope and got back up onto his knees, breathing heavily. The pink feather in his morion had snapped clean in two and now fell away and floated into the void, swirling around gently. A long time elapsed before the furious river swallowed it up.

"Are you all right?" asked Gabriel.

"Why wouldn't I be?" bellowed Candia.

Gabriel saw Hernando smiling. He stood surrounded by his henchmen up at the start of the bridge. He could see the hateful disdain concentrated in that smile even at that distance, and despite the Governor's brother's beard.

"Let's go," he growled to himself.

But the incident had altered the bridge's equilibrium, and now the structure was much more animated, strangely alive. It was not only swaying horizontally, but was also subjected to a new rolling movement like that of a wave, as though caught in a heavy swell at sea. The more they advanced, the more violent it became. The bay wavered each time the bridge jolted at the peak of the wave. Gabriel yanked on its bridle, but was himself soon overcome with nausea. In an instant, cold sweat had his shirt and doublet clinging to his body.

And then suddenly, it was all over. They were close enough to the other side for the cables to become taut. The Indian guards there grinned at them. With nausea stewing his guts and with his heart in his mouth, Gabriel accelerated and completed the crossing at a sprint. He screamed unwittingly as he did so, as though charging into battle. Seeing this, the Indian guards lost their grins and scurried away as a group, seeking refuge behind a wall surrounding a nearby group of buildings.

The Greek caught up with him on the big platform at the end of the bridge. They grinned broadly as they embraced one another and slapped each other's backs.

For almost an hour, the llamas and Indian porters streamed across the bridge without incident. The deftness with which the porters of the Inca general's palanquin negotiated the bridge was truly impressive. They seemed to literally slide along it, completely unmindful of the pitch. The palanquin itself remained stable and horizontal, and even its curtains barely fluttered.

As for the Spanish cavalrymen and foot soldiers, their own skill was no match for the Indians'. They urged one another on with loud, pointless shouts, and their movements lacked the measure and precision of the Indians'. Some even vomited, and most reached the end much paler than they had been on the far side.

Sebastian crossed the bridge without mishap and posted himself next to his two friends, greeting them with a simple wink.

The sun would soon reach its zenith. A light breeze scattered the last remaining clouds congested over the west of the valley. The green of the bush acquired the depth of emerald in the sharp light. There was no longer just one condor streaking across the intensely blue sky but two, three, ten and more spinning around in a majestic, airborne ballet. Gabriel could not help but admire them, and was delighted to see them come closer and closer. He could make out their long necks quite distinctly as well as their enormous beaks, curved like Turkish cutlasses. But it was their wings that impressed him most. They were entirely and perfectly black, reflecting the sunlight like immense sheets of damasked steel. The birds seemed to never flap their wings at all, save for the occasional slight quiver on a gust of air. As far as Gabriel could tell, the wingspan of the largest condors was easily greater than the length of a horse.

Now their whirling increased imperceptibly in scope. They fell into steeper and steeper dives, and they went farther and farther upstream. On the return they came in so low that one could hear a sort of screeching sound whistle through the air, despite the rumble of the river.

It happened when the last of the porters were halfway across.

A dozen Indians were prudently advancing in pairs, carrying between them young llama carcasses suspended from bamboo poles. Most of them had already made significant progress, and had adapted to the rhythm of the bridge's undulations. But a couple of stragglers seemed to be having trouble keeping their balance.

Suddenly, the lead porters came to a halt and looked up anxiously at the sky. It was then that Gabriel understood. One of the condors had glided so low and so close to the heads of the last pair of porters that it looked as if it were going to hit them. The two Indians, taken by surprise, raised their arms to protect themselves. They lost their llama carcass in the chasm, and it twisted about itself as it fell, chased by a second condor, before disappearing into the rapids.

Immediately, the massive bird of prey turned gracefully and climbed high, only to dive once again at the bridge. The superb and insolent creature seemed furious at having lost its prey. Its fellows joined its dance. One after the other, their wings tipped forward and their necks retracted into their spotless ruffs; they dived at the porters, who were now lying down and shrieking with fright.

Gabriel heard them cry:

"*Kuntur! Kuntur!*"

As everyone on land looked on, dumbfounded, two Indians brandished a llama carcass above the cables.

The last condor came at them majestically, so slowly that it looked as though it was going to land. It unfurled its talons, its claws as long as a man's hand, grabbed ahold of its prize, and carried it away into the sky.

Gabriel, short of breath, heard the Indians chant as the great birds made away:

"Kuntur! Kuntur!"

"Mother of God, what's got into them?" asked Pedro the Greek, still wide-eyed.

"They consider the condor a sacred animal," explained Gabriel. "The Incas see them as messengers from their Sun God, and . . ."

But he didn't get the chance to explain further. A furious roar drew him around.

Hernando, standing at the end of the bridge, was hurling insults at the porters as they arrived at a run.

"Bunch of fucking idiots! Frightened of birds! Who gave you permission to let go of those llamas?"

The porters, their eyes still full of fear, stopped dead a few steps away from the Governor's brother. Hernando grabbed Felipillo the interpreter, who had been with them since the landing at Tumbez, roughly by the shoulder, and said:

"Tell these monkeys that I will not have food wasted!"

Felipillo mumbled a few words. With his head lowered, the oldest of the Indians replied almost inaudibly:

"They say that one has to feed the condor when it is hungry, else the Sun God becomes enraged."

"Damned bunch of savages!" screamed Hernando. "Feeding birds, what next? Who gives a damn about the sun's rage? It's my rage that you should be worried about."

In three quick steps, Hernando was past the pillars. He grabbed the old porter, and in a single movement lifted him and threw him over the cables with the ease of a lumberjack.

Gabriel couldn't believe his eyes. He saw the stupor on the porter's face, his hand grasping as he tumbled into the abyss, his mouth gaping out a silent cry. In an instant the man was nothing more than a tiny, gesticulating puppet. He struck a sharp edge of a rock and bounced off it into the river as though made of dough, as though he had no spine.

Silence. Hernando turned toward the Spaniards and grinned.

"Well, it seems he was one at least who couldn't flap his wings and fly," he said with sinister sprightliness.

The Indians remained dumbfounded. They didn't dare even look at the river. Sebastian couldn't hold back a surprised gulp, and his customary grin had given way to a grimace: the slave, his face gray, trembled with impotence. Gabriel, overwhelmed with rage, approached Hernando. He planted himself in front of the Governor's brother, so close that he could feel his breath on his face.

"Don Hernando, you are filthy pig's shit."

Hernando made no reply. His eyes retracted so far into his skull that what remained were two slits through which his hatred glowered; a deep, infinite hatred. After a pause, he said:

"I don't think I heard you right, you whoreson bastard."

"Your presence poisons the air, Don Hernando. You are no man, no Christian, and you bring shame upon your name. Your blood is mud and you brain was rotted long ago."

"By the blood of Christ!"

Hernando whipped his sword from its scabbard. Gabriel had just enough time to jump back to avoid having his throat sliced.

"Haaa!"

With a cry of rage, Hernando sliced through the air again but Gabriel was too quick for him, jumping back with his arms away from his body as though dancing, and Hernando, hitting nothing, swung back in on himself.

"The day you die, Don Hernando," said Gabriel, his voice quavering less, and with a slightly amused air, "even the carrion crows won't touch you."

"Defend yourself!" growled Hernando, throwing aside his morion. "Unsheathe your sword, you bastard scum!"

Everyone around them had retreated. Gabriel's supple blade squeaked and glinted as he drew it with an easy movement of his wrist. For a moment, they seemed to be moving in slow motion, as though an invisible and insurmountable block had formed between them.

And then Hernando lunged. His blade slid along Gabriel's, who parried, his knees and waist bent, lifting the locked swords above his shoulder. The hilts slammed loudly together. Gabriel shoved Hernando back and turned as he disengaged, a smirk on his lips. The Governor's brother was heavy, breathless with rage, drunk with violence. He whipped the void with his sword as a dog wags its tail. Gabriel restrained himself to parrying with small strokes. He could read the mad rage in Hernando's eyes. Then, with a sudden jump, he was in close, his torso side-on. He slipped his blade beneath Hernando's, and now Gabriel had the upper hand. With all the strength of his arm, Gabriel heaved on the interlocked swords, and with a powerful flick of his wrist flung his arm wide to the right.

Hernando's sword tinkled like a bell as it landed at Candia's feet. The Greek couldn't help but smile.

Gabriel pushed the point of his sword into his adversary's doublet, forcing him back. His mouth twisted, and and his eyes communicated an emotion that Gabriel had never seen in him before. *He's frightened,* Gabriel thought with pleasure.

"You forget that suffering has two faces, Don Hernando," he said in a low voice, breathing heavily. "You enjoy seeing fear in the eyes of others, but how do you feel now? What have you to say to that wrench in your guts? One or two more steps and you too might learn to fly."

Gabriel forced Hernando farther and farther back as he spoke, right to the edge of the canyon, to the very spot from where the Governor's brother had thrown the unfortunate porter.

"Gather your wits, man, I'm not going to kill you. But know that Governor Don Francisco shall be the one to judge your misdeeds. Certainly, you are bringing a lot of gold back to Cajamarca, and an important general who serves the master of that place. But none of that shall buy you your redemption."

"By the Virgin, threaten me all you want! We shall see who will be the one suffering in the end."

Hernando had said this with a snigger, but everyone present perceived that it was a façade. The humiliation he had just suffered had been too great, too public, and too spectacular.

"Peace, my lords. The point has been made," interrupted Candia the Greek as he laid his hand on Gabriel's arm. "God is my witness, and I say to you that two conquistadors cannot fight one another. It ain't dignified, it ain't natural, and it goes in the face of the good of the Conquest! Don Hernando, here is your sword. Let us be on our way, if you please."

Hernando and Gabriel eyed one another scornfully. Gabriel lowered his sword. But it was Hernando who lowered his eyes.

Behind them, the hanging that enclosed General Chalkuchimac's palanquin fell down again silently.

As the column set off, Sebastian took Gabriel by the arm. He walked with him a while in silence. Then he leaned over to his ear and murmured:

"Thank you."

PART ONE

ONE

Cajamarca, April 14, 1533, dawn

"I love you," murmured Anamaya in the pale dawn rising over Cajamarca. The darkness of night still lingered, but the smoke rising over the thatched roofs was now slowly turning blue.

Anamaya was alone.

She had stolen away from the palace in which Atahualpa was being kept prisoner. She left it behind her now as she moved like a quick shadow along the narrow streets laid out on the slope overlooking the main square. Soon she was at the river and the access road to the Royal Road.

"I love you," she repeated. *"Te quiero!"*

The words came to her so easily in the language of the Spaniards that everyone was amazed, whether conquistador or Indian. It had also roused an ancient mistrust among her own people, and once again people were whispering behind her back. But she didn't care.

She ran stealthily alongside the houses, staying close to the shadows of the walls in order to evade the guards watching over Atahualpa's palace and its ransom room piled high with treasure.

The mere sight of this precious haul intoxicated those who had won the Battle of Cajamarca and who had had the audacity to lay their hands on Emperor Atahualpa. It was as though they imagined that gold would yield to them the magical powers that they lacked.

The plunder provoked a deep and silent sadness in Anamaya.

They were insatiable. In search of even more to stuff into the large ransom room, Don Hernando Pizarro had gone to sack the temple at Pachacamac far, far away on the shore of the southern sea. And because his brother was late returning, the Governor, Don Francisco Pizarro, had sent Gabriel and a few reliable men after him.

Gabriel . . . she allowed his name to settle into her heart, the sound of it so foreign, yet so tender to her. . . . She called to mind his face, his image . . . the Stranger with sun-colored hair, with pale, pale skin, with the mark of the puma crouching on his shoulder, the mark that was their bond, their secret link, which one day she would reveal to him.

Gabriel had no love of gold. Many times she had watched him stand by indifferent to, even irritated by, his companions' delirious rapture at the mere touch of a few gold leaves.

Gabriel did not accept that an Indian be beaten over a trifle, even less that they be chained or killed.

Gabriel had saved the Emperor from the sword.

Anamaya recalled Atahualpa's words, the words he had spoken when he still had all the power of an emperor. On the eve of the Great Battle, seeing the Strangers for the first time, he had murmured, "I like their horses, but as for them, I don't understand."

Like him, she could have said, "I love one among them, the one who leaped across the ocean for me. But as for the rest of them, I don't understand."

Now she had left behind the high walls surrounding Cajamarca. As she scaled the lower slopes of the Royal Road, she slowed her pace. The adobe-walled houses were fewer now, and set farther apart. Dawn was lighting the mountainsides, breathing life into the corn and *quinua* fields, rustling in the morning breeze. Occasionally she saw a peasant, already bowed beneath a burden, silhouetted against the growing paleness of day. Anamaya's heart would fill with an uneasy tenderness. She would feel an urge to run to the man and help him carry his burden. She thought about the suffering weighing on her people.

Her people! Because now, she who for so long had been the odd child with blue eyes, the awkward girl who was too tall and too thin, now she knew how much all those who lived in the Inca Empire formed what she called "her people." They didn't all speak the same language or wear the same clothes, and only superficially did they believe in the same gods. Often they had warred among themselves, and the spirit of war was within them still. Yet, in her heart, Anamaya would wish them all blood brothers.

By the time she reached the pass, the day was well established. Light shimmered on the marsh and spread across the immense plain, right up to the mountains concealing the road to Cuzco.

As happened each time she returned here, Anamaya couldn't stop the flood of her memories. She remembered those days in the not-so-distant past when the entire plain had been covered by the white tents of Atahualpa's invincible army. It had been the army of an emperor who had known how to defeat the cruelty of his brother Huascar, the madman of Cuzco.

The steam rose from the baths over on the opposing slope. Atahualpa was resting there, giving thanks to his father Inti by fasting. Her breath short, her heart constricted, Anamaya remembered, as though they were forever tattooed into her skin, those endless days when news of the Strangers' slow approach was brought to them. She remembered those days when everyone scoffed at them, and the fear that she had felt bloom within her. And then she remembered that dawn when all of a sudden he appeared, he, Gabriel. He was so handsome, so attractive that it had been incomprehensible to her.

She didn't want to contemplate what had happened after. The Emperor Atahualpa was but a shadow of his former self, a prisoner in his own palace while his temples were destroyed.

Thus had been accomplished the will of the Sun God.

Thus had been fulfilled the terrible words of the deceased Inca Huayna Capac, who had once come to her in the form of a child and said: *"That which is too old comes to an end, that which is too big shatters, that which is too strong loses its force.... That is what the great pachacuti means.... Some die, and others grow. Have no fear for yourself, Anamaya.... You are what you are meant to be. Have no fear, for in the future the puma will go with you!"*

Thus, from the other world, the former Inca had simultaneously announced to her Atahualpa's fall and Gabriel's coming!

In truth, ever since her mouth had kissed Gabriel's, ever since she had kissed his strangely marked shoulder, there were many things that Anamaya hadn't been able to understand. There were so many sensations, so many unknown emotions now living within her. And living with so much strength that it seemed as if the claws of a real puma were lacerating her heart.

There were those emotions that urged her to say, "I love you," the words that Gabriel had stubbornly labored to teach her. He had become angry as she had sat there smiling and listening to him, refusing to repeat after him.

And then there was the mystery: How could a Stranger, an enemy, be the puma who would go with her into the future?

Anamaya walked slowly to the end of the plateau that stretched across the peak of the pass. She rolled her cloak about herself and lay down on the still wet grass covering the slope's perpendicular. She gazed at the highest peaks in the east, and contemplated the sun's first rays.

Anamaya closed her eyes. She let the light caress her eyelids and expunge the tears that had formed under them. And as soon as the sun had warmed her face, Gabriel appeared to her against the red underside of her eyelids. Gabriel, the handsome Stranger with eyes like coals, who laughed as innocently as a child, and whose touch was so tender.

Once more her lips formed the words. She whispered them as though they could fly above the earth like hummingbirds: "I love you."

As they approached Cajamarca, Gabriel, unable to check his own momentum, spurred his horse on. He rode to the head of the column at a full trot. His blood boiled. He hadn't slept a wink since his encounter with Hernando three nights earlier. Three nights spent contemplating the stars or sharing the watch at a campsite or a *tambo*. But today, it was finally over.

He was going to be with her once more.

In a little while he would be gazing into her blue, blue eyes, he would be able to touch her tender mouth, so tender that her kiss melted him, made him oblivious to reality. Only two more leagues and he would be able to see her tall and slender silhouette, unique among Indian women. And the awareness of this alone gnawed at his very core.

He hoped as well that nothing had happened to her during his long absence. There had been talk, as he was leaving Cajamarca, of *mariscal* Almagro's arrival, Don Francisco's old brother-in-arms, bringing with him yet more troops and more horses.

He was trembling with joy and yet, had he dared, he would have screamed out his lungs in order to banish his fear.

He passed by stretchers borne by Indians on which the heaviest treasures lay: a great gold bowl, a gold statue, a gold chair, and gold mural plaques torn from temple walls. Gold, gold, and yet more gold! It was everywhere—in wicker baskets, in hide sacks, in woven saddle packs. The porters were bent in half, broken in two under its weight, and the llamas had disappeared beneath their charges. The column had slowed because of it, as though the entire expedition had, since Jauja, become encumbered with all the gold and silver of Peru.

And to think that it was all only a sample: rumor had it that these treasures were nothing in comparison with what would soon arrive from Cuzco. The Governor had sent three men there on a reconnaissance mission, including the execrable Pedro Martín de Moguer.

The Spanish cavalrymen were constantly on the alert. Their nerves frayed, their black gazes mistrustful of everything, they watched for the slightest stir amid the ever docile Indians. Gabriel hadn't many friends within that group. They were all Hernando's men. His personal enmity with the Governor's brother had been well known by all for some time and their duel had frozen them into an icy mutual hatred. The Governor's red-plumed brother went out of his way to avoid Gabriel, more out of caution than astuteness.

As he arrived alongside the palanquins of two high priests from the Pachacamac temple, priests whom Hernando had bound in chains, Gabriel heard a familiar voice hail him:

"Would Your Grace be in a great hurry, at all?"

Gabriel pulled on the reins. With a graceful volte, his horse compliantly came up alongside Sebastian. It had been twenty days now that the big black man, one of Gabriel's few intimate friends, had been on foot. The price of horses had become prohibitive, but more to the point, two days before they had left Pachacamac, Don Hernando had forbidden him from taking the horse from any dying or even dead man.

His insult still pierced shrill in the two friends' ears: "*Hola*, darkie! Who do you take yourself for? Have you forgotten that horses are reserved for *caballeros* carrying the sword? It's not because you kicked a few Indian butts that you have the right to take yourself for a man!"

Leaning forward on his horse's neck, Gabriel warmly shook the hand Sebastian was extending to him. The African giant had no horse, but his leather doublet was brand-new and as supple as a second skin.

His breeches were tailored with all sorts of fabrics sent from Spain to Cajamarca. They were of the latest fashion out of Castile: large green, red, yellow, and pale blue stripes of felt or satin, and even a little lace on the cords of his boots. The extravagance of his outfit gave Gabriel (who always dressed soberly) the impression of traveling with a retinue of Toledo maidens, their bosoms squeezed into their bodices!

"So where are you trotting off to so quick?" asked Sebastian.

"There's a stench around here," growled Gabriel, looking directly at Hernando's escort. "I need to breathe fresher air."

The black giant gave him a malicious grin.

"Ahh . . . and there was I thinking that you had an urgency of, how shall I put it, a higher order!"

Gabriel hinted a smile.

"Why, what else could there be other than my haste to present the Governor with my report of my mission?"

"Ho! I see nothing else, indeed."

Sebastian nodded then fell silent, not bantering anymore. Gabriel's gaze fell upon the ridges surrounding Cajamarca. A few months earlier, this alien landscape harbored nothing but menace. Now it had become familiar, almost friendly. And now, of course, it held for him the most beautiful promise.

Gabriel suddenly pulled his right foot out of the stirrup and jumped nimbly to the ground. While he led his horse with one arm, he wrapped the other around Sebastian's shoulders. He leaned in close to his friend.

"You're in the right of it," he said in a low voice, his eyes aglow. "I am in a hurry . . . and it has nothing to do with that whoreson Hernando."

"Well?"

Gabriel made a vague gesture toward the mountains.

"She says that she can't marry me. She is some sort of priestess in their ancient religion. Marriage is forbidden her, even to an Indian. But still . . ."

"But still?"

"But still, I love her. Damn and blast it, Sebastian! Just to think of her, my heart explodes like a volley of grapeshot. I love her as though I had never known the meaning of the word before."

Sebastian burst out laughing.

"Do like me, my friend! Love many of them at once! One here, one

there, but always one to want you. A tender bed here, a fiery one there
. . . then, you will know what it means to love!"

There was a certain stricture to Gabriel's smile as he returned to his
saddle.

"There are times, *compañero,* when I wish you weren't so witty."

Sebastian hinted at a smile, but his face remained as black as his skin.

"Me too, I wish it. And then again . . ."

"And then?"

The column had slowed, had grown longer, and now ground to a
halt. The Royal Road had grown narrower at the approach to the last
peak before Cajamarca.

"And then what?" insisted Gabriel.

Sebastian shook his head. He motioned to Gabriel to gallop up
ahead.

"I'll tell you some other time, when you're in less of a hurry."

The hammering that startled Anamaya from her sleep was not that of
her heart. It was the stamping of men and horses rising from the earth.
She sat up and went and hid in a hedge of acacia and agave close to the
Royal Road.

A herd of llamas that had been quietly grazing in a neighboring pas-
ture now shot past and fled, jumping nervously, to the other side of the
ridge. The instantly familiar clinking of the Spaniards' iron arms tinkled
through the balmy air. It slowly increased in volume along with laughter, bursts of speech, and the click-clacking of hooves on flagstone.

She caught sight of them coming out of a small wood at the foot of
the slope. She saw the lances and colorful plumes of the horsemen first,
then their somber-bearded faces beneath their morions, before the
Indian porters and the Spaniards on foot finally appeared. The entire
slow-moving column, led by the Governor's brother, was now visible to
her.

Anamaya breathed quick, stuttered gasps of air. She looked for him.

But scrutinize each face, each man's apparel and hat as she might,
she couldn't make out Gabriel among the men approaching the ridge.
She couldn't make out his black doublet, or his reddish-brown horse
with a long white stain on its hindquarters. Nor could she make out the

blue scarf he invariably wore around his neck, in order to "carry the color of her eyes with him," as he said, and that normally helped her pick him out from afar.

Anamaya's fingers trembled without her realizing it. Her heart beat strongly, too strongly. She was ashamed of her fear, but she pulled a low branch aside to see more clearly, despite the risk of being seen herself.

At last the blue patch of the scarf fleetingly appeared behind a palanquin. She caught a brief glimpse of the bay. She let out a little spontaneous laugh.

And then she froze.

Her eyes didn't linger on Gabriel. Rather, they remained fixed on the hangings that enclosed the palanquin. She recognized the markings and colors, the slanted lines of blood-red or sky-blue rectangles and triangles.

It was General Chalkuchimac's palanquin. Atahualpa's most powerful warrior.

So the Strangers had convinced him to travel all the way to the Emperor's prison. By what ruse, what treachery had they accomplished this?

Anamaya watched Gabriel pass before the palanquin, as though guarding it. Her heart was no longer beating so fast at the prospect of seeing him. A shadow loomed over her joy.

She understood how things stood. She knew, better than any, what was to become of the Emperor.

A cry caused her to turn around. A small group of riders was coming from the other side of the ridge, negotiating the very steep slope with some difficulty. Leading them was Governor Francisco Pizarro, the first of the Spaniards, dressed all in black, his gray beard standing out against a strange white garment full of holes. A little behind him came Almagro, an undersized man riding a mare far too big for him. He had a frightening face. A green bandana covered one eye. His pockmarked and chapped skin was covered in rusty blotches that the sparse hairs of his beard failed to hide. His too-broad mouth had few teeth. Yet when he spoke his voice was often gentle, almost doleful.

Another cry echoed through the air, followed by others. Laughter resonated; lances and pikes were raised and waved about. When the long column's horsemen were but a stone's throw away from him, Don Francisco jumped agilely from his horse and walked open-armed toward his brother.

Before they had even embraced, Anamaya had already reached the long grass and was running toward the town along the steep shepherds' path.

The ridge's last slope was very steep for the horses. Gabriel cautiously guided his steed, holding the reins chest high. The flagstones were slippery, and the porters faltered. Their talk ended as he approached; it was known among the Indians that he spoke a little of their language.

Calls and cries shot out from the column's head. Gabriel urged on his horse and moved away from the Inca general's palanquin. He saw Hernando Pizarro meet his brother Francisco high up on the flatland at the peak.

Gabriel couldn't help but grin mordaciously. Don Francisco had displayed his loveliest finery in which to welcome his brother. He wore a Cadiz lace ruff around his neck, an article that must have cost him its weight in gold, though it contrasted nicely with his meticulously trimmed beard. But whatever sartorial efforts the Governor made, it was still his brother Hernando, who was bigger and more assured in the strength of his body and the eminence of his origins, who gave the appearance of a genuine prince.

The two brothers embraced effusively before the eyes of the entire company. The Governor's two younger brothers stood a little in the background; the handsome Gonzalo with his dark curls, and the diminutive Juan, with the beauty spot on his neck, watched their embrace with their hats in their hands and grins on their faces.

Gabriel knew what those grins were worth. What really caught his attention was the ill-looking fellow with a scowling face so ugly as to frighten children. Although he had only laid eyes on him a few times, and that was years ago, before they had left for the Peruvian coast, Gabriel instantly recognized him.

So Don Diego de Almagro had indeed come from Panama during his absence! He who, out of his own pocket, had paid for Don Francisco's most ambitious adventure, who had given of himself for it, who had dreamed of becoming an *Adelantado* alongside his old companion—

now named Governor—on whom King Charles V had bestowed only the title of lieutenant of Tumbez, with a miserable salary and a *hidalgo*'s title, he had come to claim his due!

The porters resumed their long march. They advanced cautiously down the broad, slippery steps that plunged down to the outskirts of the town. The interpreter Felipillo, his thin lips shut tight, his eyes darting and evasive, stayed close to the richest and most decorated palanquin; he stayed close to Chalkuchimac.

When the palanquin and its retinue reached the square where the Governor, his brothers, and Don Diego de Almagro had already arrived, the palanquin's curtains opened slightly. Gabriel saw a powerful hand appear, large enough to crush a llama's throat.

Felipillo scurried up to the gap, bent double, and murmured a few words that Gabriel couldn't hear.

He stood tall again and barked an order. The porters fell still, their eyes lowered. The hanging enclosing the palanquin slowly rose.

General Chalkuchimac wore a magnificent blue *unku* made of a blend of cotton and wool. The tunic's weave was strewn with gold sequins. Very fine *tocapus* outlined a crimson band about his waist. His long, thick hair fell onto his shoulders, partly concealing his gold ear plugs. They seemed smaller than those worn by other nobles that Gabriel had seen. Yet Chalkuchimac's face commanded respect. It was difficult to age him, but he had the power and impassiveness of a statue, as though he had been hewn from a block of sacred rock from the mountains.

He moved forward, and glanced at Gabriel. He growled a few words: "I must see my master."

Gabriel wasn't sure if he had understood him right. Felipillo was bustling about at the foot of the palanquin. The Inca general raised a hand, pushing him back without even touching him.

Then he approached one of the porters. He took the man's load from him. The porter trembled, his hands empty and his eyes staring doggedly at the ground.

Chalkuchimac placed the enormous basket on his back. Bent double under its weight, he entered the town.

*   *   *

"Now," affirmed Atahualpa slowly, "they shall free me."

The Emperor was seated on his royal tripod, a cape woven of fine wool hanging over his shoulders. His voice was muted, and hardly broke the silence.

The room was large and always dark. Neither light nor air found their way in, and smoke from the braziers had blackened the stones, the tops of the crimson tapestries, and the building's beams. Many of the niches were empty, or else contained only carved wooden ceremonial vases, albeit magnificent, for sacred beer. The greater part of the gold pots, the silver goblets, and the statues of the gods had all long since been added to the heap in the ransom room.

The Emperor had his servants, wives, and concubines leave the room each time Anamaya visited. It was a moment of intimacy that was all that remained of their lost liberty.

Sunlight only made it as far as the threshold of the opening that gave onto the palace's patio. It threw a pale yellow rectangle on the flagstones. Atahualpa's silhouette appeared pathetically out of the shadows. Anamaya couldn't help but shiver when she thought that he who had been the Inca, the very brightness of the sun, was slowly slipping toward the Underworld.

The *llautu*, the royal band, was still on his forehead, and in it the black and white feathers of the *curiguingue*, the symbol of the Emperor's supreme power. Anamaya noticed that he no longer wore gold plugs in his earlobes. His left lobe, a gaping ring of dead flesh, hung down to his shoulder. His wives had woven him a bandana of the finest alpaca wool to wrap his hair in, and he wore it so that it concealed the torn lobe of his other ear.

Anamaya avoided looking at the pitiful signs of a power in decline. It seemed to her that a little more of Atahualpa's soul left him with each passing day. The virgins still wove his tunics for each new day. He was still served his meals in earthenware that none other used. His retinue, whether they were men or women, and including the few noblemen who were his fellow prisoners in the Cajamarca Palace, still feared his word as they always had. The Strangers bowed before addressing him, and the Spanish Governor accorded him the respect due an emperor. And yet, Anamaya couldn't help but see it all as a masquerade playing itself out. The Emperor had developed a stoop, his face had sallowed, and the red of his eyes had grown bloodier. His mouth was less beautiful, less imperial. His whole body seemed to have shrunken.

The conqueror in him, the son of the great Huayna Capac, had disappeared. Atahualpa was still the Emperor who lived in the Cajamarca Palace, but he was no longer the powerful progeny of the sun who had defeated his brother, the madman of Cuzco. He was but a prisoner without chains who dreamed of his liberation.

Anamaya wanted to tell him what she had seen on the mountain road. She wanted to warn him that Chalkuchimac was there in his palanquin. But she didn't dare, and Atahualpa repeated:

"They have their gold now. They shall let me go."

"I'm not sure," replied Anamaya, looking away.

"What did you say?"

"I'm not sure," she repeated.

Atahualpa gestured irascibly at the ransom room outside.

"I chose the biggest room in my palace, I designated a line on the wall to mark the height of the ransom pile. It has now been reached."

"I remember, my Lord," agreed Anamaya gently. "The Strangers laughed, they thought that you had been seized by madness."

"I told them where to find our gold and silver. I told them that they could take it all, from every house except my father's."

"I know, my Lord."

A sly smile lit Atahualpa's face.

"I realize that I'm talking to the wife of my father's Sacred Double."

Anamaya let a moment pass, and then replied:

"My Lord, those who went to Pachacamac have returned today."

"How do you know this?"

Anamaya made no reply. She didn't want to emphasize the weakness of his position.

Again, the Inca grinned.

"Isn't that what I was telling you? I am going to be freed."

"My Lord," she said in a voice so low that it was barely audible. "The big room is filled with gold, with all our sacred objects, whether they be the most ancient or those that the smiths have only just finished. But the Strangers will not leave your Kingdom. They shall want to go to the Sacred City. They will fill the biggest room, and then they will take the gold of Cuzco. And even if they swore to you by their god and their king not to touch anything belonging to your father, Huayna Capac, the mere sight of the gold will make them forget their promise. You know it, my Lord."

Atahualpa lowered his eyes.

Anamaya didn't want to stop talking now. She continued gently:

"More Strangers will arrive in your kingdom, my Lord. They too will bring weapons and horses, and they too will want gold."

"Yes," murmured Atahualpa. "I don't like that new one, that very ugly one-eyed man."

The words came out of Atahualpa's mouth with difficulty, as though he was a hesitant child once more.

"His name is Almagro."

"I don't like him," repeated the Inca. "His eye lies. He and those who came with him take my women without my permission. They laugh when I forbid it. He says that he is Pizarro's friend, but his eye tells me that it isn't so."

"Why would these men be here, my Lord, if not to take yet more gold?"

"Pizarro's brother will protect me," affirmed Atahualpa. "He is powerful."

"Hernando? Forgive me, my Lord, but don't trust him. His heart is false."

Atahualpa shook his head.

"No! He is powerful, and the others are frightened of him."

"You say that because he has great bearing, because he has a proud eye, and he dresses more carefully than the others, who are slovenly and as dirty as the animals that they have brought with them and that infest our streets. The feather above his helmet may be red, but his soul is black."

A look of shameful hope came over Atahualpa's face.

"He promised that he would help me. If he doesn't . . ."

His voice lowered a degree. He motioned to Anamaya to approach. A glow of naive excitement had returned to his eyes.

"If he doesn't, the thousands of warriors mobilized by my loyal generals will deliver me. Chalkuchimac is at Jauja, waiting in readiness. He will tell the others . . ."

Anamaya stifled a cry.

"Oh, my Lord . . ."

As she hesitated, they heard shouts echoing across the patio. A servant bowed at the threshold of the room. Anamaya knew what he was going to say, and her blood ran cold.

"My Lord . . . General Chalkuchimac is here. He asks whether you deign to look upon him."

At first, Atahualpa didn't move. Then the full meaning of the words reached him, and the color drained from his face.

"I am a dead man," he whispered.

"May he enter?" asked the servant again, who hadn't heard him.

"I am dead," repeated Atahualpa.

At the palace entrance, Chalkcuchimac hadn't removed the load weighing on his back. Gabriel watched him, broken in two like a supplicant carrying his cross.

Almagro muttered:

"Let us be done with this damned comedy! The only thing this monkey has to do is tell us where he has hidden the rest of the gold."

Don Francisco raised his black-gloved hand.

"Patience, Diego, patience . . ."

The Inca warriors guarding the entrance to the patio had retreated respectfully before Chalkuchimac. Water spouted from the mouth and the tail of a stone serpent set in a low fountain in the center of the patio. All around bloomed the bright red corollas of the *cantuta*, the Inca flower. A servant whose only job was to collect its wilted petals stood by them.

Once Chalkuchimac had crawled on his knees into the middle of the courtyard, Atahualpa came out of the room. Gabriel had trouble discerning him. Behind the Inca, in the shadows that half-hid her features, he saw Anamaya.

When at last she lifted her face toward his, he managed to restrain himself from going to her only with the greatest difficulty.

Atahualpa slowly seated himself on a red wood bench, about a palm's height from the ground. It was his usual seat. Some women approached, ready to serve him.

Chalkuchimac at last relieved himself of his charge, unloading it into the hands of a porter who had followed him from the outskirts of town. He removed his sandals and raised his hands toward the cloud-veiled sun, his palms turned skywards.

Tears ran down his rugged face. Words escaped from his mouth. Gabriel made out a few offerings of gratitude to Inti, and some mumbled words of love for the Inca.

Then Chalkuchimac approached his master. Without stopping crying, he kissed his face, his hands, and his feet.

Atahualpa remained as still as if the general were only a ghost brushing past him. His eyes gazed at an invisible point in the distance. Gabriel had often seen the Inca, but he had never managed to fathom his reactions or his facial expressions.

"You are gladly received, Chalkuchimac," said the Inca eventually. His voice was monotonous and cold.

Chalkuchimac straightened himself up and again raised his palms toward the sky.

"Had I been here," he said in a resonant voice, "none of this would have happened. The Strangers would never have laid a hand on you."

Atahualpa at last turned toward him. Gabriel was trying to catch Anamaya's eye when Don Francisco grabbed his shoulder. Impressed by the events, he said:

"What are they saying?"

"They are greeting one another."

"Strange way to greet," muttered the Governor.

Chalkuchimac stood up. His face had regained its usual impassive and noble composure.

"I waited for your orders, my Lord," he said in a low voice. "Each day, each time that our father the Sun rose into the sky, I felt the urge to come to your rescue. But as you know I could not do so against your wishes. And the *chaski* bearing your command never came. O my Lord, why did you not order me to annihilate the Strangers?"

Atahualpa made no reply.

The Inca general waited silently for an answer, for some encouraging words. They didn't come. They would never come.

Don Francisco asked again:

"What are they saying now?"

Gabriel felt the infinite and magnificent blue of Anamaya's eyes speak to him, and in that moment he suddenly understood. It was anger that made Atahualpa so still, that had frozen him in that terrible silence.

"The general regrets not having served the Inca better," murmured Gabriel. "He regrets that he has been taken prisoner."

Chalkuchimac took two steps back.

"I waited for your orders, my Lord," he repeated. "We were alone, isolated. Your generals, Quizquiz and Captain Guaypar and the rest, were alone. If you do not order it, they will not come to deliver you."

And with that he turned his back on his master and walked slowly out of the patio, his shoulders sagging as though they bore a heavier load than the one he had entered with.

Gabriel advanced carefully through the dark, feeling his way through the sacks, baskets, and jars.

The secret passage began from the very heart of the palace, from the end of a small room in which the *mullus* were kept, those pink shells so important during Inca rituals.

Anamaya had revealed it to him shortly after the Great Battle. He had had to promise to keep it secret. He remembered jesting with her, saying, "So, would you mind if I brought the Governor here?"

Back then, the words between them were still uncertain. Deeds had replaced their talk. They could only express and share their love through action. But they hadn't always the opportunity to escape to the cabin by the hot springs, the cabin where they had spent their first night together. So this passage had become their meeting place.

As he crossed the room, Gabriel sank his hand into a large jar of shells. Doing so evoked an oddly agreeable impression of the sea. Those trapezoid niches now so familiar to him surrounded the room. All their gold statues had been removed at the beginning of the Spanish occupation, and they were now covered with cotton hangings. He lifted one, his heart racing.

The tunnel had been dug at a slight rising angle. A thin layer of beaten earth covered the rock. During ancient times, Anamaya had explained to him, the tunnel system had crisscrossed through the entire hill, passing through the *acllahuasi* and reaching the snail-shaped fortress, the one the conquistadors had demolished upon their arrival.

The passage was remarkably clean and dry, and chests in which reserves of food and clothes had once been stored still sat in recesses at intervals along the way. A rumbling rose up from the belly of the earth: the underground rivers crossing under the mountain.

His eyes had not yet adapted to the darkness, and he uttered a surprised cry when a hand landed on his own, lightly as a butterfly.

"Anamaya!"

Her hand fluttered against his face, landed on his full lips, caressed his cheeks half-hidden under his beard, his eyelids, his forehead. He tried to kiss her, to hold her, but she wrapped him up and dodged him at the same time. They laughed low.

The moment he stopped grasping for her, she stopped evading him. Now he felt her breath close to his own and he made out her proffered face. They both smiled although unable to see one another clearly through the darkness.

"You're here," she whispered.

He sensed in her voice a timidity, or rather a sense of decency, so profound that he was overwhelmed by it. Those simple words had traveled far before reaching her lips.

She was so close that he could smell her scent.

When he drew her close, she surrendered herself modestly to him. Gabriel's arms closed around her, he felt her firm breasts against his chest, her legs against his own. Suddenly they were clutching at one another, their loins inflamed, swamped by the vertigo of desire.

All the energy and frenzy within them, all the accumulated self-constraint of waiting, gushed out in an instant, a sudden, quivering thrill that they appeased with caresses.

Gabriel wanted to be the embodiment of tenderness. His hand disappeared into Anamaya's thick hair. They held one another still for a moment. Their hearts beat so strongly that it felt as though one was beating against the other.

She was the one who placed her lips on his, who touched him, who undressed him, who pushed him back with gentle shoves so that he bent his knees and slowly slid down to the ground.

He felt her mouth traveling over him, running across his face, his neck, his chest, a wave of warmth on his body.

Then he allowed his hands their freedom, and they gripped her smooth, strong thighs, naked under her fine wool tunic. Immobile, they left their mark, and he thought he heard a new murmur, a groan that fused with the rumbling of the rivers.

Anamaya whispered a few lively, happy sounds into his ear, words that he didn't understand.

She is so light, he thought to himself, as their naked bodies burned and melted into each other.

And then, submerged in her caresses, he soared away with her.

TWO

Cajamarca, April 14, 1533

Anamaya was resting in her chamber. The small room was bathed in a gentle half-light. In the Inca's palace, the *Coya Camaquen* was privileged to a room all to herself. But unlike Atahualpa's, hers had been emptied of objects and tapestries—all its niches were bare. Delicate stone snakes slinking up the walls were the room's only ornaments. The light played on their undulating forms, and in its play the snakes sometimes appeared very real.

Anamaya dreamed of the day when she would be able to sleep alongside Gabriel the whole night through, as wife and husband. But would it happen? There were so many things in opposition to its becoming a reality.

She was still saturated from their passion: her body felt both heavy and light with the well-being of love. The door hanging fluttered in the balmy breeze. It was as though the breeze was stroking her with one final caress, an ephemeral echo of her lover's hand.

A sudden gust of air startled her.

"*Coya Camaquen!*"

It was a whisper, barely a murmur. She propped herself up on her elbows.

"*Coya Camaquen!*"

Anamaya made out a figure crouched in the shadows like some frightened, small animal.

"Who are you?" she asked quietly.

"*Coya Camaquen*, I need your help."

"Who are you?" repeated Anamaya.

All she got by way of reply was tense, quick breathing. She sat up on her matting and extended her hands toward the huddled shape.

"Come closer. . . . Don't be frightened."

The form slowly and timidly straightened itself. Two dark and lively eyes appeared beneath a head of disheveled hair. It turned out to be a young girl, almost a child. Her face was triangular, and she wore a simple tunic, splattered with mud, under a gray cape too large for her. She advanced, bent double as though she was carrying a load, and stopped at the edge of the mat. In a trembling supplicant gesture, she put her two tiny hands on it, her palms facing upward.

"What are you doing here?" asked Anamaya.

The black eyes stared at her without replying.

A feeling of infinite tenderness toward this fragile stranger beset Anamaya. She imagined the dread she must have felt while slipping past the guards and running across the patio to be here now.

"If you don't speak to me," she continued with feigned severity, "I will never know if I can help you!"

"My name is Inguill and I come from Cuzco," replied the young girl in one burst of breath. "I am from the Great Lord Manco's clan."

Manco! Anamaya felt a constriction in her throat.

Manco, her ever loyal friend, loyal to her despite the wars and the animosity between the clans. Manco, who had taken her advice and fled into the hills above Cajamarca, along with the golden Sacred Double, that terrible night following the Great Massacre and Atahualpa's capture.

Manco, he whom the deceased Inca Huayna Capac had designated as the "first knot of the future" the last time he had visited her from the Other World.

Suddenly anxious, Anamaya gripped Inguill's shoulders.

"How is he?"

"He told me to come to you," replied the very young girl, a little frightened. "He told me, 'Go to the *Coya Camaquen,* she will find a way to keep you near her. She sees the future unfurling before us.'"

Anamaya suppressed a sigh. If only it were so! What would she say to Manco if she saw him today? Would she be able to tell him "No, I no longer know how to access the Other World, and Emperor Huayna Capac stopped visiting me once a Stranger made my heart beat and touched me in a way that no other man has ever done? A Stranger unlike any other, a man marked by the puma"?

She limited herself to a smile, and lightly stroked the young messenger's shoulder.

"So he is well!"

Inguill nodded her head, finally relaxing.

"He also told me that you must not worry about him or the Sacred Double. Each is where he is meant to be."

Anamaya batted an eyelid in approval and asked:

"Now, tell me your story. You can trust me."

"As you know, Huascar, who wanted to be Inca instead of Emperor Atahualpa, died shortly after you were defeated by the Strangers. But the vengeance ordered by Emperor Atahualpa against the Cuzco clans loyal to Huascar was terrible. The order came from here, from the Cajamarca Palace. My family was annihilated. Emperor Atahualpa's soldiers entered the town and killed all its men. They crushed their heads while they slept, crushed them with bronze bludgeons. Then, as our men's blood flowed down the street gutters instead of sacred water, they took us. They took the children, the girls, and the women. They shoved us forward at the tips of their spears. They struck us with the handles of their axes and laughed. They told us that they would feed our blood to pumas, and that condors would read the future in our entrails. They..."

Inguill's calm and timid voice trembled for the first time. She didn't break down so much as lower her voice a tone, and Anamaya had to lean forward to hear her.

"They tore a baby from a mother's womb. As she lay dying they chopped it in half before her eyes."

Anamaya didn't reply. She could no longer make out Inguill. Tears blurred her vision, and she was trembling.

A vision from the distant past rebounded into her mind's eye, a vision that tore her heart and aroused a torment she had thought gone long ago. She saw the tender loving face of her own mother. She saw the misshapen catapult stone, launched by the Inca soldier, pierce her temple. She watched it take place with an unbearable precision and slowness, and once again she saw her mother tumble into the mud, never letting go of her hand. She saw her child self, standing alone, lost.

The pain suffocated her. Now, the *Coya Camaquen*, the great Huayna Capac's favorite, the one who had saved Atahualpa, had ceased to exist.

For a few seconds Anamaya was once more that young girl terrified by the brutality of warriors, that lonely young girl for whom the night brought no rest. She hardly heard Inguill add:

"One night the soldiers drank *chicha* to thank the Sun our Father and Illapa the Lightning God for having defeated Huascar's clans. I fled when they fell asleep. I didn't know where to go, so I returned to Cuzco. The Great Lord Manco was living there, hiding in his ancestors' temple. His brother Paullu had just fled to a hiding place near Lake Titicaca. I no longer had a family or home to go to, no more brothers or sisters, so Lord Manco told me that you would help me if I came to you."

"I will help you," murmured Anamaya.

She took hold of the young girl's hand. Inguill's fingers were still stiff from fear, and she hesitated a little before curling them around Anamaya's. She leaned forward and pressed her head against Anamaya's belly. Her chest burned, and her sobs punctuated her speech:

"Many moons have passed since I left. I thought I would never make it. It snowed when I crossed the Jauja Mountains. I was sure I was going to die, but then one day I saw the column of Strangers with General Chalkuchimac. I hid myself among the porters. No one said a thing! All I had to do was carry a *manta* full of gold goblets all day. . . ."

"It's over now," said Anamaya, stroking the nape of her neck. "It's over."

Inguill straightened herself, suddenly proud, and wiped the tears away from her eyes with the back of her delicate wrists. She tried to smile as she said:

"Once here, I had to watch out for the Strangers. That is why I could not come to you sooner. At first I was very frightened of them. They guffawed and tried to catch me. But they're not quick enough."

They paused, allowing the silence to return and allay their breathing. The northerly breeze had strengthened. The door hanging swung more regularly now.

Anamaya was still holding Inguill's hand. She felt her shudder. She nodded, feeling almost serene. She said in a low voice:

"The Great Massacre erased all that was before. The old order is dead. Those who claim to still know what is, and to be able to say what will be, are like blind children who see night when it is in fact day. No one here realizes that they are blind. The world has been upheaved, and that which was once strong is now weak. Tomorrow is like the blackness between two stars in the night sky. Our father and mother the Sun and Moon are watching us in silence, without telling us what we should do.

Everyone here is doing as he pleases, and many are those who are misguided. The Strangers think only of gold. And among those who serve Emperor Atahualpa, many are still fixated by the dark fire of vengeance against the Cuzco clans. You must hold your tongue from now on, Inguill. Tell no one your story."

"I know. Lord Manco warned me. He said, 'Talk only to her, she'll know how to hear you.'"

"From today onward," added Anamaya, "you must hold your tears. You must smile and show how happy you are to serve the Inca."

"I will do anything you ask if you let me stay close to you, *Coya Camaquen*."

Anamaya stood up, and Inguill jumped to her feet.

"First, I shall find you some clothes."

Inguill looked at her adoringly.

"You are so beautiful. Lord Manco told me that you were the most beautiful woman in all of the Empire of the Four Cardinal Directions. I thought he told me that because he feels so strongly for you. But you are beautiful, and your eyes . . ."

"Stop! Don't say those things!" protested Anamaya, a little too sharply. "Don't forget: when there are others present, you must speak to me only if I allow you to."

As though to mitigate the severity of her words, Anamaya took the young girl's face between her hands and brought it close to her own, placing her cheek against Inguill's.

"Everyone knows that I haven't a sister. I need you to pretend that you are my servant. But remember that in my heart you are a sister sent to me by the powerful Lord Manco."

"I am not pleased," growled Governor Francisco Pizarro, looking Gabriel directly in the eyes, "and you know the reason."

"Tell me, Don Francisco, so that I may hear it from your own mouth."

Pizarro sighed. He had steered the young man out of the palace and away from the square, across an alley running along the length of the Inca's palace, toward the hill on which stood that odd building that they called "the fortress" out of habit, despite the fact that no soldier or weapon had ever been found there.

"You seriously offended my brother Hernando, and you provoked him into a duel before the men."

"Is that the cock-and-bull he told you?"

"I forbid you to speak thus!"

But despite the severity of Francisco's tone, Gabriel was not really worried. Had Hernando's tale convinced the Governor, he would not be strolling through town but rather standing before a tribunal. Ever prudent, the Governor must have checked the facts with Candia.

"Let us save time, you and I, Don Francisco. Tell your brother that you threatened me with the worst punitive measures. And I will take upon myself the humiliation of admitting that I presented you with my most sincere repentance."

"If only it were so easy."

The Governor's appearance of despondency intrigued Gabriel.

"What in the devil is this all about, Don Francisco? Has your brother perhaps been touched by the grace of God? And now, ruing his transgressions, does he threaten to retire to a monastery to atone for his sins, and so die in the odor of sanctity?"

"Hold your jeering tongue, schoolboy. In the eyes of everyone my brother is a hero ever since he returned with that general. My brother is admired and feared by all the Indians. And my brother insists upon an apology."

Gabriel roared with laughter.

"Your brother still does not know me very well. I had thought that with the tip of my sword . . ."

"Enough!" cried Pizarro, plugging his ears. "I don't want to hear any more."

"Then ask nothing more of me, Don Francisco."

The two men had reached the high point overlooking the plain stretching before Cajamarca. They could make out the steam rising from the hot springs in the distance, from the Inca's baths where Atahualpa was waiting for them.

"I sympathize," murmured Pizarro in a subdued voice, "and if I were in your place I would no doubt refuse. But I'm asking you nevertheless. . . ."

The change in Pizarro's tone alerted Gabriel to what was to come, and he stiffened as he listened.

"I need my brother. I know him to his core, and I know all of his failings. But I need his lack of scruples, his natural authority . . . and I need his money."

"But the treasure is piling up!"

"You really are an innocent, aren't you! All that treasure is nothing in comparison to the mountain of debt that I have accumulated, nothing compared to what my esteemed associate, the one-eyed Almagro, is owed, nothing compared to the promises that I had to hand out like bread when the conquest was still nothing more than a madman's dream inside my head. If Hernando abandons me, I'm . . ."

Rather than finishing his sentence, Pizarro made a slicing motion across his throat with his hand. The gesture spoke more eloquently than a thousand words. His sincerity rattled Gabriel far more than his threat had.

"And if I don't offer my apology . . ."

". . . publicly . . ."

". . . publicly, Hernando threatens to abandon everything."

Pizarro nodded. Gabriel's heart beat hard, and a cold sweat dripped down his spine.

"I don't know about this, Don Francisco. I really don't know. . . ."

Pizarro nodded again.

"Do as you wish, my boy."

Gabriel said nothing, but he knew that in the bottom of his heart he had already accepted. An odd fusion of relief and rage made him tremble.

He didn't see the slight smile that played across Pizarro's face.

Chalkuchimac was standing still on the square, as large and as furious as a bear.

"What is the meaning of this?" he bellowed.

None of the few nobles of his suite dared reply. They stared straight ahead, wide-eyed.

Where there had once stood the elegant pyramid of the *ushnu*, there remained nothing but a pile of stones. The Strangers were building an outlandish structure with this rubble, replete with too many walls and roofs, an edifice never before seen in the Empire. Its walls were thin and twisted, and the stonework was so awkwardly chiseled that it looked as though a mere gust of wind, one small expression of rage from the sky, would knock it all over and reduce it to dust.

Chalkuchimac turned to Felipillo and barked once again:

"What is this monstrosity?"

"It is a temple they are building for their Heavenly Father. This is the name they give him who allowed them to defeat Emperor Atahualpa," replied the interpreter with an exaggerated deference.

"And who authorized them to destroy the *ushnu* to build this horror?" growled Chalkuchimac, his face dark with rage.

Felipillo turned his wary gaze to the nobles, looking for support that never came.

"Nobody."

Chalkuchimac intimated a gesture of rage, but at that exact instant a rider emerged from one of the buildings on the square. The Inca general stood frozen, stunned.

"But . . . he was in the Temple of the Sun . . . with his animal . . ." he murmured, disbelieving his eyes.

The noblemen and Felipillo stood about him in absolute silence, their heads lowered. Without taking his eyes off the horseman, Chalkuchimac extended his arm toward him threateningly and howled:

"He was in the Temple of the Sun with his animal! Is someone going to tell me what is going on here?"

Felipillo bowed almost to the ground.

"Governor Pizarro—their *Machu Kapitu*—has decided to take the temple as his house, and . . ."

Felipillo broke off. The sound of the horse's hooves on the huge square rumbled louder and louder. The rider had taken his horse to the far end, by the entrance to the baths, and there had turned it sharply. With a strike of the spurs glinting on his boots, he launched his animal directly at the gathering of Incas. Riding high in his stirrups, and with the rim of his hat flat against his forehead, he pushed his steed into a full gallop. Felipillo and the noblemen couldn't tear their eyes away from the animal's gaping ribs; they were possessed by its yawning nostrils and its eyes bursting out of its skull. But Chalkuchimac slowly closed his mouth and stood motionless, a haughty look on his face.

The din of the gallop vibrated in the hollows of their chests. When the beast was no more than a hundred paces away, the Inca noblemen cried out fearfully and retreated out of its trajectory. Felipillo bounded out of the way, taking refuge behind them. With its lips pulled back to reveal its yellow teeth, and with foam coming out of its nostrils, the animal panted as it lifted its hocks high. Now it was only fifty paces away, and still General Chalkuchimac didn't budge.

He looked at its rider, a small grimacing man, obviously having trouble holding himself in the saddle. He was a man of extraordinary ugliness, with only one eye, and the skin on his face consumed by disease.

With the rider, and his horse's hooves, approaching rapidly from dead ahead, Chalkuchimac pulled back his shoulder blades sharply, as though trying to broaden himself. Hateful disdain creased the corners of his mouth. Now he understood how the Strangers had dared destroy the *ushnu* in order to build their ridiculous house. Now he knew what they were capable of. He understood what it was that had turned Emperor Atahualpa so soft and spineless. In that fraction of a second, as he heard the cries of the wretched noblemen behind him, his fury became so immense that he seemed to turn to stone.

Just above him, the rider's fleshy lips trembled in discomposure. He extended his left arm and pulled on the reins at the very last moment and the horse's hooves kicked up a salvo of stones into the general's legs. Chalkuchimac felt the rider's boot slam into his shoulder, and the animal was so close that he could smell its acid stench. The horse flicked its tail through the air above him.

Chalkuchimac hadn't budged an inch. He didn't even move his eyes as the Stranger, laughing, trotted his animal around him, so close that the horse trampled the general's shadow.

Chalkuchimac remained absolutely still. His blood was ice. His hatred for the Strangers and his rage against Emperor Atahualpa, who had allowed this infamy to occur, were all that lived, burned, within him.

The horse turned and turned again. The beast's slaver and pungent sweat dirtied, along with the dust, General Chalkuchimac's alpaca *unku*. But he no longer heard the rider's laughter.

All of that had ceased to matter.

Only Inti and Quilla were real, along with the Apus, the stone Ancestors who lived beyond the hills, in the mountains by the sacred roads.

A ray of sun burst through the cloud-laden sky.

The rider placed himself directly before him. With a squeeze of his knees, he had his mount rear up on its hind legs. The horse neighed, furiously swiping its hooves through the air just above the defeated general's head.

Chalkuchimac remained still.

He turned his face toward the Sun God. He smiled. His face furrowed like a mountain being born at the start of time.

And now it was the one-eyed Stranger's turn to be frightened.

Compared to the one in which his brother the Governor had taken residence, the palace that Don Hernando Pizarro had taken as his own already resembled an opulent Spanish palace. By some miraculous means he had managed to have a great number of trunks delivered to him, and his residence was permanently buzzing with the work of Indian artisans. With varying degrees of brutality, the Spaniards directed the uncommon expertise of these craftsmen.

The area that he transformed into his dining room affected the regal splendor of one of Charles V's palaces: it had a massive, crudely sculpted table, candelabra, and a gold and silver dinner service. He had even got up his servants in a distinctive livery—red like his feather. Don Hernando had set out to make it clear that he was not just anybody.

When Don Francisco and Gabriel entered, Hernando was already seated at his table, entertaining his young brothers Gonzalo and Juan, Soto, and most of the Spanish lieutenants, Candia being the only notable absence. The two men were greeted by laughter.

"Ah, my brother," said the usually timid Juan, "Don Hernando was just telling us how he flung that monkey into the river, advising him to fly like a bird."

Silence followed Juan's forced laugh. All eyes were on Gabriel.

"Don Juan, did your brother tell you the rest of the story? Rumor has it that it's most amusing."

"I don't recall it," declared Hernando, "but perhaps you might enlighten us, sir?"

"My knowledge of such things is far too limited, Don Hernando, and I wouldn't dare remember what you have forgotten."

Don Francisco stood stiffly beside Gabriel, who could sense the Governor's extreme tension.

"I see that you have met with a belated sagacity, sir," said Hernando angrily.

"Merely prudence, Your Lordship, or else feebleness of spirit. I shall not bestow the noble name of sagacity on such a lapse of memory."

"Yes. Clearly something is lacking, however, something essential."

Gabriel let go a lively laugh.

"I lack so many things, Your Lordship, too many to come even close to what you infer."

"Come now, make an effort."

"It's that no matter how much I try, I cannot do it. It's simple."

"Simple, sir, yes, very simple," growled Hernando, throwing a black look at his brother. "More simple than I can describe."

Hernando, his hands clenched on the table, could no longer control himself. He jumped to his feet, knocking over his chair, and went toward Gabriel.

Gabriel turned nimbly on his heels and headed for the door hanging. With his back to Hernando, he muttered:

"I offer you my apologies, Don Hernando."

And with that, he disappeared so quickly that Hernando found himself standing stupidly in front of the flapping hanging. He turned, furious, toward the others.

"What did that whoreson say?"

"He presented you his apologies, brother," replied Juan in an embarrassed tone. "Will you tell us why?"

THREE

Cajamarca, June 1533

An awkward silence reigned over Emperor Atahualpa's court. Women were placing gold, silver, and terra-cotta vessels—the Inca's meal service—on a mat woven from green cane set before his bench. As before the Strangers' arrival, they contained the finest meats, and fish brought from the distant ocean. Yet this delicate promise of felicity was carried out in a dance of silence.

A few paces away, Gabriel and Anamaya stood side by side in the shadow of a wall, far from the braziers. They stood side by side, but not quite face-to-face, nor yet shoulder to shoulder. They had acquired the habit of standing thus whenever they were under the scrutiny of others. But nothing could prevent them from feeling the tremor of their private union: not even the sadness that pervaded every corner of Atahualpa's palace.

In a low voice, Gabriel told Anamaya how Hernando Pizarro had duped Chalkuchimac with lies, and how he had assured him that his master Atahualpa needed to see him. He described the general's contemptuous indifference in the face of the Governor's brother's insistent demands for gold and silver; Hernando's greed and veiled threats; the excitement of the troops when the rumor reached them that Moguer and his companions had reached Cuzco, and that from there they were sending a treasure even more fabulous than anything they had found thus far.

"You should have seen the madness in their eyes. . . . they wouldn't have been more excited had they been promised eternal life. Some even refused to sleep in case the treasure should arrive at night."

"The ransom room is already almost full," murmured Anamaya.

"Anamaya, it's not a roomful that they're after, not a palaceful, but a town built entirely of gold—and even that wouldn't satisfy them."

"Your people are very strange. I never stop observing them, always trying to understand in what ways they differ from you, and in what ways they are similar."

Gabriel couldn't think of a reply. He looked at Anamaya, her head lowered. Her blue eyes looked mainly to the ground, but she occasionally flashed glances at his lively face.

"Emperor Atahualpa shall never be free," she murmured.

"Don Francisco promised him that he would reign peacefully in the North, from Quito, where he was born."

"That shall never happen," said Anamaya, slowly shaking her head.

"The Governor made a promise," insisted Gabriel, his brow furrowed. "All of us must obey his command. That is how it is with us. Even the King, who is high above Governor Don Francisco, wishes it that Atahualpa remain your master."

"You just told me that gold was your only law."

"*Their* only law!" replied Gabriel proudly.

"Are you saying that you can change their law?"

Once again Gabriel didn't know what to say. Anamaya looked deeply into his eyes. He felt lost, floating, almost dissolved in the power of her gaze, in that beauty as fresh and as simple as a still lake. She was capable of communicating her convictions to him wordlessly, of thus showing him her unshakable knowledge of the truth. Each time she did it, he imagined discerning a power that he had never suspected existed until then.

Like a child unwilling to be convinced, he protested once again:

"If they try to harm him, I shall prevent it!"

He had spoken so loudly that he startled the women. Anamaya turned toward them, and the servant girls dispersed like a flight of birds. Gabriel blushed, then continued in a quieter tone:

"Ever since the day he was captured when I prevented him being killed, the Governor has requested that I watch over your King's life."

Anamaya tightened her cape, bringing it farther up her delicate neck.

"You cannot oppose what must be. . . ."

As she didn't continue, Gabriel asked, more harshly than he intended to:

"And what is that?"

"Time flees. There are forces against which it is useless to oppose oneself. Even you, who are good, cannot . . ."

Gabriel lowered his head, touched by the tenderness of her words. He didn't notice Atahualpa come out of the main room. The Emperor was wrapped in a cape of very fine brown wool, clasped across his chest by a gold *tupu* encrusted with jewels.

A woman rushed forward to sweep the little distance between him and his bench. Even from behind, Anamaya recognized Inti Palla's broadened form, her false friend and true enemy who had so often willed her end. Despite living under the same roof, they hadn't spoken to one another more than twice since many moons.

Anamaya rose and asked Gabriel in a low voice to distance himself.

At that very moment, a cry that echoed as far as the distant hills tore through the silence: a shout, or rather a roar, so clear that it chilled them. Everyone froze, and then the strident plaint came again, shredding the air.

"Chalkuchimac!" whispered Anamaya, turning toward the Inca.

Gabriel felt his guts churn.

Atahualpa continued as though he hadn't heard the cry. He extended a hand toward one of the golden bowls, and Inti Palla bent over to pick it up and bring it to him. As yet another cry shrieked through the sky above Cajamarca, the Inca brought a thin shred of vicuña meat to his mouth. A little juice dripped from his lips and a drop of boiled blood fell on his tunic.

Without waiting any longer, Anamaya and Gabriel rushed toward the entrance, disrespecting the rule of the Inca's sacred court. Raising his sword without removing it from its scabbard, Gabriel pushed aside the Inca warriors and Spanish soldiers guarding the palace's entrance.

As Inti Palla continued to hold the bowl of meat, her eyes turned toward the door through which Anamaya and Gabriel had disappeared. Atahualpa barely lifted his face toward them. He remained there for a brief moment, chewing on a few grains of corn. Then he stood up from his bench and disappeared into the tenebrous interior of his palace, walking with the slow and measured pace of a man with a mandate over time and space.

A crowd had gathered on the square, outside the defunct Temple of the Sun, now Governor Francisco Pizarro's residence. The surrounding cob wall was, as always, planted with *quinua* hedge. Gabriel and Anamaya passed through the silent group of Indians. At the entrance, Gabriel caught a glimpse of Pedro the Greek's huge silhouette and hooked nose.

"What's going on, Pedro?"

"Soto asked that fellow where the gold is, most genteel-like, but he didn't care to answer."

The Greek glanced over Gabriel's shoulder and saw Anamaya. He grinned knowingly.

Gabriel moved on, pushing aside a few men. He crossed the hall, furnished more or less in the Spanish style, and reached the light of the courtyard. There he heard Anamaya utter a little cry of surprise from his side.

A stake had been erected in the middle of the courtyard. Chalkuchimac was tightly bound to it. Under his feet was a pile of straw and deadwood. Although it hadn't yet been lit, smoke rose from the general's slightly burnt tunic, and his calves were blackened. Soto stood before him, the interpreter Felipillo at his side. The barrel-chested captain was stamping his stumpy legs on the flagstones with his hobnailed boots as though trying to flatten the ground. His face, normally so self-contained and smug, burned with rage. He was pointing his index finger at Chalkuchimac's chest.

"Let me make myself clear. You are brave, General, as strong-headed as a bull, and as stone-hearted as a crow. But I, who am only a humble captain, I want to know where your gold is!" he yelled. "I also want to know where your troops are, and what orders you have given your lieutenants. I want to know, and I will know, or else you shall burn like a pig on a spit!"

The interpreter Felipillo leaned reluctantly over the straw, as though frightened of falling there and burning with the general. He kept his eyes closed as he murmured into Chalkuchimac's ear. The Inca general's face remained unfathomable, but a vein pulsated visibly in his neck.

Gabriel came forward.

"Soto!"

The captain turned toward him, his eyes enraged.

"Stay out of this, friend."

"The Governor ..."

"... ordered me to interrogate this damned fool, and I am doing so," cut in Soto in a menacing tone.

Gabriel knew the man well enough to know that he never lied.

At that moment, the cry that they had heard from Atahualpa's palace again cut through the air. It came from Chalkuchimac. Gabriel could hear him saying something, but he couldn't tell what. He turned to Anamaya, who was now being lewdly eyed by the Spaniards. She didn't notice him. Her blue eyes were fixed on Chalkuchimac's face. Her lips moved in time with the general's cry. She was murmuring the word. This time Gabriel could make it out.

"Inti! Inti!"

The Inca general was not crying out in pain or in fear. What came out of his throat was a powerful call, like a trumpet resonating from a mountaintop.

"Inti!"

Chalkuchimac was invoking the Sun God. He was offering himself to him with all the assurance of his unshakable faith. His gaze fell upon Anamaya, and he said to her calmly:

"*Coya Camaquen.* Have my Lord, the Emperor, come to me."

"Burn him until he's a pile of ash," Gabriel growled to Soto, "he'll tell you nothing. You can't frighten him any more than a fly can. He is asking for an audience with his King. Only he can decide whether he speaks to you or not."

The captain eyeballed Gabriel, his rage barely contained. But he batted his eyelids, and, shrugging his shoulders, he sighed in resignation.

A tense calm, an uncomfortable sense of waiting, fell upon the courtyard after Anamaya had left bearing her message. Eyes darted about nervously, except for those of the Inca general, who stared fixedly at Soto with contemptuous defiance.

A noise from behind caused Gabriel to turn, as did the rest of the gathering. The Governor had arrived, with Atahualpa beside him. As Don Francisco looked from Gabriel to Soto, a smile appeared beneath the hairs of his beard. He gestured toward the Inca and announced:

"Lord Atahualpa deigns to speak with his general. Perhaps he shall succeed where your persuasion has failed, Soto. . . ."

Gabriel noticed Anamaya's hesitation. She had to take it upon herself not to go before the Inca as he approached Chalkuchimac.

From his torture post, the general looked hard at his master. He who had earlier shown himself so submissive and loyal to Atahualpa now didn't bat an eyelid as the Emperor approached. He showed no sign of affection. Quite the opposite: his mouth arched in an expression of growing contempt.

Atahualpa stopped a few steps before the pyre. He spoke in a low voice, but not so low that Gabriel couldn't hear.

"They threaten to burn you, but you mustn't believe them. They will not harm you, because to harm you would be to harm me. They haven't that wickedness in them."

Chalkuchimac remained silent for a short moment. He looked the Inca up and down, and then turned his heavy gaze toward Anamaya, ignoring the Spaniards as though they were nothing but shadows. He asked:

"My Lord, do you still know the will of your father the Sun? Are you still our Inca?"

Atahualpa quivered as though he had been slapped in the face. He straightened his spine, and in that instant the Spaniards made out in his rage the proud and powerful man he once was.

"How dare you speak to me thus?" he snarled.

"It seems to me that you are frightened of dying, my Lord," replied the general, now decided on provoking him. "Is that the case?"

"You have lost your wits, Chalkuchimac. You would do better to keep silent in front of the Strangers. You are more frightened of their flames than I of death. None will lay a hand on Inti's son."

"They already have."

"Do not see. Do not hear."

"Why not?" asked the general severely.

Gabriel felt Atahualpa's discomfort. No one among the Spaniards understood what the general meant, but Atahualpa and Chalkuchimac seemed to understand one another perfectly.

"Shut up," said the Inca finally.

"Why didn't you call for me, even though I was ready? Why did you refuse that I die to free you? I came before you, my eyes full of tears and affection, and you gave me only silence. I look at you and I see you tremble before the Strangers. They are nothing but temple pillagers, low thieves lusting after gold. It is not they who are destroying the Empire of the Four Cardinal Directions, Atahualpa, but your fear!"

With a raucous growl, Chalkuchimac spat upon his pyre. Atahualpa turned on his heel. The blood in his eyes seemed to have clouded over even his pupils. Anamaya kept her face lowered to the ground, her neck bowed. Gabriel had to clench his fists, so great was his desire to take her in his arms. But he knew that it would do more harm than good.

With a signal from Soto, the Canary Indians set their torches to the straw, and instantly it burst into small, bright flames.

In the brutal silence in the courtyard, Anamaya heard the growing crackle of the fire. She lifted her face, her mouth gaping as though she was going to cry out. Pizarro's hand gripped Gabriel's arm before he had a chance to make a move.

"Don't fret, my boy," Don Francisco murmured, "the Inca is in the right of it. This is just a ruse to loosen his tongue."

The fire jumped from the straw to the deadwood, crackling and spluttering, and billowing dense, acrid smoke. It whirled up around Chalkuchimac, who stared dead ahead, his lips only very slightly open.

Atahualpa turned toward him once again and stared imperturbably through the fire spreading across the pyre.

As the flames grew, the wood cracked loudly. Anamaya gripped her hands so tightly that the blood drained from her knuckles. Now Gabriel could feel the fire's heat on his face. Chalkuchimac looked at Atahualpa and once more screamed furiously:

"Take this lord out of my sight! Make him leave! Take him away from me! I'll talk, I'll tell you what you want to hear."

He had barely finished speaking when Felipillo shouted out the translation.

"Do as he asks, and put out the fire," ordered Don Francisco calmly.

As the Canaries threw jugs of water on the pyre, soldiers gently directed Atahualpa out of the courtyard. He left without once turning around.

The fire turned into a foul-smelling white steam. Only now did the blue of Anamaya's eyes reach Gabriel. The *Coya Camaquen*'s lovely face was as sad as it was serene.

Gabriel preferred to turn away rather than meet her gaze. He found the sight before him, and all that it evoked, unbearable.

Chalkuchimac was black with ash, and only his breathing could be heard. His ropes were untied. Below his knees, his legs were but shriveled shreds of flesh oozing blood, and his hands and arms were ravaged with blisters. And yet, when a mat was brought for him to rest on, the old warrior refused. He was carried a few paces away from the pyre. There, he elbowed the Canaries away, refusing their support and refusing to show his pain although his shortness of breath hinted at it. He remained upright and waited for the Governor to come to him.

Now it was Soto's turn to shake his head. He looked at the general as though he was a madman.

The indomitable general let loose a torrent of words.

Yes, there was more gold, a lot more, in the city of Cuzco. Yes, there were many more treasures there. If Atahualpa had forbidden that his father's, the Inca Huayna Capac's, possessions be touched, it was because he was the most powerful and the richest of all the sovereigns: he had died in this world, but lived on in the other. He drank, he ate, and his temple overflowed with gold.

But there was more: he approached Cajamarca four times at the Emperor's request. Four times the Inca had ordered his retreat at the last moment. Four times he had failed to give the order to attack, and he, Chalkuchimac, had had to retreat, his heart enraged.

Gabriel barely noticed that Anamaya had left the patio. The smoke from the pyre irritated his eyes, and filled the air with the odor of burnt flesh and shame.

Chalkuchimac talked and talked, and he spoke the words that Soto and the Governor wanted to hear. But they were words of vengeance, and no one knew if they were remotely true.

The forges lit up Cajamarca's nights. The sharing out of the spoils had begun and continued through day and night. Now that the pile had reached and even passed the line drawn by the Inca in the ransom room, loot was brought directly to the forges. They glowed red as gold streamed from them, a glinting, magic liquid. Then it cooled, became bricks, tangible measures of jubilation. It was piled up in sacks and baskets filled entirely with bricks of gold.

At first all the Spaniards stayed close, their faces as red as the burning braziers, their cheeks as swollen as the smiths' bellows. Some even burned their fingers in their impetuous desire to fondle those bricks of happiness before they had cooled. With their eyes fixed obsessively on that soup of gold that the *plateros* poured from their smelting ladles, the Spaniards consigned all else to oblivion. They forgot their bad memories, their fears, the diseases that they had suffered, their enmities and friendships. And as the gold flowed and endlessly flowed, it soon became an event as ordinary as the rising of the sun.

So much so that eventually the soldiers became reluctant to stand guard over the forges, claiming that doing so offered a mug's choice whether to roast his butt or his balls. As even the most unusual gold objects were melted down—corn ears, llamas, jugs, necklaces, ear plugs, idols, and simple plaques—no Indians, even those most loyal to the invaders, were ever allowed to approach the forges.

Sebastian observed the disparate pile of gold that had just been dumped before a forge. There were the usual vases and plates, but also tubes taken from fountains, chairs, and even gold stones.

The treasure gleamed scarlet in the light of the moon and the flames. They reflected on his face.

Gabriel grumbled to those about him:

"There are evenings when I am happy to have been deprived of a share of the plunder, to have nothing to do with it at all. My horse remains my most precious treasure!"

"Ha! But a real treasure he is, though. I'll give you three thousand pesos, going rate!"

"Forget it, he's not for sale."

"Now don't be getting sentimental about him. Why, you haven't even given him a name."

Gabriel thought for a moment.

"It's not that I don't want to . . . it's just that I don't seem able to, for some untold reason. No name seems to suit him . . . but he's my horse, and that's enough for me."

Sebastian nodded.

"Well, I wouldn't mind it at all if they gave me one . . . but Hernando forbids it."

"That damned jackass!"

The slur escaped from Gabriel at the mere mention of that hated name.

"Well may you grouse, my friend—though between you and me and the devil, you made me most uncommonly happy when you cut him down the other day—but still, that doesn't relieve me of my bondage. A slave am I, and poor I must remain."

"Bah . . . you're bound to pick up a few scraps from the forges, here and there."

Sebastian laughed a silent laugh so hard that his whole body shook. He pointed his thumb at the smithies by their forges.

"If you think that they're leaving any scraps for the picking . . ."

"Patience," grumbled Gabriel. "You're bound to find a Good Samaritan who'll slip you some of your cursed gold!"

"Is that right? Yet I have only two friends here in this forsaken land: you and Candia. And, curse my luck, you have to be the only conquistador there is who is denied a share of the spoils, and what's more who doesn't even care for gold! A madman who loves only some Indian girl's blue eyes!"

Gabriel eyeballed his mate, ready to explode in anger, but he saw in Sebastian only tenderness, amusement, and admiration. He let out a gentle laugh.

"Candia loves you as much as he loves his gold."

"Alas! You may as well say that he's no better than you and that he'll never be rich!"

Gabriel sighed, his smile still upon his lips.

"Who knows, Sebastian, perhaps you will become the richest among us?"

The black giant burst into laughter, holding his sides.

"With no horse? No sword?"

"You'll get your sword: everything in its own time and at its price."

Gabriel fell silent. His eyes followed a small group of Spaniards who were herding two Indians by. The Indians were carrying a golden idol the size of a large doll. Don Diego de Almagro was behind them, his lips pursed, surrounded by a few of his followers.

"Don Diego won't be able to watch all this gold pass under his nose for much longer," murmured Sebastian. "He's been as mad as a bull ever since he arrived."

The Indians painstakingly set the statue down on the ground as though it were a delicate child.

"The rule was set long before he arrived," replied Gabriel in a low voice. "The Cajamarca gold goes only to those who participated at the Great Battle, to those who captured the Inca!"

"Rules are made to be broken," murmured Sebastian. "All you have to be is stronger than the other."

"What do you mean?"

"Just that it won't be long before Don Diego improves his own lot."

"He would take on the Governor?"

Sebastian shrugged his shoulders.

"They're all here for the gold. All of them will have to get a share."

Gabriel watched Almagro's excited state over by the statue. He squatted down beside it, caressed it and laughed, his only eye aflame.

"Is it true that you saved his life?" Gabriel asked Sebastian, nodding at Don Diego.

"That was a long time ago. And until now, it has given me more trouble than reward."

"Perhaps he could make you rich."

Sebastian burst out laughing.

"No. He could make me free, however. He owns me. He only lent me to the Governor's expedition. His gold represents my freedom."

There was once a time, thought Gabriel as he walked through the shadowy, bustling streets, *when this city was inhabited by men busy only with living and with worshiping their gods. But now we are here, and like birds of ill omen we have brought with us our fevers and our lust for gold and glory.*

Occasionally he came across a torch burning on a street corner, a torch belonging to one of the fifty cavalrymen on night duty. These latest arrivals, Almagro's men, were the most aggressive because they were the poorest. They had no pesos, no women, and barely enough liquor.

"Soon, very soon, you shall see . . ." the Cajamarca veterans would tell them, who paid their way with gold ingots.

Coming out onto the square, Gabriel took the way heading toward Pizarro's palace. He noticed, across the square and behind the church being constructed, a gathering before the largest of the town's buildings, or *kallankas,* as the Indians called them, the one that Hernando had chosen as his domicile.

That's where Chalkuchimac was resting that night, his hands and feet burned, his nerves frayed.

A few soldiers stood guard at the entrance, tense before the crowd of Indians, who were themselves quite calm. The men spoke among themselves in low voices. It was difficult to gauge their mood.

A hand gripped his shoulder. He jumped, his hand already on the hilt of his sword.

"Don't be frightened."

"Anamaya!"

They laughed together at his surprise. A white *añaco* was wrapped about her waist, held by a crimson sash. She was gorgeous, like a star fallen to earth. She stood beside him, refraining from touching him.

"What are they waiting for?" asked Gabriel, pointing at the Indians.

"They want to serve Chalkuchimac."

"Why?"

She turned to face him, her own face unfathomable, yet she spoke with a teasing tenderness.

"They have lost their Inca, and they need a master."

"But the Inca lives yet."

"Yes, but his father the Sun no longer rises for him."

"You mean that Inti rises for him instead?" asked Gabriel, pointing at the palace door.

"No. I only say that they want to serve somebody."

"But serve whom, if not the Inca?"

Anamaya made no reply. Her gaze wandered over the distant hills, toward the moon, toward the mountains with their eternal snows.

When her gaze eventually came back to Gabriel, she allowed herself to fall gently against him.

"Come with me," she whispered.

Blind, for now, to the Indians' sadness and the Spaniards' drunkenness, they made their way along the square's wall and took the road leading to the Inca's baths. It was there that, in the autumn, Atahualpa's magnificent cortege had come to meet, in one short day, his glory and his end. It was there that they had fled together to discover the first night of their destiny.

As they went deeper into the shadows, their murmuring mixed with that of the waters. Soon, they were one with the night.

FOUR

In the shy blue of dawn, Gabriel rode along the well-lined stone path overlooking the Hatunmayo River. A great stand of trees protected him from the morning wind, and in the distance he could see the rising sun cast its pale light over the hills. It was a nice day, and last night's damp was evaporating slowly from the leaves.

Gabriel's heart grew lighter as Cajamarca slowly fell away below him. The will-o'-the-wisp wind, the intoxication of the breeze . . . it was as though he was at last escaping, in a stampede of hooves, from the tension reigning over the conquistadors.

Hernando, the Governor's brother, had returned to Spain, accompanied by a few *hidalgos*. He bore with him the good news of the victory at Cajamarca, as well as the proof of it: the King's *quint*, a ship filled entirely with gold.

Yet Gabriel hadn't found his good cheer since his hated adversary's departure. The Governor's younger brothers matched Hernando in treachery and villainy. In town, the tension between the haves and have-nots prohibited any hope of tranquillity. Their only thought was of gold, gold, and yet more gold. Yet the more they acquired, the more their avidity increased. Those already rich wanted to be richer, and those who weren't were ready to kill to become so. What's more, it was rumored that the ill feeling between Almagro and Pizarro, once comrades in Panama, had reached its highest point.

And the spread of fresh rumors further unnerved them. It was said that the Indians were amassing troops in the mountains surrounding the city, and that they were secretly being commanded by Chalkuchimac even from Hernando Pizarro's palace in which he was detained. The interpreter Felipillo claimed that the Inca's army was so massive that his generals had to divide it into three or four regiments so that it might be resupplied more easily.

Once again Chalkuchimac was interrogated. This time, however, he maintained a wall of silence. To reassure himself, Don Francisco had sent a reconnaissance mission, commanded by Soto, down the road to Cajas.

Cavalrymen reconnoitered the roads around the city on a daily basis, trying to discover an Inca vanguard preparing an assault that would never come.

And so, little by little, an insidious fear returned.

It wasn't the same as the terror that had reigned over them that past autumn when they had discovered the extent of the Empire's power, nor the panicky fear that they had experienced on the eve of the battle, when they knew that they were vastly outnumbered. It was a more muted dread, one that took hold of your guts and didn't let go. At night it feigned sleep only to return hidden in a gust of wind or the sound of an animal in the bush.

A stamping from behind caused Gabriel to turn around in his saddle quicker than usual.

"Don Gabriel! Don Gabriel!"

Gabriel recognized the dark green velvet doublet and the piebald horse with its silver-studded bridles. Pedro Cataño may have been a dandy, but he was one of the few Spaniards whose company he could stand. They were of the same age, and could have easily known one another at the university. Cataño was one of the few men of the expedition who could read and write. Moreover, he spent a lot of time writing, as though enamored of his own story. He was also one of the few who had behaved with dignity during the November battle, never attempting to insult the Inca. This attitude, in conjunction with his swarthy skin tone and cheekbones so high that he could easily have been mistaken for an Indian, had earned him the epithet *Indio*.

"*Hola*, Pedro! What a hurry you're in! Bad news?"

Cataño shook his head, smiling, his breath short.

"I should say not! It was only that I saw you leaving, and the desire came upon me to accompany you."

"I am not so certain that I need your company," said Gabriel, but not unkindly.

"Gabriel," replied Cataño without dismounting, "I thought that we had been ordered not to wander into the hills alone."

"Ah yes, orders . . ." sighed Gabriel fatalistically.

Riding at a slow walking pace, the two men reached the first peak. The river meandered gently down below. The day was well advanced, and a light breeze prevented the heat from becoming oppressive. It was hard to believe that thousands of men armed with axes and slings were hidden in the surrounding splendor.

Cataño brought his horse up alongside Gabriel's. The two men sat shoulder to shoulder in silence, admiring the beauty of the city, smoke rising from its roofs.

"What damned inventions these rumors are," griped Gabriel. "I wager you all the gold I don't have that there isn't an Inca warrior within leagues of here!"

Cataño grinned.

"Now there's a wager that can't be lost!"

"They're lying to us, Pedro! And we know why, don't we?"

Cataño pondered. He was at once timid and abundantly audacious, and his speech was on occasion disarmingly direct.

"Are you inferring that Almagro's people want to rid themselves of their Inca Atahualpa? That they are so impatient to reach Cuzco and make their own fortunes that they would contravene the Crown's orders?"

"Atahualpa's ransom has been paid, even overpaid," said Gabriel. "Those recently arrived, Don Diego most of all, find that they cannot wait any longer. Atahualpa's presence, and the supposed risk of an assault by Chalkuchimac's troops to free him, frays their nerves. And the fact is we can't remain holed up here forever. Is that not your opinion?"

Cataño hesitated slightly.

"Don Francisco will not allow it to happen. The Inca to be killed, I mean."

Gabriel stroked his horse's neck. Whenever anyone propounded the Governor's rectitude to him, he couldn't help but remember the smell of burnt flesh at Chalkuchimac's pyre.

"By the faith, I hope so."

"Is he aware of this danger?"

"Don Francisco understands and is aware of everything. No one here has a better view of the situation than he. And everyone knows that he has cheated Don Diego a little. They set out on this adventure together ten years ago, against the winds and the tides, being particular friends. But today one is rich and a Governor, whereas the other has lost his fortune and is a mere captain."

They admired the splendor of the plain for a few moments in silence, as the implications of Gabriel's words found their weight. Then Cataño nodded with a weary smile:

"I understand now why the Governor's brothers hate you as they do, Don Gabriel. Until now I thought it mere jealousy of your intimacy with Don Francisco. But your eye is too sharp. They will not let you off the hook."

Gabriel laughed quietly and gave his companion a friendly look.

"Well, may you be the only judge of whether your own eye becomes too sharp, Pedro. Not forgetting the tribulations such a fine, clear view can bring you."

Pedro considered this silently. But his half smile, one of affectionate appreciation, told that he had already decided.

Gabriel said a short good-bye and, without another word, set off at a full gallop toward the town.

Putting on her straw sandals, Anamaya found a hefty spider on one of the straps, its massive limbs covered in a sheen of hair. After an initial moment of repugnance, she let the arachnid crawl up her bare leg, and it hesitated awhile around her knee before climbing back down and fleeing across the flagstones. As nimble as a shadow, it disappeared beneath a mat.

She remained still a moment. She no longer enjoyed mornings as she once did. She often awoke these days in a cold sweat, her heart racing, terrified by premonitions, her spirit confused by the lies and the heavy silences weighing down the palace's *cancha*. Things were being hidden from the Inca: his servants who died or fled, the imperceptibly gradual crumbling of everything. He existed in the center of an invisible shrinking circle drawn around him by others, and within it he was still an absolute ruler. But outside it chaos, confusion, and disorder ruled.

Hers was a strange state of being now, and Gabriel's love brought her no certitude: on the contrary, it brought her even greater disquiet.

"Are you dreaming, Anamaya?"

Inguill had never lost her habit of slipping into Anamaya's room with the agility of a *viscacha*. It had helped her survive so far, and she continued to move thus about the palace. In all the chaos, few questions were asked about the sudden appearance of another servant girl. All spare hands were needed.

"Yes, but I'm trying to reach the conscious world," said Anamaya cheerfully.

"May I have permission to speak to you?"

Inguill had the serious manner of children that always made Anamaya feel like a mother.

"You have heard, as I have, the rumors that are being spread about Inti Palla."

"I'm not interested in Inti Palla."

Anamaya spoke spitefully despite herself. Her hatred of that woman, once such a very beautiful princess, had never subsided. Inguill stared at her, taken aback.

"Forgive me," said Anamaya more gently. She took Inguill's hand in hers.

"So tell me, what are these rumors?"

"They say that Inti Palla allowed herself to be seduced by he who serves the Strangers and translates all they say."

"Felipillo?"

Inguill nodded.

"Inti Palla goes to Felipillo's bed?"

"You mean you didn't know?"

Anamaya shrugged contemptuously.

"But such a thing is impossible! Inti Palla is a wife of Atahualpa! How could she dare?"

Inguill took on a stubborn air, squeezing Anamaya's wrist, insisting in her certitude:

"But it's true! I saw them! I couldn't sleep last night and I went to the *cancha* before hiding in the Temple of the Divinities. And I saw them. . . ."

"Them?"

"Felipillo had his hands on her, and she was happy."

The specter of Anamaya's dormant hatred toward the false-hearted princess flared in her heart. She asked coldly:

"Did they see you?"

"I don't think so."

"I told you to watch out for yourself, Inguill!"

"But *Coya Camaquen!* I heard them pronounce Atahualpa's name! I had to tell you!"

"Yes, that's true . . . thank you. But don't forget to be very careful. And now let me be, little one."

Inguill's eyes lingered a moment on Anamaya before she reluctantly obeyed.

Once alone, Anamaya sat perfectly still. She felt a pain rising in her kidneys. Shame, fear, and a sense of having been deceived ran through her body like poison. She should run to the Inca and tell him, she thought; warn him of the danger as she had on so many previous occasions.

But this time, she felt only sorrow and a longing for solitude.

"Fucking idiot! Damned fool!"

Gabriel heard the insults through a gap in the wall. He dismounted and handed the reins to one of the Indians who were always hanging about in front of the *canchas*. He entered the courtyard. A Spaniard was hitting an Indian with the hilt of his sword, hammering him on his head, his ears, and his neck. The Indian, bleeding, howled in pain.

"What's going on here?" demanded Gabriel.

The Spaniard turned around, his disheveled brown curls framing his cherubic face. Gabriel hadn't immediately recognized him from behind: it was Gonzalo Pizarro, the Governor's youngest brother, and the handsomest man in Cajamarca. But his good looks were but a mask for his black soul.

Gonzalo smiled with feigned amicability, and pointed with the tip of his sword at a table. There was an adze at its legs.

"What's going on is that I ordered this monkey here to make a table. A table, do you hear? Not a rood screen or a damned pulpit, but a table! And this is what he does!"

Gonzalo leaned on the table. It wobbled very slightly.

"Well?" asked Gabriel, forcing a smile as unstudied in appearance as Gonzalo's.

"Well, it wobbles."

Gabriel approached the other end of the table and leaned his hand on it.

"It doesn't wobble," he said quietly.

"I tell you that it wobbles."

Gabriel bent down to pick up the adze. He handed it to the terrified Inca.

"Here, take it," he said in Quechua. "Don't be frightened."

The man hesitated an instant, then timorously took the tool and glanced fearfully at Gonzalo.

"In my opinion this table doesn't wobble," said Gabriel agreeably for Gonzalo's benefit. "Yet even if it wobbled so much that everything slid off it and shattered on the ground, your brother the Governor would agree with me that it wouldn't be worth a poor wretch's life."

Gonzalo's hand was gripped around the hilt of his sword. The evocation of his brother's name, the Governor's name, made him thoughtful.

"Be very careful," he said eventually.

"Santiago," continued Gabriel in his friendliest tone, "I'm on my tiptoes night and day."

Gonzalo reddened at the jeer.

"I shan't be as kind to you as my brother Hernando was," he spat.

"I hear you, Gonzalo. It's just that I miss your big brother and his big red feather. But I'm as frightened of you now as I was of him then. Do you not see how I tremble?"

And with that Gabriel turned on his heels and left the courtyard. He slipped a fruit to the Indian who had looked after his horse.

Gonzalo gave the artisan one final thump, the poor man keeping his eyes turned toward the ground.

"Make it again, you confounded idiot!" he hurled. "And this time make sure that it doesn't wobble!"

He turned around and shook his fist at the door through which Gabriel had left.

"Be very careful," he said to himself.

And then he smiled.

*   *   *

Seated on his *tiana*, his royal throne, the Emperor had his eyes closed. His face was impassive, and he sat utterly still, as though he was already a mummy. When he opened his eyelids, his pupils were two tiny black points lost in the middle of two blood-red lakes. Anamaya remained silent. An old feeling overwhelmed her, something stronger than her anger against Atahualpa, or her sadness, or her bitterness.

Tenderness.

But suddenly, as though he had read that emotion, the Emperor did something astonishing. He slipped from his bench toward the ground covered with guanaco skins and vicuña wool blankets. He reached out his hands toward Anamaya. He murmured so low that it was barely louder than the sound of his breath:

"*Coya Camaquen!*"

She crawled to him on her knees and placed her hands in those of the Sun King, palm against palm.

The Emperor trembled. His entire body trembled, his lips, his hands, his chest, everything in him trembled from the unhinging of the world. He trembled so much that his teeth chattered. He trembled like the stones in the temples, their edges polished a thousand times, did whenever *Pacha Mama*, the Mother Earth, moved from deep within.

And so the Inca wrapped his arms around Anamaya and held her close. He held her like his father, Huayna Capac, had once gripped her hand for the entire night before he died. He held her against his heart as he had in the old days when, guided by the comet, she had foretold his destiny of glory and triumph.

They heard boots stamping in the courtyard. When Don Francisco Pizarro crossed the room's threshold, he found them thus intertwined.

Pizarro hesitated, embarrassed. From behind him, Felipillo's wily gaze was flabbergasted by what he saw. The Governor waited a few more seconds and then, as though there was nothing out of the ordinary, he called out gently and with respect:

"Lord Atahualpa!"

The Inca opened his arms, and Anamaya rose with no particular haste. She stood behind Atahualpa, who had returned to his *tiana*. She stared at Felipillo. The interpreter looked away, ill at ease. She thought about what Inguill had told her, but the three words that came out of the Governor's mouth captured her attention.

"You are free!"

She was not certain of having clearly understood.

The Governor stared intensely at Atahualpa.

"You are free," he repeated, "but I don't understand you."

Felipillo interpreted, looking furtively at Anamaya.

"What is the meaning of this?" asked the Inca. "What is the *Machu Kapitu* saying?"

Anamaya repeated it, looking hard at the Governor, but unable to decipher him.

"I hear rumors, Lord Atahualpa!" continued Pizarro, more comfortable now. "I try to ignore them, but they keep on coming . . . almost every day your caciques come to my palace and tell me that you're sending orders to every province in the empire to mobilize your troops against us. Your general Chalkuchimac is here with us, but you send orders to your other lieutenants, Quizquiz and Ruminavi. But I like you, and I don't believe everything my ears hear. Nevertheless, I ask you: Am I right not to believe them?"

Anger flashed across Atahualpa's face.

"Of course you are right! It is all rubbish."

The Governor listened to Felipillo's nervous translation and nodded.

"So much the better. In that case, you will soon be able to go to your northern kingdom as I promised, and there rule in peace, with my protection of course, for the glory and in the name of our Emperor Charles V and Our Lord. Meanwhile . . ."

Atahualpa was listening intently. He waited. But Pizarro fell suddenly silent, showing no intention of continuing.

"So, I'm going to die," said Atahualpa eventually.

"How do you mean, die?" asked the Governor, astonished.

"I shall soon be with my father."

Pizarro didn't deny or protest his words.

Anamaya saw Gabriel's silhouette suddenly appear through the door hanging, and he came up next to the Governor.

"Forgive me, Don Francisco," he whispered, out of breath, "I couldn't come more quickly."

Pizarro didn't look at him. He didn't take his eyes off the Inca.

"Please don't say such things, my friend," he said gently, "you are not going to die. If you have enemies, we will protect you against them. And we will guard you from those Christians who don't understand you. I value your friendship too much."

"I am weary," replied the Inca in a even voice.

"Then rest. Be at peace, and have a nice day."

Pizarro bent his lean person down low, then left, followed by Felipillo and Gabriel.

"Where are they?" he asked out in the courtyard.

Two soldiers approached. Gabriel was stupefied to discover Sebastian, his face tight, carrying a chain with links as big as a child's wrist.

"But what in the name of God are you doing with that?" he asked.

Sebastian made no reply. Gabriel turned to the Governor.

"Don Francisco, please explain to me what's going on."

"Come," said Pizarro to Gabriel after having directed the two soldiers to the Inca's room. "We need to talk."

Anamaya had remained behind Atahualpa. When she saw the door hanging rise once more and the chains in the Spaniards' hands, she involuntarily stepped back.

"Don't worry," said Atahualpa, "all is as it should be."

Sebastian approached the immobile Inca. His gaze darted away, caught Anamaya's blue irises for a moment before darting away again.

"Tell them to do what they must do," said Atahualpa calmly.

The African giant placed an iron collar around the Inca's neck. He made sure not to set it too tightly. A chain was hooked onto the collar, then looped about the room's lowest supporting beam and padlocked.

Atahualpa still hadn't moved. A wan smile lit his face and even his eyes.

"You see, Anamaya. I am free!"

FIVE

The Strangers had transformed, with what little means they had at their disposal, the biggest room in the Temple of the Sun into something approximating a lavish Spanish palace. They had even fashioned some rudimentary Spanish furniture such as tables surrounded by high-backed chairs, albeit mostly rickety. Faded tapestries hung on the walls above stacks of travel trunks. In the niches stood statues of the Virgin Mary, so cherished by Governor Pizarro. They had replaced puma masks and llamas made of gold or silver, long since smelted down into bricks. As for the pottery, it had all been stolen or smashed.

Four places were set around the big table, its candelabras dripping wax onto it. At the moment there were only three guests, however. Don Diego de Almagro sat facing Gabriel, while Pizarro remained standing.

Don Diego wore no eye patch across his pockmarked face that evening. Gabriel wasn't sure which eye to look at. The one that had been destroyed by an Indian spear was oddly fascinating in its unsightliness. It was a dry, black mass, which on occasion seemed to move in coordination with the good eye. Don Diego (who, it was said, was as courageous as ten men) was, in fact, beneath his boorish, uncut façade, a sophisticated and wily man, and he knew how to make the most out of his disability.

"I saw him," he said, his accent betraying his La Mancha roots. "I went to his cell and told him to calm down."

"Who are you talking about, Don Diego?" asked Gabriel.

"Pedro Cataño! Your friend, apparently. He kicked up a fuss at the Council this afternoon, interrupting Don Francisco to claim that you and he had foiled a plot against the Inca! Why, in the name of God, he went so far as to declare that he would give his life for him! One would think that he's one of the Inca's twelve hundred sons, to say such things! Though I can't help but wonder, given the color of his skin."

Pizarro grinned. Gabriel went pale, and had to clench his teeth to prevent himself from insulting the one-eyed man.

"The Governor had him thrown in a cell to cool off," said Don Diego, laughing. "What else could he do?"

"He could've let him be," growled Gabriel, "and simply advised him to hold his tongue."

"Enough, gentlemen!" intervened Pizarro, rubbing his hands together. He had removed his gloves, for once. "I have invited our friend Cataño to sup with us. Was that not a good idea of mine, Don Diego?"

Rolling his only eye, Almagro raised his arms toward heaven.

"I know too well the unfathomable depth of your magnanimity, Francisco. It is unfathomable indeed, and also, if you will forgive me, dangerous."

Pizarro's face lit up. Despite the causes and the bitterness of their rivalry, Almagro had the privilege of being one of the few men able to draw a smile from him.

"If your lordships, in all your beneficence, would be so kind as to grant me an explanation?" asked Gabriel sardonically, wary of what he would no doubt hear.

"At the Council of War that your friend Cataño so rudely interrupted, we were discussing what to do with the Inca. Father Valverde and I are of the opinion that he is a human being and that we can make a Christian of him, but there are some . . ."

The play of the candlelight cast sinister shadows across Almagro's face.

". . . there are some who feel that it is a dangerous situation," finished Almagro in his shrill voice, toying with a goblet of bad wine, "and there are others who think that it is no longer possible to launch an expedition against the Empire's capital. Moguer and Bueno were adamant on their return to Cuzco. There are treasures to be found there far more considerable than anything we have seen up to now—I mean anything *you* have seen up to now, all of you who were with my cherished friend the Governor Don Francisco, the treasure that *you* have amassed, melted down, and carefully stashed away in your pockets."

"Nonetheless, none of us are in doubt that we must demonstrate a very Christian spirit throughout this adventure," continued Pizarro impassively. "We must ensure that our Emperor Charles V is gladdened by our efforts when news of them reaches him."

"The royal decree is clear," intervened Gabriel. "It dictates that we protect as far as is possible the lives of all Kings, Princes, and Lords of the Indies."

"As far as is possible, so therefore not in the case of treason," said Almagro hoarsely.

"What treason?" demanded Gabriel, raising his voice.

"Easy, Gabriel . . . none so far," said the Governor quietly, approaching the table. "It is possible, and possible only, that there is a case of treason, Diego. It is possible only, and in the absence of any solid evidence of it, we must continue to protect the Inca's life and await Soto's return."

"But we have evidence!" shouted an exasperated Almagro, slamming his goblet on the table.

"What evidence?" asked Gabriel.

"The Indian witnesses!"

"Lies, Don Diego! You know very well that that is all the result of their internal politics and intrigues."

"Lies yourself, sir! You want truths? I'll give you one: we can't march the roads to Cuzco with that feathered monkey on our backs! All the Indians in the world will fall on us!"

"How do you know? He appeases them with a mere word. I've seen him do it."

"You've seen nothing at all, mate. I have but one eye, but I've seen far more than you can imagine! I've been seeing what this rabble is capable of for more than forty years! And Francisco knows them as well as I do, don't you?"

"I like to do things according to the law, Don Diego. I like there to be order."

"Ha! Is that so! Then put things in order, Governor! Set a date for our departure to Cuzco, and make sure that Featherhead can't come up behind us!"

"But that's disgraceful!" yelled Gabriel, standing up. "You cannot . . ."

Don Francisco waved him back down, and then turned to face the Virgin.

"The Inca is under my protection. If he is guilty, it shall be a court of law that decides, just like in Spain."

Almagro shook his large, misshapen head, angrily bit into a piece of corn bread, and screamed.

"Diego! What's wrong?"

"By the devil! I've broken a tooth," he mumbled, furious. "Forget about your damned Virgin, and have them bring us meat, Francisco. I'm hungry!"

Don Diego de Almagro spat his canine into the dirt.

Shadows reigned in Atahualpa's palace. The Emperor had given the order that no torches were to be lit. He had turned away all his meals; refused visits from his *curacas;* and turned away from the attentions of his wives and concubines.

He wanted only Anamaya as company. While the light of day still reached the gold puma in its niche, he remained silent. It was only long after nightfall that he said:

"I am a jungle cat who no longer knows how to pounce."

There was no bitterness or sadness in his voice. It was a simple observation. He touched the collar around his neck, and shook the links chaining him to the wall.

"Come nearer, *Coya Camaquen.* Put your arms around me. . . ."

Anamaya put her hands on the Emperor. She felt his exhausted body through the softness of his clothes, the heat already dissipating from him. He was dying of his own volition. He was a man who already belonged to the Underworld.

"Now I know everything," said Atahualpa calmly. "It is too late now. I regret nothing, because life is the price of this knowledge. I know what my father said to you the night before he died because I am in that same night now, and soon I shall be at his side. It is his voice, not mine, speaking to you. So listen: behind mine there is my father's! My voice is infinitely older than I, and it will continue to speak long after I'm gone. *Coya Camaquen,* gentle young girl with eyes the color of the lake, never forget to heed the voice of the son of Inti!"

"I have known for many moons that you would be leaving us, my Lord," murmured Anamaya, "yet now that the moment is upon us, I'm frightened."

"I am not. Stay with me as you stayed with my father."

Anamaya's breath joined Atahualpa's, and they were one in the night.

"There are no more Cuzco clans," whispered Atahualpa. "I carried out my vengeance like a drunken fool, an unjust man ruled by anger. There are no more brethren; no more enemies. The children of the Empire are today bound in chains just as I am. They cry tears and suffer, and it is my fault."

His knees gave and Anamaya tried to hold him up, but the collar ground into the Inca's neck. A rumbling of pain juddered from his chest. He said hoarsely:

"The North and the South have been weakened by my doing, the blood of the Sun has been shed because of me. Chalkuchimac was right: this is not the doing of the Strangers! They are like the birds that wait for their prey to exhaust themselves. I, Atahualpa, son of Inti and of the great Huayna Capac, I have fractured the Empire of the Four Cardinal Directions, and the Strangers are making the most of it. But they know nothing of the power of the Other World. They are building with mud on a mountain of fire that will, one day, wake and so utterly consume them that their ashes shall be blown back to the ocean that bore them here."

His voice no longer came from his chest. It was as harsh as winds blowing from the bowels of the earth. It was the voice of all the Ancestors, of all the fathers and sons who had carried the lineage since the birth of the world.

"I have long renounced my brother Manco. Now I see what you have always seen but never dared tell me: that he is the first knot of the future."

"And the Puma?"

The question came out of her mouth despite herself. Yet there was no surprise in Atahualpa's voice when he answered:

"The Puma is no longer with me, but you must place your trust in him. Follow my father's orders, and heed his advice. . . ."

Anamaya felt the shackles of silence that had been constricting her throat now break against the relief his words brought her. At last, the Emperor had managed to see and understand that which she had seen and understood for so long. At last, he was again close to the Ancestors of the Other World. Now he was truly on the path that concluded with the death of the body.

The Emperor and the *Coya Camaquen* shared their joy long into the night, with their eyes closed and their spirits relieved. The lines between their dreams and their wakefulness, between night and day, between flesh and the absence of flesh, had been removed. Like transparent birds they spread their wings and traveled above the mountains and plains of their beloved country, into its past and into its future, into the lake of its origin, into the Sacred River in the sky, into the silver of the moon and the Sun's gold.

Prisoners, they had found freedom.

They were already peeling their fruit when Pedro Cataño walked unsteadily into the Governor's dining room. Rage and fear from having been locked up ruined his features. Don Francisco rose and placed a hand on his shoulder, a gesture that Gabriel knew well, for it was the Governor's way of calling for submission under the guise of affection.

"Calm yourself, Pedro! Sit down and eat something."

Cataño slid into a chair and promptly launched into a tirade that clearly had been long premeditated. He glared at Almagro seated directly in front of him.

"Gentlemen, Governor, I thank you for bringing the justice that Lord Atahualpa deserves upon his head."

Almagro chuckled and picked at some mango flesh caught between his teeth. Pizarro, acting as though he hadn't heard, asked:

"What do you say to a round of cards?"

"Cards!"

Gabriel couldn't believe his ears.

"Does our noble Gabriel consider himself above such amusements?" jibed Don Diego.

"Excellent," continued Don Francisco, making a sign to the Indian servant girls. "Diego, you team with our friend Cataño, but first let him eat his dinner."

Almagro took the deck with a bored expression on his face while Cataño ate ravenously from his pewter porringer.

Just then a quarrel broke out outside, and angry voices could be heard. Gabriel went out onto the threshold. The palace guards were blocking three men: two Spaniards and an Indian slave brought from Nicaragua. Gabriel recognized one of the Spaniards as Pedro de Añades, a little man with a sparse beard who never stopped sweating. If ever there was one loyal to Almagro, it was he.

"Well, Añades," called Gabriel, "what's going on?"

"They're preventing me from getting through," shouted Añades, indicating the guards. "I need to see Don Diego de Almagro this instant."

"This instant? That's a little presumptuous, isn't it? Don Diego is playing cards with the Governor."

Añades's face lit up at the news.

"The Jesus is watching over me, Don Gabriel. I also need to see the Governor."

"May I ask why?"

"I feel that their Lordships would take umbrage at me should I not bring them this fellow's testimony directly," he said with a grandiose air and pointing at the Indian.

"What testimony?"

Añades put his finger to his lips.

"Forgive me, Don Gabriel, but this matter is of such import that I can allow this man to speak only before the Governor and Don Diego."

Smug satisfaction was writ large all over Añades's face. Gabriel reflected on it for an instant, thinking that there was something cruel in it. He gestured at the guards.

"Let them in," he ordered.

"Your Lordships," began Añades pompously, once in the dining room, "it is of the utmost importance that . . ."

"Get to the point," snapped Pizarro.

Disconcerted, Añades glanced at the table, the dishes, the cards, as though looking for the quickest way to reach his goal. In the end he thrust forward the reluctant Indian and said:

"Speak, then."

The Indian remained silent, rolling his terrified eyes. His lips moved but no words came out. Añades, his forehead glistening, said:

"This man says that he saw a multitude of Indian warriors three leagues from Cajamarca marching on us."

"From what my ears hear, this man says nothing at all," remarked Pizarro coldly.

"Hold on, Francisco," intervened Almagro, throwing his cards down and jumping up from his chair. "By all the saints, we are in danger of annihilation and you speak as though we were in a Seville court of law!"

"This man either speaks or he doesn't. I want to hear what he says."

"Talk to us," said Gabriel gently. "Just tell us what you saw, and we will be satisfied."

The slave gathered himself. He spoke in short, chopped sentences:

"I saw those warriors. Many, very many of them . . . from the North . . . I was hiding in a village . . . they razed a cornfield. They were singing. They spoke about attacking the town tomorrow night. . . ."

Gabriel knit his eyebrows and pinched his lips as he listened to the Indian continue his story. Pizarro nodded with each sentence.

"And so?" asked Añades, looking smug.

His question met with silence.

Then Almagro's voice echoed sarcastically:

"Does Your Lordship wish that we all die for Cataño's love?"

Pizarro looked at him blackly and replied:

"Spare me your idiocies, Diego, I've heard them all before!"

He squeezed his fist into his glove and left the room without even glancing at Gabriel. Almagro, already standing, went after him, followed by Añades, his companion, and the slave. Despite the light of the flames, young Cataño's usually tawny face had turned gray.

"It's over then," he murmured. "They're going to murder Atahualpa. We've lost, haven't we?"

Gabriel shook his head gently.

"Pedro," he said in a low voice, "you were with me this morning, yes?"

Cataño nodded unhappily.

"You saw what I saw, didn't you? Pastures, air, silence. There is no army outside Cajamarca."

"But that man said . . ."

"That man is lying!" burst out Gabriel.

SIX

Cajamarca, July 26, 1533

"Prove to me that he's lying!" barked Pizarro.

"I don't need to prove it. I saw the mountains and fields with my own eyes, and there is no army there! I give you my word on it! I tell you: that fellow is lying. God's blood, Don Francisco! Is not my word worth more than that of a mere slave?" said Gabriel, deeply vexed.

He had forced his way into Pizarro's room at the hour when the Governor was dressing. Don Francisco was carefully setting his white lace ruff around his neck. Along with a few colored feathers in his hat, it was the only finery he wore that counterbalanced his perpetual black garb.

"Don Francisco," he continued, "at least wait until Soto returns! We shall know more then. He and his men will have explored every ravine between here and Cajas. If there are more than three armed Indians gathered anywhere, he will have seen them, or at the least heard of them."

His voice was hard, his eyes furious. He wished himself calmer, more measured. He knew that the Governor hated being pressured. And in any case, the Governor rebuffed his proposition by merely raising his eyebrows disdainfully.

"Wait? But my boy, what will I tell the Council this morning? What could I say to Almagro and to the King's officers?"

"My Lord, if my memory serves me well, you were hardly so concerned with the King's officers at our departure from Seville ... and even less so with the Council or with Don Diego! You wished things to happen according to your own lights, and that events follow rather than precede you."

Mirth flashed across the Governor's wizened eyes. He liked being reminded of that caper. Nevertheless, he shook his head.

"The past is behind us, my boy. Henceforth I am responsible for this town, for you, and for your companions. I am Governor, and this country must abide by Spanish law."

"Precisely!" said Gabriel bitterly. "If the King learns that Lord Atahualpa was executed without proof . . ."

The Governor's fingers quivered on the edge of his hat. His exasperation showed when he rapped out:

"How many times need I tell you? You haven't given me any proof that Don Diego's Indian is lying. No more than you have that Atahualpa isn't feeding us poppycock to lull us into complacency!"

"Just give me the time to find that proof and you shall have it!"

"Enough!"

For the first time, Pizarro raised his voice and his black-gloved hand against Gabriel.

"Enough! That will do, Gabriel Montelucar y Flores! You forget yourself! Remember who you are and what you owe me! And remember your promise!"

Gabriel stiffened. The allusion to his illegitimate birth and to that hated name made him pale. As for the rest of it, he remembered it as though it had happened yesterday.

But the Governor was already biting his lip, feigning embarrassment, and now he said, more calmly:

"Oh, I don't give a damn where you come from. I'm like you. But as for the rest, don't forget . . . you promised to submit yourself to my judgment. And this condition makes you . . . yes, it makes you a son of mine."

The Governor's voice faded as he voiced that secret, ambiguous affection that bound them together. *Cunning old dog* . . . thought Gabriel, unable to hold back his emotion.

"I need your trust, Gabriel," continued Don Francisco as he took his arm. "Don't let yourself be overly influenced by that Indian girl, that sorceress from Atahualpa's entourage. It doesn't bode well."

"That is my affair and mine only, Don Francisco!"

"I'm not so sure. . . ."

They sized one another up for a moment, eye to eye. In the end Pizarro waved his hand as though brushing aside a fly.

"Bah, women, they're not important. I only tell you this because my brothers are grieved to see you with that strange girl."

So, here we are then, reflected Gabriel, almost amused, *the old dog is trying to change the subject and get at what he thinks is my weak point.*

"You know my opinion of your brothers, Don Francisco. I decline to have an opinion of their Indian women, whom they take and discard according to their whims."

Gabriel was almost sure that he detected a gleam of amusement in Pizarro's haggard face. He used the opportunity to add:

"We were discussing serious matters, Your Excellency."

"Yes . . . yes, you're right. In that case, listen to me carefully. I'm not only exercising power here, enforcing the King's authority. You know me well enough to know that that doesn't suffice. No one has a greater sense of duty and justice than I. No one, d'you hear?"

"I know, Don Francisco."

"Do you think that I spend my nights praying for no reason, merely making sounds with my mouth? Or do you believe that I listen to what the Sacred Virgin tells me?"

"I know," repeated Gabriel.

"I am not here for the gold, Gabriel, nor to grab myself enough land to work thousands of slaves on. I leave that to Don Diego de Almagro and the rest of 'em. . . . No, I'm here to write into the annals of history a legend dedicated to the glory of our Lord Jesus Christ and our King Charles V."

"Then do not stain that legend with blood."

Pizarro pulled his hat low on his forehead and stared into the shadows. He briskly tightened the buckle of his scabbard and placed a hand on the hilt of his sword, as though he was about to sit for a portrait.

"You insist that Añades and his slave lie?"

"Yes."

"Find me the proof."

"And then?"

"And then nothing. Just find me that fucking proof, that's all."

Gabriel was shocked by all the nervous activity taking place on the square at Cajamarca at such an untimely hour. Groups of Indians murmured among themselves, and Spanish patrols walked about menacingly.

The guard roster had been doubled. A hundred troopers had super-vened one another patrolling the roads and streets on the outskirts of Cajamarca. All the Spaniards had slept with their weapons at hand. At dawn Father Valverde had given a Mass in the unfinished church. His sermon reminded the Cajamarca veterans, their pale faces telling their devotion, of the one given before the Great Battle of November.

"Gabriel!"

The call startled him. Sebastian approached. His perpetual grin revealed his teeth, the whiteness and health of which provoked the jeal-ousy of the European conquistadors.

"Walk with me for a minute, will you?"

Side by side, they walked around the church. The walls of the nave were still only waist high. On the stone altar a simple wooden crucifix had been erected. The as yet roofless columns reaching for the blue Andean sky had an ethereal quality about them.

"Why did you put the Inca in chains?" asked Gabriel harshly.

"Because they ordered me to," Sebastian said simply.

"They?"

"Almagro and the Governor himself."

"But you? Why you?"

Sebastian uttered a sinister chuckle, and his voice was full of bitter-ness when he said:

"My friend, why do you always need to be reminded of the most self-evident truths? They chose me because I am Don Diego's possession; me, because my skin is black and because no God-fearing Spaniard wants to sully his hands by chaining a King, even a Peruvian King wear-ing feathers! You never know what tomorrow's mood will be, especially if you're white, Spanish, and your name is preceded by *don*. But I know what *my* tomorrow will be like: the same shit as yesterday and today."

Gabriel lowered his eyelids. There was so much pain in his friend's voice that each word hit him like a fist in the gut. The early stonework of the church seemed to him in that moment as hideous as a rosary of lies.

"It was a stupid question. Forgive me, my friend."

"There is an ocean between you and me, Don Gabriel," said Sebas-tian unhappily, "and sometimes friendship isn't enough to navigate between its shores."

"I told you: I know what it is for you, and I ask you to forgive me. Do

I have to get on my knees and beg you?" said Gabriel, feeling guilty. "God almighty, very well! You are not to blame. It's just that I'm tired of having the wool pulled over my eyes. What's more, last night seemed to me blacker than most."

Sebastian's smile returned.

"As for that, I can bring some light to bear on it. That Indian who testified yesterday . . ."

"Añades's man?"

"Exactly: that Indian, and slave above all, and who doesn't even know who he belongs to, the bugger! In any case, last night I drank with him— some of that beer of theirs that slips smoothly down your gullet and unties your tongue in no time at all—and by the third goblet, he was no longer sure whether what he had seen had been an Indian army or a herd of llamas; by the fourth, he wasn't sure if he had even been out gallivanting in the highland pastures at all; by the fifth, he was showing me the lovely gold pin generously given to him by Añades for telling his tale."

"You are my guardian angel, Sebastian. Where is he?"

"If only I knew . . ."

"How do you mean?"

"As he sobered up he grew frightened and regretful, and now I can't find him anywhere."

"Christ's blood!"

"Yes. And if you don't get him to spill his guts to the Governor, then I shall play Judas: they have chosen me to garrote the Inca."

Gabriel stared into his friend's eyes. Had it been ten minutes earlier, he would have exploded into a rage. But now he felt only immeasurable bitterness. Only one last hope kept his heart alive.

"You're not going to ask me why?" grouched Sebastian.

"Don't start!"

Sebastian took hold of his friend's wrist and plunged his dark eyes into his as he declared, his voice sharper than a saw squeaking through an old piece of wood:

"If I break the Inca's neck, Don Diego will personally present me with a sword, and Don Hernando Pizarro himself will no longer oppose my placing my noble ass on a horse's back. Moguer will call me *Don Sebastian*. Not a bad deal, don't you think?"

Gabriel held back the fury bursting from within. He ground his jaws together to prevent his mouth from spitting useless words. Sebastian was right: it was not a bad deal.

Anamaya blankly watched the crowd of Strangers enter the Inca's chamber. She recognized all of them: the Governor led, followed by one-eyed Almagro, the priest Valverde, his Bible in hand, and the King's officers. Then came the interpreter, Felipillo, and the Governor's two younger brothers, the diabolically beautiful Gonzalo, and Juan, with his odd mix of pride and timidity.

She hadn't left Atahualpa once throughout the night.

Pizarro motioned to a soldier to remove the collar. Atahualpa rubbed his neck. He eyed the Strangers one by one, looking at them with disdain, with distaste, with indifference. He looked at the Governor.

"Why did you do that, my friend?"

Pizarro made no reply. He kicked aside the iron collar as though to distance it from the Inca and to erase its very existence.

"You've come to play chess, haven't you?" said the Emperor.

A murmur grew among the Spaniards as Felipillo translated. Anamaya wanted to smile. Atahualpa had spoken with such quiet assurance. The Emperor had found consolation in the night. . . .

The Emperor signaled a servant to bring a table made of pleated bulrush. A bench was set beside Pizarro, and then the chessboard on the table. Atahualpa had developed a fondness for the game during his captivity. Not far from the palace, beside the now empty weaving workshops, his people made chess sets for him, the materials and sizes of the pieces being carefully chosen by him.

"You be white," declared the Emperor, "and I shall be black. It is in keeping with the natural order of things."

If the Governor was surprised, he didn't show it. He removed the black glove from his right hand. Anamaya saw that small, dry hand nervously set the pieces.

Still standing, the Emperor removed the accessories that symbolized his power and handed them to Anamaya: the breastplate of pink and red *mullus*, an astonishing piece of workmanship; the *llautu*, the royal head wreath; and even the handkerchief hiding his torn earlobe. There was total silence. All the Spaniards had their eyes riveted on Lord

Atahualpa. The more royal adornments he removed from his body, the more regal he became.

When he had nothing left but his tunic, he said quietly to Pizarro: "Let's play."

All his servant girls and wives and all the noblemen of his suite crowded into the recesses at the back of the room. The Spaniards ebbed back out onto the patio, leaving the two players to their game. Felipillo remained prudently behind Pizarro, occasionally glancing furtively at Anamaya.

From the brightness of the patio, another Spaniard was persistently trying to catch her eye: one of the Governor's brothers; but which one? Gonzalo? Juan? Each time she thought she had caught one of the brothers' gaze, she received only a slanted smile, as though they were but playing with her.

Outside, the Spaniards were in consultation among themselves. They spoke over one another, becoming increasingly heated.

Atahualpa ignored their squabble and advanced his pawns with calm self-assuredness. Pizarro's moves were less regular, less well thought out. Soon, one-eyed Almagro entered the room. He came and stood so close to the Governor that he brushed his shoulders with the pommel of his sword.

"Don Francisco, we are not here to watch a game of chess."

A murmur of agreement rose from the patio. Anamaya observed that the Governor had already lost a lot more pieces than Atahualpa.

"Don Francisco!" insisted Almagro.

Pizarro barely turned his head.

"What is it, Don Diego?"

"Bloody hell, Francisco! I mean, really, Your Lordship! We are not here to play, but to notify the Inca of his sentence."

Felipillo had stopped translating. Anamaya took over, murmuring in a low voice into the Inca's wounded ear. He stiffened slightly at the word "sentence." Then he nodded.

"Well then do so, my friend, do so. . . ." growled Pizarro.

As Almagro turned his head toward the Royal officers and shook his head in vexation, the Governor stared hard at the indecipherable enigma on the chessboard. His hand fell haphazardly onto one of the few pieces that remained to him before fluttering indecisively to another.

When he eventually raised his eyes toward the Inca, Anamaya was taken aback to discover his face full of confusion.

But now the youngest of the officers had entered the room and unrolled a piece of paper. He began to read, pausing after each sentence to recover his breath. Ridiculously, Felipillo did the same. With a click of his tongue, the Emperor ordered the interpreter to stop. Meanwhile the Spaniard continued to read the litany of accusations. Kneeling near the Inca, Anamaya translated only the most serious: duplicity, fabrication, treason, assassination, hostile armies. . . .

Atahualpa's smile broadened with each word.

When the Royal officer had at last finished, the Inca addressed Pizarro:

"Those are not the reasons why you're going to kill me, are they?"

It wasn't a question. Pizarro grew disconcerted and dropped the piece that he was trying to move. Emperor Atahualpa bent over, picked it up, placed it back in his hand, and gently curled his fingers around it.

His smile was beautiful, so tender that it softened the redness of his eyes.

"Are you sure that you don't want more gold? More lovely plates, pretty statues, fine fountains?"

The Spaniards had come into the center of the room. Their breaths were the only audible sounds in the heavy, threatening silence.

The Emperor moved one last pawn. Pizarro had almost no pieces left, whereas the Inca had almost all of his.

"You are in checkmate, brother," said Juan with contrived liveliness.

Atahualpa took his own king and lifted it above the board. He turned it around in his fingers as though it was the first time he had ever seen it.

"He is a great king," he said, "with powerful forces. And yet he must have committed some grave errors."

In one fell swoop he broke the piece against the edge of the board. Its head rolled about on the ground like a die. No one dared pick it up.

Silence returned. Don Francisco Pizarro picked up the glove beside him on the bench and wiggled his fingers into it.

"A great king, but an unhappy game," he sighed. "There is nothing I can do."

"Are you sure?"

The question asked for no answer, and got none. The Spaniards squinted with apprehension. When the Inca reached out for Anamaya's hand, some even took a step back. Everyone watched that dark hand squeeze the *Coya Camaquen*'s, squeeze it so tightly that it looked as though it might break.

They didn't understand the true meaning of the gesture. They told themselves that the Inca was frightened and that he needed the comfort of a woman.

When the Emperor released his grasp, Anamaya advanced forward into the room and picked up the head of the chess king. She enclosed it in both her hands. Atahualpa smiled, and nodded slightly.

"There. Now, do with me what you must, my friend Pizarro."

SEVEN

Upon arriving at Añades's lodgings, Sebastian and Gabriel found the place empty save for an ancient, tottering slave seated in a rocking chair propped up against the wall who only muttered incoherently when addressed. They had spent the entire day running through town, searching every alleyway, every palace, every *cancha* whether rich or poor.

In the end they found him in a squalid courtyard, amid guinea pigs nibbing away at rotten leaves and scampering between naked children. Four groaning slaves were working a heavy millstone. Outside the *cancha*, some Indian servants were waiting for sacks of corn flower. Sebastian pointed at a man sitting on a stool:

"Here he is at last!"

Gabriel saw the man's fearful eyes recognize him.

"Yes, it's definitely him," he said.

Gabriel and Sebastian hastened simultaneously toward the poor fellow before he had a chance to move. Their jostling caused the guinea pigs to take flight in a cacophony of squeals to which the children added their cries.

Motivated by a sound sense of caution, the Indians abandoned the millstone and took refuge in the shade of a squalid room.

"I'm not going to kill you," muttered Gabriel as he pushed the fellow out of the yard.

As they appeared, the line of waiting servants fled to the end of the alleyway.

"I'll let you take care of it," said Sebastian. "They're waiting for me. Do it quickly."

As the giant black man left at a run, Gabriel backed the slave up against a wall.

"What's your name?"

"I don't have one."

All the frustration that had accumulated in him through the course of the day, coupled with his rage at the prospect of the great injustice soon to be committed, snapped Gabriel's self-control. He slapped the man with the back of his hand, as hard as the flat of a sword. Blood flowed from the slave's nose and mouth.

"You can't even remember your own name? How many *tupus* did they give you to forget what you know and remember what you don't? How much was it?"

But what Gabriel received as a reply was the same wry, ironic look that Sebastian had given him that morning when he had said "There is an ocean between you and me, Don Gabriel. . . ." And his rage left him as quickly as it had come, replaced by a deep sense of shame and weariness that drained the strength from his arms. He let go of the man, who fell into a crumpled heap, his dripping sweat mixing with his blood.

"What's your name?"

Two wary eyes rose up to meet his, two eyes blinded by fear. Gabriel bent over and took the slave by the shoulders with unexpected gentleness.

"Don't be frightened, I won't strike you again."

He sat down beside him, on the same dirt and filth. When a guinea pig began nibbling at the points of his boots, he made no motion to shoo it away. He caught a glimpse, through an opening in the wall, of the silhouettes of two crouching women. The sinister sound of distant trumpets came to them carried on the breeze.

"Tell me what happened," he insisted. "What did your master ask of you?"

"I was ordered not to tell anyone," said the man in a low voice.

"I know. Yet you must tell me anyway."

"The Stranger Lord said that we would all be killed unless I said the things he wanted me to. He said that your master would be gratified and that he would spare us. He gave me a gold pin."

"You didn't see any soldiers. You didn't see the Inca's warriors."

The man rubbed his feet into the dirt, saying nothing. He caught a guinea pig, and then released it tenderly. Finally, he shook his head.

"What story would you tell if I were to take you to the Governor now?"

"If I speak the truth, they'll kill me as soon as I'm finished."

"No," said Gabriel, standing up and dusting himself off. "I can promise you that you shall not be killed for speaking the truth."

Troops lined a path through the crowd from Atahualpa's palace to the execution post that had been erected in the center of the square. When the Emperor, chained and bareheaded, came out of his palace, the Indians threw themselves to the ground, crying out mournful cries, as though they were all drunk.

Atahualpa had the priest Valverde, the interpreter Felipillo, and a Spanish captain at his side. Anamaya followed a few paces behind. The Inca turned to face her:

"Stay with me until I can see my father," he ordered her.

She simply nodded, her throat so constricted that she was unable to reply.

"Ask them why they are putting me to death," Atahualpa said calmly to Felipillo.

The interpreter became flustered. Hoping that Anamaya wouldn't be able to hear him, he said in a low voice to the captain and the priest:

"The Inca asks if he can buy his life with more gold."

It wasn't the first time that the interpreter had misinterpreted the Emperor's words. Anamaya was about to protest when Atahualpa, not bothering to wait for a reply, said in a voice loud enough for the crowd to hear:

"Ever since I have been in your hands, Strangers, what have I done other than bring you gold and yet more gold, silver, and precious stones? What have my wives, my servants, and my sons done other than obey your every command? You claim that my armies are marching on you. . . . You have imprisoned me and bound me in chains, and you torture the powerful Chalkuchimac. Is there a will here that is not your own? Now you have grown weary of me. You want to take my life from me. Take it. You are only taking my presence in *this* world. I am the Emperor of Tahuantinsuyu; nothing can prevent my reaching the Other World. Many seasons ago, my father the Sun scattered his seeds of gold on these mountains to ensure my birth. My mother the Moon let flow her silver milk into my mouth so that I would be strong and powerful. I feel only joy and peace at the prospect of at last returning to Inti."

When he had finished, a heavy tremor of suffering ran through the crowd. Tears flowed, shining on their cheeks. Even those who had complained of the Inca's indifference and severity now bent double with grief. Today, like the sun at last tearing through the clouds, his courage and suffering was theirs. With him, they bore the weight of helplessness of being citizens of the Empire of the Four Cardinal Directions, and with him they suffered the wind of destruction raised by the Strangers.

Two men took his arms and tied him tightly to the cedar post. Anamaya recognized the black-skinned one, Gabriel's friend, the one who had placed the collar around Atahualpa's neck the previous evening. She looked at him closely, and read in his face only deep resignation.

"Where is the Governor, my friend Pizarro? I wish to speak with him," said Atahualpa.

Father Vicente Valverde sighed, and motioned to the captain to fetch Don Francisco.

At that moment shouts silenced the crowd's wailing. Anamaya turned around to find Gabriel breaking through the line of soldiers, dragging an Indian behind him.

"Where's the Governor?" he yelled. "I've got his proof! I've got the proof that he asked me for! Añades's slave lied, d'ye hear? There is no Indian army! The Inca is innocent!"

After a moment of surprise, an irritated Valverde replied:

"What do you want of the Governor?"

"Father Valverde, the Inca is innocent!"

"Innocent of what? Of scorning God's will? Certainly not! My friend, if you want to be useful to this creature, you should be praying for him rather than shouting like a madman."

Gabriel brought up before him the trembling slave and shouted:

"Father Vicente, need I remind you that you are going to murder the Inca not in the name of God but under the pretext that he wants to annihilate us with his armies. But Añades ordered this man here to lie to us. There isn't a single Indian warrior within fifty leagues of here. Are you going to ignore this fact?"

The Dominican said nothing.

"By the blood of Christ, Father Valverde, give me an answer!"

But Valverde never had a chance to reply. A cry distracted them:

"Milords! Milords! We cannot find Don Francisco anywhere! No one knows where he is."

"You see how it is," said Valverde quietly. "There's no reason to complicate things."

Gabriel, dumbfounded, turned to Felipillo, who was still interpreting for the Inca. He caught a glimpse of Anamaya's lips, which were also moving. Atahualpa, slightly astonished, looked directly at Gabriel. He silenced Felipillo with a wave of the hand and spoke directly to Gabriel:

"Tell the Governor that I remain his friend and that I place my children under his protection."

Before Gabriel could react, Valverde, his crucifix raised high, stepped between them.

"Forget about your children, Inca!" he exclaimed. "Forget about your wives! Think only of God, think of the face of God and die a Christian!"

"My children are many, and all so young," insisted Atahualpa, still looking at Gabriel over the priest's shoulder.

"God wills it that you die for all the excesses you committed in this world. You have to repent all that so that God may forgive you."

"My children are weak, defenseless. . . . They need protection."

Gabriel could hear Atahualpa's voice, but the priest's arms hid his face from him. But now it was Anamaya's eyes that weighed upon him, that touched him as though she had placed her hands on his chest. He shouted out in Quechua, raising his voice above Valverde's sermon:

"Have no fear, Emperor, I will speak to the Governor about your children."

Livid, Valverde turned on his heel, his cheeks crimson, menacing him with his crucifix.

"That's enough! Hold your tongue!"

Behind him, Atahualpa almost smiled.

"Might I not be burned?" he asked quietly.

"Your sentence compels that you be," said Valverde, sighing, "unless you die having accepted the word of almighty God."

"How so?"

"Then God will forgive you and indulge you with his clemency."

Atahualpa looked away from Valverde. For a moment he gazed at the crowd, as though he wanted to commit each face to his memory. And then he suddenly declaimed:

"People of Tahuantinsuyu, I am going to die!"

A clamor rose from the crowd, a sound more profound than that of horns, more deafening than that of drums.

"I am leaving you to rejoin my father at last! I am going to the Underworld to begin my long voyage. I shall return to you in the form that I have done once before, as a snake. The Strangers say that they won't burn me if I turn Christian, like them. They wish me to submit to their god."

The crowd fell silent. Atahualpa's chest swelled impressively despite the ropes binding him.

"People of Tahuantinsuyu, my body must not be reduced to ashes. It is the vessel that must transport me to my father. So I shall do what they ask of me. But remember: I am the son of Inti!"

These last words were spoken with so much pride that the crowd began to chant:

"It is so, Emperor!"

"I am the Son of the Sun!"

"It is so, Emperor!"

And it was thus, amid all the cries, wails, and tears, that Atahualpa permitted Valverde to baptize him.

Anamaya closed her eyes and let her memories rise to the forefront of her mind. She remembered the day that she had helped the Emperor flee, the dumbfounded guards finding only a snake slough in his cell. She remembered the morning of the Great Massacre, when he had hailed the crowd with exactly the same words.

The shadow of night was already upon the great valley, and the mountain peaks glowed red. Torches burned here and there. Gabriel wanted to go to Anamaya and hold her body close to his. The Indian whom he had dragged along watched him in a daze. Gabriel motioned to him to disappear into the crowd. When he raised his hanging head, he met Sebastian's gaze. Despite himself, and unaware of the meaning of it, he nodded.

Sebastian placed the leather strap around the Inca's neck with singular tenderness. He slipped two withes into the garrote's aperture. It was a wooden screw, the same as those used to crack nuts. He turned the handle, and the leather cut into Atahualpa's flesh.

With a single twist of his wrist, Sebastian gave it another turn. The

Emperor's dun skin whitened under the pressure of the strap. His glottis quivered, and his mouth opened in a silent scream, his well-defined lips curled with pain.

Anamaya had opened her eyes, and she stared into Atahualpa's blood-filled eyes as though she wanted to melt into his last view of life. As the crowd continued to wail, and Valverde chanted as forcefully as he could, she barely heard Gabriel order:

"Quicker, Sebastian, quicker!"

The giant black man now turned the garrote with all the strength in his body. A cracking sound tore through the noise. The Emperor's spine had snapped. His eyes rolled back to see what no one else could see.

Gabriel realized that Anamaya was now so close to him that their shoulders and hips were touching. He felt the back of her hand brush against his. She murmured:

"No one can stop that which must be, not even you."

The women's wails rose sharply into the darkening sky. The men tore their clothes and scratched at their bare chests. The torch flames danced madly. Anamaya closed her fingers around Gabriel's.

"All is well," she said.

Sebastian sat down at the foot of the pyre. His cheeks were dry, but his shoulders were shaking as though he was being destroyed by fever.

EIGHT

Cajamarca, July 26, 1533, night

Quilla, the Moon Goddess, did not shine that night. The Inca Emperor Atahualpa's palace was drowned in a darkness that would never end. Everywhere, in its vast halls as in its small chambers, in its courtyards and storerooms, wailing could be heard throughout the night. As recently as the previous day some of the Emperor's wives, concubines, and servant girls had dreamed of serving the Strangers. They had complained about the Inca, his indifference and callousness—but now, there was only pain. No amount of blood flow would be enough to match it.

Anamaya felt as though she was burning up, and she stopped by the fountain on the patio to plunge her hands into its diaphanous water. But the water streamed off her face without bringing her coolness.

Inguill came to her, and without uttering a word she pressed herself into her bosom.

Anamaya let her do so and tried to console her. She too, the young Cuzco girl, Manco's protégée, grieved the death of the man whose cruelty had caused the death of her mother and brothers.

Then, slowly, Anamaya pushed her back a little. She looked at her for a moment in the shade, her small and birdlike face bathed in tears.

"Leave me now, little one," she murmured tenderly. "I have much to do. . . ."

And Inguill disappeared into the night.

Anamaya slipped into Atahualpa's vast chamber. Only one torch was lit, and that at the far end of the room, illuminating nothing, but giving the impression of a boat sinking slowly through the night to the Other World.

She banged her foot against something, and a metallic sound resonated: it was the collar, the one that had earlier been around the Inca's neck. She squinted until her eyes adjusted to the feeble light. She saw all the things that had surrounded the living Inca: they still carried his afterglow, the marks of his now fading power: the redwood *tiana,* the woven rush table, the overturned chessboard.

"So, you've come back too."

A terrible fear streaked through her.

"Inti Palla?"

The young woman's silhouette appeared from the shadows. Anamaya stepped back and tripped on the Inca's bench.

"Don't be frightened."

This wasn't the voice of the old Inti Palla, the one in whom she thought she had found a friend, the one who had betrayed her with honeyed words, words concealing a lurking jealousy.

"Please, take my hand."

Inti Palla was almost imploring her, and yet her words seemed to be coming from a world already faded. After a slight hesitation, Anamaya took her hand. It was icy cold, despite the balmy night's humidity.

"Remorse plagues me by night. Whether asleep or awake, my soul tries to escape it, but in vain. My remorse is a *quipu* whose knots are beyond undoing."

Inti Palla uttered a little laugh that turned into a cough, her chest shaking.

"I am nothing, and yet I shared the Inca's bed. When you and I were together in the house of virgins in Quito, I had no other desire than that. And I got what I wanted. And then, I no longer know how, treason began to visit my bed more often than the Emperor, and revenge and deception followed in its steps."

The princess moved closer to Anamaya. Her arm and shoulder brushed against her. Her skin was unusually dry and coarse, as though her body was preparing itself for the Other World.

"You saw those treasons all too clearly, and I was frightened that you would steal him from me. I was frightened that I would be rejected like the forgotten concubines whom the troops share among themselves. I couldn't face it, I'm too delicate!"

That joyless laugh again.

"My remorse, you see, is not because I lied, or even because I betrayed Atahualpa with Felipillo. What I regret is you, blue-eyed girl. I admired and loved you more than anyone else."

Anamaya, startled, tried to pull her hand away. But Inti Palla tightened her grip, her nails digging into the *Coya Camaquen*'s palm.

"You don't want to believe me, do you? You're very wary of me, aren't you? You don't believe a word I say."

"I believe you, Inti Palla."

"I want you to so much! Anamaya, no other moment of my life torments me as much as that day when you arrived at the *acllahuasi*. That day when you first looked at me. Your strange eyes were so beautiful, so deep, that jealousy instantly shredded my heart. You possessed something that I would never have . . . and over time I realized that your eyes asked only for friendship and fidelity. A friendship for life. But my pride and my fear immediately denied those things to me. And now, I am going to die. This very night, I am going to die with that remorse in my heart."

"You *are* my friend," whispered Anamaya.

Her own words surprised her. She wasn't lying. The words brought up a very old, long-lost emotion, something she could give to the doomed princess.

Inti Palla's hand stiffened in hers. She seemed warmer now.

"How strange it is," said Inti Palla, her voice even lower than before, "I'm not frightened anymore."

The two young girls hugged one another in the chamber-turned-prison. Anamaya felt Inti Palla's breathing subside and her body relax, driven by a renewed will, stronger than before.

"I want you to help me now," asked the once beautiful princess.

"Of course," said Anamaya.

Pizarro, bareheaded, wore a black armband over his customary black clothes. He raised his silver goblet as Gabriel walked in.

"Guess what I'm drinking."

Gabriel made no reply. His rage had been lifted from him while he had been with Anamaya, but had then returned after he had left her, and had grown with each step that had brought him to the Governor now.

"Thank you, but I'm not thirsty," he said dryly.

"Oh, go on, taste it, my boy!"

The Governor's tone allowed for no reply. Gabriel grabbed the goblet proffered to him and gulped down its contents, then immediately spat it out. Don Francisco nodded soberly, without a hint of a smile, and took back his goblet.

"It's vinegar! I shall drink it all week, as will one-eyed Almagro and all the rest of them."

"Don Francisco, if you think that that will in any way . . . Soto!"

Soto walked heavily into the room without removing his hat. Several men followed him. The captain wore the black look of someone who had just been through difficult days. His eyes looked tired, his beard was unkempt, and his clothes were covered in dust. Gabriel knew what he was going to say before he had even opened his mouth.

"Nothing! Nothing at all, Don Francisco! No army, no column, not a single goddamned soldier within a hundred leagues in any direction from here. There is nothing, I tell you! The roads are as empty of Inca armies as is the back of my hand. The only weapons we saw were the peasants' spades! Nothing: we've been had."

Pizarro sighed. His eyes half-closed, he swirled the vinegar in his goblet.

"I was lied to."

Soto turned to Gabriel. His tiredness made his voice hard:

"What's going on here? I'm told that the Inca is dead? As I crossed the city, I heard such wails that freeze your blood!"

Gabriel shivered. All his muscles ached, as though he himself had been in the saddle for days on end, searching in vain.

"Garroted," he murmured.

"Garroted? Without a trial?"

"With a trial."

But . . . since I was out on the roads . . ."

The captain's mouth quivered. He understood. He fell silent.

"So, Almagro won his argument."

He lowered his head for a moment, removed his hat, and shook his head as though trying to shake away a gadfly.

"Governor," he said in a severe tone, "it is true that the Inca's presence made the Cuzco expedition difficult, but there were other solutions than execution. I regret the Indian's death extremely. It is a very bad thing, for you as well as for all of us."

And you didn't even see it, thought Gabriel, who was still haunted by the image of the steel collar.

Pizarro returned Soto's stare for a moment, then poured more vinegar into his goblet. He sipped it without blinking.

"I too regret it extremely, Don Hernando."

Pizarro's voice was so full of solemnity and sadness that it commanded respect. Soto looked at him in silence, searching his face, and waiting for something more to be said. Nothing came. He put his hat back on and left the room, returning to his men outside.

"Tell me," said Don Francisco to Gabriel, "tell me how he died."

They were in a little room at the back of the palace, surrounded by piles of *unkus* of an astonishing variety of shapes, weaves, materials, and colors. There were enough there to dress emperors for generations to come.

The women hadn't found any agave thread in the storeroom, so Inti Palla had stolen one of those long leather straps with which the Spaniards tied their horses. Without a hint of a smile, she handed it to Anamaya.

"The Emperor Atahualpa died from a strap just like this one."

Anamaya slipped her hands around Inti Palla's neck. She adeptly tied a strong but movable knot into the strap. Against the princess's fine, supple flesh, covered in skin the color of dark honey that had fanned the flames of lust in so many men, the leather strap made almost an alluring sort of necklace.

She looked at the princess. Inti Palla gave a little nod.

"Should it break," she said, "I'll fall into the piles of the Inca's tunics, and I'll dream that I was the concubine whom he enjoyed during his last night on earth."

She set a bench atop another, and climbed deftly onto the wobbly structure. She adeptly slung a rope around the main beam supporting the thatched roof.

"Now, leave me alone."

Anamaya left the room without looking back. From the courtyard, she heard the muted sound of the wooden benches collapsing.

It was the only noise that Inti Palla made during her voyage into the Underworld.

Anamaya didn't check her pace at all. She went to the fountain—it was still running—and drank some refreshing water.

That night, in Atahualpa's palace, in Cajamarca's *canchas*, in the *acllahuasi,* dozens of women killed themselves, following their Inca into the Other World.

In order to fulfill the court's edict, a feeble pyre still had to be lit. A few flames pawed at the dead Inca's clothes and burned his skin and hair slightly. That way, they would be able to say later that he had been burned.

The stench produced by this sham was still floating in Cajamarca's air when Gabriel left the Governor's residence. The valley's air was already unbreathable, stifled as it was by the wails and cries.

The execution post still stood in the middle of the square. Atahualpa's cadaver remained tied to it, a sort of Indian Christ, night's martyr wearing the lament of an entire people. The suffering begotten by his death hadn't subsided. It was like a slow-moving arrow, reaching into the depths of their hearts, breaking them.

Gabriel moved through the crowd with his jaw clenched tight. Their faces, usually so inscrutable, were glistening with tears. The highly strung Spaniards had tried to clear the square a number of times throughout the evening, but it had been an impossible task. The Indians—both men and women—had lain down on the dusty ground like corpses, and no boot or spearhead could move them. They were equally indifferent to fear or pain, so much so that some let themselves be trampled by horses and their heads be crushed.

Horns and drums echoed in the distance, their sound spreading over the hills that surrounded the town, and farther still from what was before the living heart of the Empire of the Four Cardinal Directions, reaching as far as the high, distant mountains, their sound mingling with that of the rivers and the thunder of a coming storm. The eternal river of stars flowed gently across the expanse of the sky.

The breath of the Inca gods passed through the night.

Once at the pyre, Gabriel did something that he had never been able to do for anyone until this day. He kneeled in silence and put his hands together before Atahualpa's body. He, who had sworn to never again pray after his experience in the Inquisition's jails, now found the words with an ease and fervor that astonished him.

"I knew that you would come. . . ."

It was only a whisper, but he instantly recognized the voice and its accent. He didn't turn around. His heart beating, he sensed from behind his closed eyes the presence of his beloved.

"I did everything I could to stop them killing him," he murmured. The stench had evaporated, and he inhaled her perfume. She wrapped her arms around him and stopped him by placing her hand lightly on his lips.

"I know."

"I had proof. Soto has returned. . . . The Governor is convinced now. But it's no use. It's too late."

Anamaya embraced him gently, her chest trembling against his arm.

"No. It is neither too early nor too late. It happened as it was meant to happen. I told you: all is well. The Emperor is now where he is meant to be. You did what you were meant to do. Like one of our heroes, a living warrior amid stone soldiers."

"Stone soldiers?"

She nodded, peaceful, serene. Their breaths became synchronized. With all the horror about them, he was surprised by the intensity of his sudden desire to have her. Slightly embarrassed, he felt his member stiffen as Anamaya slipped her slender, agile fingers under his shirt. She traced the outline of the mark of the puma on his shoulder.

"There are some things that you should know," she whispered, "about this mark on your shoulder. The one that I kissed during our first night together."

Her caress was delicious, her tenderness spreading throughout his body.

"I remember. . . ."

"It represents an animal that dwells in our mountains, a magnificent and powerful animal that we worship because it carries the strength and will of our ancestors."

"The puma?"

"Yes, the powerful Lord *Puma*. One night, many seasons ago, when I was still a frightened little girl, Atahualpa's father, the Inca Huayna Capac, called me to him. He confided to me not only the secrets of the Empire's history, but also its future."

Anamaya spoke in a soft voice, caressing his hand and mouth. Gabriel let himself be carried along by her, utterly at ease, and unsurprised by her revelations. She told him how she had become the *Coya Camaquen*, wife of the Sacred Double of the great Huayna Capac's mummy. She told him how she had accompanied him, lost him, then found him once again in the heart of the *huaca*, the labyrinth of sacred stones.

"It was there, in the shadows and fear of that place, that I saw you for the first time. You were the puma with the glowing eyes, with the frightful claws, the puma who could cross the mountains in a single bound. I wasn't sure if you weren't going to devour me . . . and then I heard Huayna Capac tell me: *Trust the puma.*"

Gabriel wasn't sure if he fully understood what Anamaya was telling him. Her words traveled into the depths of his spirit like night birds, and they would later return in his dreams.

"When I saw you before me, when I saw the puma on your shoulder, I knew that you had come for me. I knew where you came from, and to where you would return."

She looked up at Atahualpa's corpse.

"We have one life here, and others elsewhere, in many different worlds. We travel from this world to the Underworld, and from the Underworld to the Other World in the sky, the most beautiful and perfect world. We return, we transform ourselves. . . ."

"You too? You've taken this . . . trip?"

She didn't reply.

She turned her blue eyes toward him, looking into his, and a smile lit her face. Her eyes were the color of the lake, the sky, the night: he dived into them, totally surrendering himself to her, and so began a journey from which he already knew that he wouldn't want to return.

PART TWO

NINE

Huayhuash Cordillera, October 5, 1533

"Watch out!"

The cry echoed over Gabriel's head. Instinctively he raised his shield and clenched his horse's bridle, bringing it up close against a wall. Rock fragments plunged into the ravine like grapeshot, the larger ones whistling down like cannonballs. The impact of the stones on the flagstones and on the iron bands across their bucklers echoed as though they were being struck by clubs. All of them held their breath. A few stones pelted the horses' hindquarters, making them neigh. And then there was silence.

Almost simultaneously, Candia's and Sebastian's long silhouettes straightened themselves. Like Gabriel, they brought down their shields and looked up toward the top of the gully.

The rockfall must have had its origin just beyond the overhang that hid the summit from them. Gabriel was worried, and he turned back toward the porters following behind. But all of them had managed to find shelter, and only a very few bundles had been damaged.

"Very warm artillery work," muttered the Greek, "and I consider myself an authority on the matter!" A predatory glow emanated from Candia's eyes. The three friends simultaneously had the same thought: had the rockfall been an accident, or had it been set off by Quizquiz's or Guaypar's warriors? In actual fact, from where they were it was impossible to tell.

"That's the third time this morning," remarked Sebastian, grimacing ironically. "If they didn't set this one off themselves, then they must've got one of their gods to do it for them."

Candia grumbled an insult, but it was lost to the void.

"Let's go," ordered Gabriel, cracking the end of his reins on his horse's rump. "There's no point freezing to death here."

Behind them, the long, long column stretched out across the whole breadth of the mountain, steam rising from it. It was as though an entire people was migrating. The four hundred Spaniards, led by the Governor, Soto, and Don Diego de Almagro, were lost in the crowd of thousands upon thousands of Indians: slaves, Canary Indians and their allies, warriors from the coast, servants, and minor local noblemen, all of whom had joined the fascinating and powerful newcomers either willingly or by impressment.

The weather was terrible, cold and wet, with a low, heavy sky. The mountain peaks and vales rose before them menacingly. The mountain rose up and up, becoming lost in the fog and icy air. The column produced a concert of coughs and moans, of cries and curses mixed with the sporadic click-clack of hooves.

Chalkuchimac's palanquin was situated more or less in the middle of the column, just after the cavalry platoon surrounding Governor Don Francisco Pizarro. The rainbow of colorful feathers decorating it made it stand out from afar, even through the gray light. A file of Spanish infantrymen, relieved every five hours, surrounded it from the moment they set off in the morning to the moment they collapsed in exhaustion in the evening. Torture had drained the Inca general of his strength, but had not diminished his reputation of fearlessness among the Indian warriors. Not a day passed without the Governor and his men fearing an attack sent to free the general.

The Royal Road to the capital followed ever tighter twists down the steep and slippery slope. The cavalrymen had all dismounted some time ago to relieve the overworked horses, which were snorting in strong, quivering breaths.

The fog would now dissipate, now aggregate, at the whim of invisible gusts of wind. Occasionally Gabriel, approaching a pass, would find himself blinded by the harsh light of the sun, and he would see a sky as deeply blue as an ocean.

He felt as though he was traveling into a supernatural world. The slopes became as gentle as a rolling swell, washed by rain and swept by violent gusts of wind. The short yellow grass was covered in dust worn from the rocks that was in turn covered in frost. The monotony of the red and ocher earth was broken only by occasional black boulders rising from it like colossal blisters. Man was unwelcome here, and only fortune could determine the success of a voyage across it.

It was almost impossible to breathe. They felt as though they grew heavier with every step they took, as though all the gold of Cajamarca had been smelted down and slipped into the soles of their boots.

The previous night had been an interminable nightmare for Gabriel. He had woken with a start at least twenty times, both freezing and sweating, his mouth gasping for air, convinced that he was suffocating. Twenty times he had dreamed that he was walking through a land devoid of air, a vacuum, and each time he woke he jerked up on his bedding, and moaned like a wounded animal. Each time he had heard similar moans from his companions all around him, all gripped by the same dread.

He ate very little breakfast. In the afternoon he tried to banish the thought that he wouldn't have the strength to continue, that he would collapse by the side of the road. He had started out by counting his steps in sets of hundreds, then in dozens, and now he counted them one by one, surprised that he was still able to put one foot in front of the other.

His bay slipped on a flagstone, and the yank of the bridle pulled him down, making him lose his balance. He had to hold on to the pommel of his saddle while he recovered the strength in his legs.

Every effort exhausted him further. But the continual effort was also what kept him from succumbing to the numbness that occasionally overwhelmed him like a drug.

His face was becoming frostbitten, despite the blue scarf he kept wrapped around his mouth. He could no longer feel his fingers, despite his thick leather gloves. Yet he could feel a cold, clammy sweat covering the small of his back. His temples throbbed so much that his vision became blurred. He felt a burning sensation in his desiccated throat.

Anamaya's advice whirled around in what little remained of his mind: "Don't stop, above all, don't stop, even if you can't take another step, because if you do you won't feel rested but rather even more exhausted. When you feel tired," she added, caressing him with her fingers, "chew slowly on these leaves."

Of course, the leaves she gave him. Why hadn't he thought of them earlier?

His numb fingers searched sluggishly for the cloth pouch, the *chuspa* she had strapped around his shoulder. The wool was covered in frost. He drew a few green leaves from it and immediately put them into his mouth. They tasted bland, slightly bitter, and he almost spat them out immediately. But he let himself chew them for a while, and eventually a sort of lightness came over him, and his headache subsided.

In parts, the road ran parallel to a wall over thirty feet high. Its stones had been put together with that expert masonry that he had become accustomed to in this land, and that seemed almost magical.

Once again his horse shied, as though it could sense his own apprehension. The cliff seemed suddenly dangerously close, and Gabriel, despite himself, whined, "Why the devil build a wall in the middle of nowhere?" Yet he felt a sort of euphoria brought on by facing the elements thus, and he was almost indifferent to the flurries of ice whipping his face.

The road described a sharp bend after the wall, and from it they could at last make out the peak. Gabriel turned around and looked at the column advancing as well as could be expected. He saw horses slipping and falling, porters struggling, the men toiling through the freezing rain that went right through their clothes and got into their bones. Occasionally, an ill man, overcome by exhaustion or nausea, would collapse in the middle of the road.

"Did you see?"

Gabriel made out Sebastian's grin through the rain, like that of a ghost. He looked up at the peak once again. Two colossal dark blocks of stone marked the way, as though chiseled by giants. He nodded, and grinned. Each climb that they had undertaken had been longer than the descent preceding it, and he could not help but feel a sort of absurd hope that this would be the last.

When they had left Cajamarca a few weeks earlier, the rivalry between Pizarro's and Almagro's followers had been dangerously strained. The Governor held the lieutenant personally responsible for a wrongful execution, one that might upset the Crown. Almagro fumed against the subversion of the commitments undertaken with him, and against the fact that during the distribution of the gold, he and his companions had not been deemed entitled to a share for they had arrived after the Battle of Cajamarca. But here in the mountains, their peaks scraping against the sky, the men, walking along seemingly fathomless cliff faces, with rocks falling on them, suffocated by snow, and in their silent, ever-increasing, shared anxiety, had forgotten their enmities, so that now there were no longer rich men or poor men, or men loyal to one leader or other, but rather simply a group of men trying to survive.

Gabriel saw the sky through a breach in the clouds, a calming and vivid blue through the milky white cover. A huge black bird, the end of its wings shaped like fingers, appeared in this glade of light. The condor was gliding, dancing through the air, and gave an impression of strength and unbounded freedom. It was a beautiful sight, but Gabriel couldn't help but remember the attack on the bridge at Huaylas, the porters brought to their knees, and his duel with Hernando.

For a moment he forgot about his fatigue and the cold.

Then the clouds shut out the sky as abruptly as they had revealed it, and a glacial wind brought thicker and thicker flakes of snow. He could only open his eyes for split seconds to make sure that the silhouette of the person in front of him, bent by the wind and by effort, was still there.

And in that moment of extreme solitude, when all his strength was drained from him, he felt an inexplicable confidence warm his exhausted limbs and melt away his fear.

He drudged on, reassured that Anamaya was actually there, right next to him.

When they reached the peak, the storm and the wind suddenly died away, and the sky gradually began to clear. Gabriel blinked and breathed slowly, his face burning, while a few Spaniards, who had arrived just after him, took long drafts from their gourds.

The Indians lay down their burdens and squatted on the ground, their faces bearing their usual indifference. One of them raised his eyes to Gabriel, who greeted him with a smile. The man grinned, revealing his green teeth, then pointed at Gabriel and laughed quietly. "*Coca,*" he chortled, deeply amused. "*Coca!*"

One of Almagro's men, a young man whose name Gabriel didn't know, was sitting against a rock a few paces away. His face was gray and bloated, and a vicious, dry cough ruptured his irregular, wheezing breath. Occasionally he turned away to spit out a sort of red foam, which landed like crimson flowers on the snow.

"What's wrong, *compañero?*" asked Gabriel.

"I see it . . . I see it . . ." he repeated deliriously.

"What do you see?"

The man didn't reply, instead putting his head between his hands and squeezing it as though he wanted it to explode, as though the pain was too much to handle.

"Gold . . . I see gold," said the young man, "plenty of gold, and that knight in arms guarding it . . ."

His words were interrupted by fits of coughing, and Gabriel felt overwhelmed by a feeling of profound tenderness toward this young stranger, who was dreaming of adventure and fortune, and who, without a doubt, was now dying of some strange disease on this mountain peak, far from home.

He knelt down beside him and took his hand between his own, trying to share his warmth with him. The young man's hand was as cold as that of a corpse.

So Gabriel wrapped his arms around him. He put his ear against his chest and listened to his body through his soaked vest. What he heard was like a lake being devastated by a furious storm. The young man's breathing would occasionally cut short, but that seething inside his body never ceased.

Gabriel drew his ear away without touching him.

"Where are you from?" he asked in a tone he hoped was strong. "What's your mother's name?"

The young man had closed his eyes. He could no longer control his convulsing body. When he spat, his whole body shook violently.

As the rest of the column arrived, the other men kept their distance. Only Gabriel stayed at his side.

The youth fell asleep for a while, as though a corporeal sluggishness had taken hold of him. Yet Gabriel could still feel his heart beating in his wrist.

"Extramadura," he murmured eventually, so softly that Gabriel had to lean closer to hear him. "Maria . . ."

"Why, I come from the same country, and my mother has the same name! Don't be frightened, I'm with you."

The man's fingers clenched Gabriel's, and his face became twisted by a bout of unforgiving pain. His whole body rose upward, as though he wanted to tear himself away from the earth.

"I'm boiling," he said. "I'm suffocating! Open the window!"

"You're going to see our sunburnt native land long before I do, *compañero,* and your mother shall look upon you as she did when you were a child."

He gave a final shudder as he died. He was beyond suffering or joy now. He had seen, before dying, either his mother's face or that of the knight guarding the gold. He was dead.

Gabriel stood up. He became aware of his own vitality, of his own freezing, sweating, lamentable existence. Life was a strange shore on which one never overcomes anger, or fear, or greed.

He walked unsteadily toward the crowd of men who had closed their ears and turned their eyes away.

The storm sped away in the gathering dusk. Gabriel looked to the sky and saw a black dot, then another. The condors had returned to drift over the mountain in all their sinister majesty.

One of the great boulders at the entrance to the pass had had a cavity hollowed out in its back, a nook not unlike the apse of a church. The rock stood out sharply against the blue-black sky, and Gabriel's heart skipped a beat as he looked at it: it was exactly the same shape as the mountain on the horizon, the snow-capped summit glowing gold in the setting sun. Gabriel turned toward the few Spaniards around him. They had their heads lowered, their shoulders hunched, and they were murmuring along with the words spoken by the priest. Under this star-speckled sky, in this biting cold, with a dead man beside them, over whom they had quickly placed a blanket so that the Indians didn't see him, they were returning to their long-neglected God.

Gabriel found no consolation in prayer. The young man's inscrutable gaze haunted him, and he felt a hand tugging at him from beyond the veil of night. He stared at the rock and the mountain behind it for a long time. His eyes naturally followed the arrangement of stones surrounding the small group before returning to the table set on two great stone blocks, situated in the center, and behind which stood the priest. It was an altar high in the mountains.

Gabriel turned and walked away, his step crunching through the snow. He came out from behind the natural protection of the rock and walked into a light but freezing wind. There was no other source of light but the millions of stars twinkling in the sky, and that couldn't fail to fascinate them: whether they were from Extramadura or Castille, from Galicia or even Greece, the conquistadors were all born under the same sky. But this was a different sky, and it looked as though a mischievous god had entertained himself by sprinkling stars about according to some divine whim. Yes, it certainly was another world.

He could hear the murmur of his companions' prayers and responses behind him. And from down below he could hear a sort of drone, a sad and monotonic music, coming from the enormous Indian tents set up on the natural platform just below the pass. There were no drums or horns playing. It was simply the murmur of the Indians, who had gathered in clans to tell their stories and invoke their gods.

And so, ignoring one another, not understanding one another, and divided by war, the Spaniards and the Indians allowed themselves to be simply human beings, united in their fear of death and their admiring awe of the sky.

Gabriel heard voices coming from a tent set up behind a cluster of snow-covered rocks. He went to it. Three men were inside, breathing heavily and encouraging one another, trying to dig into the frozen earth with a sort of hoe that became hopelessly dented with each strike, the blade being made of bronze rather than steel.

"Fucking useless tool," grumbled Sebastian.

Gabriel caught a glimpse of his friend's sweating face, as well as that of Diego Mendez, a weasel-faced follower of Almagro, whose face had become so swollen that one of his eyes was barely visible through a narrow slit. He was afflicted with that mysterious mountain illness that chose its victims randomly, killing some while leaving others with their lives.

"Gabriel! Come break your back with us!" called Sebastian. Gabriel disappeared wordlessly into the night.

The Inca tents had been set up around Chalkuchimac's. They were made distinguishable by the geometric patterns that decorated their white cotton canvases.

They lowered their voices or fell silent altogether as Gabriel came nearer, the men and women wrapping their blankets tighter around themselves, and diverting their eyes when he tried to make eye contact with them.

"They're not frightened of you."

Gabriel turned around. Anamaya had surfaced next to him, wrapped in a large black and gray woolen cape. Gabriel grinned privately into the darkness.

"I was looking for you."

"I was frightened for you."

With no firelight to see her by, Gabriel could only surmise the concerned look on Anamaya's face. But he could hear the concern in her voice. He could feel her body close to his, and he experienced a shiver not brought on by the cold. He had to clench his teeth to distract himself from the longing to take her in his arms, to abandon himself to his desire.

"Quizquiz's warriors are in the mountains," she continued, "and Guaypar is with them."

"Guaypar?"

The mention of the Inca lieutenant's name brought the image of the man to his mind's eye, a man with a proud forehead and nose, and with eyes immured in hatred.

"They know who you are now," said Anamaya, "and they know that you are not immortal. They won't be as foolish as they were during the Great Massacre. You are in their territory now, and here your horses slip, your swords weigh you down, whereas their stones fly easily and find their mark."

Gabriel said nothing. He had been experiencing that inadequacy and anxiety she had just described for days now, as had every Spaniard.

Gradually the Indians around them returned to their conversations. He felt surrounded by their peaceful presence, their hostility dormant. For the moment at least. He noticed silhouettes moving in front of the glow of a fire behind a tent. He turned to Anamaya.

"They found wood to burn?"

She didn't reply, and he didn't persist. Sometimes he felt intimidated by her silences. They walked together toward the rock near which the priest had earlier given Mass.

They passed a group of Spaniards laughing and mucking about around a sort of small square fort made up of trunks and sacks. They had attached small bells to the horses' harnesses, so that any suspicious movement would wake them during the night.

"Gold," sighed Gabriel.

"They guard it better than they do themselves."

Gabriel gave a gesture of helplessness. Because he had fled the battle with Anamaya, Pizarro had denied him his share of the booty. Yet that humiliation had turned out to be a blessing in disguise, and he felt joyful in his penury and in his total lack of interest in gold.

They reached the black rock, now barely distinguishable from the night.

"Do you know this place?" asked Anamaya.

"No."

"The mountains are gods for us, like the sun and the moon, and like the spring of the wind. And so are these rocks, the shapes of which mark the presence of a god. This place was shaped by the hands of our Ancestors to indicate the presence of divinities here. We have been making sacrifices here ever since, to give thanks to the gods for their gifts. We call them *huacas*."

A voice emerged from the darkness.

"The God of Christians has also known sacrifices. But he held back Abraham's hand against his son Isaac, he broke the pride of man, and he sent them Jesus to redeem them of their sins."

It was a gentle voice, very different from Fray Vicente Valverde's vengeful tone. But Gabriel still instinctively placed himself protectively before Anamaya.

"Have no fear," said the soft-voiced man, "we know one another."

His outline emerged from the shadow of the rock and approached them noiselessly across the trampled snow. The man raised his right hand and said to Gabriel, grinning, "Do you know me now?"

Gabriel, dumbfounded, looked at his blue-gray eyes set in his clean-shaven face, which was both very young yet very old, and then at the hand he had raised peacefully above him as though to bless Gabriel and Anamaya, his ring and middle fingers joined together. Old memories came flooding back to Gabriel through the haze, until he cried out:

"My God!"

"You see, you do call upon him when you feel the need, friend of Erasmus."

"Brother Bartholomew!"

"When I think," said Bartholomew to Anamaya, "that we spent two months together and that this fellow had erased everything from his memory, except for one sad accident of nature."

Gabriel was overcome with emotion. He hadn't thought about that jail, hadn't brought to mind his memory of being terrified of being tortured, hadn't remembered the rage and humiliation he had experienced before his father, nor the memory, and of this he was almost ashamed, of Doña Francesca, for so long, that he now felt disoriented as the familiar face brought them flooding back.

"That was in another life," he said.

"And yet it's the same one."

The two men stared at each other for a long time before clasping one another in their arms.

"When did you join the column?"

"I arrived in Cajamarca a few days after it had left but I caught up with it easily."

"But then, how can it be that I haven't seen you until tonight?"

"Yes, it's odd, isn't it?"

"Don't play the theologian with me, Brother Bartholomew, by answering questions with questions."

"When there is no answer to a question, one might as well ask another. Or else keep silent."

"Silence . . . that was your advice to me all those years ago, wasn't it? . . . And I still don't know if I'm capable of it!"

"Oh, you seem capable of many things to me," said Bartholomew gaily, glancing at Anamaya.

The two men and Anamaya had returned to the tent in which Sebastian and his companions were digging the grave.

"I must give the last rites to this ill-fated fellow," said Bartholomew.

"What are you doing here, Brother Bartholomew?"

The monk didn't bat an eyelid.

"The work of God," he said eventually, grinning.

"When there is no answer to a question . . ."

"Haven't I just given you an answer?"

Bartholomew disappeared into the tent.

Gabriel remained there for a moment, staring into the night, before Anamaya led him away.

"That man isn't like the rest," she said. "He isn't like you, but he isn't like the rest either."

"Yes. I think him strange as well."

"Is he capable of massacring us?"

Gabriel searched the magnificent starlit sky, trying to pierce through the night that all the birds had taken refuge in, to feel beyond the cold.

"I don't think so," he said at last, "but I'm not sure."

TEN

When the first gray light of dawn revealed the field to them, all the men fell silent. It wasn't the delicate mauve of *quinua* that had been sown here, however, or the gold of corn. It was death.

The battle between Huascar's and Atahualpa's men had taken place a few weeks earlier, but their warriors still lay where they had fallen, this one with his head in the mud, that one with his eyes turned to the sky. Gabriel detected something atrocious in this scene of eternal peace: the pestilent odor of decomposing bodies, the grass growing around them, the worms swarming in their wounds, the hollow cavities where their eyes had been pecked out by birds. In all, over four thousand bodies lay strewn across the plain, a sinister harvest that the earth would reabsorb and that the grass would soon cover.

It was a beautiful day. Men were vomiting.

Gabriel turned his eyes away and tried to absorb the verdant landscape. After the harshness of the mountain passes, of the snow and the cold, that dawn seemed mild, and held the promise of warmth.

Only Governor Don Francisco Pizarro, at the head of the column, seemed as indifferent to the scene of carnage as he was to beauty. He frequently stopped the Indian guides to have them explain some anomaly in the terrain to him. He kept the *curaca* of the town close by him, after having made a long declaration of friendship to this long-haired Huanca Indian who wore a crown four fingers wide on his head. "We'll take care of you," he frequently told him. "We'll free you from the bondage of the Incas." When this was translated to him, the man's eyes lit up, and he nodded enthusiastically.

Pizarro spent his nights praying, as he had at the beginning of the conquest. The veterans of Cajamarca felt a familiar apprehension in their guts, one that both excited and frightened them.

"We're going to fight soon."

*   *   *

The mountain loomed over the town of Hatun Sausa. It was a beautiful
Inca town, with its Temple to the Sun, its *acllahuasi*, its *ushnu* in the
standard pyramidical shape in the middle of its huge square, its walled
canchas, its warehouses, and its narrow alleyways. It was a beautiful town
set in the bottom of a broad valley, next to a fast-flowing river.

It was a beautiful Inca town, and it was burning.

Higher up on the mountain, Pizarro had found himself held up by
the slow progress of Chalkuchimac's palanquin. Although the general
never showed himself, and although the wounds he had sustained under
torture prevented him from walking, the Governor was persuaded that
he was more or less secretly directing the movements of the Indian
troops. That's why, as the battle loomed closer, Pizarro didn't let him out
of his sight.

The Governor had to check his brother Juan's and Almagro's impa-
tience, and he ordered Soto to lead a company of cavalrymen into the
town.

The days when Gabriel had to beg to be part of the vanguard were
long past, and Pizarro motioned to him to go with Soto "just in case, as
usual," gibed Gabriel. With a kick of his heels, he urged his bay on and
took his position among the fifteen or so cavalrymen, who had aligned
themselves in pairs.

Once they reached the edge of town, Soto raised his hand to halt the
column. The majority of the Indian troops were massed on the other
side of the river. Soldiers in colorful tunics were torching the main buildings, beginning with the *collcas*, the food depots.

"They're burning the warehouses! We must hurry!" cried Diego de
Agüero, one of the more hotheaded *caballeros*.

"Easy, *hombre*," countered Soto.

"You are unusually cautious, Captain de Soto," said Gabriel, surprised.

Soto grinned.

"I am simply obeying the Governor's orders. There is to be no major
engagement until he arrives."

"But everything is burning, Soto. In a couple of hours, not a single
ear of corn, nor a strip of dried meat will remain in this town," carped a
caballero.

"Soto," continued Gabriel, "let me take a patrol in, along with Agüero and Candia."

"And me too," called a cavalryman from the back.

"And him too," said Gabriel without looking back. "A well-executed charge might repel them before everything is turned to ash."

Soto thought about it for a moment.

"By the faith, it's your head, after all! But try to stay alive, my friends, until we arrive with reinforcements."

"Don't worry, Captain. We shall set the table. Just don't be late for dinner!"

They forded the river at a trot. Then Gabriel launched his horse into a gallop at the small group of buildings, shaped like truncated cones, where the Royal Road narrowed into an alley. A thick and bitter smoke already billowed between the houses. At the entrance to the main square stood an Indian waving at them, his tunic torn to tatters, his face blackened by soot. He appeared completely unsurprised by their presence, and, running after their horses, he called in Quechua, "Save us! They're torching everything!"

The Huancas were one of the tribes conquered by the Incas who had never really completely surrendered to them. Gabriel turned toward his three companions and cried, "They're welcoming us as liberators!"

"Well then, let's liberate them," cried Candia, pointing at the biggest building on the square, a *kallanka,* which the Inca soldiers were about to set alight, "or else everything is going to be reduced to ashes, us included!"

Gabriel, his eyes irritated by the smoke, drew his sword, then patted his horse, which also found the acrid smoke offensive. The soldiers coming out of the *kallanka* were armed with axes, lances, or slings. An officer, catching sight of the newcomers, bellowed an order to his men. The deep sound of a trumpet echoed across the square, and twenty warriors were already running at the Spaniards, utterly heedless of the horses.

Candia let fly a savage cry, a "Santiago!" so deep that it could easily have been emitted by an animal. All four Spaniards, moved by the same instinct, bent down low on their horses' necks and held their swords out, the blades of which gleamed in the pearly light. The horses seemed to also find some furious stimulation in their gallop, as though they found it easier to breathe.

Their first charge split the group of Indians. Their steel swords sliced through the lances and the straps of the slingshots, and cleaved through the Indian hands holding clubs and axes. One man fell to the ground howling in pain, his shoulder slashed open. The others fled down the narrow alleys. Gabriel chased them, with Candia at his side. Through the thick smoke, they made out Agüero and his companion heading toward the river.

"Watch out!" cried Candia.

The alley before them was too narrow for two horsemen to ride down it abreast. Gabriel went first, bent down low on his horse's neck. As he went through, he felt a man stumble and fall beneath his horse's hooves. He was horrified when he felt the man being trampled under the horse. A stone whistled past the animal's ears, and Gabriel saw the man who fired it hiding in the door of a *cancha*. When he reached the man, he pushed his horse close enough so that he was able to thrust his sword into the man's chest. The man stared at him with bulging eyes for a fraction of a second. Gabriel felt the death shudder of his first kill.

Soon there was only one man left trying to escape, his rapid pace showing no sign of weakening. He was a long-ear wearing an officer's helmet with blue feathers. The enormous gold plugs extending his ear-lobes tossed about on his shoulders as he bolted.

With a glance, Gabriel realized that he was trying to reach the river. The rest of the Indian troops were waiting on the other side. He urged his horse over to the riverside, intent on cutting off the officer's route. But when the officer realized this, he stopped running. Gabriel was astonished when he recognized him through the dust and soot covering him. He could never have forgotten those proud eyes, and that nose as straight as a rock edge.

"Guaypar!" he cried. "I know who you are!"

"You speak our language?" yelled the other angrily. "How can that help you kill me?"

"I've often thought of you, Guaypar!" said Gabriel, grinning.

Guaypar's expression remained impassive as Gabriel hesitated. To see this man before him now, the man who had tried to protect Ana-maya during the massacre at Cajamarca, weighed on him terribly, as though his sword was suddenly made of lead instead of steel.

"You should kill me," said Guaypar, sensing his doubt.

Gabriel kept his horse perfectly still. Smoke floated out over the river. On the other side, the warriors had identified their officer, and were gathered on the bank, crying out. Other cries rose from the village. But still Gabriel didn't move, nor did Guaypar, who seemed gripped by his own doubts.

At that moment a thatch roof, not twenty paces from them, burst into flames. Gabriel turned his head for an instant to look at it, and he saw flames rise into the sky. But he didn't see Guaypar leap deftly past the horse, jump onto the sparsely grassed riverbank, and throw all his gold finery into the river.

"You should have killed me while you had the chance, because now it's me who shall kill you!" he cried, before diving in.

Everywhere he went, Gabriel met groups of men, women, and children coming out of the houses and *kallankas,* all crying tears of gratitude. He felt uneasy, and he rebuffed them with scant ceremony.

Yet one group of them managed to lead him to a *cancha* where an Inca soldier lay on the ground, his leg broken, holding an axe, and surrounded by a gang of young Huancas who were hurling insults at him but didn't yet dare approach him. A child yanked on Gabriel's scabbard.

"I haven't the time!" he yelled.

He set off at a gallop across the square. He found no trace of Agüero or Candia. He went down to the bridge. Anamaya drifted into his thoughts, but he pushed her as far away as possible, to a place of purity, away from the bloodshed.

Across the river, over two hundred Indian warriors had gathered, protected by another fifteen or so at the rear, and they were trying to set the straw and rope bridge alight. Agüero and Candia were already fighting, in vain, to cut a passage through the bulk of the group to prevent them from burning the bridge.

Agüero was fighting bravely, windmilling his sword in wide circles, dodging sling stones, and staving off swipes from clubs, and was simultaneously managing his horse well. Candia's movements were more deliberate, but equally efficient. What struck and horrified Gabriel, meanwhile, as he rushed to join his two companions, was the resignation with which the Indians before him were ready to die, just like those at

Cajamarca, simply to allow their companions the time to fire the bridge, and so prevent the Spaniards' crossing.

In order to encourage himself and blot out his doubts, Gabriel howled like a maniac as he launched his horse into the fray. He heard Candia laugh out loud, an absurd and comforting guffaw.

"Well! You took your time getting here," said the Greek giant.

Gabriel struck out with such incredible violence, slicing off arms, piercing holes into chests, and destroying faces, that he became delirious with death. None of the Incas' traditional armor offered them any protection against his carving blade. First ten, then twenty fell, powerless against him. Some died suffocating under the bodies of those who fell on top of them, others crawled away to drown in the river, wounded and mutilated. But still their kinsmen continued the fight, their clubs and axes raised high, and with insane looks in their eyes.

Gabriel noticed one warrior who stood out above the rest. He was taller and seemed stronger and nobler than his companions, whom he never tired of haranguing. He avoided death as though dancing around it, and many times he dodged a sword or a hoof. Then, in one agile stroke, he jumped onto the rump of Candia's horse, grabbed the Greek by the shoulder, and brought his axe up to strike him in the side.

Gabriel charged down on them on his bay. His sword arm burst forth like a shot from a crossbow, and he felt the steel shudder through the Inca's flesh.

The warrior cried out and straightened up, putting all his weight on the sword. For a moment, everything seemed suspended. The Indian's legs remained clenched around the horse, and Gabriel thought that he was holding him there with his sword. Then the warrior let go, and he fell down beneath the horses' hooves.

"Fucking hell!" bellowed Candia, rubbing his ribs, "you're a welcome arrival, Don Gabriel!"

"The bridge has gone, it's burning already," replied Gabriel, pointing at the rising flames.

But now the Indians were retreating, abandoning the dead and dying behind them. The battle ended as if by magic. Agüero and his companion joined them, looking distraught, their boots and breeches covered in blood. They dismounted and lifted the visors of their morions. Their faces were drenched in sweat and blood, their cheeks and lips still tense with fear.

"Gentlemen," growled Candia, "I have some good news: we're still alive!"

Soto and the other cavalrymen joined them, and then, around midday, Pizarro and the rest of the column. The entire town was filled with rejoicing, but the Spaniards didn't linger for the festivities, or for the gifts offered to them.

Pizarro reached the riverbank along with his brothers Gonzalo and Juan, Captain de Soto, and Almagro.

"How do we stand, Gabriel?"

Gabriel pointed to the other side of the river, where around five or six hundred Inca warriors stood facing them.

"We gave them chase, Don Francisco, and as you see we managed to discourage a few of them. But I regret to say that they managed to destroy the bridge."

"Recreant coward!"

The slur had come from Gonzalo's mouth.

Gabriel wiped away the sweat still on his forehead. Then he came in right up close to the curly-haired fop, a menacing smile on his face, a grin that he had acquired earlier, when he had been killing Incas, and which remained with him now, like a gash across his face.

Gonzalo took a few steps back, before barking again:

"We all know how you carried yourself in battle, you coward, letting their chief go."

Gabriel, surprised, wavered for a moment before understanding that Gonzalo was referring to Guaypar.

"That's enough, Gonzalo!" decreed Pizarro.

The Governor's abrupt tone invited no reply. Gonzalo and Gabriel stared one another down for a moment, pride and hatred warping their features.

Don Francisco phlegmatically took stock of the piling up of the bodies, then the deep and fast-running river that ran between them and the road down which the village's attackers had gone. Without turning around, he asked for volunteers to carry out another attack.

"We must teach them a lesson," he said, "and not let them think that they can get away with this so easily."

Why was Gabriel one of the first to volunteer? He didn't know himself. Rage made his blood pump faster. He barely heard the others.

"Me too!" said Juan.

"And me!" said Soto.

"And me," growled Almagro, as though waking from a long sleep.

Pizarro grinned. The four horsemen, followed by a few foot soldiers, descended the bank down to the river. Some young Huanca men, eager for vengeance, jumped with them into the freezing water and admired the horses swimming with their nostrils above the swirling river.

The current was strong. They had to describe an arc in order not to exhaust their horses. But the slope of the opposite riverbank was gentle and easy to climb. As soon as they reached the road, Almagro and his men galloped away toward the mountain to come at the Incas from behind, while Juan and a small group followed the course of the river. Soto and Gabriel went directly after the Indian warriors, intending to force them back.

Gabriel didn't feel any fatigue. Gonzalo's insult still whirled around in his brain. He held on to his bay tightly with his thighs, and his hand, clasped around the hilt of his sword, weighed on his right thigh as if all the weight of the world was concentrated in it.

The first group of warriors rushed at them. They were waving their arms stupidly in the air. But as Soto cried "Watch out!" a storm of sling stones came down on them. Gabriel's bay, struck on the shoulder, stumbled and shied. The Indian warriors were already dispersing, having learned not to stay gathered as a group.

But another group of Incas with slingshots had taken up position a hundred paces on, and this time they let fly at Juan Pizarro's group, forcing them to retreat.

It was at that moment that a crazy idea occurred to Gabriel. He launched his horse forward as another group of warriors, formed in a perfect line, reloaded their slingshots. Howling like a lunatic, he charged straight at them. The Indians, transfixed, stared at him as he approached screaming, "Santiago! Santiago!"

He had the taste of death running through his veins, and his spirit was blinded by a violent rage. The Indians stared, gaping. Once upon them, Gabriel slipped down the side of his saddle, hanging on to the pommel with his left hand. He didn't see a bronze axe swipe just above him. He kept his eyes fixed on the warriors' throats. He was aware only of the rhythm of his horse beneath him. His right arm was harder than oak. Crouched thus, he held his sword with its blade angled back. He was upon them.

"Santiago!"

The steel sliced through throats, one after the other. One after the other, as quick as lightning, Gabriel severed the breath of life out of twelve men before they had the chance to cry out.

When he heaved himself up and pivoted his horse about, he saw twelve men crumple to the ground, their arms and legs waving about grotesquely, their blood pumping out onto the grass.

He became aware of a vacant silence flooding the valley. A bright white light stunned him. He had to grab on to his horse's mane to prevent himself falling from the saddle. Over to his left, the terrified Indians sought refuge in the safety of the bushes.

"Recreant coward," he murmured to himself, not understanding his own words.

He heard shouting from behind him. Almagro and the Huancas were giving chase to the fleeing Incas. Gabriel wiped the sweat from his face.

Soto came up to him. They stared at one another. The Captain nodded at Gabriel, and Gabriel thought he detected a perplexed fear in the other man's respectful nod. They turned their horses about simultaneously, like two exhausted men.

An hour later, over six hundred corpses were littered along the riverbank. Only a few fleeting shadows remained of Guaypar's battalion, trying, in vain, to escape by diving into the muddy, foaming river.

ELEVEN

Hatun Sausa, October 15, 1533

Nightfall, and the roofs and beams of Hatun Sausa glowed red as they burned. The air was infested with smoke and the smell of blood. Jubilant cries of victory echoed through the valley. A strange music could be heard, punctuated by the laughter of women and children. The music consisted of a deep-throated flute mixed with the insistent song of young girls and endless beating drums.

Gabriel hadn't yet found the strength to cross the river again and join the festivities. His horse wandered along the riverbank, grazing on the trampled grass between the unclaimed corpses of Inca warriors.

Every now and then one of his compatriots hailed him from across the river. Soto himself shouted a few words to him. Why will he not join them? Is he wounded?

No, he hasn't shed any of his own blood. But he felt poisoned by the images of the carnage. In the gathering darkness, he watched images, still fresh in his memory, of his sword cutting through flesh, slicing limbs, piercing into lungs, killing.

No, he wasn't wounded. But his chest was suffocated with an agonizing repugnance that he couldn't shake. He thought of Anamaya. He dreamed of her tender lips on his own, her kiss on his burning eyes. He wished he could embrace her in his arms, aching from the effort of having killed. He wanted her to whisper a few words of love, of forgiveness, to him.

And yet he knew that in these circumstances, he wouldn't even dare utter her name. He wouldn't be able to support her gaze or her touch.

Only after night was well advanced did Gabriel at last call his horse and cross the river. The freezing, turbulent water rushing past his boots did him good. Once he reached the other side, he broke into a short trot. He avoided people's glances, ignored their exuberant cries as they hailed him when he passed, their voices made hoarse by their unrestrained victory celebrations.

He reached the town's main square just as Almagro's men, in the presence of the Governor himself and of the cacique of Hatun Sausa, were taking the treasures out of a smoldering *kallanka*.

Dozens of gold plates, goblets, masks, and statues were piled up outside, a now familiar scene. The pile gleamed under torches despite the soot covering them. And the Spaniards' eyes gleamed even more. They were laughing and flinging gold porringers into the air with the tips of their swords, treasures saved from the blaze just in time by slaves, but still somewhat deformed by the heat. The local Indians watched them from a safe distance, intrigued.

Don Francisco's face remained impassive through all this. His eyes watched the gold accumulate, but he seemed not to be registering it. Hidden behind his perfectly trimmed beard, his lips were moving, murmuring something. Gabriel, without having to hear him, knew that he was praying to the Sacred Virgin. Don Francisco was not one to give up his old habits. He was offering the blood, the dead, the suffering, and the joy of the gold to the Virgin, feeling that by doing so he was purifying himself. For a few moments, Gabriel envied him.

Eventually Don Francisco turned around and saw Gabriel close by, who had dismounted and was holding his horse by the bridle.

"Ah! There you are," said the Governor, eyeing him fondly.

He looked Gabriel up and down, took note of his torn and soaked breeches and his dirty doublet, its right sleeve torn open and stained with half-dried blood. And when the Governor looked at Gabriel's face, at the scratches on his cheeks and his vacant eyes, his affection gave way to bemusement.

"What a state you're in, my boy! Not such a bad performance, for a coward."

Gabriel didn't acknowledge the compliment or the repudiation implicit in the Governor's words. Shivering with cold and exhaustion, he turned his gaze toward the men piling up the gold in great wicker baskets brought by Indian women.

Suddenly the Governor made a motion to the trumpeter Alconchel.

"Sound to quarters," he said calmly.

Alconchel raised the instrument to his lips. The town's Indians, astonished, took a step back. Those who had been with the Spaniards since Cajamarca laughed at them and explained to them the source of the wail rising above the thick air in the valley.

"What's going on, Don Francisco?" asked Gabriel.

"Those whom you carved to pieces were only a small company. The bulk of their army, over fifteen thousand warriors, is about six leagues to the south of here. Now that the men and horses are rested, I want fifty cavalrymen to go after them."

Gabriel was dumbfounded.

"I'm not thinking of you, my boy. You must rest now. Your day is over. Relax, enjoy the dishes and women that our new friends are offering us."

Pizarro gave him a hug.

A cutting snigger rose from behind them as they broke their emotional embrace.

"What a lovely sight this is!"

Gonzalo Pizarro was sneering still, his chest thrown out arrogantly, his doublet open over a dirty and torn shirt, and his breath stinking of beer. He gave an exaggerated, farcical salute.

"Well, well, brother, that's a real hero that you're holding in your arms!"

"And you another, Gonzalo!" replied the Governor, ostentatiously opening his arms to him. "And if you might find happiness in the embrace of your Governor, then it is happily that I offer it to you!"

Ignoring his brother's open arms, Gonzalo turned toward the group of cavalrymen fawning around him and spat:

"Gentlemen, please doff your hats. Having at last had the courage to gut a handful of Indians, Don Gabriel has become one of us. Welcome, bastard son!"

The Governor paled at the insult. His features became hard, as if the affront had been directed at him. His left hand gripped Gabriel's wrist to hold him back, and Gabriel spat through clenched teeth:

"Gonzalo, the day shall come when you shall die poisoned by your own venom. And I doubt that I shall be among those mourning you."

Gonzalo immediately dropped his smug smile. He looked at Don Francisco, stupefied. He opened his mouth to reply, but shut it again as

Gabriel disengaged himself from the Governor and stepped up to Gonzalo. He eyed the fop up and down.

"You're in the right of it, Don Gonzalo. There are only bastards here. But none stink of pigs' shit as much as you do."

As he turned on his heel, Gabriel didn't hear a snigger, only the orders given for the march. Don Francisco's voice was calm once again, as though nothing at all had happened.

Walking with what he hoped would be perceived as an unhurried gait, Gabriel crossed the square. His body still ached from the afternoon's violence. It was only a little later as he was heading back to the tents set up outside the town that he came across Chalkuchimac's palanquin, guarded by a few warriors. Half a dozen old noblemen followed in his retinue, and Anamaya was surrounded by their severe old faces.

Reflexively, Gabriel ducked into a tiny alleyway that stank of stagnant water. He would not have had her see him for anything in the world, with his breeches, his heart, and his eyes still sullied by the blood of the Indians whom he had killed today.

The flicker of the torches fixed to the walls at the bottom of the *ushnu*'s stairwell made their features seem indistinct and blurred. With a mere bat of his eyelids, Chalkuchimac ordered that the tar-coated torch poles be brought forth.

A dozen young boys came forward so silently that even their sandals couldn't be heard rustling across the flagstones. As there were no holders set in the nearest walls, the boys stood around the Council of Noblemen, holding the torches at arms' length, perfectly still.

Now Anamaya could see their faces more clearly.

There were nine of them forming a circle around a brazier in which some coca leaves were burning: four old men, exhausted by the trip, two high-ranking noblemen from Cuzco, the Governor of the region nominated by Atahualpa, Chalkuchimac, and herself, the *Coya Camaquen*.

General Chalkuchimac was the most impressive. His face showed no sign of the tortures that he had endured over the previous weeks, although he couldn't walk or even feed himself. His hands and feet, tortured with fire in Cajamarca, were still raw. The women nursing him did their best, smearing his wounds with unguent and changing his ban-

dages every morning and every evening, but still his blisters wept con-
tinuously, worsening as though they wanted to infest the courageous
warrior's entire body.

And yet as he sat there on his matting, leaning back against a chair,
wrapped in a great *manta* from which only his head emerged, he seemed
to Anamaya the strongest and most determined of the men present. It
was he who had convened this meeting now taking place as the
Spaniards celebrated their victory, feasted in the town's still-standing
canchas, and laughed at the dead rotting in the river.

Chalkuchimac surveyed each of their grave and silent faces before
fixing his piercing gaze on Anamaya. The whites of his eyes glowed red
in the torchlight. For a brief moment, she saw Atahualpa in his gaze. But
Chalkuchimac turned his eyes away as he said:

"We follow them like blindfolded children. We are neither brave nor
shrewd. The Strangers want to enter the Sacred City, so we lead them to
it by the hand! And yet we know what they will do there. Look around
you: they're pillaging the clans' *canchas*, and they're stealing all the gold
from the temples. And yet, Noble Lords, when I see your demeanors
and listen to your words, it is as though you are completely indifferent
to it. Indifferent to the fate of the Empire!"

One of the older Lords raised his hand and interrupted him in a
sharp voice:

"You still behave and think like a warrior, Chalkuchimac. You speak
only the language of force. That served you well while Inti blessed you
with his power. But now that you are weak and yield to the will of the
Strangers, you speak only the language of defeat. See only what has happened today! Hundreds of your brave warriors are dead by the hands of
the Strangers, although they were only a handful! Whether you like it or
not, their horses give them a strength that you don't have."

"Chalkuchimac, listen to the people of Hatun Sausa rejoicing!"
yapped another elder furiously. "Can you not hear them singing and
dancing? Your men had come to torch this valley so that the Strangers
would find only ashes and smoke on their road. Listen to how happy the
inhabitants of this province are now, as the Strangers empty the Inca's
warehouses and help themselves to their women as if they belonged to
them! Is this what you want to see throughout the Empire of the Four
Cardinal Directions?"

"That's enough!" ordered the most high-ranking of the Cuzco noblemen. "There is no point in arguing."

They remained silent for a moment, as cries and laughter floated in from the tents by the river outside the town.

The high-ranking Cuzco nobleman was a round man, with very high cheekbones and skin so bronze that he looked like some painted piece of earthenware. Chalkuchimac remained impassive under his gaze. His gold ear plugs dangled against his shoulders, gleaming. He hadn't batted an eyelid throughout the accusations against him, and his jaw seemed as large and strong as a puma's.

"Chalkuchimac has spoken one part of the truth," continued the Cuzco nobleman, "and I, Tisoc Inca, agree with him when he says that we follow the Strangers like blindfolded children. It is time to elect an Emperor. It is time that Inti finds a son among us."

Anamaya watched the old men lower their faces. Chalkuchimac grinned disdainfully.

"I suppose that the Noble Tisoc wishes that one of his clan be chosen!"

"Your anger is in vain, Chalkuchimac. He who is elected must have the blessing of the Sun God and the support of our Ancestors in the Other World. That is all that I ask."

"It surprises me that you have no one in mind," growled Chalkuchimac.

"How can we elect an Emperor when we have neither a priest nor a soothsayer to tell us the will of Inti and Quilla?" asked another Elder, speaking for the first time. "How are we to choose him, since Emperor Atahualpa didn't hand down the royal *mascapaicha* to any of his sons before dying?"

"He didn't because he didn't need to," replied Chalkuchimac dryly. "Everybody knows that Atoc Xopa was Atahualpa's favorite son. It is he who should wear the two-feathered *curiguinge* on his head, as his father did."

Once again Chalkuchimac's words were met with a heavy silence. Some of the Elders looked at Anamaya. She knew what they expected of her, but she bided her time, preferring to hold her tongue until all of the noblemen's words and ulterior motives had come to the fore.

"Atoc Xopa is only a child," remarked the Cuzco nobleman. "What's more, he lives in the northern capital, far from here, and far from the Strangers. How will he be able to impose his will?"

"Tisoc, you have completely missed what Chalkuchimac's words imply," scoffed one of the Elders. "You are right, Atahualpa's favorite son is only a child. He lives in the North, and none here have seen his face. He has never even been to Cuzco. But that is precisely what endears him to General Chalkuchimac!"

"If we choose him," added another, "he will be nothing more than a shadow under Chalkuchimac's influence. Chalkuchimac will be the real master of the Empire, even though he isn't the son of Inti!"

All eyes were on the general. He stared back at them without twitching a single muscle in his face. Anamaya couldn't help but admire his strength and composure. The tension in the room was so high that she noticed that the hands of a few of the Noble Lords were trembling. Then the oldest of them said, as he raised his crooked and buckled hand:

"I heard what Chalkuchimac told the Strangers' *Machu Kapitu* through their intermediary who speaks their language. He told them, alone and without our consent, that Atoc Xopa should be our Emperor."

"Chalkuchimac, is this true?"

Before replying to Tisoc Inca, the old warrior turned his gaze toward Anamaya. He plunged his eyes into hers deliberately and for a long time, as though trying to read her soul. Then he looked up and said:

"Yes."

An angry cry of dismay rose in unison from the Noble Lords. But now Chalkuchimac appeared to be addressing Tisoc Inca alone as he said:

"What has happened to you all? Are you like Atahualpa, who believed that the Strangers would simply leave after taking all the gold we offered them? Atahualpa has gone, and no one among us knows whether he was able to join his father in the Other World!"

Another angry howl rose from the Noble Lords. Chalkuchimac, in a choleric gesture, pushed back the *manta* that was covering him. Everyone saw his blackened hands. They had no skin left at all, and glistened with blood. The flesh on his feet and legs had been reduced to roasted shreds oozing yellow pus.

"Why do you think that I suffered this?" roared Chalkuchimac. "The stench of my scorched flesh fouls the air of the Empire of the Four Cardinal Directions! My agony rises into the blackness of the sky so that

Inti may find it when he rises each morning! And Inti prevents me from healing so that every one of our warriors may smell the odor of my wounds and so know that I will never prostrate myself before the Strangers. Tisoc! They are not kind and gentle! They feed on gold, and their hunger is insatiable! Tisoc Inca, don't you realize that when they reach Cuzco, they will take everything without giving anything in return? They will take your livestock, your women, your children, and your servants. They will take everything and they always will, because that is why they are here! I, Chalkuchimac, tell you this: we must annihilate them while they are still few in number."

"In that case, why designate an inexperienced child?" grumbled an Elder.

Chalkuchimac grinned like a demon from the Underworld, and Anamaya couldn't help but shudder.

"Because then the Strangers will think themselves the Emperor's master! They will tell him, Do this, do that. And we will smile at them. We will give them their gold. But meanwhile, I shall be freed. And then I can lead our warriors into a great battle, and all the Strangers shall die."

"Like today?" sniggered Tisoc cynically.

"You are nothing but cowards!" yelled Chalkuchimac, waving his wounded hands. "Inti shall reduce you all to ashes!"

"Inti is not with you, Chalkuchimac!" replied Tisoc dryly, "you forget that he who is hungry always ends up by either eating or starving to death. Your choice is neither wise nor sound. We all know whom we should elect Emperor. It must be Manco, the son of Huayna Capac and the Lord of the northern clan. He is the wisest and strongest of those who are still alive. He will bring peace and unity to the Empire."

Chalkuchimac's derisive snigger sounded almost like a full-blown laugh. He turned toward Anamaya.

"Is it you who has elicited this choice, *Coya Camaquen?* You are very quiet, I find. I've known you more talkative when you were at Atahualpa's side."

"Chalkuchimac!" called out one of the elders. "How dare you taunt the *Coya Camaquen!*"

Chalkuchimac accidentally brushed his flayed hands against his clothes, and he grimaced in pain. He shook his head, and then said in a lower voice:

"No, no, Noble Lord, I do not mock her. I know who the *Coya Camaquen* is."

"Chalkuchimac," continued Tisoc Inca in a conciliatory tone, "this argument is pointless. We are running out of time, and we must choose an Emperor. There is no soothsayer here, no servant of Inti who might interpret the oracles for us. But the *Coya Camaquen* can. She designated Atahualpa Emperor even before the comet crossed the sky above Quito. He trusted her in all the decisions he took, as you know. And we all know that he spoke his last words uttered in this world to her, just as his father, Huayna Capac, did in Quito."

"Yes!" agreed one elder loudly. "That is what we should do."

"Chalkuchimac, agree that the *Coya Camaquen* choose the new Emperor, that she choose between Manco and Atoc Xopa."

Chalkuchimac hadn't taken his eyes off Anamaya. For the first time she detected fear, doubt, and even a glimmer of goodwill toward her in them. Then he exhaled suddenly, like a smithy's bellows, closed his eyes, and asked:

"So, what do you say, noble Anamaya?"

Anamaya's heart was beating so strongly that its thud almost drowned out his words. She was aware of the immense consequence of what she said. All her muscles became as hard as rock, and her bones stiffened. But the sentences rose from her throat and came out of her mouth as though spoken by a will other than her own, as had happened on so many other occasions. Even as she uttered them, it was as if they were spoken by someone else.

"On the eve of the great massacre at Cajamarca, Emperor Huayna Capac visited me from the Other World. He came in the form of a child. He told me, *'That which is too old comes to an end, that which is too big shatters, that which is too strong loses its force . . . that is what the great* pachacuti *means. The world is shrinking and being reborn. Everything has changed.'*"

An astonished murmur rose from her audience. It didn't occur to anyone to doubt her: it was as though the great Huayna Capac himself was speaking to them through her lips. They were on tenterhooks, and she saw their tense faces absorbed in every word she uttered. She continued:

"Emperor Huayna Capac continued: *'Take care of my son whom you saved from the snake, for he is the first knot of the future.'* A long time ago, when I was still an inexperienced young girl without any learning, I watched the ceremony in which the noble Manco became a man. He won the race that day. But during the course of it, a venomous snake had placed itself in his way, in order to bite him. I got rid of the snake, and saved Manco's life."

Absolute silence reigned over the room. The laughter and singing had ceased in the night outside, as had the din out on the plain.

"And so, *Coya Camaquen*, Manco is your choice," murmured Chalkuchimac.

"Noble Chalkuchimac," replied Anamaya with an audacity that surprised even herself, "it is not my choice. It is the Ancestors in the Other World who designated Manco a long time ago now. But allow me to add that he is noble and honest. He is fair, and he is no coward. He will know how to unite all the parts of the Empire without having to submit to the Strangers like some child. And to wage the war that you wish for, if it must happen, then it must happen after a reign of peace. The wounds of the civil war between the brothers that so weakened Emperor Atahualpa must be given time to heal. Yes, Chalkuchimac, you are a noble warrior. But today, war takes the guise of peace. Only peace will allow us to be strong when the day comes, should Inti and Quilla wish for it."

"Well said! She is right," said two of the Elders approvingly.

"Chalkuchimac," said Tisoc, "all of us here agree with the *Coya Camaquen*. We trust her. Tomorrow, at first light, she will leave to meet Manco and tell him of our decision."

With his eyes half-shut, Chalkuchimac gazed at his wounds. Then he looked up at Tisoc and asked bitterly:

"What would happen if I were to disagree with the *Coya Camaquen?*"

Tisoc didn't reply. The Elders' tired breathing could be heard through the heavy silence, the breaths of old men who now drew their strength from only the memory and the words of a young girl. Anamaya looked at Chalkuchimac with both admiration and regret.

"What would happen?" repeated Chalkuchimac in a deeper, more menacing tone.

Anamaya looked at Tisoc for a moment, but she didn't wait for his approval before saying with prodigious calm:

"Nothing, my Lord. Nothing would happen. I shall leave at dawn."

Chalkuchimac stared into her eyes. For once, she saw an emotion that was neither anger nor defiance. She saw resignation.

And an infinite sadness.

Dawn rose over a thick fog that lacquered the rocks and tent canvases with damp. The air was still full of ash. There was no noise save the constant rumbling of the river and an occasional bird cry.

Wrapped in his long horsehair cape, Gabriel sat on a tree stump a little apart from the Inca Lords' camp. He had slept badly, waking often from a nightmare in which he repeatedly saw horrifying images of yesterday's battle. He would wake with his heart beating hard with the violent desire to run to Anamaya's tent. He imagined himself taking her in his arms, losing himself in her caresses and between her thighs, erasing the burning memory of all the violence in a physical love that never ended. But he didn't dare.

Nor did he dare join her now, as she prepared to leave on her journey.

Don Francisco had warned him: the Inca noblemen had chosen a new king. "With my consent, of course," he had said, without giving any other information, before adding, "Their priestess has been designated to take the news to the Emperor-elect, and I have given her leave to withdraw from the column." At the word "priestess" Pizarro's black eye had looked directly into Gabriel's, who had turned away, almost ashamed.

Now, in this damp and silent dawn, near the river, Indian porters were preparing the *Coya Camaquen*'s palanquin. She was to be escorted by a dozen warriors commanded by a young officer, and they stood waiting a few steps away. But Gabriel stared only at the group gathered between the tents of the noblemen.

Anamaya looked resplendent as she stood in the center of a group of Elders paying their respects to her. She was draped in a vicuña cape decorated with blue, scarlet, and bright yellow patterns. She wore a sort of gold tiara with three yellow feathers rising from it. Her wrists were covered in gold plaques. She held an ear of corn made of gold in her hand.

Gabriel had never seen her so strikingly dressed. She was like a stranger, a princess from a world still so inaccessible to him that he experienced a puerile jealousy.

"Aren't you at least going to bid her farewell?" asked a voice from beside him.

"Brother Bartholomew!"

A smile spread across the monk's curiously pale face. His gray eyes displayed a degree of tenderness. He pointed his fused fingers at Anamaya, before whom some Elders were bowing.

"I know what that woman means to you, my friend. But not because of any indiscretion on my part: everybody in the column whispers about it. As you know, lies spread as easily as truths, but then one needs to scratch only a little to tell them apart."

Gabriel hesitated before replying:

"I can't tell if this is one of those situations where it is better to keep silent, as you have so often advocated, Brother Bartholomew. What do you think?"

"*Mihi secretum meum,* yes? Do what your heart tells you, my friend. But you cannot prevent me from reading in your eyes the answers that your lips won't give me."

Gabriel nodded slowly and examined the scene before him. Anamaya, surrounded by Indian soldiers and three of the Noble Lords, and followed by a handful of servant girls, approached the palanquin. Gabriel knew that she had seen him.

"They say that she isn't like other princesses," said Bartholomew, looking at Gabriel.

For the first time since the battle, Gabriel cheered up, half-smiling. It was easier to surrender to intelligence than to spitefulness.

"She has abilities that inspire fear and respect in the Indians," he replied, "and the dead King, Huayna Capac, confided in her some secrets on which they believe their future depends."

Gabriel paused, hesitating.

"But perhaps this all seems heathen, or even the work of the devil to you, Brother Bartholomew."

The priest grinned.

"I'm not one to see the devil in everything, Gabriel. On the other hand, I can recognize beauty when it stands before me. And is not beauty always the work of God?"

Gabriel felt a real joy in rediscovering the monk's subtle and affable mind. And his natural smile attracted Anamaya's attention. She was only a short distance from her palanquin now. She seemed to be hesitating a little. But ceremony dictated her path. An old nobleman motioned toward the palanquin, the porters, and the escort.

Bartholomew laid his hand on Gabriel's forearm.

"Let me ask you another question: Why don't you go and wish her a safe and happy journey?"

"Yesterday," said Gabriel in a muted voice, "I killed a lot of men. A lot of Indians."

"Are you frightened that she will reproach you for it?"

"I don't know. But I'm disturbed by the memory of having wanted to kill, and even of enjoying it."

Bartholomew laughed quietly.

"As for that, you should speak to me, not to her."

Brother Bartholomew gazed at Anamaya's cortege with his gray eyes. He said nothing further as they watched Anamaya take her seat in the palanquin. Then he said in a lively voice:

"Yesterday, Gabriel Montelucar y Flores, you did your duty. You became a hero in the eyes of many of your companions, and many of them admire you for it today. Probably you couldn't care less, because you are immensely proud and you find your compatriots a little uncivilized. But it makes no odds. If it makes any difference to you, tell yourself that you have already returned the lives you took to God. As for the love in your heart, Gabriel, don't look to me to call it a sin."

Gabriel was so surprised that he turned to look the priest in the eyes.

"What things you tell me, Brother Bartholomew! That woman hasn't even been baptized! If I were to heed the words of Fray Vicente Valverde, then . . ."

Bartholomew interrupted him impatiently:

"And if you were to heed mine, then to deny the force of love is a sin. The apostle Paul says as much, and St. Augustine."

"But they're talking about the love of God!"

"And now the freethinker takes himself for a theologian! Do you pretend to teach me what the force of divine love is? I tell you that there is a spark of the divine in your love."

Bartholomew's words were almost lost to the wail of the bronze trumpet sounding the cortege's imminent departure.

"Now go! Hurry!" insisted Brother Bartholomew.

Gabriel, at last released from the moral shackles that had been hob-
bling him since the previous day, walked through the crowd of warriors
and noblemen toward the woman he loved.

The palanquin was already on the outskirts of the town by the time
Gabriel reached it. The Indian soldiers looked a little surprised as they
watched him fall into step with them. Anamaya ordered her porters to
stop.

Gabriel felt a slight shiver run up his spine as she stepped out of her
palanquin and approached him. He had never seen so much nobility and
dignity incarnated in one person. She led him a short distance away. He
noticed that none of her porters, guards, or servant girls dared look in
their direction.

"I am so happy that you came," said Anamaya.

She was quiet for a moment before adding:

"I was worried that you wouldn't. I didn't want to leave without seeing your face up close."

She raised her hand to his lips. When he tried to kiss her, however,
she stepped back slightly. But she continued to smile at him.

"We can't, it's impossible," she said gently, "not here, and not now."

Gabriel's gut was twisted into knots, and he was unable to speak the
words his racing heart wanted to say. He was trembling slightly. It
seemed intolerable to him not to hold her body against his before their
separation.

Anamaya stepped closer to him. They were so close that their bodies brushed against each other without actually touching. When he
opened his eyes again, he saw Anamaya's blue irises looking into him, as
though searching the depths of his soul.

"I know what war is," she murmured. "We also kill our enemies."

"I'm going to miss you," said Gabriel at last. "Not an hour shall pass
when I won't yearn for you."

"Soon we shall return to a time of peace. We have elected a new Inca.
He is like a brother to me, and he is wise. He will know how to negoti-
ate a peace with your Governor."

The members of the cortege behind them stood perfectly still. Not
one man or woman moved an inch. Gabriel thought of Guaypar, whom

he had faced during the battle the day before, and whom he had let escape.

"Peace is still a far way off. Be careful."

"You are the one who must be careful," said Anamaya.

Suddenly her eyes were filled with such intensity, such anxiety, as she looked at him that he felt disturbed.

"You have come a long way to find me. I don't want to lose you. You have opened a weakness in me, a fissure that has grown into a ravine, and I'm more frightened for you than I have ever been for myself."

She spoke these words without looking at him, and although her voice was muted and firm and her face impassive, he sensed the depth of emotion in her.

And he found himself incapable of saying a word.

He reached out for her hand, and this time she let him hold it, and she even leaned against him with an energy that made them tremble. She gripped his hand so tightly that it hurt, scratching and grinding it, and there was perhaps more abandon in this grasp than she had ever given him during their lovemaking.

Gabriel caught people looking at them, and he recollected her words "not here, and not now." He tore himself away from her. His heart was warm and his back cold.

They stood beside one another for a little while, the ground uncertain beneath their feet. They found themselves unable to move or speak. Gabriel smelled the scent of flowers in the air, and he took refuge in it, closing his eyes.

She made to return to her palanquin, then stopped and turned around.

"Look after yourself," he said, his throat constricted.

She opened her mouth to speak, but then closed it again. He remained hanging on her eyes, on her lips. She said:

"I love you."

And before he had realized that it was the first time she had spoken these words to him, she had run back to the cortege.

TWELVE

The Apurimac Valley, October 30, 1533

He was a small man. Wooden plugs hung from his ears and he wore the tunic of a bridge warden. He got down on his knees on the flagstones and prostrated himself before the palanquin. The officer of the guards, club in hand, eyeballed him warily.

"Welcome to the Apurimac Valley, *Coya Camaquen*. It is my honor to help you cross the river."

Anamaya had to smile, so much did the man seem to fear her. Not a day had passed since departing from Hatun Sausa that she did not discover how much her reputation and cortege impressed both the humble villagers and the Empire's officials.

The bridge warden had a few reasons of his own to be worried. Two hundred paces below them rumbled the furious Apurimac River, studded with giant boulders. Its rumble echoed throughout the entire valley, which broadened substantially to the south. But in front of them, where there should have been hanging a long rope bridge, was nothing.

"Stand up," ordered Anamaya, "and explain to me why the bridge has disappeared."

"Ten nights ago, *Coya Camaquen*, some soldiers came and burned it. I tried to stop them, and I ordered my guards to defend the bridge against them. But we were only ten, whereas General Quizquiz's company consisted of over a hundred men!"

"Quizquiz?" said Anamaya, astonished.

"Yes, *Coya Camaquen*. That is how they introduced themselves, as the men of the Emperor Atahualpa's great General Quizquiz."

"Did they say why they were to burn it?"

"To prevent the foreign gold robbers from reaching Cuzco."

The little man pointed toward the southern end of the valley and added:

"They say that there are troops throughout the mountains, and on the road to Cuzco."

"But how can we cross the river now?" asked Anamaya brusquely, wanting to stop the prattle that she sensed was coming.

The little man seemed delighted by her question. He bowed respectfully again and said:

"A messenger announced your arrival three days ago, *Coya Camaquen*. We have prepared the necessary rafts."

"Rafts?"

"Yes, *Coya Camaquen*. But we cannot cross here, where the bridge was, because the currents are too strong and dangerous. There is a better place not far from here. Shall you allow me to lead you there?"

"*Coya Camaquen*," interrupted the young officer commanding the escort, "it is unwise to leave the Royal Road. It might be a trap!"

"As you can see, Lieutenant," replied Anamaya, "the Royal Road has ceased to exist over the river. And I must absolutely reach my destination. You shall do your duty, then, and protect me."

It took them almost an hour, hiking along a steep and tricky path, to reach the place in the river where the current ran somewhat slower.

Set between two tree-covered slopes, the Apurimac ran slower and more evenly here. It described a wide curve between some pastures, passing through a small valley. But at the far end, it broke once more into a foaming mass against a large gray boulder that marked the start of more rapids.

Here, the river broadened and ran easy. But one only needed to glance at it from the bank to realize that the current was only slightly less dangerous than it was downstream.

"You see," explained the bridge warden, "the rafts must be launched from that spot over there. We must reach the other bank before the big gray rock."

"Where are the rafts?" asked Anamaya.

"Under the cover of those trees over there, *Coya Camaquen*. We didn't want the soldiers to find and destroy them before your arrival."

"Have you already tried crossing the river?" asked the officer suspiciously.

"Once already!" said the bridge warden with a broad grin, "there and back."

"Well then, this will be the second time," said Anamaya calmly.

The little man, flattered by her encouragement, began to exert himself vigorously in the moments that followed. His men pulled two heavy rafts built of logs and poles from the edge of the forest. Deftly rolling them on smaller logs, they brought them across the field to the bank of the Apurimac, where they launched the bigger of the two.

A dozen men held on to it with cables while six others set Anamaya's palanquin on it. Once the seat had been properly fastened, the Governor's men prostrated themselves and didn't get up until the *Coya Camaquen* had taken her place on the raft. Then, using long poles, they tried to keep it as stable as possible.

The current was so strong that Anamaya felt her palanquin sway back and forth. The tree trunks, tied together to allow a degree of flexibility, moved in an extraordinary way.

While the men struggled to keep the raft by the riverbank, a furious argument broke out between the officer of the guards and the bridge warden.

"I must accompany the *Coya Camaquen* with at least five soldiers!" said the officer.

"Impossible! That would overburden the raft, Lieutenant. We would not be able to navigate it safely. Two men at the most. Look: the logs are sinking as it is."

"Because you did a poor job of it!"

"No, it's just that the palanquin is heavier than we imagined. But there is always the second raft. Your men can follow the *Coya Camaquen* on it."

"That's enough!" intervened Anamaya. "Lieutenant, come aboard my raft, and you too, Warden. If this raft has been badly built, well then, we shall suffer the consequences all together!"

In truth, once the raft was released into the flow, Anamaya understood the concern of the men trying to navigate it. In addition to its increasingly violent rocking motion, the raft accelerated significantly as it neared the center of the river. The power of the current seemed bound to overcome the strength of the men as they poled along with astonishing speed.

Suddenly one of them let out a cry. An unexpected eddy appeared, deeply hollow. The six men quickly gathered on one side of the raft to shove it toward the right. But everything was happening too quickly. The shock threw Anamaya upward. The raft's logs jumped as they ground over the hidden rock. The palanquin was thrown upward once again, and tilted to the side. The officer of the guards threw himself onto one of its shafts to prevent it from slipping away. Anamaya grabbed on to the palanquin's posts, and bent double in counterbalance to its tilt.

The palanquin righted itself with a thud, but one of its legs sliced through a cord holding the logs together, which had already been weakened by the impact with the rock.

The gray rock marking the start of the rapids seemed to be getting closer at an alarming rate. The bridge warden barked an order, then another, and another. At that moment, the six men shoved together with perfect coordination.

It was like a ballet. Their poles rose, plunged, gave way and slipped, then rose again, plunged, gave way. Sweat pearled on the napes of their necks, and the raft stabilized. Even better, it began to move out of the center of the flow. The warden's barks continued, the poles bending so much that they seemed on the point of snapping. But at last, as the rumbling of the rapids rolled menacingly through the air, the raft slowed down, and began gliding toward the bank.

The warden grinned. He turned toward Anamaya and saluted her. Each of his men realized that the *Coya Camaquen* hadn't said a word, hadn't cried out in fear despite the danger.

She smiled back at him, and was surprised by the gentleness with which the raft met the bank.

As the palanquin was taken off the raft and set on the grass, she observed the men, absorbed the freshness of the air, and savored the odd feeling of pleasure she had just experienced: their gazes upon her were full of admiration and a newfound respect.

"Are we far from Rimac Tambo?" she asked the bridge warden.

"Less than a day's walk. But if you should like to do us the honor of accepting our hospitality for the night, then . . ."

Anamaya didn't let him finish.

"I thank you, and I will be sure to mention your competence to Lord Manco. But we must be in Rimac Tambo tonight."

*   *   *

The rumble of the river rose like a soothing murmur. The mountain slopes surrounding the village seemed like sheltering petals in the gathering dusk. From the *cancha* one could see a deep and narrow valley extending to the east. The lucent fog filling it glowed pale in the failing light. Anamaya knew today where the valley led: to the sacred city the name of which must never be spoken aloud: Picchu!

Nothing had changed at Rimac Tambo. It was a strange feeling.

Many years earlier, she had stood here in just such a sunset. The beautiful, perfectly joined walls surrounding the ceremonial square had possessed the same peaceful quality then as they did now. The sharp slopes surrounding the valley, like giant triangles or rectangles embedded in the earth, reminded her then, as they did now, of the weavings that the virgins created daily in their *acllahuasis*. Even then they had had that same, slightly alarming, power. Only Anamaya had changed. She had been nothing more than a frightened little girl whom the sage Villa Oma had done his best to change into a vigilant and confident woman.

It was from this very same spot and in a sunset identical to the one that night that, much to their surprise, the comet identifying Atahualpa as Emperor had appeared to them in the hollow of the forbidden valley.

Anamaya merely had to shut her eyes to see it again.

A ball of pale yellow fire, like a sun in the night. It had climbed up between the early stars to the black horizon. Its long hair trailed behind it, lifted by the wind of the Other World.

She could call to memory the sound of the sage's voice as he had said, "Let go of your fear, *Coya Camaquen*. Let your Spirit be your guide. Remember your voyage into the rock of our Ancestors. Let go of your fear."

A bird screech startled her and she opened her eyes.

The square around her was deserted. She felt a little cold. Her ceremonial cape wasn't warm enough for the mountains. She had made herself wear it since two days earlier, so that she would be sure to have it on when the new Emperor Manco arrived at last. But as night fell, she felt shivers of cold run down her neck and her back.

She heard the bird screech again, now closer to the river. And then another, this time behind the *tambo*.

Night was falling fast. Now the valley seemed dark and menacing. She could still make out the flagstones of the Royal Road between the bushes on the steep slope that blocked the valley to the south. The road created a strange impression, as though the mountain had been cleaved by a bolt of cold, hard lightning.

Anamaya repressed a shiver, a shiver due more to worry than to the increasing cold of dusk.

Many of Rimac Tambo's peasants had heard the bridge warden say that there were hundreds of soldiers roaming in the surrounding mountains, pillaging *canchas* and destroying villages. Their officers refused to obey the orders given by the Noble Lords following their peace agreement with the Strangers. Some proclaimed that they would obey only General Chalkuchimac, and that they would never allow the Strangers to reach Cuzco. The more time elapsed without a sign from Manco, the more Anamaya worried that he had fallen into the hands of the warrior hordes.

Would this always be the way? Would there always be violence, hatred, fighting between brothers despite the will of the Ancestors, and despite the grave danger that should have united them all?

This valley, despite its apparent calm, had buried in its earth so many melancholic memories that menace rose from it like mist. Anamaya remembered very well the massacre of the Elders who had been accompanying the mummy of the Emperor Huayna Capac, a massacre that had taken place on this very same spot.

The bird cries multiplied as the forest grew darker. In the darkening night, the rumble of the river sounded increasingly mysterious and insistent. Anamaya drew her cape tighter around her shoulders, but decided not to return to the *cancha,* as though her vigilance might protect Manco as he traveled toward her.

She hadn't moved since nightfall. Now it was the depth of night. A brazier had been brought alongside her by which she might warm her hands and face. Time passed slowly as she watched the stars rise.

From time to time animal cries echoed from the dark mountainside. And although she had been listening intently, she didn't hear the steps on the grass until the very last moment. She hadn't time to turn around before a broad, strong hand covered her mouth, preventing her from crying out. She felt herself embraced and lifted into the air like a doll.

"Manco!"

"Aaah!" murmured Manco as he released her, "you recognized me too quickly!"

They stood facing one another. Her eyes shone with tenderness. Anamaya immediately forgot the official salutation that she had planned to greet Manco with. The man standing before her glowed with strength and dignity. She felt profoundly happy to see him again, and to see on his face the marks of the time that had elapsed since they first met at Tumebamba. He too seemed moved at seeing her. He took a step back to admire her better.

"It is night, and you shine like a star, my beloved sister," he said gently.

"I'm so happy to see you, Manco. And so very happy as well to see that . . ."

She stumbled on what she was about to say. She wanted to tell him that he had acquired the beauty and bearing appropriate to an Emperor; that he possessed, in the line of his lips and in the sparkle of his eyes, the determination and self-assurance of a Son of the Sun. But she didn't dare. In a flash she remembered the eruption of her love for Gabriel. The *pachacuti* had overturned not only the world but also her heart. And in this troubled state of mind, she didn't want Manco to misinterpret her words as those of seduction.

". . . and so very happy to see that you have arrived without mishap," she said.

"Yes. Quizquiz's and Guaypar's troops are everywhere. But those northerners don't know the mountains quite as well as I do!"

He smiled, a little disdainfully, and then continued:

"But how is it that you didn't take fright and that you recognized me so quickly? Does the *Coya Camaquen* now have eyes in the back of her head, in addition to her other remarkable powers?"

"Oh, I've been waiting for you for hours! I was worried about you, and I was listening to the noises in the night as I waited for you . . ."

She paused, grinning, then continued:

". . . and then, you already surprised me like that once before, and in this very same place!"

They laughed together, both self-consciously happy.

"Come," said Manco, "let's go into the *tambo*. I'm hungry, and we'll be able to talk more comfortably."

Lord Manco's arrival created a great commotion inside the buildings. The few noblemen who had accompanied him had settled into a communal room with the commander of Anamaya's guard. The servant girls fluttered back and forth, stoked the braziers, prepared food, and brought the men *chicha*, blankets, and torches.

As soon as the door hanging had fallen behind them after they had entered the room that had been set aside for Manco, Anamaya fell to her knees and prostrated herself twice.

"Anamaya!" exclaimed Manco, abashed.

"Emperor Manco . . ."

"Anamaya! Why do you address me thus?" interrupted Manco as he leaned down to her. "You and I are brother and sister. . . ."

Anamaya shook her head and looked up at him.

"We won't be for much longer. The Council of Noblemen has met. They have elected you Emperor."

Manco straightened. His lips drew tight.

"The time has come," murmured Anamaya.

Manco looked at her for a moment. Then he took her by the shoulders and had her rise to her feet. He looked at her directly in the eyes.

"I remember the first time that I saw the color of your eyes. We were still children. That day, the blue of your eyes entered my heart. Even Paullu, my beloved brother, was a little jealous!"

Anamaya felt troubled once again, as she did every time he expressed his feelings for her. She pursed her lips, hoping he wouldn't go further. Manco, to her relief, noticed her discomfort. He remained silent, wearing a dreamy smile.

"I miss Paullu," he sighed. "He has been at Titicaca for three months now. He only likes being there."

Manco's gaze hardened as he continued:

"I also remember the last time we saw one another, Anamaya, my sister. That horrible night of the great massacre at Cajamarca haunted me for days and days afterward."

"That night, noble Manco, I warned you that Emperor Atahualpa was heading toward his end in this world, and that you would soon have to take his place. That time has come."

"Yes. Your words have stayed with me. I haven't forgotten. Just as I haven't forgotten that you have always marked out for me the road leading to the world of my Ancestors."

"But it's not me!" protested Anamaya. "I'm merely the medium through which they speak. I'm just the wife of your father Huayna Capac's Sacred Double. It is he who has designated you Emperor. And it is he who has placed the future of the Empire of the Four Cardinal Directions in your hands."

"I must try to understand, Anamaya, what happened that night. So many things were said—that the Strangers were gods, that they spat fire and were bodily joined with their animals. In Cuzco there is a rumor that the Sun has extinguished itself ever since they laid their hands on my brother Atahualpa."

Anamaya considered his words.

"I don't understand everything that is happening to the Empire, Manco. Your father no longer visits me to offer me guidance. My dreams are full of silences. But I have lived alongside the Strangers for many moons now, and I can assure you that they don't come from the Other World. They are men just like us! But men insatiable for gold. They neither spit fire nor possess any powers greater than ours. Their weapons are simply more powerful than ours."

Manco nodded, released Anamaya's shoulders, and sat on a thick pile of matting at the back of the room.

"Come sit by me," he said.

"Emperor . . ."

"No! Not yet. I'm not Emperor yet. Come, don't be frightened. I only want to feel your warmth next to me, little sister, like before."

Anamaya joined him, a little hesitantly. Manco held out his hand, and she placed her fingers in his palm. He closed his hand gently.

"Tell me more about the Strangers," he said. "Help me understand them. Must we hate them, or can we respect some of them and love them like humans in our own land?"

Disconcerted, Anamaya felt her heart beating prodigiously fast. Did he know about Gabriel? Of course not. Manco was merely curious and concerned.

"They're all a bane for us," she said sincerely. "Well, almost all of them . . . they are strange and difficult to understand. They worship their own strength as though it were a goddess. Most of them say one thing but do another."

"Do they frighten you?"

Anamaya didn't reply straightaway.

"No," she finally admitted. "No. But they're frightened of us. Their fear makes them cruel and devious."

"Then isn't it dishonorable to make peace with them?"

"I think that peace with them is necessary for the moment, and that peace is needed throughout Tahuantinsuyu. There has already been too much bloodshed, too many fallen. All the clans and all the families are suffering, but none know why. We must gather our strength before leaping toward our destiny."

Manco sighed and nodded.

"Chalkuchimac opposed my ascension, didn't he."

It wasn't a question but rather an observation. Once again, Anamaya was impressed by the future Inca's maturity.

"Yes."

"How did you manage to convince the others to elect me?"

"All the Noble Lords, led by Tisoc, opposed Chalkuchimac. I simply acted as a channel for your father, telling them what he told me when he came to visit me the night before the great massacre. That was enough."

Manco nodded approvingly.

"It seems that I am not the only one who appreciates your gifts, girl. But we must be careful. I don't trust Chalkuchimac. I know he controls all the soldiers in the mountains. He'll do anything to prevent me from placing the royal *borla* on my head. What's more, some *chaskis* have brought me the news that Guaypar is preparing an assault on the Strangers."

Anamaya went pale, but didn't say a word.

Manco wasn't looking at her. His gaze was lost in the night, meditating on his destiny.

"They want war. They want war with the Strangers, and they want war with us, the Cuzco clans. They prize war and they don't believe that peace is in the best interests of the Empire. Anamaya, you must warn the Strangers of this threat to them. If Chalkuchimac's men attack them, it's mostly to get to me. They hope to provoke the Strangers into retaliation against us all, and prevent me becoming Emperor!"

Anamaya said nothing. She knew that Manco was right. But she also knew, without being able to explain why, that neither Guaypar nor even Chalkuchimac could prevent Manco from wearing the royal *mascapaicha*.

Manco looked at her closely. His gaze was so intense that Anamaya felt it burning into her cheeks, her lips, and on her forehead, as though it was a real caress. Manco raised his hand, and Anamaya felt it brush against her neck.

"My happiness is great when I'm near you," he murmured. "It makes me happy to inhale your perfume and to know that you're close by. I have missed you terribly, sister Anamaya. No woman I know is as beautiful or as strong as you."

She smiled and bowed her head demurely.

"I have also missed you, brother Manco. But I knew that the day would come when I would have to prostrate myself before you and call you my Lord Emperor. Where is the gold Sacred Double?" she asked so as to avoid responding to the invitation contained in his caress.

"Carefully hidden in Cuzco, *Coya Camaquen!*" replied Manco, perhaps a little brusquely.

"I miss him too," murmured Anamaya, without reacting to his ill humor, "and I shall be very happy to be reunited with him. Emperor Huayna Capac hasn't transported me to the Other World once since the great massacre."

"You're a consummate woman these days, I find," said Manco melancholically, "and perhaps it is no longer possible for you to be the Sacred Double's wife? If you were with me, your influence would be great."

Anamaya plunged her eyes into Manco's and saw in them affection as much as desire. She took the young prince's hand and put it on her lips as she whispered:

"Brother Manco, you know as well as I do that that is not how things are meant to be. Tomorrow, when you leave at dawn, you will be Emperor. Tomorrow, only you will be able to prevent the Empire of the Four Cardinal Directions from crumbling into dust. No one will be permitted to touch you or even to look at you, not even me, because your father the Sun God forbids it. It's the law. You must observe the law so that the Empire is strong and united. Only then will you have the support of your father the Sun God. Meanwhile, you know that you can always depend on me, no matter what happens."

Manco scrutinized her face. A hard look flashed across his eyes, perhaps even anger. Yet he too brought Anamaya's fingers to his lips and kissed them.

"Tell me everything, little sister. Tell me everything that you have seen in the last few months. Tell me about Atahualpa's death and about the Strangers' *Machu Kapitu*. Tell me everything, until your mouth is dry and my ears tired, because I must understand."

THIRTEEN

Vilcaconga, November 8, 1533

The Indian looked at Gabriel with a cool grin on his face as curious as it was fearful. He repeated his answer more slowly so that the Stranger might understand him better:

"Yes, she was here three days ago. I saw her."

"The *Coya Camaquen?*"

"I am only a humble *hatunruna*. I don't know the names of the Inca princesses."

"Well then, how can you be sure that it was her?"

"Her eyes. You told me that she had eyes the color of the sky. I have never seen another princess with such eyes."

Gabriel nodded. He smiled faintly and almost said that he hadn't either.

It was dawn, and the abrupt slopes of the mountains surrounding the village of Rimac Tambo were veiled in a light fog that was already rising in transparent strands. The slopes and ridges created a beautiful illusion of protective petals. Gabriel gave them a disappointed glance. The river rumbled on. Perhaps Anamaya was not so far off; perhaps she was somewhere in the forest. The preceding days, as he had ridden along the Royal Road with Soto, he had constantly hoped to see her palanquin returning from her mission. But he had hoped in vain, and his disappointment had gradually turned into worry. Had she met with some strife? Or had she gone on all the way to Cuzco? But that hadn't been her original plan.

"She was with a Cuzco nobleman," continued the man, as though reading Gabriel's thoughts.

"Do you know what direction she took?"

But the man hadn't time to reply. A voice startled them:

"Good news or bad?"

Soto smiled amicably. Gabriel noticed that he was wearing his padded cotton vest over his doublet. What's more, his left hand, resting on the hilt of his sword, was already protected by the big leather glove adorned with metal plates that Soto wore in combat.

Gabriel pouted:

"Neither one nor the other for the moment."

He turned back to the Indian. He waved at the surrounding mountains and asked:

"Do you know if there are warriors in the forest?"

The man hesitated. Soto's battle outfit had perturbed him. Gabriel insisted:

"Soldiers from the northern clans, the soldiers who are pillaging your villages and destroying your bridges?"

The Indian gathered his resolve. He pointed, with his peasant's hands, toward the steep mountains in the south.

"Two nights ago, just before you came, there were a lot of fires burning up there. But there haven't been any since."

Soto didn't need Gabriel to translate.

"Of course they're there," he murmured. "They must be a few days ahead of us, destroying all the bridges leading to the capital."

The two men looked at the mountains. Less than a league from the village, the Royal Road climbed up a slope steeper than any that they had yet encountered. It was unpaved, and rose so abruptly that, in the mist rising over the forest, it seemed almost vertical.

"That slope is going to be hard going, especially for the horses," remarked Gabriel. "The animals haven't been properly rested after the tough journey we've just made. We would do better to wait for the Governor here."

Soto shook his head, scowling.

"I don't like this valley, and I don't like this river. No, I don't like it at all," he said.

With his bare hand, Soto pointed at the strange, narrow gorge in the east beyond the sturdy Inca buildings. Whereas everywhere else the fog was lifting to reveal a blue sky, there it remained dense, immobile, threatening. Its translucent curls gave it the appearance of a giant, savage beast.

"Not once did the fog lift from that gorge yesterday," added Soto, "as though it led to nowhere, or else straight to hell."

Gabriel grinned, amused.

"I never knew that you were so superstitious as to fear the forms of the natural world, Don Hernando!"

"A natural anomaly, I'm sure. But you're unwise to scoff, Gabriel. Consider the topography of the place. Those damned Indians can remain hidden in that fog-filled valley forever, and then attack us here when we're least expecting it."

"We'll be equally at their mercy if we climb that slope, and the horses won't be of any use to us. Quite the opposite, in fact."

"Then we must do it quickly. It will be worse if we wait for the weather to turn against us. Look at the sky: today is going to be beautiful, clear and blue."

"By the faith," muttered Gabriel, unconvinced by the serene sky, "you're the Captain."

"Whoa, my friend!" bantered Soto. "I've known you more adventurous before. Is it that you suspect me, as our beloved leader Don Francisco does, of being impatient to reach Cuzco?"

"Certainly I suspect it," replied Gabriel in the same bantering tone, "and I think that this time I suspect correctly, Soto. But it doesn't matter. It's that slope that's bothering me."

"And it's that valley that bothers me."

"Then one of us is wrong," said Gabriel, grinning.

"Not at all, my friend! Let us hope that we are both wrong."

As they headed back toward the buildings where the Spaniards were bustling about, the Indian called out to Gabriel. He pointed at a mountain overlooking the valley from the north and said:

"Noble Stranger, the princess with the sky in her eyes left for that mountain two days ago."

It didn't take the sixty cavalrymen long to saddle the horses, don their padded cotton surcoats, or even, for some, their mail armor. And the day was in fact too promising to worry about rain.

The three harquebuses were primed with very dry powder and loaded onto packhorses. Those cavalrymen who possessed shields attached them to their saddles. The catgut cords of the catch-trigger crossbows had been greased the night before and, if they were stiff, changed for more supple ones. Some were already cocked, the handle pulled back on the trammel, and the quarrels were within arms' reach in the saddle quivers.

What took the most time was designating a dozen men to guard the gold in Rimac Tambo until the Governor arrived. In the end, as no one volunteered, Soto assigned a dozen foot soldiers and the two youngest cavalrymen to the job. Gabriel and the more experienced horsemen would accompany him, including Rodrigo Orgoñez and one of their bravest, the proud Hernando de Toro.

And it was with closed, resentful expressions that those asked to stay behind heard the order to depart, just before midday. The sun was as heavy and as hot as a smithy's fire. It weighed on their morions as much as it reflected off them.

Yet they began their ascent with a great deal of enthusiastic anticipation. Soto even had to order them to slow down, lest they tire the animals too early.

They quickly realized what they were in for, however. The paved road soon gave way to a dirt one, equally steep, and where it wasn't muddy it gave way underfoot. The horses found the climb so onerous that they couldn't even carry themselves, let alone their riders. Sometimes they could advance only by vaulting forward like mountain goats, and they quickly spent their breath.

About a quarter of the way up the slope, the road narrowed and the forest thinned. There was less and less shade, and the sun beat down brutally. Both the men and the horses advanced openmouthed, gasping for breath, their tongues dry and furred. Soto gave the order that they were to advance in groups of four only.

Gabriel and his three companions decided to ride alongside the road rather than on it. Their boots slipped on the grass and got caught on the thick branches of the bramble bushes and wild cotton plants, but the horses were more comfortable here.

Men began to undo the padded armor vests under which they were suffocating. They loosened their belts and undid their shirts. They blinked in the blinding brightness of the sun. Their hands were clammy on their bridles. No one said a word, but there was a fair amount of noise: the shuffling of boots, the thumping of horses' hooves, and the labored breath of men filled the crystalline air. Their hearts beat heavily in their chests. Their veins pulsed out of their necks and temples. They bared their gums and teeth through their beards, which made their faces look like they were wearing the rictus of the dead. Everyone forgot about the Indians. Their only thoughts were for the vast mountains before them, mountains that they would have to overcome one by one.

By midafternoon, they had conquered only half the slope.

The heat was overwhelming. There wasn't a cloud in the sky. Under their helmets, sweat streamed down their mud-spattered faces, twisted with effort. They had ended up attaching their crossbows to their saddles a long time ago. The horses were exhausted. Sweat foamed up on their ribs and forelegs, and the leather straps of their saddles were soaked with sweat. A few animals rolled their eyes and wheezed continually, as though each breath was tearing their lungs.

They reached a point on the slope so vertiginous that it afforded them a bird's-eye view of the country around. Below them the narrow valley of Rimac Tambo appeared no bigger than a tablecloth. And if it wasn't for the unremitting rumble and the sudden appearance and disappearance of foaming whirlpools on its surface, one would have thought that the gray-blue river was utterly still, like a giant, sleeping snake.

Soto, who had been pushing on since the bottom of the slope, yelled a long-awaited order. The men raised their faces to see a large, flat, grass-covered ledge, a kind of giant balcony halfway up the mountain.

"Half an hour's rest," shouted the Captain.

"Make it an hour!" yelled back a man with a nose so big that it seemed as though it had been chiseled from a cucumber. "It's not only the horses who need a rest!"

"Then have a horse blow up your ass, Soytina, if it'll make you go quicker!" replied Soto quickly. "A half hour, no more. Water the horses and feed 'em the corn we've carted up here: it'll do better in their bellies than on their backs."

The men collapsed onto the ground and removed their morions, which had become unbearable. They lay around for a few moments in a stupor before splashing themselves with water from their gourds and wetting the horses' quivering nostrils.

Gabriel remained standing in order to better gather his breath. His bay, although its whole barrel shook spasmodically, was holding up well. Gabriel whispered reassuringly as he made it drink slowly. The animal, its ears pricked, was too conscious of its own pain to pay him much attention, but the refreshing water and Gabriel's caresses had their effect.

Once his horse had settled a little, Gabriel fumbled around mechanically for the cloth pouch that Anamaya had given him. He drew some coca leaves from it. The tasteless, thick juice was gathering in his mouth when Soto and Hernando de Toro joined him. Seeing him chewing on his ball of coca leaves, Soto frowned for a moment, but then smiled wearily as he remarked:

"Another hour and I'll be proven right. The hardest is behind us."

Gabriel squinted up at the peak. Apart from the path, the slope was nothing but rocky scree thinly covered in vegetation.

"I'd say another league or so," he said, "a league of slope so steep it makes me think that we're climbing to heaven on Jacob's ladder."

"That's a lovely image," sighed Soto.

"Horses don't climb ladders," remarked Hernando de Toro.

"My point exactly," said Gabriel, stroking his horse's withers.

Soto pointed at the slope.

"What bothers me," he said, "is that we're now obliged to stay on the path. If we lead the horses off it, they'll break their legs on those rocks."

"No doubt," agreed Hernando de Toro, "but that serves us as well. No man can run across such terrain without breaking his neck."

Gabriel said nothing. He sensed that the two men were just trying to reassure themselves. All three of them stared at the slope ahead for a while, perhaps hoping that it would disappear.

"They're nowhere to be seen," murmured Soto, "not a glimpse, not even one of their damned llamas."

Hernando de Toro wiped his face with his glove.

"It'll be up there that we'll have to be on our toes."

"I'll lead," said Soto, "and we'll go in groups of four, at intervals. You two bring up the rear."

*   *   *

Soto ordered them back on the road. They advanced in groups of four on foot, yanking their horses by the bridle. Their boots became heavier with each step. No one wore his padded vest anymore.

The sun was lower now, and their shadows were longer. They watched their own shadows on the path ahead of them, feeble, flickering silhouettes. Their strength, recovered during the rest, quickly evaporated. In only a few minutes, they were once again swimming in sweat and short of breath.

And then it happened.

They heard a roar so loud that they thought the sky was being torn in two.

They all looked up at the summit simultaneously. And they all froze in terror.

"Fucking hell!" murmured Hernando de Toro.

The entire summit was covered with Indian warriors standing shoulder to shoulder. It was impossible to tell how many of them there were, but Gabriel guessed at least two thousand. He felt his throat constrict.

Over two thousand yelling, howling warriors, banging on their shields to the same cacophonous rhythm as the war drums. Over two thousand warriors stamping their feet, waving their axes and clubs, and whirling their slingshots around. Over two thousand men forming a fringe of fierce colors against the mountain's dull green peak, like a flood of liquid poison about to carry the Spaniards away.

"Fucking hell," repeated Hernando de Toro.

"Into formation!" ordered Soto, sword in hand.

"Cavalrymen, mount!" shouted another voice.

The Indians up on the ridge were still shouting, but they had broken their line. The first waves of warriors came hurtling down the slope. Despite what Hernando de Toro believed, these men knew how to run through the onerous scree.

"Watch out for stones! Watch out for their damned stones!" bawled a voice.

Gabriel didn't realize that it was his own. Panic had taken hold all around him. The men were trying to simultaneously button up their padded vests, take advantage of a narrow rocky ledge to climb into their saddles, draw their swords, detach their morions from their shields, strap their shields to their arms, draw the cords back on their crossbows, and set quarrels in the grooves. But it was all a mess.

"The hackbuts, the harquebuses!" bawled another voice. "By the Virgin, get the hackbuts set up!"

But it was not to be. The harquebuses were unreachable, packed too deeply on a pack animal behind Soto, who was himself madly whipping his own gelding. The Indians' roar never let up, and in fact became more high-pitched and frenetic. The Spaniards stumbled, fell over, gasped for air, showed the whites of their eyes.

"Mount your horses, by the blood of Christ, mount your goddamn horses!" screamed a voice that Gabriel didn't recognize through the din.

Yet those who were already in the saddle couldn't make their horses climb the slope. The Indians spread out through the scree, as agile and as ferociously beautiful as pumas. They were so many, so close, and so colorful that they seemed like an enormous fabric unfurled from the mountaintop.

"Watch out for the stones! The stones!"

Like everyone else, Gabriel placed his shield over his horse's neck. Hundreds of stones came whistling down onto them, hammering into their shields, thudding into their padded vests and on the grass, and smashing into their exposed legs, faces, and necks. It was horrific. Cries and moans erupted from the length of the entire column. The horses shied, fled into the scree, or tried to bolt down the mountainside, utterly terrified.

"Hold the horses!" yelled Gabriel and Hernando de Toro simultaneously.

Gabriel caught a glimpse out of the corner of his eye of Soto and Ortiz at the head of the column, already engaged with the Indians, striking at them violently with their swords, which threw up showers of sparks each time the steel blades came into contact with the Indians' bronze axes.

A long period of chaos followed. The Indian warriors swarmed at them by the hundreds from all around, continually howling their demented war cries, slinging stones, throwing spears, firing arrows, aiming for the horses as much as for the men. But they were still reluctant to engage in direct, hand-to-hand combat. They danced like butterflies around the panicked horses and the Spaniards, who found themselves hindered by their armor. The Indians made terrifying faces, lunged forward, and sliced through the Strangers' leather shields with their axes, or else smashed off their armor with their clubs, before quickly retreating to avoid the whistling swords. And then they would start their horrific howling again.

"To the peak! Push for the peak!" growled Gabriel as he pushed Hernando de Toro on.

But half the men hadn't even saddled up. They impeded one another as they stumbled up the narrow path, incapable of mounting an adequate defense.

Suddenly, an appalling neigh, followed by another, rose above the din of battle. Marquina's horse had fallen into a trap, a ditch lined with sharpened spikes and covered with branches. Spikes pierced through its neck and belly, and its spine tore audibly apart, leaving crimson flowers blooming in its back. Its eyes bulging in terror, the animal struggled desperately, exacerbating its agony, and pissed blood like a fountain. Marquina, unhurt, managed to clamber out of the pit with a helping hand from Soytina. They tried to climb back onto the road, but they weren't quick enough: half a dozen Indians pounced on them. An axe cleaved deeply into the foot soldier's back while a club smashed into his face, exploding his nose and instantly transforming his face into a gruel of blood, smashed cartilage, and hacked flesh.

As for Marquina, he had fallen to the ground with three Indians upon him. All three clubbed his head in a coordinated effort, splitting his skull in two. The Spaniards, stupefied, watched as the Indians dragged the cavalryman's corpse into the scree, roaring with joy as his brain streaked across the stones.

The deafening noise echoed through the air like a flight of blackbirds. "Stop!" ordered Anamaya to the porters carrying her palanquin.

Since leaving Manco the night before, they had taken only the less frequented mountain paths on their return trip to Cuzco in order to avoid Guaypar's and Quizquiz's men.

The cacophony continued, shockingly violent. Its force made the very leaves of the trees shiver.

The officer of the guard turned to Anamaya:

"Those are battle cries."

Everyone listened intently. Still the violent noise persisted.

Anamaya found that she was holding her breath. She felt a knot harder than stone develop in her gut.

"There are a lot of them," remarked the officer.

She didn't need to close her eyes to imagine the scene.

She knew that she shouldn't worry for the Strangers' safety, yet she was deeply, deeply concerned for them.

"They're at Rimac Tambo," she murmured.

"Yes," agreed the officer. "The Strangers must be trying to cross the Vilcaconga peak. It's a good place for a trap. Quizquiz relishes it up there."

The din seemed to subside a little, but then grew even louder and more high-pitched, even more ferocious. Anamaya imagined in her mind's eye the innumerable warriors hurtling down the scree, down a slope so steep that even the palanquin's surefooted porters sometimes used ropes to conquer it.

She tried not to think about him. But the moment she had heard the battle cries she had remembered Manco's words, and the chill that she had felt when he had spoken them. Gabriel was in peril.

She felt it: her whole body felt it. She knew that he was over there in the thick of the battle.

She wanted to be reasonable with herself about it. But her love for him actually caused her physical pain in her back, as though a great weight was upon her.

The cries continued echoing through the cold forest air of the pass.

Anamaya was trembling. She began murmuring a prayer to herself without realizing it: *"O Inti, O Force of the Other World, O Sun, Father of all our Ancestors, O Quilla, our Mother, do not block the Puma's bound. O Emperor who elected me, do not abandon me on the road to which you led me. O you who divides day from night, do not carry him away to the Underworld and leave me here alone."*

With a great effort, she regained her composure, and she saw that all the soldiers and porters around her were watching her, utterly amazed. But they all looked away as her gaze turned upon them.

Suddenly thunder roared above the war cries echoing through the air. Anamaya recognized the sound of the Strangers' fire-spitting sticks.

Another explosion startled the porters. Yet its echo had hardly faded before the warriors resumed their furious howling, now with even greater rage and power.

In a flat voice, she gave the order:

"Let us turn around. I want to return to Rimac Tambo as fast as possible."

How long had they been fighting? Gabriel had no idea. Their blood-covered bodies cast long shadows.

The chaos of the battle and the Indians' cries were unremitting. The stones, blows, and arrows never let up. The horses' flanks shone with blood. They had climbed only half a league when they had fired their crossbows at point-blank range, sometimes killing two Indians with the one shot. Yet the Inca warriors, instead of being discouraged, fought with even greater fury. They were familiar with these contraptions now: they knew that they took time to reload, and in the pauses they fell upon the cavalrymen with terrifying cries.

Gabriel maneuvered his bay around the ditch-trap and then whipped its croup hard, giving the horse its head. The animal bounded forward furiously through the fray, plowing itself a passage for the peak. A group of Indians grabbed hold of the tail of the horse under the cavalryman right beside Gabriel in an attempt to stop the animal and bring down its rider. With a mad cry, Gabriel lunged forward and brought his sword whistling down, slicing clean through an Indian arm and the horse's tail. The Indian stumbled backward, howling in pain. Gabriel made out the fear in his eyes. He crossed his dagger and his sword and parried a blow from an axe, then kicked his assailant hard in the gut, sending him tumbling down the slope.

Hernando de Toro yelled from above:

"Soto is at the peak! He's made it!"

He was interrupted by a berserk charge by a group of Indians.

He and Gabriel defended a passage by the pike-lined ditch by which the rest of the column passed. The two men seemed to be everywhere at once, increasingly short of breath, blocking the strikes from the Indians' axes and clubs without ever finding the opportunity to counterattack.

Then Hernando de Toro let out an agonized cry. Gabriel saw him stagger, a pike lodged in his thigh. He rushed toward his companion, windmilling his long sword through the air, giving Toro enough time to tear the spear out of his flesh.

"Go on!" shouted Gabriel. "Go up to the peak, I'll guard your back!" His voice was lost in the report of the two harquebuses, fired simultaneously.

But the Indians felled by the shots were ten paces away from Soto at the peak. Hundreds more stood between Gabriel and him, so many in fact that they hindered one another.

The smell of powder floating through the air seemed to unleash their wrath.

The rear of the column was advancing at a snail's pace. The horses were exhausted. Hernando de Toro was dragging himself along the ground, pulling himself along by grabbing rocks and bushes, while Gabriel, guarding the right flank, kept the Indians at bay, slicing through their arms and chests. The veins in his temples throbbed, his pulsating blood disturbing his vision. His sword felt increasingly heavy, and he was using it less effectively, its blade now slicing through air more often than flesh. He felt overcome by an indescribable weariness, as though he too was crawling on his hands and knees. He felt suffocated by the stench of blood and fear. He hardly registered it when an Indian bounded forward and landed on Hernando de Toro.

The fight was over quickly. Toro, in a last, desperate effort to live, thrust his dagger as the Indian brought his star-shaped club crashing down on Toro's head, one of its spikes piercing through his cheek and shattering his jaw. Hernando de Toro, wide-eyed, watched helplessly as the Indian brought his club up one more time to deliver him the death-blow.

Gabriel spun around and instinctively bounded forward. Blood streamed off his sword as it flew through the air. Its steel blade sliced through the Indian's neck. But Gabriel had struck at him so hard that the force of impact jolted the sword out of his hands.

And Gabriel felt the most odd, unlikely experience: his fear was lifted from him. Time seemed to slow down. Exhaustion and blood-soaked weariness overcame him.

He slowly picked himself up, his dagger hanging from his dangling arm. From his place of stillness in the center of all the chaos, he looked at the faces of the warriors of the Empire of the Four Cardinal Directions. They were not the resigned faces of those who had allowed themselves to be massacred at Cajamarca or at Hatun Sausa. They were the faces of warriors who had recovered their lost pride.

He heard Soto calling out to him, his voice so faint that he could have been shouting from a great distance. But a sling stone flew at him even quicker than the sound of his name.

He heard the sound of its impact against his morion, and then, blackness.

Night was closing in by the time Anamaya, from her palanquin, made out the terraces of Rimac Tambo in the distance.

Shouting and drumming could still be heard from the heights of Vilcaconga. A number of wounded warriors had made it back to the river. Some were in such shockingly bad states, their arms missing, their chests or backs cut to pieces, that they collapsed on its bank and died the moment they touched its icy water.

Anamaya had ordered the officer of the guard to send two men ahead for news. Now the men had returned and were kneeling before her palanquin. Despite the growing darkness, Anamaya could tell from the looks on their faces that the news was terrible.

"Speak!" she ordered dryly.

"Two thousand soldiers from General Quizquiz's army, under the command of Captain Guaypar, lay in wait for the Strangers at the mountain peak. They let the Strangers climb most of its height, so that they would exhaust their own strength and that of their beasts, and wouldn't be able to move as quickly as they usually do."

The man fell silent, his eyes lowered, his neck bent subserviently. Anamaya could tell that he had yet to tell her the most important news.

"Continue," she commanded.

"Five Strangers were killed by the soldiers, *Coya Camaquen*, and many were wounded. Two of their big llamas were also killed."

She had to use all her strength to conceal her fear.

She said in a measured voice:

"And now?"

"The Strangers have managed to reach the peak. They have taken

refuge there and are resting their horses. Guaypar's men have suspended
their attack. But tomorrow at dawn, the commanders shall give the order
to bring down a rain of flaming arrows on them, to frighten the horses."

The drums and night war songs echoed down from the mountainside. Anamaya thought about Guaypar for a moment, of his murderous
rage, his insanity, and his consummate knowledge of warfare and of the
Strangers. He was surely up there, and no doubt he had ordered all the
noise in order prevent the Strangers from sleeping, from gaining a
moment's rest through the night. At first light, massacring Gabriel and
his companions would be child's play.

She caught the eye of the officer of the guard. She could see that he
was troubled, and she easily guessed why: the Empire's warriors were
killing the Strangers for the first time, and were on the point of winning
a real battle against them. He wanted to rejoice, but didn't dare do so in
front of her.

She stepped down from her palanquin and gestured to the young
officer to accompany her away from all the people. Down below,
between the river and Rimac Tambo, she saw fires burning, and by their
light she made out peasants bringing food to the injured warriors as they
arrived in small groups. Many seemed to have broken limbs, and they
collapsed into the scree.

"Officer," said Anamaya, "you know that I have conferred with
Emperor Manco."

At the mere mention of his name, the man bowed.

"I know it, *Coya Camaquen.*"

"He wishes for peace throughout the Empire, and peace with the
Strangers. Those attacking them up there are violating his wish."

The officer said nothing.

"The Emperor wishes that we help the Strangers reach Cuzco, where
he wishes to receive them and demonstrate to them the extent of his
power," she said in a clear voice, "and we must do this even if we have to
fight our own people who are disobeying him! There is but *one* Emperor,
and we must all obey his will. Do you understand me, Officer?"

The officer said nothing for a moment before slowly lifting his head.

"Yes, *Coya Camaquen.* I will do as you command."

"I thank you for it, and I shall not forget your loyalty."

But she could see the sadness in the officer's eyes as he said quietly:

"I have learned that there is a troop of Strangers on horseback not far from here, on the Royal Road to the other side of Apurimac."

Anamaya had to stop herself from crying out joyfully.

"Then you are to send men to meet them," she ordered. "Let them cross the river as soon as possible. The Strangers must be here before dawn."

As he regained consciousness, Gabriel knew that it was night. He also knew that the hellish pain in his head was not going to subside anytime soon. He felt a fine rain falling lightly on his face.

"Dreadful blow, Gabriel, an absolutely dreadful blow," muttered Soto as he stood up, his fingers sticky with blood.

Gabriel sensed that there were a number of men around him despite being unable to see them. Soto's face was obscured by shifting shadows.

"Don't try to move, my friend," said Soto, his voice hoarse from shouting. "We're looking after you, and we're all going to make it out of here."

But Gabriel doubted it. He wanted to smile and say something to Soto, to ask him how many men they had lost, if Soto could mount a reasonable defense with the remainder, if the wounded could be saved. Wounded other than himself, that is, because he was sure that he was going to perish. And he accepted this fate with unusual calm, completely composed. In fact, the idea of dying calmed him greatly.

But he was unable to utter a word coherently, only a long groan that he couldn't hear himself. What was also strange was that his head no longer hurt, whereas his left arm ached unbearably.

He couldn't remember the exact sequence of events after Hernando de Toro was killed. He remembered being dragged to the top of the slope, surrounded by charging Indians. That's when his arm had become stuck between two rocks, and was almost broken.

But he was sure that while his arm was aching, death was eating away at his head. He had lost a lot of blood, and his face was covered in a sticky crust. His head had been bandaged with the blanket of a dead horse. But no part of him was functioning normally, not his hearing, not his vision, not his voice.

He could see that it was night, but he didn't know whether it would be his final one.

He wondered whether the battle was over.

He wondered whether the Indians were still howling their battle cries.

He thought he made out some cries, and the sound of a horn. He wondered whether he was entering the realm of the dead, and whether these trumpets and cries were accompanying him into it. He mused that he was not unlike a fragile boat being carried away on an unstoppable tide. The sound of the trumpets became increasingly terrifying, increasingly unbearable. He had but one desire left: to slip even deeper into the darkness, to be delivered from the agony by death.

He surrendered to the comfortable numbness gaining on him.

FOURTEEN

They didn't pause once, not even to gather their breaths. Indians and Spaniards marched without respite to Rimac Tambo, stopping neither for the night nor for the weather turning against them, the sticky humidity causing their clothes to cling damply to their skin.

Anamaya remembered, during her climb, the dreadful ambush in which the Elders, Huayna Capac's loyal servants, had lost their lives, victims of Huascar's madness. And as she came across the first evidence of the battle—the broken weapons, the moaning wounded, the dismembered corpses—it seemed to her that that atrocity was repeating itself, or that this latest horror was a reply to the first.

She and her escort, along with the Spaniards accompanying them, came across the pike-lined ditch in which the bodies of a horse and two white men lay, their faces battered by the stones fired from slingshots. The Strangers cried out in anger, and for a moment Anamaya was frightened that they would turn their rage against her. But Almagro was already haranguing his men, ordering them to push on.

"We can do nothing for these poor souls! We must get up to the peak where Soto is waiting for us, at the mercy of those damned Indians about to massacre them all!"

From the nearby mountain they could hear Guaypar's men shouting triumphantly, the muffled sound of their war chants, the roll of their drums, and the wail of their horns. Anamaya knew that the Incas, as a rule, never fought at night. Nevertheless, with a leader like Guaypar, anything was possible. What if, emboldened by their initial success, they resolved to massacre the Strangers in the night?

She could hear the labored gasps of the Spanish soldiers behind her struggling up the scree-covered slope, leading their horses by the reins.

She shut her eyes every now and then and thought of Gabriel, imagining that she was being drawn up the mountain to him by her violent desire to be with him, to touch him, and to reassure herself that yes, he was still alive.

When they reached the peak, Guaypar's warriors stopped their racket. Perhaps they were on the move, having been warned of the arrival of Spanish reinforcements. The horses were so exhausted that they didn't even lift their heads to watch the newcomers arrive. But Soto's men ran to meet them, crying out joyfully. Anamaya looked on as the Spaniards embraced one another, and she saw what seemed to her a gathering of shadows, standing tight one against the other and utterly motionless at the very edge of the rock mantle. They were as black as the night surrounding them, and seemed to belong neither to this world nor to the other.

What remained of Captain Soto's column had made no fires in order to avoid creating easy targets in the night. A horse lay to one side, and two exhausted men, lying on the muddy ground, tried wearily to get up. A faint moan reached her from farther away. Almagro rushed up to the Captain.

"Soto!"

Soto barely moved. He was too tired to speak, instead saluting his compatriot with a wave. The upper part of his chain mail, torn to pieces, and his breeches, stiff with congealed blood, bore witness to the fury of the battle. But the icy, troubled mask of rage on his face told far more.

"How many have we lost?" asked Almagro.

"Five, as far as I know," sighed Soto. "Marquina, Soytina, Hernando de Toro, Ruiz, and Rodas. And a sixth probably won't make it through the night, if he hasn't died already."

"Who?"

"Gabriel."

"Montelucar y Flores?" asked Almagro with the thinnest of smiles. "Francisco's protégé?"

Soto nodded. Anamaya startled him when she grabbed him by the arm and said:

"Where is he?"

"What are you doing here?" growled Soto, pulling his arm away.

"Her escort brought us the news of the attack," said Almagro.

"Please," insisted Anamaya, "where is he?"

Soto pointed his chin at the group of shadows that she had noticed earlier.

"Over there, with the other wounded."

She ran. The *Coya Camaquen,* to the utter astonishment of her escort, ran all the way to the wounded, those moaning bodies that seemed about to disappear into the night.

None of the Spaniards tending to the wounded protested when she pushed her way through them and kneeled at Gabriel's side. A blanket lay over him, covering him up to his neck. Another, rolled up, lay under his head, which was wrapped in a ragged blanket. He was breathing, albeit very slightly, through barely opened lips, and his eyelids shivered feverishly. Anamaya brushed her fingers against his cheek, and they became coated with his cold sweat.

She was breathing heavily, searching for a calm center within herself, refusing to surrender to her fear. Yet when she felt a hand settle gently on her shoulder, she cried out in terror.

"Let me do this."

She recognized Bartholomew's quiet voice, and looked into his gray eyes.

"I can help him," he said.

"What are you going to do?" she asked in a low voice.

"My duty: help him pass into the other world in a Christian manner."

Anamaya stared at him for a moment, and then shook her head violently. She shoved him away and said:

"No! If that's your duty, then take it elsewhere and leave me with him!"

There was no bitterness in her words, only a determination that kept Bartholomew from replying. He watched her lower her head down to Gabriel's and whisper into his ear. He heard her murmur to him in a strange mix of Quechua and Castilian. Then she slipped her hands under the blanket, onto the wounded man's chest. She began slowly massaging the spot on his thorax above his heart. Without lifting her head, she commanded in Spanish:

"Light a fire to each side of him and bring more blankets."

She seemed unconcerned whether she had been obeyed or even heard. She repeated her order in Quechua to the soldiers of her escort, who were standing to one side and watching her with looks on their faces as incredulous as the Spaniards'.

"Do as she says!" barked Bartholomew.

A few moments later, as the first flames rose from the piles of dry twigs, Soto ran up, shouting:

"Have you lost your minds? I said no fires!"

Anamaya had bared Gabriel's torso and was rubbing fine mud into it. She answered Soto without stopping her ministrations.

"The battle is over, Lord Soto. You will not be attacked, not tonight nor tomorrow. Have you not noticed that the war drums have stopped?"

And, without waiting for a reply, she gave further orders in Quechua before lying on Gabriel as though about to make love to him. Indians ran off and came back with *mantas*, which they piled up on the pair.

Soto's rage was broken by his bewilderment. Bartholomew raised his joined fingers and said:

"She is right, Captain de Soto. Let her be, I beg you."

Soon two great braziers blazed at their side, flooding the rock ledge with light and revealing the vacant, weary faces of the wounded.

Anamaya never stopped caressing Gabriel's inert body under the blankets. She blew on his naked flesh as though trying to stoke the flames of life back into him. She took her pouch of coca leaves from her belt, chewed some quickly, and let the juice run from her lips into her lover's mouth. She continually massaged his chest, forcing his heart to keep beating. Eventually, long after the noise of the camp had subsided, she heard a faint groan rise from Gabriel's throat. Soon after, his belly shook with spasms.

She made him take more coca juice. Gabriel's breath became heavier, deeper, and more hoarse. His heart beat against his ribs. Anamaya put first her lips and then her reddened cheeks to his chest. She was overcome by a timid, fearful joy, as though life was being reborn in her as much as in him.

FIFTEEN

Vilcaconga, November 10, 1533

Brother Bartholomew paused on the threshold of the tent. He saw them through its raised flaps.

Gabriel lay awake on a pile of blankets at the back of the tent, his face washed and shaved, his head wrapped in a sort of blue turban. Wide-eyed, he was kissing his pretty friend's hands, the young Indian girl who was some sort of influential princess among the Incas. And also some sort of magician.

For a fraction of a second, Bartholomew hesitated, unsure whether to continue or to turn back. He realized that the two young lovers hadn't noticed his presence, and so he did neither, allowing himself to indulge in the petty sin of curiosity.

Brother Bartholomew smiled. Certainly the young Indian girl was a magician! What he had seen her accomplish two nights previous would have earned her the Inquisition's stake back in Spain.

The two lovers were now kissing one another tenderly. She gently put Gabriel's injured arm to one side, and stroked his cheek, giggling. For a fraction of a second, she looked just like every young girl in love in the universe.

But in the following moment she straightened and transformed once more into a reserved princess who kept her movements carefully measured, and who wore a severe expression that did her beauty a disservice. She had seen him.

Gabriel followed his lover's gaze and saw him too. Brother Bartholomew stepped forward and greeted them without a hint of embarrassment.

"Well now, it seems to me that we have a real Lazarus here, brought back to life!" he said humorously.

But his laughter was lost. His attempt at lightness notwithstanding, the princess's gaze never failed to make an impression on him. He greeted her with a brief nod.

"Don't be afraid of me," he told her.

She stared at him with a blank expression. In fact, he was the one who was a little uncomfortable, as though she had the ability to see right into the depths of his soul, to see even the darker complexities of his thoughts that he himself would have preferred to forget. He was irrationally relieved when he thought he saw the briefest good-humored flash in her sumptuous blue gaze, but it had crossed her eyes so furtively that he couldn't be sure of it.

The princess said something quickly to Gabriel in Quechua. Then she gracefully fastened the clasp of her silk *manta* and left the tent with a poise that would have impressed the Queen of Spain herself.

Bartholomew followed her with his eyes. He heard Gabriel say to him from behind:

"Please don't misunderstand her, Brother Bartholomew. Anamaya appreciates you. But she mistrusts all Spaniards."

"Well, you shouldn't complain about that."

"Why not?"

"You should have seen how she pushed me away from you. I, like everyone else, had given you up for dead, whereas she still saw the life in you."

The monk spoke with a lightness of spirit that charmed Gabriel, whose own spirit was still fuddled from the blows he had received in battle. He smiled wearily as the monk continued:

"One thing is for sure, though: she saved your life. I saw her do so with my own eyes."

Bartholomew considered Gabriel for a moment, who had shut his eyes. Without opening them, Gabriel smiled as he said:

"Pray tell me all about it, Brother Bartholomew. She wouldn't tell me anything. And I remember nothing, except for the cold." He shivered as he remembered it. "And seeing the blue of her eyes when I regained consciousness."

"Everyone but God had given you up for dead, Captain Soto being the first," said Brother Bartholomew. "And in fact you were responding to nothing. We could no longer hear your breath. Soto asked me to give you the last rites. I was about to do so when she reached you."

Gabriel couldn't help but grin as he imagined the scene.

"And do you know what she did?" continued Brother Bartholomew. "She lit a fire to either side of you and lay against you until morning, to warm you. I must say that the two of you were quite a sight. Everyone was impressed."

Gabriel let his imagination run. His throat constricted from the strength of the emotion he was feeling. He opened his eyes and tried to hide his emotion with irony, asking:

"And you allowed this scandalous behavior?"

Brother Bartholomew nodded. He ran his joined fingers pensively across his chin.

"Yes. I admit that it was a little . . . unorthodox, shall we say. But amid all the chaos that night, amid all the suffering, her actions seemed almost . . . normal."

He paused, then added:

"Although having said that, my friend, it would be best if those who weren't there never hear about what happened. Do you understand me?"

Gabriel didn't react. He felt the warmth growing in his body, and reflected that he must have been on the threshold of death for Anamaya to abandon herself so completely to him. He thought to himself, *To think that I wasn't conscious enough to make the most of the opportunity.* He smiled wickedly at the thought.

Brother Bartholomew shook his head and added:

"The next day, as soon as you were lodged in this tent, the princess smeared a clay that she had brought from the riverbank over your wounds. After that, she had you drink vast quantities of some concoction of her own devising."

"That's all?" asked Gabriel, surprised.

"That's all. And it was plenty."

"How do you mean?"

"Because you are alive."

Brother Bartholomew said this in a tone that put Gabriel ill at ease.

"Certainly," continued Bartholomew, "you were a little delirious. But in a happy way. You took yourself, it seemed to me, for some kind of wildcat. I had trouble understanding you because you spoke the language of your pretty friend rather than Castilian. I'm learning it, as you know, but I have yet to progress beyond the most elementary level."

"It must have been a pain-relieving decoction," said Gabriel. "The Indians are well versed in the analeptic qualities of plants, and Anamaya . . . I mean, the princess, knows their secrets well. It's not unusual in these parts."

"No doubt. But the strangest thing, do you see, was that your head wound immediately stopped bleeding and weeping. You can see for yourself that it is already cicatrizing, as is the gash on your arm."

The gentleness of Brother Bartholomew's tone made Gabriel shudder a little. It reminded him of conversations he had had a long time ago now, back in Spain. It reminded him of that quality peculiar to men of the cloth, that insidious smile they wore when they were laying a web of words in which to ensnare the unwary.

"What are you trying to say?" he asked.

"The beautiful princess has led me to think a lot about our situation," said Bartholomew, with acute earnestness. "Is it true what they say, that she has certain powers, and that she has influence over the Inca Emperor himself?"

Gabriel straightened, his face hard. His friendliness toward the monk had completely evaporated, and his old distrust had returned.

"If you're thinking, even for an instant, of orchestrating some political intrigue, then you are completely in the wrong of it, Brother Bartholomew. Anamaya is not some sort of demon disguised as a woman."

"Did I say that?"

"I would prefer it if you didn't even think it."

"You are mistaken, my friend."

Brother Bartholomew seemed genuinely surprised. He laughed with real candor, and placed his strangely deformed hand on Gabriel's shoulder.

"What do you think, Gabriel? That I wish your friend harm? Or else do you resent me for having helped you see clearly the truth in your heart when you would have otherwise succumbed to confusion and doubt?"

Gabriel dismissed the monk's allusion with a disdainful grimace.

"I've never seen a man of the cloth put up with what he doesn't understand for very long."

"No!" protested Bartholomew, sitting up straight. "No, you have not understood me at all, Gabriel. I did not come to this land to add to the suffering, but to fight against it, if such a thing is possible. You must believe me!"

"We shall see," replied Gabriel dryly, returning to his pile of blankets.

Brother Bartholomew looked at him for a few moments.

"As Christ is my witness, my friend, let me tell you that what interests me most is precisely that which you mention: experiencing that which seems unknowable."

Gabriel watched him leave the tent.

He closed his eyes, exhausted. Despite the hostility still within him, he remembered that if it were not for that strange monk and his disconcerting benevolence, he might never have had the courage to say goodbye to Anamaya, and would never have heard her say "I love you" to him, words that remained in him still, and which perhaps saved his life.

But it was too late to call him back.

Gabriel fell asleep with a smile on his lips.

SIXTEEN

Rimac Tambo, November 13, 1533

"Go in peace," said Valverde.

The Spaniards, all of them armed, were standing as a group in the vast square of the *tambo*. They had listened to the Mass with exceptional reverence, and there had been none of the usual muttering or whispered conversations, no noise at all, in fact, except for the occasional neigh of a horse and the continual murmur of the nearby brook in the background.

Despite the priest's signal that the Mass was over, none of them moved.

In the middle of the square stood a hastily built rostrum on which lay the shroud-covered corpses of those Spaniards who had died in battle. All those gathered there that day could not take their eyes off it.

Gabriel was cumbered by his wounded arm, stiff and in a sling. He hadn't donned his chain mail as the others had, but rather wore only his usual leather-covered cotton-padded breastplate, now stained with his own blood.

Even the most loyal of their Indian allies averted his eyes whenever he crossed a Spaniard. As for the noblemen accompanying Chalkuchimac, it was as if they had disappeared in the mountains: the general himself hadn't left his palanquin since daybreak.

Don Francisco Pizarro walked through the ranks to stand before the bodies on the rostrum in the center, along with Valverde. He wore his full suit of armor, from which only his small head emerged, like some blackbird. He looked at each of those gathered there individually, and each man met his commander's gaze. And as their eyes met, they experienced that fervor once again, just as they had the night before the battle at Cajamarca, when the distinctions between noble cavalrymen and lowly foot soldiers and between rich and poor had disappeared.

"You are grieving," said Pizarro in a firm voice, "and you are angry." He turned around and pointed at the corpses wrapped in sheets.

"They were our friends, and they were brave soldiers and I want you to remember their names: Juan Alonso de Rodas, Gaspar de Marquina, Francisco Martín Soytina, Miguel Ruiz, Hernando de Toro." He enunciated each name as though he was invoking the saints. "They came from the Basque country, from Seville, from my own dear Extramadura. Some were light-skinned, others dark, some could read and write while others knew only how to fight, some fought on horseback, others on foot. They died victims of treachery, but they died nobly, as men."

Gabriel glanced at Hernando de Soto's impassive face. Pizarro continued:

"I know that some of you are asking why. I will tell you."

With a broad motion that made his armor clang, Pizarro pointed at the mountain above Vilcaconga. His hand remained pointing at the peak and the horizon beyond it.

"I remember," he said, almost laughing, "I remember those who doubted that we would find this kingdom of gold. But I always knew we would, my children, I always knew we would. Well then, here we are at the gates of the capital of this kingdom of gold. Do you hear me?"

His eyes shone as though they were black nuggets of gold themselves, and the eyes of his men began to blaze with the same luster. Pizarro lowered his voice a little as he turned his eyes back to the dead bodies.

"But do you imagine that for mere gold—even for all that the capital of the kingdom of gold has to offer—do you imagine that I can forget who killed these men, these brave soldiers, so far from their homes in Spain?"

"No! No!"

As the cries rose from the crowd, Gabriel sensed their growing spirit of vengeance.

"Then keep the memory of your fallen comrades close to your hearts, my dear, dear children," insisted the Governor ardently. "Keep it in the very pockets of your hearts, and know that one day you shall bring it to light again by the blades of your swords!"

*   *   *

As he climbed up Vilcaconga Mountain, Gabriel had the unreasonable sensation that ghosts lurked behind the bushes and rocks and in the riverbed. His watchful eyes kept deceiving him with the image of thousands of warriors charging at him, and his ears with the phantom sounds of their battle cries and the neighing of terrified horses. It was a cool day and he was walking slowly, yet he was saturated with sweat.

He had insisted on walking ahead, but his step was heavy on the slippery flagstones, and the impact of each step sent shooting pains through his injured arm.

"Does Your Grace grow tired?"

Without turning around, Gabriel shot back:

"His Grace almost had his head cut from his body trying to save your African butt!"

Sebastian, dressed in his usual spectacularly colorful outfit, guffawed and came up alongside his friend.

"My master marched us at double pace in order to reach you in time . . ."

He paused, and then continued:

". . . but they say that Soto is so eager to get to Cuzco that he . . ."

"By God! What is that?"

Gabriel pointed at the rapier dangling from Sebastian's side.

"Why, have you never seen a sword before, *caballero?*"

"Where did you get it?"

"It was presented to me with all due pomp and ceremony by Don Diego de Almagro himself, as a reward for my past services and on the condition that I swear my allegiance to my God, my King, and to Don Diego de Almagro himself," recited Sebastian like a schoolboy.

Gabriel whistled, impressed.

"In which order?"

"In the order of whosoever asks for my services first."

"And may one inquire as to how you intend to use it?"

"Ah! As for that, well . . ."

Sebastian shrugged. The air around them had grown darker, despite the cloudless, almost white sky. They were walking now through a thick stand of trees and could sense that the peak was at the end of it.

"I had hoped that you would give me a few lessons," said Sebastian timidly.

Gabriel looked at him vaguely.

"You're determined to get yourself killed, aren't you?"

"Me? You're talking nonsense, schoolboy. What's more, I'm bound to my sword."

"Ah yes? What does its engraving read?"

"*Mi dama es mi ley.*"*

"It's a nice thought."

"Yes . . . still, it didn't bring its previous owner much luck."

"Who was that?"

"Miguel Ruiz."

The two men fell silent. Ruiz was one of Gabriel's comrades who fell during the battle at Vilcaconga. Certainly, he had been a nasty piece of work, but now he was one buried in the ground. What's more, he had been the son of a gentleman of Seville and his African slave girl.

They came out of the trees and were blinded by the brightness of the sun. As his eyes adjusted, Gabriel made out the peak.

And seven black shadows standing silhouetted against it.

Anamaya had been lurking around Chalkuchimac's palanquin all morning. She had invited Inguill to take her place in her own, herself walking alongside the Inca general's, despite the hostility of the Spanish soldiers, who had put him in chains again, and despite the smell of fear and death that surrounded him.

She leaned toward the hanging of fine alpaca wool decorated with a black-and-white checkered motif against a red background that enclosed the general's palanquin.

"Chalkuchimac?"

"I hear you."

She smiled. The seasoned Inca warrior's gruff, unyielding voice held a special distinction for her.

"I listened to the Strangers speaking among themselves this morning, and they spoke of you with particular hatred. They hold you responsible for what happened."

---

* "My lady is my law."

"Don't worry about me."

"If you want to escape, now's the time."

A bitter laugh came through the hanging.

"If I had wanted to escape, I would have done so a long time ago."

Because the path was so narrow, Anamaya managed to keep some distance between her and the Spanish soldiers, who were obliged to march in front of and behind the palanquin. The general continued:

"They have no proof whatsoever, and only I can convince Quizquiz and Guaypar to lay down their weapons."

Anamaya felt fear flutter in her heart.

"You know as well as I do that they don't need any proof. And as I am the one who chose Manco, and you can't . . ."

"It wasn't you who chose Manco, you strange girl, but our father Huayna Capac. Today you are all going to make peace with the Strangers, but tomorrow . . ."

The rest of the general's words were lost in a murmur. The road was widening now, and already the Spanish soldiers were approaching her menacingly.

"Tomorrow, all the Incas and all the Indians shall unite to fight a war against the Strangers, and you shall lead them. . . ."

A Spanish soldier shoved Anamaya.

"What treacheries are you plotting now?"

She looked at him contemptuously, but made no reply. The anxiety that Chalkuchimac's words had planted in her heart grew as she distanced herself. She foresaw war, destruction, and bloodshed.

And she saw Gabriel's face, and Manco's face, so close together that they were almost touching one another, forehead against forehead, mouth against mouth, the blond curls of one becoming intertwined with the long black hair of the other.

"So that's him," Gabriel said to himself upon seeing the young Emperor wrapped in his yellow cotton cape, standing a little in front of the others, his expression both proud and timid.

Over time Gabriel had learned to distinguish between the Inca's faces, faces that at first had seemed to him all identical to one another, not unlike those gold llama figurines that the Spaniards had amassed by the thousands in Cajamarca and which, each one practically indistinguishable from the next, had been smelted down into ingots.

He remembered Atahualpa's bloodshot eyes, Guaypar's arrogant gaze, Chalkuchimac's rugged face. But what he saw on this young man's face was something altogether different.

He saw an august stateliness, the evidence of suffering, and the marks of strength. He saw a youthfulness that had already lived a thousand lives, a young man who had seen death firsthand at an age when most children are still playing games.

The small group of Incas watched the Spaniards arrive one by one on the peak. They appeared to be completely fearless of the Strangers, or else determined not to move an inch. Gabriel, the first to reach the peak, approached them straightaway, without waiting for Pizarro or the interpreters. The young Emperor said to him in a firm voice:

"I am Manco Inca Capac. I am the son of the Inca Huayna Capac, and I have been elected by the Elders to be Emperor of the Empire of the Four Cardinal Directions."

"I know it," said Gabriel in Quechua.

Manco showed no sign of surprise. He stared intensely at Gabriel.

"Is your *Machu Kapitu* far from here?" he asked eventually.

"He will be here soon."

Gabriel took in the breathtaking view offered from the peak. Beyond the steep slopes of the Apurimac Valley, the landscape broadened into a vast plateau surrounded by gentle hills. He could see the houses of Jaquijaguana clustered together on their slopes, and a mountain pass beyond them.

The last pass, beyond which lay the city of gold.

He turned back to the Incas, who were themselves watching the Spaniards and their horses stream out onto the peak. Five noblemen of about Manco's age stood behind him, large gold disks stretching their earlobes. A little farther back stood another Indian, shorter and older than the others, his skin darker. He wore an odd square hat over his long hair, hair that streamed down to his shoulders. He was looking not at the Spaniards, as were the others, but at the distant mountains.

Don Francisco arrived at the same time as his brothers, and was followed by Almagro, Soto, Candia, and the rest of the Spanish commanders.

The Governor took Manco's hand between his own and lavished him with compliments and declarations of goodwill. The young Inca smiled somewhat shyly, but showed no other emotion as he listened to the Spaniard's protocol.

"The Cuzco clans and I," said Manco, "have had to endure the crimes and vengeance of those from the North, who wished to rule over us, in violation of my father Huayna Capac's will."

"I know," said Pizarro cheerfully, "and that is why I have crossed these godforsaken mountains to help you."

"It was they who attacked your army, not my people. We want peace."

Pizarro's smile grew broader.

"Then we are brothers, for I too want peace, and I have not come all this way to go to war with you or to steal your treasures!"

"What I call peace," said Manco without batting an eyelid, "means that I rule over my people, who are at peace with the Strangers who visit us."

"We have the same understanding of peace, then. Please be assured that we have come to help you and your people return to your capital in peace, and to make sure that you will not have to suffer the treachery of the northern clans any longer."

The two men smiled.

"I want to tell you," continued Manco, "that the armies of General Quizquiz and Captain Guaypar are marching on Cuzco, and that they intend to raze it to the ground so that you shall find no treasure there at all, nor any food for your men."

"We shan't let them. And we shall put an end to the treachery of him whom we had welcomed as a friend, and who has ever since been giving orders to destroy us by secret messengers. I am talking about that worthless dog, Chalkuchimac."

Pizarro had spat out the word "dog" like an arrow from a bow. He stopped and looked at Manco, expecting a reaction.

Manco said nothing.

"Do you not agree that it is time for that dog to die?"

Manco kept his silence. He turned his eyes away from Pizarro, and looked to where the road came out of the trees. Anamaya appeared, carried by eight porters. They came to a halt, and she stepped down from her palanquin.

"The *Coya Camaquen* must come with us," asserted Manco. "She must stay with us all the way to Cuzco."

Pizarro looked at Gabriel, then nodded to Manco.

"By the faith, my friend, if that is your will, then it shall be so."

Gabriel's breath was cut short. He tried to catch Anamaya's eye as she walked past him. But she seemed determined to ignore him. So he looked straight at Manco instead. And in the young Emperor's black eyes, he was astonished to see not only a challenge, but also a sign of respect.

SEVENTEEN

Jaquijaguana, evening of November 13, 1533

Manco, sitting in the *cancha*'s courtyard, stared into the curling flames of the recently stoked brazier. He couldn't decide whether to sleep or not. Anamaya had stayed at his side, along with the longhaired Indian whose name she now knew: Katari. She sensed Manco's disquiet. He seemed unable to get used to all the noise the Strangers made, their grating voices, their loud laughter, their indelicate shouting.

Anamaya wrapped her *lliclla* tighter around herself against the night's humidity. It was too thin for this climate. She felt her convictions slowly evaporating. She thought of Manco facing Gabriel, so close and yet so far apart, each coming from entirely different worlds and yet united together in the strange domain of her heart. For a fleeting moment, she reproached herself for not having spoken to Gabriel. But what could she have said to him? How could she explain her feelings to him? There was once a time when her visions had given her a sense of clarity, of conviction. But now that the Spirits were silent within her, she had to walk on with her eyes closed, seeing only the path immediately before her. *Trust the Puma.* Those words, spoken so long ago, now took on a fresh and mysterious significance. *Tomorrow, all the Incas and all the Indians shall unite to fight a war against the Strangers, and you shall lead them.* She could not envisage Chalkuchimac. She wondered if he wasn't already half in the Underworld when he had spoken these words to her. All these words lived within her, and acquired power through her.

She looked at Katari.

Manco had introduced him as the son of a great Kolla warrior who had been raised by his maternal uncle. He had been imbued, during his upbringing, with a great respect for and knowledge of the ancient divinities, before learning how to sculpt stone. For as long as he could remember, Manco had said, Katari had always been there to protect him and to reveal to him the presence of the gods.

He had a flat face with jutting cheeks, and his eyes shone out of two slits extended horizontally by wrinkles, two lines that divided his face, and that were lighter than his swarthy skin. His long hair fell freely to his shoulders.

"It is time," said Katari, without looking at Manco.

The young Inca jumped to his feet and signaled to a startled Anamaya.

Everyone was asleep now, except for the Spanish soldiers assigned to guard Chalkuchimac. Manco, Katari, and Anamaya left the *cancha* and darted silently down the narrow alleyways of the mountainside town.

Soon they were alone in the night, alone with the stars and the moon that, almost full, bathed them in its gentle pearl light.

Katari led. He seemed very confident. Soon they left the houses behind them and arrived at a natural esplanade, with four large black boulders standing at its corners.

Manco took Anamaya by the arm to allow Katari to go on alone.

The Kolla walked ahead a few paces, removed his cape, lay it on the ground, and sat on it. He remained there immobile for quite some time, his head slightly tilted to the right, blending into the calm night.

Then he took a piece of cloth and spread it before him. He fiddled with it for a moment, arranging it so that its four corners were aligned with the four surrounding boulders.

Anamaya suddenly saw, like a bolt of lightning slashing through the night, the totality of the alignment: behind them, this side of the Forbidden City, rose Salcantay Mountain, its snow-capped peak shining silver in the moonlight; dead ahead of them, beyond the pass, and much beyond the City of the Puma, lay the forbidding bulk of the twin Willkanota Mountains.

The two mountains towered majestically in the night, two Apus watching silently over Cuzco nestled in the bottom of the valley somewhere directly in front of them, midway along the line between the mountains and where Anamaya was standing.

The three Indians felt their souls stirred by the presence of the deities that Katari had evoked merely by aligning his piece of cloth between the sacred peaks. They sat there in silence.

Katari now took out his *chuspa* and emptied half its contents onto the piece of cloth spread out before him. He took three of the best leaves, fanned them out in his hand, brought them up to his mouth, and blew upon them while facing the Apus, which he invoked in a low voice, before setting down the leaves on one of the corners of the piece of cloth.

He repeated the ritual for each of the other three corners.

When he had finished, Manco came up to him and picked three leaves out for himself and blew on them, turning to face the Apus as he did so, before putting them in his mouth and chewing on them.

Katari did the same.

The two men's eyes were half-closed. Wordlessly, and without looking at one another, they moved with a perfect synchronicity of action and intention. Anamaya remained perfectly still and quiet in the light of her mother, Mama Quilla the moon. She wasn't asked to participate.

Manco took a handful of leaves with both his hands, held them over the cloth, and let them sprinkle down like rain. Katari leaned over the leaves and discreetly pointed at Anamaya.

She looked at the cloth. The petiole of the biggest leaf was pointed right at her.

Manco gathered up the leaves and repeated the ritual three times, letting the leaves slip from his hands onto the cloth, then picking them up again.

Each time the biggest leaf fell away from the rest and pointed at Anamaya.

There were no other sounds in the night except for the shuffle of Manco's hands and the occasional beating of a bird's wings, flying on the nocturnal breeze.

Anamaya felt light and free. That night, she was no longer the woman who had to interpret her visions, or decode the words spoken to her from the Other World. She was simply the one designated by the coca leaves, the one who offered protection and direction. The one who opened the way.

Manco took a polished black basalt stone from his *chuspa*, a stone as hard as a sling stone. He put it in Katari's strong hands, who squeezed it between his palms so hard that it seemed as though he wanted to crush it into dust.

When he opened his hands again, Anamaya saw that the stone now shone brilliantly, as though it had acquired the quality of the moon above them.

Katari slowly raised his hands, offering the stone to the night sky. When his arms were level with his face the stone continued to rise on its own. It rose up, then became suspended in the night sky.

Time stood still.

And at that exact moment, a roar tore through the night.

Fueled by rage, Fray Vicente Valverde scampered to the middle of the esplanade. He looked angrily at the piece of cloth for a moment, then threw it on the ground and stamped on it, picked it up again and flung it away.

"Pagans!" he spat. "Idolaters!"

The two young men stood still. They turned to Anamaya. Manco was wide-eyed with surprise, whereas Katari's feline eyes remained hidden behind their lids.

Before she had a chance to reply she saw Gabriel approaching with Bartholomew, the young priest with the joined fingers.

"Fray Vicente, please . . ." began Bartholomew in a pacifying tone.

"Heathen practices, soothsaying, human sacrifices . . ."

"I cannot hear the cries of children having their throats cut, can you?" interrupted Bartholomew in a slightly ironic tone. "Please calm down, Fray Vicente, I beg of you."

Anamaya was impressed by the young man's cool authority. But she was still in shock from the Dominican's choleric episode, as well as being a little unsettled by Gabriel's presence.

"The alarm was raised earlier," said Gabriel in a flat voice. "You had disappeared. The Governor gave the order to find you."

"We were . . ."

Anamaya stopped midway through her sentence. She realized that it was still too early to explain to him what they had been doing: the Apus, the coca leaves, the stone-which-makes-time-stand-still, it was all much too early. They stood facing one another in silence, and the young man's confused expression dismayed her. One day, soon, she would tell him. But not now.

Bartholomew approached Katari. The contrast between the physical appearance of the gray-eyed monk and the longhaired young sage could not have been more striking. Yet the same serenity, the same spiritual energy, radiated from both of them.

"We are still learning your ways," said Bartholomew gently, "and we shall guide you to the Truth of Almighty God with love rather than swords."

Katari listened without understanding, but smiled anyway. Bartholomew turned to Valverde.

"Fray Vicente, I understand your zeal and believe me, I am as committed as you are to the spreading of the true faith, but . . ."

"But you are far too interested in their so-called customs!"

"Knowing their ways makes it easier to guide them, my brother."

Valverde said nothing, perhaps embarrassed by his excessively violent reaction. A calm returned, despite all the shouting in the night, and the stomping of approaching soldiers.

Gabriel approached Manco, his heart raging.

"It would be better, for your own security, not to wander off thus."

Although Gabriel had addressed him in Quechua, Manco did not answer him directly but turned to Anamaya instead and said:

"Tell him that the Apus watch over me. That is security enough. I don't need foreign soldiers."

Gabriel interrupted:

"I thought you needed us to fight Quizquiz and Guaypar. Isn't that what you told our Governor?"

"Tell him that our nights are our own."

Anamaya sensed the defiance between the two men, the violent rivalry between them. They were like two wildcats challenging one another, each one young, strong, angry, and each sure of his own supremacy.

"We're leaving, Gabriel. Please tell the Governor that we regret the trouble we have caused. May the remainder of the night be peaceful for all."

Gabriel stared at her, imploring her with his eyes. It hurt her to see him so pained. Then he turned and headed back toward the town with Valverde, Bartholomew, and the soldiers.

She was alone once again with Manco and Katari. Silence had returned. But her peace of mind hadn't, the marvelous serenity she had felt when she had become aware of the alignment of the mountain peaks, and when the stone had left Katari's hands.

Manco broke the silence:

"Who is he?"

She couldn't find a reply.

EIGHTEEN

Jaquijaguana, November 14, 1533

The Spaniards had ordered, at dawn, that a stake be erected in the middle of the town's square. They hadn't found the need to use the whip on the Indian slaves in order to encourage them to bring the necessary fagots of wood to the stake.

The slaves all harbored a wicked desire for vengeance against Chalkuchimac, whom they held responsible for the attacks by the northern Incas. The prospect of the spectacle of seeing him burned at the stake filled them with a gruesome joy, and they carried their loads of wood as though they were as light as feathers. They told jokes to one another in muted tones as they added more wood and straw to the pile growing around the stake. They looked apprehensively to the sky, worried that it might rain and drown the flames.

But there wasn't a cloud to be seen in the vast expanse of blue above them.

The principal Spanish commanders—Soto, Almagro, Juan, and Gonzalo—stood in a circle around Francisco Pizarro in a dark room lit by only one torch. The palace they were in was said to have belonged to one of the Ancestors. But they saw only a sad and dark old house, each room of which had niches carved into its walls, niches that were now empty, their treasures having been pillaged. The house's guardian was a frail and trembling old woman.

"What does Manco Inca say?" asked Soto.

"He is with us," said Almagro confidently.

Pizarro nodded in agreement with the one-eyed captain.

"We have all the evidence we need, should anyone ask for it: the messengers he dispatched, the jewels he used to send coded messages by, as well as those cords of theirs."

"*Quipus,*" specified Gabriel.

Pizarro stared at him. Gonzalo and Juan chuckled.

"*Quipus, puquis,*" crooned Gonzalo. "He's a friend of the Inca, and so we must heed what he says."

Pizarro raised his hand authoritatively to silence his two younger brothers.

"*Quipus,* then, if that's what he says, my brothers. We also know that Chalkuchimac revealed to them the fact that our horses are mortal, and that we are too. The vast majority of their troops used to believe that we were some kind of gods without having ever laid eyes on us. If it were not for that traitor, Hernando de Toro would be with us yet."

"But what about Manco?" insisted Soto.

"He hates him from the depths of his soul. Only his pride prevents him from asking us outright to burn him. And in any case, we don't have a choice."

There was no trace in Pizarro's voice of the doubt and hesitation that had weighed on him before Atahualpa's execution. His guilt about that came back to haunt him at times, especially when he prayed to the Virgin in the evenings. He said to Valverde:

"Try to convert him, but do it quickly!"

"But Your Grace!" protested the priest.

"Quickly, I tell you! I shall burn him whether his soul has been redeemed or not! After the terrible attack he brought upon us, Fray Vicente, there shall be no mercy given to that dog. And I have learned that there is no worse fate for them than to be burned to death. I want them to know that the curse of God is brought upon them by our hand!"

Bartholomew had disappeared, the morning's events being contrary to his spirit. Gabriel no longer felt the intimacy they had shared at Hatun Sausa, when the monk had pushed him toward Anamaya. The sympathy he felt for him was now clouded by some shapeless unease, some indistinct disquiet.

"Gentlemen," said Pizarro, "we are on the threshold of Cuzco, the city of gold. I know that you are eager to live up to your roles as Spaniards and as Christians."

There was a dark glee in the Governor's tone, and his cruel irony prevented them from laughing wholeheartedly. *How well he knows his men*, thought Gabriel, *and how deftly he fans their avidity, yet despises them for it all the while.* Almagro, Soto, Juan, Gonzalo, and the rest followed the Governor from the house, the only large, stone-built house in the town, which he had commandeered as his quarters for the night.

The Indians had gathered in the square while the Spanish leaders had been in council. They parted willingly to let the Spaniards through to the *ushnu*.

When the Spaniards reached the bottom of the pyramid's steps, they turned around and watched the General, bound in chains, being brought forward. The General had declined to come in his palanquin, so that all the Indians—whether they were Northern or Cuzco Incas, allies or rebels—could see how the Strangers had treated the General, and what color their vengeance took.

He walked painfully slowly, his entire body racked with an agony that would have overwhelmed anyone else. He held his burned and blistered hands out in front of him. None of the usual Inca natural remedies applied to them had had the slightest effect, and decoctions of leaves brewed by even the wisest healers had not caused them to heal one bit, or even help him stand the pain.

But his eyes burned with immense pride in his inscrutable face. His tight, straight lips showed his unbreakable will.

Chalkuchimac faced death defiantly.

Pizarro didn't say a word to him. The General didn't even glance at the Spanish captain, or any of the Spaniards for that matter. He behaved as though they didn't exist.

He had to be carried up the steps to be tied at the stake. He was so close to collapsing from exhaustion that being tied to the stake was all that kept him from falling to the ground.

Only Valverde approached him, and uttered a few stifled words about God, heaven, and hell. But Chalkuchimac didn't give Felipillo the chance to translate.

"I curse you and despise you, and your religion as well, with its foreign gods unknown to me, and which I shall never acknowledge."

The strength of his voice contrasted greatly with his feeble, failing body.

"Enough, Valverde!" shouted Pizarro. "Let us get on and be done with him."

As the torches were brought forward, and as the first flames flickered up from the fagots of dry wood, licking at the General's legs and torso, he shouted:

"Burn me, then, burn me like you have already. But you shall not kill me. And you shall not kill our gods, Viracocha, creator of the universe, or Huanacauri. You cannot burn me any more than you can burn Inti himself."

He was almost completely hidden by the crackling flames now, but his voice seemed to survive as his body burned, as though detaching itself from him and rising up over them.

"Quizquiz! Guaypar! All you Inca generals, captains, and soldiers! Avenge me, and destroy these traitors, destroy these filthy, greedy Strangers!"

Pizarro signaled to the slaves, and they fed more wood into the fire, the flames now dancing into the sky. Its roar was so loud that the General's voice could at last no longer be heard, swallowed by the flames.

The fire was reflected in the fascinated eyes of thousands of silent Indians. The showed no joy, nor did they moan and wail as they had at Atahualpa's execution. They seemed only amazed and bewildered by this furious battle between gods.

When the fire began to subside a little, and its flames began to settle down, a final, terrifying cry burst from its center, a cry that fell upon them all as hard as stone from a slingshot:

"NO!"

And when the echoes of this cry had faded away, the fire subsided in an instant. Only a few tiny flames still flickered away at the feet of the horrifically charred corpse, now as black as coal. Bizarrely, Chalkuchimac's eyes were still open, staring with lifelike intensity at a distant point beyond the horizon, beyond his executioners, beyond the silent crowd, beyond the town and its mountains.

A point over there.

At the very moment of the Inca general's death, the sky had abruptly clouded over and it had begun to rain.

It hadn't stopped since. It was a cold rain, one that found its way through their chain mail and clothes, and chilled them to the bone. Black clouds bearing more rain raced through the lead-gray sky. The Incas had built a causeway, flanked by two long ramparts, through the middle of the swampy plain. The long cortege, over a league in length, was at the foot of the last hill from the crest of which one first saw Cuzco.

Rumors that the city had been sacked or burned had spread through the ranks of both Indians and Spaniards. The names of Quizquiz and Guaypar were on everybody's lips. The porters, fearful, stumbled more than usual, and even the battle-hardened cavalrymen, weighed down under their armor, felt the twitchy nervousness of their horses, which had spent the night saddled and bridled.

Manco's palanquin led the column. Bizarrely, he had inherited Chalkuchimac's, and he had had all signs of its ownership by the general removed. It was now crowned by a banner of yellow cloth—the same golden color as the cape he had worn when he had first met the Spaniards—and it fluttered irregularly in the cold wind.

Pizarro's brothers, along with the other Spanish leaders, followed just behind. Gabriel rode beside Don Francisco, his eyes searching the surrounding mountains for signs of an invisible enemy.

"You seem glum, my boy," said Pizarro. "Would you be pining for that young girl, at all? What do they call her, *coya* something or other?"

"*Coya Camaquen.*"

"That's right. And she's certainly a most attractive girl. I sympathize with you, my boy."

Pizarro let a silence pass. Once again Gabriel found himself surprised by the man's intuition, this man who appeared completely untouched by the most horrific barbarities, yet was capable of the deepest and most surprising sensibility.

"Yes, I understand you," continued Pizarro, "and so I shan't give you the advice that I would normally give to anyone else: that if you don't have her, than you shall certainly have another."

Gabriel stiffened.

"Easy, Gabriel," murmured Don Francisco, looking directly at him. "Women are just women, after all, and we're not here for them."

He pointed at Manco's palanquin with his eyes.

"You heard what he said as well as I did. He wants her for himself. I don't know why. I thought she was married to the sun or the moon or to a condor or something. But the fact remains, he claims her. An ally of ours claims her. Do you understand my meaning?"

Gabriel nodded. He understood Pizarro all too well, much to his own unhappiness.

"I need him," continued Pizarro. "He's a rebel, but a rebel who has suffered. We need to rest before the war, and to gauge the strength of this country. For that, we need him as a friend, for as long as possible. Are you still following me?"

The causeway had grown gradually steeper, and now they were climbing broad steps up to the peak. The rain had stopped, but heavy clouds still darkened the sky. Although they had adapted somewhat to the high altitude, their breathing still grew more labored with each step.

"I'm not sure if I follow you, Don Francisco," grumbled Gabriel. "I'm not sure if my spirit is open to what you are talking about."

"My, how touchy and proud you are," said Pizarro with a crafty smile.

"Don't forget that I owe her my life. And this second life of mine is not the fruit of pride, but of love, despite what you might think. She must choose between me and him."

The Governor was now staring at him with his bearded face, and his words stung like darts when he said:

"No, Gabriel Montelucar y Flores. It won't be she to choose, or you. It'll be I. Don't forget your oath to me, nor what you owe me. Nor should you count on my indulging you, or think that I'll allow you to bring down everything that I have built in this land."

Gabriel didn't reply, instead spurring his horse into a gallop, bolting away from Pizarro. The move sent pain piercing through his wounded shoulder, but his fury was greater than his agony. He pushed his horse harder than was wise, bolted ahead of the column, all of whom looked at him with astonishment, and galloped to the hilltop.

When he reached it, his heart beating furiously, he dismounted, pulled off his morion, and flung it to the ground. He followed it with his eyes, watching it spiral to a standstill, and it was only then that he saw the valley before him.

He was so stupefied that he thought he was looking at a new world.

He saw first the washed-out, diaphanous blue sky, the clouds now having cleared from it.

He saw the peaceful mountains immediately surrounding the valley, and the snow-capped peaks beyond them.

He saw the valley itself, crammed with agricultural terraces stepped neatly one above the other. The sun hadn't been shining long enough to warm the wet ground.

And he saw the city itself.

He had been led to expect, from Moguer's and Bueno's descriptions, a massive pile of gold. But what he saw instead was rather a magnificent ship, built of silver and gold, moored in the heart of the valley.

The walls of the temples, palaces, and houses glittered iridescently in the sunlight. It was like a multicolored pile of treasure in which one wanted to plunge one's hands. He saw the two emerald rivers winding their way to the city from the far end of the valley.

He heart skipped for joy, and he had an urge to clap his hands ecstatically. He didn't notice when those at the head of the column arrived alongside him, and drank up the scene for themselves.

"*Najay, tucuyquin hatun Cuzco.** You see it for yourself now," said a gentle voice in his ear.

He didn't turn to face her, but he could feel her breath warm against his neck, more refreshing than the still cold morning breeze.

"Do you know what we call it?" she asked him. He shook his head.

"The City of the Puma," said Anamaya, "the city born of the Puma. It is here where you and I shall find the path to the future."

Standing there in the sunshine and eddying breeze, Gabriel felt all his doubts and fears evaporate as Anamaya spoke these tender and promising words to him.

---

*"Great City of Cuzco, I salute you."

PART THREE

NINETEEN

Cuzco, November 15, 1533

The Spaniards, crossing through a green cornfield, noticed the contour of what they thought was a hill to their left. As they progressed, however, they realized that the hill was in fact a fortress. Its massive outer walls rose as vertiginously as natural cliffs. Three towers, one round and two square, rose at its eastern, western, and southern corners, towers far more imposing than any in Castille.

The Spaniards carried on in an odd silence, hardly noticing their weapons clanging, the click–clack of horses' hooves on the flagstones, or their leather saddle girths squeaking. Not a word was spoken. The horses clearly disliked the steep climb, and they shuddered as they threw their heads back, eliciting reassuring caresses from their riders.

At the foot of the slope, facing the meticulously kept terraces, were the first houses of the town. Its streets, arranged in a neat grid pattern, were lined with men and women dressed in fabulously colorful clothes, clothes that shimmered in the early morning light. Smoke rose up from fires burning amid the flower beds in the courtyards. Groups of Incas stood perfectly still in the great square, a square surrounded by *canchas* and magnificent buildings. All eyes were focused on the Spanish column. Gold glittered on the walls. Gold glittered on the noblemen's clothes as they watched the Spaniards draw nearer. Thousands more Incas standing in a tent city farther down the valley, an extension of the stone one, watched the new masters of the Empire make their way down through the sacred terraces.

Pizarro rode at the head of the column. He focused his black gaze on the city, wanting to absorb its every detail. His brothers, the one-eyed Almagro, and his main commanders rode at his side. No one dared speak a word.

They couldn't see a single Indian warrior.

"Gabriel!" called Pizarro.

Juan and Gonzalo turned back in their saddles at the same time. Gabriel, ignoring their jealous glare, clicked his tongue as he urged his bay up alongside the Governor's black horse.

"Don Francisco?"

"Stay by me. I want you to savor the full gusto of our triumph."

Pizarro spoke in a voice so low as to be practically inaudible. He glanced disdainfully at Almagro and his retinue.

"They weren't at Tumbez or Cajamarca. They're here only to stuff their pockets with gold. But not you, my boy. You're just like me. So stay close to me and make the most of this day, for it is ours."

They had now come to the first houses on the outskirts of the city. The houses had stone foundations, and their walls were made of sun-baked clay bricks. The Spaniards, riding up the steep slope, looked over their low, thatched roofs from atop their horses. Dozens of Indians now surrounded them. They were streaming out of everywhere, and if they were frightened of the newcomers they didn't show it. Gabriel was astonished by their diversity, by the different ethnic features of their faces, by the variety of their clothes and languages.

Pizarro ordered the column to a halt.

"Fetch the Inca," he commanded. "I want him to lead us in."

Gabriel moved back along the column at a half-trot, ignoring his companions' quizzical looks. He could feel Manco's gaze upon him from some distance. Manco's palanquin was of an unequaled luxury. Its interior was decorated with constellations of jeweled stars, a sun made of gold, and a moon of silver. His seat was carved of precious wood and was strewn with cushions stuffed with gaily colored feathers, feathers plucked from parakeets taken from the heart of the jungle. The young Inca was himself wrapped in a huge, billowing cape of yellow cotton embroidered with gold. He turned his face away at Gabriel's approach, pretending not to see him.

Anamaya, sitting in the next palanquin and wearing a red belt around her white *lliclla*, smiled furtively at Gabriel. But Gabriel perceived her as some haughty princess now so distant from him that he found it hard to believe that she was the same woman whom he had once held in his arms. He found himself once again plagued by doubts.

He saluted the Inca stiffly, then said in a cold voice:

"Lord Inca, Governor Pizarro requests the pleasure of your company at the head of the column."

Manco looked at Gabriel as though he were looking into the depths of his soul. He motioned to Anamaya to join him. They spoke a few words to one another, too quickly and too quietly for Gabriel to hear. She took her place at the Inca's feet with a submissiveness that fueled the jealous passion raging through Gabriel's veins.

He turned his horse around abruptly. He kept his back as stiff as he could while he accompanied the imperial palanquin to the head of the column.

A great uproar rose from the crowd as they approached and recognized their Emperor. The entire town and the sky itself echoed with the cry of:

"Sapa Inca Manco! Sapa Inca Manco!"

The clamor rose in waves from the crowd and made the hair on the Spaniards' arms stand on end. For a moment the valley air became as thick and palpable as sand.

Don Francisco Pizarro grinned. A broad smile, something rare for him, bisected the white beard on his emaciated face. He raised his feverish eyes to the sky and gave thanks to the Sacred Virgin, whom he considered his blessed fairy godmother and whom he was sure was looking down on him from the heavens at that very moment. He was so excited that he stood up in his stirrups and shook Gabriel by the shoulders.

"Sapa Inca Manco! Sapa Inca Manco!" shouted the crowd over and over.

Don Francisco spun around in his saddle so that all the Spaniards could hear him and cried:

"Gentlemen, remember this noise. They hail their chief, but in fact it is us that they unwittingly hail. Pay close attention to the sound of their cries, gentlemen, for you shall never forget it."

Gabriel shuddered. Nearby, almost within hand's reach, Anamaya stood by Manco. Her beauty dazzled him and he became deaf to the shouting all around. When she turned her head to look at him he told himself that yes, the Governor was right. He would never forget this moment.

*   *   *

Thousands upon thousands of Indians bowed before the young Inca. Anamaya observed the extraordinary scene from his palanquin. It was as though an enormous blanket of bodies had covered the sacred terraces, the streets, and the city square. The city of Cuzco, the "navel of the world," was a great weave of men and women, a giant *unku* decorated with a pattern new to the world. And from this human tapestry of faces and eyes rose the endless cry:

"Sapa Inca Manco! Sapa Inca Manco!"

"Do they call me to war or to peace?" asked Manco in a flat voice.

"They're asking you to become their Emperor."

"Will you help me?"

Anamaya burst out laughing.

"You're no longer the young boy frightened of heights and of snakes, Emperor."

"Yes I am. Will you help me?"

Anamaya, surprised, turned her head away and looked at the crowd. But Manco was right. He still had the face of a boy, and the crowd made such a strong impression on him that instead of showing his joy, he clenched his lips tight to prevent them from trembling.

"You're coming home, Manco, home to this city, to Cuzco, which for so long has given you only fear and pain. But today you are Emperor. Aren't you glad?"

"I don't know, Anamaya. My heart wants to shout out, and my heart wants to cry tears. I cannot get it out of my mind that my brother Paullu is so far away."

"You are emerging from a sea of chaos, my Lord. It is natural that there remains a little within you."

Manco's expression relaxed a little.

"I shall show you Cuzco," he said. "I shall show you my Ancestors' palace."

"I know it already: I lived there once."

Manco was honestly surprised.

"I thought you'd never been here."

"Forgive me, my Lord, you are right. But the stones of your capital are so sacred that some of them were taken to Tumebamba, where I grew up in the *acllahuasi*, and the girls there told me stories about the city at the navel of the world. And then that night, that terrible night when

your father Huayna Capac passed on to the Other World, he took me
through all his palaces."

"Was it my father who told you that I was the designated one?"

Manco touched Anamaya lightly on the shoulder. She trembled
almost imperceptibly, but the young Inca sensed it. He pulled his hand
away without saying a word.

The road leading into the city ran alongside a river. Its clear water
streamed along between the expertly constructed houses. Although it
was a wide road, the Spaniards could progress only two abreast, squeezed
between the massive crowds stretched along the stone walls. A cacophonous din rose from the crowd, a noise not unlike the rolling thunder of
a thousand drums.

When the Indians saw the Inca's palanquin, they raised their
upturned palms to the sky, a sign of veneration and subservience.

Gabriel's fear slowly evaporated, as did his distress at being apart
from Anamaya and his feeling of being a stranger to her. While he certainly didn't feel the heady joy that the usually impassive Pizarro was
displaying, he felt himself nonetheless carried along by the general fervor greeting the Inca and those accompanying him. The Indians now
surrounding them were a hundred deep, and although they surged forward at them, they made sure not to touch them. The newcomers were
themselves extraordinarily quiet, speaking only in murmurs.

"Are you dreaming, my friend?"

Bartholomew had appeared from out of nowhere, and now walked
alongside Gabriel's horse. He placed his hand with the deformed fingers
on Gabriel's thigh, looked at him with his laughing eyes, and said:

"You have certainly come a long way since I first met you in the jails
of Seville."

"Don't delude yourself. That jail is as close to me here as it was
there."

Each time he spoke to Bartholomew, Gabriel felt conflicting emotions toward him. He felt a strong intimacy with the monk, so strong
that he often felt the urge to reveal to him all the demons tormenting his
soul. Yet he also felt instinctively distrustful of the man.

They came out onto a vast square, the surface of which consisted of fine sand rather than the usual flagstones, sand on which the horses' hooves crunched. A magnificent round stone fountain stood in its center. Water streamed from it toward the river bisecting the square.

To one side of the river—the side that they had just crossed over to—there were no buildings of any note, only a wall that had just begun to be built. But on the other side stood the façades of palaces the likes of which the Spaniards hadn't seen anywhere else in the Empire. One of these was built of red-veined, green, and white marble. A massive circular tower, topped with a high conical roof, partially obscured its door, which was lined with plates of silver and other precious metals.

Here, an old, old Lord sat on an expertly chiseled throne under its magnificent lintel. The ancient nobleman sat perfectly still as he watched the Spaniards stream into the square. His evident nobility and impassivity intimidated the newcomers. A dozen women, dressed entirely in white, quietly busied themselves around him in a graceful ballet. Two of them fanned him with shimmering feathers, and two others looked after a fire burning at his feet.

He gave an impression of incredible power. The passing of the Spaniards, with their steel helmets and horses, seemed not to disturb him in the slightest, as though he was privy to the secret order of the universe.

The crowd streamed silently into the square, careful to stay out of the way.

"My God!" cried Bartholomew. Gabriel turned around.

"What is it?" he asked.

"Don't you see?" said Bartholomew, pointing at the old man's throne.

Sweat streamed down Gabriel's face, bothering his vision. Everything seemed slightly blurred to him. He saw only the perfectly still Lord, surrounded by his faithful servants.

"He's dead," said Bartholomew.

"Dead?"

"He's a mummy."

TWENTY

Cuzco, November 15, 1533

It was a humble *cancha,* set back a little from the southern road leading to Collasuyu in the district known as Pumachupan, the puma's tail, and within sight of the Temple of the Sun. Whenever a ceremony took place on the Intipampa, one could hear the priests' stentorian voices, the wail of trumpets, the rolling drums, and the chanting from within the *cancha's* walls.

Anamaya passed timidly through the door in the simple, unadorned wall enclosing the *cancha's* central courtyard. Its rooms, which gave onto the courtyard, were all dark and silent.

Yet she was sure that this was the place.

A roar made her jump, and she almost cried out.

She stood face-to-face with a puma, tied to a post by an agave rope. She took several deep breaths, straining to calm her beating heart, and then plunged her eyes into the beast's.

The feline paced about imperially, never taking its gaze away from hers.

"So, Princess," joked a voice from behind her, "have you forgotten your old friends?"

A frieze made of gold as wide as a palm and as thick as a finger was fixed to the stone wall surrounding the Temple of the Sun. The fat Pedro Martín de Moguer pointed it out to the small gathering with proprietary pride.

A half dozen of them, including the Governor and Don Diego Almagro, stretched their necks to better see the gold.

"There's some that you missed, Moguer. There's some you didn't ship back to Cajamarca."

"Gold falls from the skies in these parts, Your Excellency. It grows from the earth. They replace it as quickly as we take it from their walls."

Moguer had "discovered" Cuzco, along with Martín Bueno, a few months earlier, and he had organized the first transports of treasures to be sent back from the capital to the ransom room in Atahualpa's Cajamarca Palace. Now he moved his massive bulk about it with childish glee, proudly playing the guide to his compatriots. Meanwhile, an Inca priest wearing a long, fringed tunic appeared through the door. He was carrying a statue hidden under a wool covering. Gabriel was startled by his piercing gaze, and noticed the green coca juice dribbling from his thin lips. Two warriors bearing spears, clubs, and axes made of gold followed him. Two young boys in yellow livery preceded him, sweeping the flagstones with brooms, flagstones that seemed to Gabriel already immaculately clean.

The little group seemed astonished to find the Spaniards there.

"What are they doing?" asked Pizarro.

"We're interrupting their ceremony," said Gabriel.

Juan and Gonzalo burst into laughter behind him.

"What things he tells us," sniggered Gonzalo, "as though we were interrupting Easter Mass at Saint James's."

"Moguer, how well do you know your way around this temple?" asked Pizarro, ignoring his brother.

"Well, my Lord."

Pizarro grinned.

"In that case, gentlemen, let us go in and learn a little more about their ceremonies."

"I'll come too," said a gentle voice. Without waiting for Pizarro's permission, Bartholomew went ahead of them briskly.

They ran into the two Inca warriors beyond the trapezoidal door. The warriors crossed their spears, barring the Spaniards' passage. Their weapons could hardly be taken seriously, yet the Spaniards nevertheless hesitated for a moment.

Gabriel noticed a sort of cloister behind the soldiers. He watched as the priest placed the statue on a gold-leafed stone bench in the center of the cloister.

Having done this, the priest now turned his gaze upon the Spaniards.

He looked at them for a while. Then, at a disconcertingly slow pace, he approached them.

"Every morning, I'm amazed to see the sun rise again," said the dwarf. "I'm amazed that I'm still alive."

Anamaya smiled.

"I've missed you, dear friend."

"And I you, Princess, and I you. Do you remember the day when that despicable priest abandoned me in the mountain?"

"Yes! How you cried, 'Princess! Princess!' in a pathetic voice."

"I might have died, yet you were utterly indifferent."

"Oh, how silly you are," said Anamaya, amused. "I've thought of you a thousand times since."

She looked around the room they were in. Although its exterior appeared humble, it was in fact sumptuously appointed inside. Its mats and luxurious blankets were made of feathers and wool. Finely worked stone statues of pumas, condors, and snakes stood in its alcoves.

"You haven't done too badly for yourself, for a poor, abandoned soul."

"The job of Guardian of the Puma is one that no sane, healthy Inca will touch. It is only right that it is duly compensated."

The dwarf was wearing one of his too long red robes, its fringes sweeping along the ground. He couldn't stand still and kept bouncing nervously around Anamaya.

"How did you come to be entrusted with such a high office?"

"You mean you haven't heard?"

"I was told only that you were still alive."

"Alive . . . in a manner of speaking, yes, I am alive. When we arrived here with the mummy of my master Huayna Capac, I went to the head of the cortege and, to banish my fear, danced about, shouting: 'Here I am, I am Chimbu, the son of the great Huayna Capac! Make way, make way, here comes Chimbu!' But no one did. Instead, the local noblemen captured me and threatened to carve me up into little pieces. 'You little runt,' they called me, and they shouted, 'Woe, why did the Sun God take our beloved Emperor, our father, who loved us and looked after us, and leave us this stunted fool in his place!' They insulted me thus, they spat on me, they hit me, they ignored my tears and my pleas. But luckily for me, others came to my defense, and they arranged it so that I was put with the other prisoners."

The dwarf's face darkened at the memory.

"Do you know the prison at Sanca Cancha?"

"No."

"It is like your worst nightmare of the Underworld. It is in fact underground, a maze of underground caves. Deadly sharp flints are fixed to its walls, but the absolute worst . . ."

"The worst?"

"The worst is that there are no guards in this prison: only wildcats, bears, and vipers. They left us there for three days. For three days we howled in terror, for three days we cried until our eyes were dry. For three days, we were so close to death, it was as though we were already dead. But we survived."

"And then they freed you."

The dwarf nodded.

"Of all the terrifying things that happened to me, that is the only thing that I can look back on with joy. I have died many times in my life, but I'm far more attached to this particular life than to any of the others."

Anamaya was fascinated by the dwarf's tale. She murmured:

"And then?"

"I stuck as close as possible to the brothers, to Manco and Paullu, and I served them. That's it."

"You served them?"

"Yes," replied with dwarf, with an amusing, affected air. "I served them. I hid Manco in this very place, before he was able to slip away from the city. And I risked my miserable life time and again to carry messages to Paullu in the prison."

"Paullu was imprisoned?"

"Yes, but not for anything serious, I promise you. He was rather forward with one of Huascar's favorite concubines, so . . . but when the northerners arrived, he pretended most convincingly that he had been persecuted because he supported them. So they freed him, although they remained suspicious. He didn't wait for them to change their minds, however, and he scampered off to Lake Titicaca."

Anamaya looked pensive. She recalled the two young men she had helped all those moons ago, during the *huarachiku*. Now, one was the Sapa Inca while the other was in hiding.

"Manco spoke affectionately of you. He told me how to find your house."

"He too frightens me. Who knows how he will change, now that he's Emperor."

"Don't worry so much, my friend. Have you forgotten that we vowed to watch out for one another, you and I?"

"If I had forgotten it, Princess, then a very important person took it upon himself to remind me of it."

"Who?"

The dwarf came and stood directly in front of Anamaya and raised his round eyes to hers.

"Don't tell me that you don't know, Princess."

Gabriel watched as the green-lipped man walked up to the Governor, so close that he could have touched him.

"My name is Villa Oma, and I am the high priest of this Coricancha, this Temple of the Sun, built by our powerful Ancestor Manco Capac. Strangers are not permitted in here."

Gabriel translated. Pizarro replied, with an appeasing gesture:

"Tell him that we have come to protect him and his people from the northerners."

"And tell him as well that we have come to show them the one true God, and to put an end to their pagan practices," added Gonzalo.

"As for that, my friend," intervened Bartholomew, "leave that to the men of God."

Gabriel couldn't help but smile as he translated the Governor's words.

But the priest remained unmoved. He stood there, his arms out-stretched from his tall, lanky frame, like some Indian Christ, barring their way.

"How dare you barge in here like this, when the law dictates that he who wishes to enter this sacred place must fast for an entire year, and then only enter barefoot and bearing a stone on his shoulders?"

Gonzalo burst out laughing.

"Tell this featherhead that we have fasted for far longer than that, and that our shoulders are far more burdened than he can imagine. And as for our boots, well . . ."

Gonzalo pulled off one of his boots, and the Spaniards guffawed when he shook it at the priest and said:

"You see, Brother Bartholomew. I have only the highest respect for the customs of these . . ."

A pebble fell from his boot as he put it back on with an exaggerated grimace on his face, provoking more laughter.

". . . these barbarians. Let us leave the affairs of God to the men of God, then, and the affairs of men, well, let us deal with them as men."

He shoved the Inca priest aside, and stomped into the temple.

The small group of Spaniards followed him into the center of the courtyard. They glimpsed their own indistinct reflections through the doors into the rooms surrounding it. A strip of gold plate, set high up off the ground, ran all the way around the walls.

Four recesses, not unlike tabernacles, were carved into the walls. They were finished with extremely accomplished moldings, their interiors gilt with gold and set with precious stones. The Governor turned to Villa Oma:

"We are aware of the terrible threat that casts its shadow over your palaces and temples, and we have seen for ourselves the dreadful destruction brought upon some of your other towns by your enemies. But we are here in the spirit of peace."

The priest Villa Oma narrowed his eyes. He looked at them for a while in silence. Then he said:

"I don't believe you."

Villa Oma's voice echoed through the cloister. Pizarro didn't blink as Gabriel translated the priest's words. He smiled.

"Assure him that we shall win his trust. Meanwhile, we shall carry out a reconnaissance mission of this temple, in order to better guard both him and it. Don Diego?"

Almagro's only eye shone avidly at the thought of all the wealth hidden in the temple.

"I am sure that you shall take it upon yourself, as I do, to ensure that nothing from this temple is excluded from the King's fifth."

Almagro growled incomprehensibly in reply. The small group of

Spaniards began moving toward the door of the building facing them, leaving the priest Villa Oma behind. He raised his arms to the sky and cried:

"O Noble Sun God, send us some tangible sign of your magnificent power!"

Mummies sat in their thrones at either side of the Sun's path, mummies not unlike the one that the Spaniards had seen earlier in the square. They were dressed in gold-sequined tunics made of the finest wool, and spangled with precious stones. They all wore royal bands on their foreheads, from which colorful feathers emerged. Gold disks hung from their ears. They were in remarkably good condition, and one of them was missing only the end of his nose—a sight that caused Pizarro's two younger brothers to giggle ridiculously once again.

They moved slowly around the courtyard, going from room to room. They found one room covered in silver and dedicated to the Moon Goddess. Here, Moguer had to restrain himself from invoking Venus. They came across another lined with the usual gold plates, but with the added beauty of a jeweled rainbow, its colors running from one wall to another.

They had begun their visit in a state of excitement, like a band of young lads setting out to drink and chase girls. But they were increasingly quiet with each room they entered, increasingly serious.

Once they had visited the six rooms and had returned to the courtyard, they found that the high priest and his attendants had disappeared. Moguer stood there in silence, and Almagro had a dreamy look in his one eye. The Governor's younger brothers were unusually sedate.

Then they walked through a passage on the courtyard's eastern side. They discovered that the inner sanctuary of the temple was far larger than they had at first imagined. They discovered more buildings in which they found servants who hid their faces as they appeared, and who were storing provisions in quantities large enough to wait out a siege of many weeks.

Gabriel's heart grew heavy as he saw the greedy looks in the eyes of his companions at the sight of all these treasures.

"There was a story going around," said Moguer, "when we first arrived. . . ."

"Well, what is it?" asked Pizarro impatiently.

But Moguer didn't reply. No one asked him anything more about the story.

They had just unwittingly entered the garden of gold.

The dwarf continued telling his story in a muted, even voice.

"As soon as word arrived that the Strangers were approaching, Manco summoned me from Yucay, where I was living at the time. His men took me to him at Chinchero. When I found myself alone with him and that abominable high priest on one of the terraces below the *collcas*, I was sure that they had reconciled their differences behind my back and that they had some bloodthirsty plan in store for me."

"Manco and Villa Oma together?" asked Anamaya, astonished.

"Yes. Strange, isn't it? At the time I didn't think about it much, because I was too busy working out how to save my own hide. But luckily for me, they had something else in mind."

Anamaya grinned, amused, as always, by the irresistible mix of fright and comedy that was forever at the heart of the dwarf's tales.

"Perhaps, if you're lucky, you'll live long enough to tell me what it is," she said.

"Mock me if you must, Princess," sighed the dwarf, "but first let me tell you that they asked me to look after your noble husband, the Sacred Double."

"You!"

Anamaya was unable to prevent the exclamation bursting from her mouth.

"That's exactly how I reacted. But they ignored me. They told me that the Strangers, who are despicably greedy, would try to get their hands on as much gold as they could. Manco and the priest were themselves indifferent to this because they know that there is gold in such vast quantities, oceans of gold that the Strangers could never dry up. But they were not to lay their impious hands on the Sacred Double, which was then at Coricancha."

Anamaya was overwhelmed with emotion, one that sent hot and cold shivers down her spine.

"Is he here?"

The dwarf looked at her with the utmost seriousness.

"Do you think that I would be so foolish as to keep it here, even with a ferocious puma to guard it? No, we shall go to it under the cover of night. The Sacred Double is waiting for you."

Everything in the garden was gold: the grass, the flowers, the trees, even the animals, whether big or small, domestic or wild, were made of gold. Gold lizards and snakes slithered along the ground, and gold butterflies and birds hung in the air, suspended by invisible threads.

There was a terrace with golden corn growing in it, and another with that grasslike plant that the Indians called *quinua*. There were gold llamas grazing, and a gold fountain from which silver water ran. There was a patch of golden vegetables, trees of golden fruit, and even piles of gold firewood.

The Governor stood there, flabbergasted.

"Touch nothing," he said, his mouth dry.

"The story was," began Moguer at last, "that there's a statue made of solid gold, one that is the exact image of one of those mummies we saw. It is said to be bigger and far more beautiful than any we have yet seen, and not hollow like so many of them are."

"How big is it?" asked Almagro.

"More or less life-sized, I was told."

"And how much does it weigh?"

"Several hundred pounds, surely."

No one thought of disbelieving Moguer. Each man silently calculated the value, in pesos, of that legendary statue, which doubtlessly increased in size in their own imaginations.

"Where is it?" asked Almagro.

Moguer shrugged his shoulders.

"We have to find it," said Gonzalo.

Juan agreed, his eyes ablaze.

"What's this statue of yours called?" asked Gabriel.

"Oh, that I know," said Moguer proudly. "It has a strange name, which was translated to me as 'the Sacred Double.'"

Gonzalo glanced at Gabriel.

As they left the garden, his companions overcome by the sight of this land of gold, a land that had previously existed only in the most fabulous fairy tales or in their own overheated imaginations, Gabriel remembered Anamaya's words, and he vowed to himself that he would never repeat them.

She had told him that she was the Sacred Double's wife.

His soul was confused, and he didn't know what significance this had for the Incas.

But he knew what it would mean to his companions.

TWENTY-ONE

Cuzco, evening of November 15, 1533

The city of Cuzco didn't sleep.

The city of Cuzco never slept.

The hustle that kept the Empire running allowed for no rest. Young virgins continued weaving in their *acclahuasis*, goldsmiths and sculptors continued hammering their works, and priests carried out their rituals. Clans continued maintaining their *panacas*, attending to their dead sovereigns, bringing them food and honoring them, recording their messages from the Underworld and implementing these in this one.

In the square towers at Sacsayhuaman, guards relieved the previous watch. And in the round tower at Moyocmarka, the people were continually ready for a visit by the Inca.

There was a lot of whispering that night, both in the palaces and the more humble houses, and the waters of the Huatanay carried fearsome secrets.

The mummies slept, wide-eyed, in their palaces.

The mummies knew what the living didn't.

The dwarf ran ahead of Anamaya and guided her through the dark, narrow alleyways made slippery by the falling fog, which penetrated through her *añaco*.

He froze every time he heard a suspicious noise, or else dragged her to safety under the lintel of a trapezoidal door. He led her across a bridge spanning the Huatanay.

Upon setting out, she had tried to figure out what part of the puma's body she was in. But all she knew now, as they rose higher and higher, and as the lights burning up ahead in the towers of Sacsayhuaman came into view, was that they were heading toward the puma's head.

She came out at the top of a steep slope and, short of breath, discovered a vast esplanade covered in the same kind of sand as that at Aucaypata. She saw the evenly spaced recesses carved into a palace wall at its far end, at the base of a cliff. The lights of the city shone brilliantly behind her, and fires and torches burned on the mountain slopes.

"Where are we?" she asked the dwarf.

"Colcampata, Princess."

The very word made her heart beat quicker. It was one of the largest districts of Cuzco, located just below Sacsayhuaman, and it was here that the Chima Panaca, who were descended from Manco Capac, worshiped the founder of the Inca dynasty.

"What now?"

The dwarf didn't reply. Instead he took her by the hand and led her toward the palace wall. All its niches were empty, their gold statues no doubt pilfered by the Strangers during their first visit. Where there had been a finely worked gold frieze, there were now only the mutilated holes where it had once been fastened. And yet, even on that dark and damp night, the place still had a power about it. The sloping walls had a majestic quality about them that their perfectly fitted stones accentuated.

They followed the wall around a corner. The palace seemed to merge into the cliff here. Now hidden from the city's lights, they had entered the kingdom of shadows. They followed the wall, blending into its black rock, slipping through each new door they came to.

After they had gone through three, the dwarf leaned against the wall with all his weight. Slowly, silently, it pivoted open.

The veil before Anamaya's eyes was lifted.

Don Francisco Pizarro gave his orders on the great square. He commandeered as his quarters the palace situated on its northern side, by the river. Its main room was so large that it could have easily accommodated sixty cavalrymen to play a game of *a cañas*. His brothers Gonzalo and Juan were given the neighboring palace. Soto was to stay in another across the square, the walls of which were decorated with snakes carved from stone.

"Let the tents be pitched," said the Governor.

Gabriel stared at him, taken aback, and pointed at the palaces.

"I know, but I want us to remain on our toes, and I won't have any disorder. Let no one enter any house without my permission. I want to remain at peace with that young man."

"Young man?"

"Manco. The Inca. I want his trust in return for our good behavior. Almagro, Soto, and my brothers shall have all they wish. But none of them understand that we are here to stay, and that now is the most crucial moment for us. If we abandon our discipline, if we let ourselves go to pillaging, then we are dead. I shall see the young man tomorrow. Together, we shall raise an army against the northerners."

Pizarro's eyes were ablaze, and Gabriel sensed that strange mix of calm and excitation so characteristic of him in critical situations. He gave his orders to his lieutenants, and soon Gabriel witnessed a forest of tents rise in the square.

"And afterward?" he asked.

Pizarro looked at him for a moment, smiling.

"Don't ask me questions that you won't like the answers to."

Gabriel began to move away, but Pizarro set his dry, bony hand on the young conquistador's shoulder and said:

"There's a matter I must discuss with you."

The passage was broad enough for one to advance through the growing dark with a degree of ease. But then they came to a flight of high-stepped stairs, and they climbed these cautiously, making sure that they found their footing with each step.

It was said that Tupac Inca Yupanqui had had this tunnel dug all the way through the mountain to the Sacsayhuaman fortress, which was then being built.

Anamaya heard the dwarf's voice muffled through the fog. His face was wet from its humidity.

They followed a passageway around a corner, after which she made out a faint light flickering through a door hanging up ahead. The dwarf passed through it ahead of Anamaya, then held it aside to allow her through.

It was a round room without any recesses in the wall. It was lit by only one torch, fixed to the wall. There was nothing on the ground, no mats, no blankets.

There was only a simple wooden bench on which sat the Sacred Double.

A shudder ran through her body, and she had to close her eyes to keep her balance.

She extended her hand toward the Sacred Double, but stopped short of touching it. She spread her arms and murmured to herself.

When she reopened her eyes, the dwarf had disappeared, and the room was dark once again.

But it wasn't a threatening darkness, for from its heart the Sacred Double's golden body burned like a night sun, calming and eternal.

She thought that she could make out on the walls traces of shapes familiar to her: forest animals, perhaps, or armies meeting one another on the field of battle, sling stones flying through the air like lightning, axes raised, about to strike.

Slowly the images of that shadowy battle dissolved, and as her heart settled she was overcome by a marvelous peace, a serenity that brought her to the ground, to the feet of the one whom she was to accompany and protect throughout his meanderings on the surface of the earth.

You are here.

Was it someone else's voice speaking? Or had she whispered those words herself? It didn't matter—she could hear him at last, whom she had thought had forsaken her.

You are stronger than peace, and stronger than war itself. You are older and wiser than the Inca, and you have crossed the deserts and the rivers to be at my side. All that is yours is given to you by the night.

All was silent. Anamaya could no longer feel cold or heat, humidity or dryness. She was now at the secret heart of the universe, at the junction of all the worlds, and she was filled with a wondrous serenity.

My words are eternal. You cannot forget them.

The voice traveled through stone and air to reach her. Sometimes it sounded very, very deep, sometimes as resonant as a sea conch. But when the voice spoke the words that she had been hoping for, hoping for without admitting it to herself, it was in an almost inaudible murmur:

Trust the puma.

She hadn't time to enjoy the sensation of well-being that now spread through her body, relaxing her every muscle.

The light returned, blinding her.
She cried out.

"Which one do you want?" Pizarro asked Gabriel, pointing at the palaces, their solid walls lining the street.

"None. I want my tent."

Pizarro chortled quietly.

"You surprise me yet, my boy. God chased you out of Spain, and you aren't here for gold. . . ."

"I thought that I was here for the same reason as you, Don Francisco."

"Only God and the Sacred Virgin know why I'm here. There are times when I'm not so sure myself."

Their boots clicked against the flagstones as they walked. A child could be heard crying through the night, its wail blending with the gentle rustle of water running in the stream.

"You wanted to ask me something, Don Francisco."

"Ask you something?" The Governor snapped out of the stream of his private thoughts.

"Yes, ask me something," he said. "Something important."

Gabriel held his breath.

"It's no secret that you've bedded that girl, my son, that blue-eyed girl. Now please understand, I'm not leveling any reproach at you, far from it: even an old dog like me grows warm in the company of some of those Indian girls."

Gabriel felt his heart beating hard, and his mouth was dry. Pizarro pretended not to notice his discomfort.

"Still, for some reason unknown to me, the young man seems to attach some great importance to her. I have no idea what he plans to do with her. Make her one of his wives, perhaps, or else a royal concubine, or a priestess of his cult. I'm not happy about these idolatries of theirs, as you know, but there is a time and a place for everything, as it says in Ecclesiastes. In short . . ."

Pizarro paused and glanced at Gabriel, who was now trembling uncontrollably.

"In short, my boy, it seems to me that of all the women here to choose from, you've chosen the wrong one."

"I love her, Don Francisco."

Gabriel regretted having said this the moment it left his mouth. What could the word "love" mean to the Governor?

"Have you ever loved before, my boy, to use the term so blithely now?"

"No, Don Francisco, I haven't. That is why I now understand the meaning of the word."

"It's a serious affair, then."

There was no teasing in Pizarro's voice. Rather, Gabriel sensed an unexpected sadness.

"And yet you must end it, Gabriel. Or at least act with the greatest of care, so that the young man has no cause to give me any trouble whatsoever. Do you understand me?"

Gabriel couldn't reply. He felt Pizarro grab his arm and squeeze it, squeeze it until it hurt.

"Do you understand me, son?"

"I'm trying to."

"Try harder. And I have something to help you forget this unhappiness of yours."

Gabriel chortled nervously.

"You've found me another woman?"

"Better than that, my boy. I have a mission for you."

"What is it?"

"Find me that statue. Find me the Sacred Double that they carry on about so much. I would like to see it for myself."

Gabriel hoped that the Governor hadn't noticed it when his face had blanched.

The torchlight revealed Manco's face.

He came up close to Anamaya and stared at her without saying a word.

Anamaya had trouble regaining her breath, and she desperately tried to contain her rage at having been interrupted.

"Your father was speaking to me," she said simply.

"I'm very sorry."

He spoke these words with such simple sincerity that Anamaya's anger melted away.

"He was silent for so many moons. He hadn't spoken a word to me since the night of the Great Battle. I lived with a cold solitude within me."

"Have you found him again?"

"He has never left me. I am his protector. Sometimes I think that he speaks to me only in order to remind me of what he had already taught me, back when I was but a young girl learning her lessons in the *acllahuasi.*"

"Does he speak to you of me?"

Manco's voice sounded touchingly naive. He was but a child, this Emperor, a child looking for reassurance.

"I told you, he marked you out a long time ago as the first knot of the future. Nothing that is happening now is new. Everything is as it should be, and the order of the universe is as your father told me it would be. You mustn't be frightened. You must be determined, and go onward. You must allow yourself to be guided by your own power and that of the Sun-God, just as you did the day of the *huarachiku.*"

"You cannot prevent me from being frightened."

"Your fear is an illusion. It isn't real. Your father never mentioned your fear to me, and I never spoke of it to the Elders when they elected you. Was your father frightened? Was Tupac Inca Yupanqui frightened before him, or Pachacutec? Maybe . . ."

"And Manco Capac?"

The mention of the founder of the Inca dynasty left Anamaya wordless. She knew Manco held him as his ultimate role model.

"Come," he said.

She turned her palms reverently upward toward the Sacred Double before leaving him.

"I must return with *chicha* and corn, with coca and . . ."

"The dwarf fed him and quenched his thirst regularly. But you are right. He does need you."

They passed quickly through the passage. Manco deftly pivoted the secret wall by placing both his hands on it. They found themselves back in the night outside, a night darker than the darkness that they had just come from.

On the esplanade at Colcampata, Manco took Anamaya's arm. He led her to the edge of the stone parapet overlooking the town and the valley. Although it was an inky black night, moon- and starlight occasionally shone through gaps in the clouds, revealing the shadowy peaks of the Apus.

"My Ancestor Manco Capac arrived here by coming across that mountain there, the Huanacauri. Mama Occlo was with him. They had made a long and difficult journey from the lake of origin, Lake Titicaca, from the depths of which the god Viracocha had created all that is. Manco saw this rich, fertile valley, and . . ."

Manco interrupted himself, and turned toward Anamaya.

"You are right. He may well have been frightened, but it is of no consequence. He had plenty of reasons to be frightened: travel fatigue; the certainty of his destiny, which he alone could see; doubt, that insidious enemy, which eats you from within and leaves you exhausted even before your battle has begun. The legends don't tell us which of these fears Manco Capac had to overcome before he took possession of his golden bar, his *taclla*, with which he tested the fertility of this valley soil for the first time. The legends are silent on that subject."

Occasionally, the clouds would part wide enough to allow them a glimpse of the great river of stars in all its splendor. For a moment, the lights of the sky matched those on earth, of the torches burning in the city, and for that moment the world would be in perfect harmony. Then a sudden gust would close the gap once again, and once again the black night returned, with its cold, its hostility, and its fearsomeness.

"The story goes that he was with Mama Occlo. The story goes that a woman helped him found the empire."

Anamaya suddenly realized what Manco was trying to say. She reproached herself for her slow understanding.

"I have stayed at your side as often as I have been able to, Manco, and you know that I shall continue to do so."

"That is not what I'm talking about."

"Do you want yet another wife? It's impossible. I haven't royal blood running through my veins. Do you want another concubine for your bed? You have dozens already and, what's more, my skills in that particular art are negligible."

"I know that, Anamaya, you've already told me so, and I don't want to lie to you with pretty words. And yet, I don't think that you would speak to me like this if it wasn't for . . ."

"If it wasn't for . . . ?"

Anamaya spoke defiantly. Manco lowered his tone.

". . . if your heart wasn't already with another man."

The silent night fell upon them. Anamaya measured her breathing and made a concerted effort to rid herself of the fear that had overcome her when she had sensed the violence underlying Manco's words. Manco, whom she had once protected in his youth, but who was now Emperor of the Empire of the Four Cardinal Directions.

"It's true," she said at last, "I love one of them."

"A Stranger?"

"Yes."

Manco had let go of her arm some time ago. And yet she could feel him as though he were still touching her, she could feel his breath growing heavy. His profile, silhouetted in the night, had something of a bird of prey to it, a hawk about to swoop, to attack.

"His arrival was foreseen by your father a long time ago."

Manco shouted out in rage, and his fist came crashing down on the parapet.

"Manco!"

Anamaya's voice quivered with indignation.

"You know that I cannot tell a lie. Do you think that I would be so audacious, so *impious* as to invoke your father Huayna Capac's name in order to hide from you some sordid affair?"

"No, of course not. It's just that . . ."

He broke off. Manco's rage had passed as quickly as a squall. What remained was a moving, infinite sadness.

"Your father told me to wait for the puma's coming. This man is the puma."

"This man is a Stranger. A Stranger cannot be the puma."

"I find it as hard to believe as you do, Manco. And yet it is so. In my heart, I wished desperately for it to be otherwise. I've tried everything. But each time that I distanced myself from him, your father's voice reached me, and instructed me to trust the puma."

Manco remained silent.

"He is generous, Manco, and good. You have met him, you see that he already speaks our language, that he isn't like the rest of them, that he doesn't crave gold. What's more, I know for sure that he wants to help us. I've seen him try with my own eyes."

Manco let Anamaya list Gabriel's noble qualities to him. Or rather, he let the silent, black night absorb her words. Soon Anamaya, feeling a little ridiculous, stopped herself.

"And now?" asked Manco.

"Now?"

"Now that union with the Inca is beneath you, now that you prefer some puma, come from who knows where . . ."

"Your rage is no better than your fear, Manco. It might even be worse."

"I often speak to my rage, you know, I speak to it as though it were a person and as one does to become familiar with one's enemy. I ask it to let me be. I childishly believed that becoming the Sapa Inca would rid me of it. I know now that it's not the case."

His joyless laugh rang through the night.

"He cannot have you, you know," he said.

"I know."

"You are the Sacred Double's wife, the *Coya Camaquen*, and you cannot be wife to any other, whether he is a puma or not."

"I know, Manco. I didn't ask for this destiny of mine. But I accept it."

As she spoke these words, Anamaya's voice cracked despite herself. She had a vision of herself leaning over her mother's face, her mother who no longer spoke those tender words to her that reached into her very soul. Anamaya trembled as her old suffering returned. Then she said, with great dignity:

"I served at your father's side, and I never failed Atahualpa. I saved you from the snake, and it was my voice through which your father designated you to be Emperor. Do you need yet more proof of my loyalty?"

"I trust you, Anamaya," said Manco in a conciliatory tone. "I do not doubt you, and I know the difficulties that you have overcome. I am grateful to you, as I am to all those loyal to me. What's more, I need you for what is to come."

"That which must be."

"That which must be."

Manco's words echoed Anamaya's, and the universe's natural order was restored. But still, he stopped short when he reached out his hand to touch her arm. True, he had given his pain a name: that which must be, must be. But that which mustn't be would not be, and that was just as cruel.

TWENTY-TWO

Cuzco, end of November 1533

The *acllahuasi's* only door opened onto Aucaypata Square. Its buildings were wedged between those of Hatun Cancha, where the Spaniards were setting up their quarters, and those of the palace of Amaru Cancha, which Governor Pizarro had allotted to Captain de Soto. The twenty guards supposed to preserve and protect the house of virgins had fled the moment the Strangers had arrived. Only one remained, either because he was unshakably loyal, or else because his blindness kept him from fleeing. Anamaya called to him:

"You may let me pass, old man. I am not some bearded Stranger come to ravish a virgin or one of the Sun King's wives."

"You shouldn't joke about such things," grumbled the old man, "one day such a thing may very well happen."

"Impossible. You'll be here to defend us."

He waved his hand wearily, and turned his white, unseeing eyes toward the sun.

Anamaya headed down the alleyway that ran alongside the *acllahuasi's* buildings, passing first the workshops, then the warehouses filled with *piruas,* those large jars in which all that was needed to maintain the Inca was kept. She walked across the courtyard in which the idol of the Sun God was worshiped every morning, passed the buildings that housed the servant girls, the ordinary *acllas,* most of whom had already returned to their families, and finally reached the end of the alleyway, where the wives of the Sun King were lodged, and where it was forbidden to enter under the penalty of death.

Anamaya was regarded as some kind of queen in the *acllahuasi.* Even Curi Ocllo, Manco's *coya,* didn't dare challenge her authority. The women who had remained behind, priestesses who had devoted their lives to the cults of various divinities, felt threatened by the Strangers, who were steadily taking over the surrounding palaces and temples. Rumors of the rapes that they had committed in all the towns that they had passed through had reached Cuzco, and the women looked to Anamaya with a certain illogical expectation, perhaps because her blue eyes, the color of a peaceful lake, appeased them, or because she always had a kind word for those terrified young girls and their servants.

Anamaya's own room was located just before those of the Sun King's wives, and no one was allowed to enter it without her invitation. Her room was completely bare save for a simple mat, a woolen blanket, and a snake carved from stone in the room's only niche.

As Anamaya passed through the door hanging, she heard sobbing.

"Inguill!"

The young girl was rolled up in a ball at the bottom of Anamaya's mat and didn't rise to greet Anamaya, who had never before seen her gripped by such a terrible despair.

"Inguill! What happened?"

She turned her small, careworn face toward Anamaya and said:

"What good did it do me to obey him? What good did it do me to cross great mountains and slip past soldiers who wanted to rape me and cut me up? What good did your protection do me?"

"Inguill, if you don't tell me what happened, I'm going to leave you to sob by yourself."

"He's not going to take me."

"Manco?"

"He promised me he would a long time ago, but he's not going to do it. He despises me more than even the lowest of his concubines."

"But have you lost your mind?"

"He hasn't spoken to me once since we arrived in Cuzco."

"But he had to leave the very next day with Captain de Soto's horsemen and give chase to the northern armies, those who had mistreated you."

"But I so hoped that he would have me, Anamaya, I so hoped for it."

"Inguill, listen to me. . . ."

Anamaya couldn't tell Inguill that she was responsible for Manco's suffering the same pain that Inguill now suffered because of him. But she could tell her that this world was full of inexplicable emotions, and that one can never know whether to love and be loved is a blessing or a curse. And when she told her about the puma, about Gabriel, Inguill's teary eyes suddenly burned with pleasure and surprise.

"A Stranger!"

But Inguill didn't seem disdainful or frightened, as the men had been. She asked Anamaya questions that only a woman would ask. She asked her if his hands were gentle and what his lips tasted like. Anamaya told Inguill the delicious details, told her of his tenderness, and of how she would have to hide her eyes from him whenever they filled with tears when he was in her arms, inside her.

"But I cannot see him anymore," she concluded rather dryly.

"Why not?"

"Manco has ordered me not to. He wants me to remain faithful to my husband, the Sacred Double, and to the service of the Empire."

Inguill said nothing. Her feminine instinct fell short of knowing the mysteries of the Inca's destiny.

"I will speak to Manco about you," said Anamaya after a pause. "I won't leave you alone, my friend."

Inguill curled up in her arms.

"The other women love you because you see and hear secrets that they cannot understand. But I love you because you are good."

Anamaya was hardly listening to her. Speaking about Gabriel, being able to at last share her secret openly with someone, had been charmingly agreeable. But as soon as she had spoken the words she wanted to say them again, and her heartbreak was even greater than before. Obeying Manco was a burden that wasn't becoming lighter with each passing day. On the contrary, it was a pointless ordeal, and one that led nowhere.

She wished that there were no more words, that he was simply there, with his eyes and his smile, with his way of silently desiring her, and that he would come to her, confident, noble, magnificent.

The first time that Bartholomew had stopped Katari one morning on the gray, empty Cusipata Esplanade, the young Kolla had been startled. He had stared at the Stranger with his black habit girdled with a white sash, his head completely void of hair, and his two fingers joined together. And then he had stared directly into the monk's gray eyes with his own black gaze, and he had held his gaze until a smile had lit the Stranger's face, a smile with no hint of malice, violence, or fear. It was the smile of a man who had unexpectedly recognized himself in another.

Katari had flicked his long black hair and pointed at the towers and thick walls of Sacsayhuaman rising above them. Then he had swept his hand around at the entire city in its cradle of fields and terraces and at the slopes of the mountains surrounding them, before finally pointing at the first rays of the sun now rising from the east, from the direction of the distant and invisible ocean.

The two men began walking alongside one another.

And they had been doing so ever since. Rarely a day passed when they didn't meet to ramble together through the more obscure corners of the city, or else into the mountains overlooking Cuzco, the mountains with their sacred stones, their streams, and their spirits.

Gradually, their silent partnership had given way to an exchange of a few words, and anyone observing them would have had the impression that the language of one somehow matched and penetrated the language of the other, even if neither man ever understood more than a third of what his counterpart was saying. Katari was frequently astonished to see the monk take from his robe a rectangular piece of fabric and some sort of paintbrush, similar to those used by potters, and trace a few patterns on the fabric. But he asked no questions. He breathed in the air and allowed the breeze to carry him. He showed the monk the steps that led, upside down, into the depths of the earth. He heard him pronounce the name of God.

Today the storm had forced them home earlier than they had planned, and Bartholomew led Katari to the simple house in which he was quartered in Cantupata, the district where flowers bloomed with a magnificence that he found richer and more beautiful than all the gold in the world.

Katari examined the few simple pieces of furniture with some curiosity. There were a table, four chairs, and some shelves on which sat a few books. He stared for some time at the crucifix fixed to the wall. Bartholomew gave no explanation. Instead the monk pulled out a chair and invited his guest to sit down. Katari looked at him with some confusion, and the monk gently pushed him down by the shoulders until he was seated. Katari had the impression of floating above the earth. He was not lying down, nor squatting, nor standing. It was a position utterly alien to man.

The monk took out a piece of his white fabric and placed it before him, along with another brush. He dipped the brush in some black liquid contained in a tiny, narrow-necked jar, shook a drop or two from it, and then began tracing signs on his white fabric again.

"Look," he said, "and do as I do."

He held his brush toward Katari, and the young man clumsily dipped it in the small bottle. He tried to trace a few signs on the fabric, but he managed only to make a mess, causing Bartholomew to burst out laughing. He looked at the monk furiously, and Bartholomew simply started over again, patiently guiding his hand.

"That's good," he said eventually.

Katari looked at what he had traced. It was some kind of sign, a poor facsimile of what Bartholomew had done on the other piece of fabric, but he had no idea what it represented. He looked at the monk inquisitively.

"*Amigo,*" said the monk, pointing at the signs.

Katari looked from Bartholomew to the piece of fabric and back again.

Bartholomew pointed with his two joined fingers at each of the signs on the fabric, saying patiently:

"A-M-I-G-O. *Amigo!*"

And, smiling, he placed his hand first on his own chest, then on Katari's.

"You and me: *amigos!*"

Katari's face suddenly lit up with understanding.

"*Amigo!*" he said, enthusiastically nodding.

TWENTY-THREE

Cuzco, evening of December 4, 1533

The dwarf had waited for night to veil the city before daring to venture out into its streets. Whenever he heard the sound of hooves hammering the flagstones, he would duck into a doorway, or else flatten himself against a wall. He did not follow the Huatanay, which led directly to the Aucaypata, his destination, but rather went the long way by dark alleyways, stopping often to look over his shoulder.

When he reached the square, he stood for a long time in the shadow of a wall, watching the Spanish soldiers' tent city. Why had he said yes to Anamaya, he asked himself, and put his own life in danger once again? He sighed and stepped tentatively forward. She had told him that it was the tent closest to the Amaru Cancha. "He speaks Quechua," she had said, "and I have told him about you. When he sees you, he'll know straightaway that you were sent by me."

The soldiers he came across barely noticed him, or else elbowed one another in the ribs and burst out laughing. He felt his legs weaken as he approached the tent. Just as he was about to enter it, a voice burst out from within and startled him.

There was an odd atmosphere inside the tent. The sight of the Strangers, their bare torsos covered in black or red hair, quite alarmed the dwarf. He saw weapons bigger than himself lying about, along with those metal carcasses that made the Strangers invulnerable. He was tongue-tied, but they wouldn't have understood him anyway. He rolled his eyes from one to the other, trying to stay as far away as possible from them, all the while hoping that some miracle would show him which one was the one he was looking for.

But the Strangers, gesticulating and making odd sounds, approached him, and he scurried backward, waving his arms before him. He tried to scramble out of the tent, became wrapped up in the canvas, and fell over.

As the Strangers pealed out in laughter he thought, feeling somewhat ridiculous, that this time there was no Huayna Capac to protect him.

"What are you doing here?"

The Stranger had accidentally kicked him as he had entered the tent. He had blond hair and light eyes, and he seemed less barbaric than the others. He perfunctorily helped the dwarf to his feet.

"Are you the one they call Gabriel?"

Gabriel looked at him, taken aback. Then comprehension flashed across his eyes, and he muttered a few words to the others, who sniggered.

Gabriel wordlessly followed the dwarf through the sea of tents until they reached La Cassana, where they started down the alleyway leading to Colcampata. Here, Gabriel grabbed the dwarf by the collar and growled, "Are you going to tell me where you're leading me or not?"

"I cannot. You must trust me, and follow me."

Gabriel shoved him away with ill feeling, but he continued to follow him, never once noticing the shadows following behind.

As the dwarf placed his hands on the wall Gabriel suddenly felt very alone and very foolish. If this was a trap, he had walked into it willingly, unthinkingly.

What had he based his decision on? Some vague old story Anamaya had told him in Cajamarca about her friendship with a tiny man. And what of the dwarf's odd way of pronouncing his name: GA-briel?

The passage was completely dark. He called out, but in vain. He turned around and placed his hands on the wall to find his bearings, but he met with nothing but air. He was overcome by a vertiginous terror, an old fear from his childhood that knotted his guts. He could feel the violent thumps of his heart beating in his chest and temples.

He advanced, feeling his way with his feet, checking that the ground was solid before him. The ground had the same sandy quality as that in the great square. Then he grazed his hands against the hard stone of the walls. This reassured him, and although he didn't advance any faster, he was less panicked now.

But a moment later his hands met air again. He thought he could make out a gray light high above him, a light that illuminated nothing.

He stopped in his tracks, and his entire body experienced a sensation of spinning and of falling into a pit.

"You're here," said his beloved gently.

He grabbed her with a passion that he had not thought himself capable of, a passion greater than the terror he had just now almost surrendered to. And as his hands took hold of her body, he uttered a sound like that of a wounded animal. He had conflicting urges to love her and hurt her at the same time, to cover her in kisses while beating her until she cried.

And even though he thought himself in charge, it was she who pulled him down to the ground, to a pile of matting covered in blankets made of the softest wool, and her tenderness inflamed both his desire and his rage. He desired her with a necessity he had never yet felt, an ardor without limits.

He slipped her tunic off her shoulders, and he felt her abandon herself to him, give herself without any restraint, as though all the days that they had spent apart had removed every barrier between them. Her hot skin quivered beneath his touch.

He felt as though every part of his body was charged with desire, that if she kissed his neck, if her breast brushed against his, or if her leg found its way between his thighs, he would have to cry out to release all the knotted tension contained within him, and perhaps also his anger at the fact that she had let so many days go by without contacting him, and had even seemed to avoid him deliberately.

Her belly snaked its way up and down against his in a passionate frenzy of release, and he thought of those snakes that she was friendly with. He allowed himself to be surrounded by her, overwhelmed by her, and he surrendered to her serpentine power. When he entered her, he sensed her holding her breath, and her long silence left him surprised and immobile. Then, slowly, she resumed her undulating movements, subtle and irresistible.

It was so dark that he couldn't make out the features of her face, and this accentuated his excitement. What man has not fantasized of a mysterious woman, a magical woman with perhaps malign powers, who leads him into forbidden love by the blackness of night? He knew that it was Anamaya, but the sense that she had become a stranger to him incited in him a fury of which he was terrified, and over which he had no control.

"Put your hands around my neck," she said. He was so startled by this that he almost withdrew, but she was so much in him that she effortlessly controlled his rhythm. He was the one who now remained immobile. Then his hands, suddenly docile and obedient, left her smooth, willowy thighs and her arched back, its curve leading the dance of love. At first he simply stroked her neck, but then his fingers joined together around it, like the clasp of a necklace. He could feel her flesh palpitate like a fragile bird, while the rest of her body accelerated its pace frenetically. He squeezed her to the point where he felt her suffocating, while her body continued to surge like a sea swell above his own, and at the moment he released his grip on her, tears welled in his eyes as he let go of all his anger and released all of his desire into her.

She wrapped a blanket around them and nestled her head in the crook of his neck. He couldn't stop crying, and she licked away his tears like a cat. Slowly he calmed down, and he realized that he still had more questions than answers.

"I didn't want to hurt you," he said.

Then, after a pause, he corrected:

"No. I did want to hurt you."

"I wanted you to do both. Not hurt me, and hurt me."

"And?"

"You did both well."

They laughed with relief.

"Ours is a strange world," she said. "A secret door opens in the middle of the wall of a *huaca,* and you fall through it to the center of the earth, and then, lost in the absolute darkness there, a light suddenly blinds you. When you go out again, you are reborn. You are changed, transformed into something else. I'll take you there one day."

"Haven't you just done so?"

"You still know nothing."

He whistled between his teeth, and she giggled once again.

"Where are we?"

"Are you like the other Strangers then, who can't stand not knowing, and who want to know, to own, everything?"

"You seem to know everything about them. About the Strangers."

"You taught me everything I know about them. We are in the only place in Cuzco where we may meet without your people or mine bothering us."

"Manco, right?"

"Manco won't harm you. But he needs me near him, and I mustn't shirk my duty to my father."

"Your father? But I thought . . ."

"My father Huayna Capac."

"Anamaya, I don't understand any of this. I thought you were married to that king . . ."

"The Sacred Double, yes."

"Where is he?"

He felt her stiffen, then slip out of his embrace.

"What's wrong?"

"Why are you asking me this?"

"To protect you against my people's greed. The younger Pizarro brothers—their souls to Satan—have heard rumors of a statue made of solid gold, and they think of it now as the finest prize to be had in Cuzco, perhaps because they've never seen it. And to cap it all off, the Governor has ordered me to find it."

"And what would you do if you did?"

"Why, like the others, of course. I'd take possession of it and smelt it down into ingots. I'd make myself rich. Wasn't it my avarice that seduced you?"

"Tell me what you would do, seriously."

"I'd help you hide it from their greed. Because if I can find it, then so can they."

He reached out to embrace her, but she dodged him. His voice echoed into the void. He was naked and cold.

Just then a torch appeared, revealing the room by its feeble light. It was a circular room, like a baptistery, and before his eyes adjusted, Gabriel saw only dancing shadows. Then he saw her, also naked, and despite their recent lovemaking he was still attracted to her supple body. In the center of the room was a gold statue on a plinth, glowing red by the torchlight. It was seated on a throne in the same posture as the mummies Gabriel had seen. It was absolutely perfect except for its nose, which was missing its end.

Gabriel shivered, but not from the cold. They had barely had the time to recover from their lovemaking, or to enjoy the delicious abandon that had been denied them for so long.

"Isn't it a terrible thing with your people to disobey orders, as it is with mine?"

"Yes, it is. But when orders are merely a cover-up for immoral greed, then even what they call treason is a preferable course of action."

"Perhaps you are decorating a simpler emotion with honorable words."

"It's that emotion itself that inspires honor in me."

"You shall be exposed to great dangers, Gabriel."

"Hide this statue tonight."

"We must not stay together any longer. You must trust me, no matter what you see, no matter what happens, you must trust me without being able to see me, you must trust me despite all the evidence to the contrary."

"What do you mean?"

But Anamaya's voice was already trailing off, although he wanted to touch her once more, to hold her in his arms, to feel the fleeting caress of her lips.

"Trust me as I have trusted you. I will be there, Gabriel, when I need to be. Close your eyes."

He obeyed her, using all his strength to resist the instinctual urge he was feeling to do otherwise. He wanted to take her with him. He wanted to defy Pizarro, Manco, and the brothers. But instead he listened to the soft echo of her words: *Trust me as I have trusted you.*

When he at last reopened his eyes, he met with the dwarf's froglike gaze. He didn't even turn back to look at the Sacred Double as he set out down the passage. He felt empty and weak.

When they emerged into the night, he walked along the Colcampata Esplanade. He looked to the stars, and made out shapes in the Milky Way, shapes that, one after the other, she had shown him after Atahualpa's death—the dog, the llama, the condor.

Suddenly, in the middle of that celestial disorder, he clearly saw a cat looking at him, its paws raised, its mouth open.

The puma.

He walked fearlessly to the square.

TWENTY-FOUR

The Temple at Cuzco, December 20, 1533

Anamaya had trouble distinguishing between the silhouettes of the two men preceding her through the damp fog. Yet Villa Oma and Katari could not have been more different in appearance. The fog extended the Sage's already unreasonably tall and lean body, whereas it flattened the young Kolla's already compact one.

No one said a word.

They were but a short distance from Cuzco, but the weather was so bad that they might as well have been lost in the mountain, in the heart of the wilderness. The Sage was leading them along a narrow path lined by two low walls to the temple in which Manco had retreated for three days to complete the ritual fast required before receiving the *mascapaicha*.

Turning around, they could see the houses of the city, indeed the entire valley, engulfed in fog. Yet the play of the light streaking across the sky sent shapes of boulders, animals, and warriors to meet them, and the gusting wind made these cry out indistinct, doleful cries.

What was Viracocha's will?

The bulk of the Poquekancha Temple now rose before them, with its vast esplanade and its blocks almost as perfectly hewn as those at Coricancha. It was surrounded by corn terraces, the widths of which exactly matched the height of the walls.

As Villa Oma greeted the guards standing at the only door cut in the wall, Anamaya turned around and allowed herself to absorb the harmony of the place. Majestic and almost vanished, the view of this world had never been closer to that of the other.

The temple's courtyard was thick with fog. It seemed to rise from the ground and was streaked with silver filaments, like a hummingbird feather. It muffled the regular lapping sound of the fountain, which was fed by a cleverly constructed system of pipes.

Manco sat alone at the entrance to his room.

Tomorrow, he would don the Inca's costume, which included an *unku* that a hundred virgins had woven in the *acllahuasi*, ensuring that each of its strands emanated gold and other colors. He would wear a necklace made of many thousand *chaquiras*, a *llautu* and a *curiguingue*, heavy gold ear plugs, and the royal breastplate. But for the moment he wore only a simple white *unku* and straw sandals, and he was seated on his *tiana* gazing at the pearly sky.

Anamaya, Katari, and Villa Oma came before him in silence, their heads bowed. He looked away from the sky to gaze at them. He gave them the most fleeting of smiles, a smile that in no way lightened his haggard expression.

"It looks like the Son of the Sun is lost in the fog," said Katari.

Anamaya was taken aback, and Villa Oma almost choked. There was an awful pause, and then Manco burst out laughing, so hard that his whole body shook and he finished with a fit of coughing. Katari's face lit up and Anamaya relaxed, but the green-mouthed Sage remained unmoved, severe, disapproving.

"The Son of the Sun in the fog . . . you're the only one, Katari, whom I can forgive such a transgression. Isn't it so, Sage Villa Oma?"

The priest made no reply, but his moral disapproval was palpable. Anamaya found him more reserved and severe than ever, as though a deep, deep fury was raging in his guts.

"Follow me," said Manco.

He led them to one of the rooms giving onto the courtyard. Unlike many other temples, this one hadn't yet been ransacked, and it still had not only its gold frieze running along the top portion of the wall just below the expertly worked beam supporting the *ichu*'s roof, but also thick gold plaques on which, with a single, unbroken stroke of the awl, the outlines of animals had been etched. There were still idols in the niches, statues of gods with precious stones as eyes, turquoises and emeralds, eyes that followed one around the room.

But above all, there were still paintings.

Anamaya's breath was cut short. They were on wood panels hung on all the walls around the room. She had never seen them before, but she recognized in the blink of an eye the most famous scenes of Inca history: the construction of Coricancha by Pachucatec and the battle against the

Chanca. She was fascinated by them, and she could not dwell on one long enough before feeling the urge to go to the next. The scenes seemed so alive, so powerful, their colors so vibrant, the characters so close to reality that she wouldn't have been surprised if the painter was not still there with them, hidden among them.

Even Villa Oma seemed impressed by the solemnity of the place. The entire mythology of the Inca world was painted here in strong, simple images, stronger than words, and far more durable than the roar of battle. Anamaya suddenly felt her heart jump in her chest.

She recognized, in one of the paintings, the great Huayna Capac's inscrutable face, as cracked as old wood, and so true to life that it left her nonplussed. He was pictured reclining on a mat, his body hidden by wool and down blankets that protected him from the cold. And at his side, her face half-hidden in shadow, stood a little girl looking on, her timid blue eyes revealing dread as the old Emperor placed his hand on her.

Manco watched Anamaya as her eyes filled with tears. She could not escape from the role she had played in the Empire ever since Huayna Capac had died. But nothing could match this painting to make her realize to what point she had now become part of its history.

"Tomorrow," said Manco slowly, "will be a great day for the Incas."

Anamaya looked away from the painting to her friend's aquiline face, and she saw a vital flame burning in his dark eyes.

"But tomorrow," he continued solemnly, "is fraught with dangers. My fast has relieved me of many pointless concerns. But it has not dissipated all my confusion. I need your help to see clearly."

He looked at Villa Oma, who didn't bat an eyelid, and then at Katari, who smiled faintly.

Finally, he rested his eyes on Anamaya and maintained his gaze.

A few days before Christmas, Don Francisco Pizarro at last gave the order to strike the tents on the square, and that the men go to their quarters. Gabriel was staying with him, in the La Cassana Palace, and not across the square with the rest of the men. He was alone in a modestly sized room and enjoying his only concession to luxury: a window, an exceptional little trapezoid of light that he had refused to cover with greased paper so that he might continue to enjoy the spectacle of the street, the motley crowd of men and women flowing along the Huatanay.

"Gabriel?"

Gabriel made out Bartholomew's silhouette in the shadows, and he did his best to suppress the nameless dread gripping him.

"What news?"

The monk approached him, smiled, and brushed past him. He stood before the window, and watched the passersby on the street.

"They're hopeful," he said lightly.

"What do they hope for?"

"What all men hope for: peace, food, a woman's body. Our men hope for more: gold, silver, and the like."

"True. The Governor has promised that the paying out will begin immediately after the coronation."

"You say that so joylessly."

"You know very well that gold holds no glitter for me."

Bartholomew looked at him curiously.

"You have only one motive for being here, then?"

"Which is?"

"The same as me: for the glory of God."

A twinkle in Bartholomew's eye started both men into fits of laughter.

"By the faith, my friend, given the circumstances in which we met, I find it most generous of you to accord me with such a religious zeal."

"Am I so wrong?"

Gabriel, pouting, suppressed his irony.

"It's up to you to decide. But have you come here to ask me to help you prepare for Mass?"

"No, my friend. You know that for that purpose dear Father Valverde is irreplaceable. He has already dedicated the palace that the Governor gave him to Our Lady of the Conception, after having exorcised it of demons, of course. I imagine the demons fled at the mere sight of him, howling at the top of their lungs."

"Will the church be built in time for Christmas?"

"Most likely not. But only because we no longer believe in miracles."

"You don't think I can perform them, do you?"

"I wish you would stop mistrusting me, Gabriel. You have some problems I can help you with. Come."

The two men crossed the palace's vast courtyard, which was patrolled by soldiers night and day. It was here, in the Governor's own palace, that the treasures looted from the palaces and temples were amassed in piles under the treasurer's watchful eye, and where these piles sat waiting to be smelted down into ingots from which the royal fifth was levied and the remainder divided among the conquistadors.

They came out onto the square which, now that the tent city had disappeared, had regained its normal appearance. Bartholomew led Gabriel to the fountain in its center. Dawn's thick fog had now dissipated, and they stood in the light of a warm sun.

"They saw you," said Bartholomew.

"Could you speak Castilian so that I can understand you?"

Bartholomew raised his two joined fingers in an appeasing gesture.

"A few days ago, you were guided by night to one of their temples. You then 'disappeared into a wall'—forgive me the expression—before reappearing a few hours later."

"So?" said Gabriel defiantly.

Bartholomew paused. Then:

"You can reply to me any way you wish. But I'm not so sure that the Governor will accept the same reply."

Gabriel turned pale.

"I think I know whom you visited that night, and believe me, I'm not judging you in any way, no matter what you might believe."

Gabriel scrutinized the bald-headed monk's gray eyes to see if he could discern a trap in them. But he found only the wrinkles of genuine concern.

"Your problem is that the two Pizarro brothers have a different theory. And your problem is that they are trying at this very moment to bring the Governor around to their way of thinking."

"And what do those two curs think?"

"They think that you've found this famous gold statue that the Governor entrusted you to find, but that you've hidden it away safely and hope to keep it all to yourself."

Gabriel felt the ground give way beneath his feet. Bartholomew plunged his gray eyes into his and said:

"In the name of God, is my Castilian clear enough for you now?"

*   *   *

It was a long and grim argument. More often than not, it was Manco and Villa Oma who disagreed as Katari looked on. While they carried on, Anamaya stared at the painting of Huayna Capac's death, experiencing the odd sensation of looking at her own memories.

"We must go to war, and we must do it now," insisted Villa Oma. "We must not repeat your brother Atahualpa's mistake. We must destroy them while we still can. We must raise an army from all the villages. We must summon your brother Paullu, and perhaps even make peace with Quizquiz and Guaypar."

At that, Manco roared:

"No! I will hunt those two down unto the Other World if I have to. They elude me now, but . . ."

". . . but only with the help of the Strangers! Do you really believe their false smiles, their sweet words? Do you really believe the things they tell you to lull you into complacency? Do you really want to serve under their king, and under their god? You will serve them like a slave."

"Villa Oma!"

"You go too far, Sage," intervened Anamaya.

"But I'm not accusing Manco of cowardice," raged Villa Oma, "I'm just saying that we know what the Strangers are now, we know that they only want to strip us of our treasures, to take our silver when our gold runs out, our emeralds when we have no more turquoises. We know that they want to destroy our temples. How much longer must we wait before we fight back?"

"We're not ready, Sage Villa Oma," said Anamaya simply, motioning to Manco to say nothing. "We're not ready yet. It's as simple as that."

The Sage stared at the young woman to whom he had taught, many moons ago now, the most sacred rites of the Inca world. A sad smile crossed his gray, wrinkled face.

"You have changed, young Anamaya."

"I have listened," she said, "and I have learned. I know these Strangers well." She looked away from Manco as she said this. "And I know their motives. But our father Huayna Capac's message is that Manco must reign, and that at first it must be the reign of the snake, who slides silently between the stones and disappears into the leaves. It is not yet to be the reign of the condor, master of the skies."

Manco turned to Katari.

"What do you think?"

The young man flicked his long hair.

"Anamaya is right."

"And you, Villa Oma?"

The Sage made no reply, but simply nodded, conceding defeat. For now.

"Is the Sacred Double secure?"

Manco had uttered the question like an accusation.

"He has left Colcampata and Cuzco for a secret destination," Anamaya said simply.

"Will the blond Stranger be shown this place as he was the last?"

Anamaya, flabbergasted, grew pale with shame, but didn't ask how he had found out.

"No."

Katari and Villa Oma said nothing. The Sage wore a severe, disdainful look on his face. Anamaya felt a gust of self-defense rise within her, but Katari stepped in before her, and said:

"It's not what you think, Manco."

The young Inca wavered for a moment. He trusted Katari absolutely, but he was caught between conflicting emotions.

"The *Coya Camaquen* has always been the Empire's most loyal servant," said Villa Oma, in his usual abrupt manner. But Anamaya sensed that his words carried weight. Manco touched her furtively on the shoulder.

"I need you, Anamaya. The Empire of the Four Cardinal Directions needs you."

His voice was so shy that Anamaya found it touching. She saw in him the echo of the adolescent frozen in fear before the snake for whom she had cleared the way.

"Everything is ready for the *capa cocha*," said the Sage, green coca juice dribbling from his lips.

Anamaya froze, stared at him.

"But it's impossible!" she exclaimed, turning to Manco, who didn't react.

"Impossible?" chortled the Sage. "The children of the highest families are arriving as we speak from every corner of the Empire. They are coming to receive the honor of being sacrificed for the glory of the Son of the Sun."

Anamaya dryly declared:

"The Strangers will never allow it."

"The Strangers!"

Now Villa Oma turned to Manco for support. But still the young Inca showed no reaction.

"Who are these Strangers," spat Villa Oma, "that they think they can interrupt our traditions that have existed since the foundation of the Inca Empire? Who are they to impose their laws, their gods, over us?"

Anamaya stared at the Sage. Her anger inexplicably gave way to an enveloping calm.

"You are wrong, Sage."

Throughout this confrontation between the young girl and the old shaman, Katari hadn't opened his mouth once, hadn't moved any more than Manco had. But at these last words, he came and stood by Anamaya, his long hair sweeping across the *Coya Camaquen*'s shoulders.

Villa Oma spat on the ground to show his contempt.

"Well, Manco?"

Anamaya had tried to speak as gently as possible, but she hadn't been able to stop her voice from breaking. A bitter memory had flashed before her mind's eye: that of the very young girl who had been saved by the condor, many moons ago, on the summit of the mountain overlooking the secret city.

Manco looked away.

"The Strangers mustn't see a thing," he said. "But . . ."

"But?"

". . . my reign cannot begin without the *capa cocha*."

Anamaya said nothing. She tried to catch his eye but he looked obstinately away. She held back from spitting out the words of disgust and great vexation that had formed in her mind.

The words *capa cocha* reverberated in her head like a terrible echo sent out into a narrow mountain gorge.

When they eventually left the temple and came out into the exquisite day, the sky a beautiful blue, the dreaded words were still echoing in her head.

*   *   *

The great hall of La Cassana was crawling with people. Local caciques, wearing colorful tunics and gold disks in their ears, were gathered in groups not far from the soldiers. Some were looking for a step up or abettors to plot with, while others were fishing for information on behalf of the Sage or Manco. Many were acting for both sides, keeping their options open, and Gabriel, passing through this crowd, was uncannily reminded of the court in Toledo, that seething mass of ambition and mediocrity. Human nature, it seemed, was universal.

"Well, my son?"

On the eve of his triumph—triumph, because Manco's coronation was Pizarro's victory—the Governor seemed to have relaxed at last. He wore neither his armor nor his chain mail, and he had slipped a crimson vest, of all things, over his usual black garb. Even his crisp white ruff suggested spring, as did the feathers in his hat, which jiggled as though still attached to the bird from which they had been plucked.

Don Francisco broke away from the group fawning around him to join Gabriel, who noticed the brothers glaring at him rancorously, as well as Soto and Pedro de Candia smiling at him amicably.

"I haven't seen much of you, these last few days."

"Don Francisco, I must speak with you."

"I believe so, yes."

It was the same friendly and paternalistic face, but Gabriel sensed a degree of menace in his voice. He privately thanked Bartholomew for having forewarned him. Pizarro took Gabriel by the arm and led him back to the group despite his reluctance.

"Gabriel wishes to speak to us," he said smugly.

"I said I wished to speak to you."

"What is there to hear? Are my brothers' ears too delicate, perhaps? Captain de Soto's too large?"

Gabriel hadn't been mistaken: his words, husked of their humor, promised a severe reprimand. Soto raised his hand in an appeasing gesture, and bowed before turning on his heels and disappearing without having said a word. Candia was about to do the same, but the giant Greek remained after Gabriel gave him a look imploring him to stay.

"Only traitors and thieves speak in such riddles," spat Gonzalo.

Gabriel reddened at the insult, and placed his hand on the hilt of his sword.

"Hold your tongue, Gonzalo. Were you not the Governor's brother, I'd have it out in an instant."

"I know who you are, bastard son. My brother Hernando told me all about you, and I warn you . . ."

Gabriel glanced sidelong at Don Francisco. The word "bastard" hadn't caused him to bat an eyelid. He even seemed to be deriving some strange pleasure from the confrontation. All conversation had ceased, and a circle had formed around them. Everybody awaited the natural outcome of the confrontation with bated breath. Gabriel noticed Sebastian giving him a friendly and slightly concerned look.

"I'll teach you a lesson, you cur. And I won't show you the mercy that I showed him."

"I know all about you, damned swine. I'll have your sword and your balls. And I'll have the gold statue you've hidden for yourself. And then I'll have your blue-eyed wench, and I'll part her legs and show her what a real *caballero* is made of."

Gabriel threw himself at Gonzalo. He landed a round swing just above his eye, and blood burst from the split.

"Enough!" barked Pizarro, but to little avail. Gonzalo was as eager to fight as Gabriel, and it took two or three men and his brother Juan to tackle him. There was no longer anything benevolent left in Pizarro's black eyes as he turned toward Gabriel.

Gabriel was breathing heavily, like a smith's bellows. He glared back at his master the Governor.

"Gabriel," he growled, "when in God's name will you cease your childish capers? You have all the ingredients of happiness within your grasp: my friendship, my trust, and the respect of all those who have seen you in battle. Why do you insist on forfeiting it all? Why continue with these petty squabbles with a man whom I do not rate, never mind that he's my brother? Do you see me, the Governor, seeking to quarrel with him over any of his idiocies?"

Gabriel brusquely freed himself, and eyed Gonzalo, who was trying to stem the not inconsiderable flow of blood from his brow.

"You are, of course, in the right of it, Governor. Such idle prattle has no end. Follow me, then, those of you who crave so much to know where I've hidden my treasure."

As he walked, the rest made to follow him. Gabriel stopped short, turned around, and pointed at the Governor's brothers. "Not you. Don Francisco, Candia, and Sebastian only. Not one more." And with that he turned on his heels. Pizarro pretended not to be surprised. He ignored his brothers' furious protestations, and winking at Candia, he fell into pace at Gabriel's side.

Day was fading.

Gabriel and Pizarro hadn't said a word to one another since they had started out on the road to Colcampata. They entered the passage alone.

Sebastian and Pedro de Candia waited silently out on the esplanade.

"Well?" said the Greek.

Sebastian said nothing at first. Then:

"I hope so."

The Greek spat out the end of the wick he had been chewing on.

When Pizarro and Gabriel returned at last from the passage, the two giants—one white, the other black—looked at them expectantly. Candia was the first to surrender to his anxious curiosity.

"Well, Gabriel?"

Gabriel pointed at Pizarro.

"There's nothing there," said the Governor, "nothing but endless, infernal steps leading down a narrow passage, plus a few rats and snakes."

"The statue?"

"There is no statue."

The two friends withheld the sigh of relief that had simultaneously risen in their lungs.

"Leave us now," said Pizarro.

Candia and Sebastian walked away. The silence between the Governor and his protégé had yet to be broken. Gabriel gazed away at the distant mountains, golden in the setting sun.

"I don't blame you for seeing her despite my express orders not to do so," Pizarro said kindly.

Gabriel turned to face him, but didn't reply.

"And I don't hold it against you for having perhaps lied to me about that statue. I punish thieves when I catch them, but I know very well that if I rid my army of all its thieves and liars, then I would be on my own."

He uttered his characteristic dry laugh.

"And perhaps I would have to get rid of myself."

A smile flashed across Gabriel's face.

"In the end, I blame you for nothing. But I am a little grieved. You know that I love no one in this army. That is to say, I love them when I see them banded together, when I address them, when I see them in battle, when I hear their voices united in prayer. But as for them individually, well . . ."

He whistled disdainfully.

"They're thieves and liars, hypocrites, drunkards, criminals, almost to the man, and my own brothers first and foremost. Do you imagine that I'm unaware of this?"

Gabriel shook his head.

"But you," continued Pizarro, with a certain amount of emotion, "you I recognized, I chose you myself. I adopted you."

Gabriel was startled by that word "adopted," although he still said nothing. But he felt the hostility knotted in his gut begin to unravel.

"And that you should lie to me, that you should hide something from me, it makes me . . ."

He waved his pale, thin hands in the air, as though trying to show the shape of the word he couldn't find.

"Look, Don Francisco!"

Pizarro looked in the direction Gabriel was pointing to.

"And over here! And there!"

Gabriel's arm moved about like a confused compass needle. The two men saw, through the dusk, entire columns of men coming from every direction at once, all slowly converging on Cuzco, and appearing from afar like an immense human compass card spread out across the entire area of the valley and its mountains.

"What's going on?" asked the Governor, stupefied.

"An army? I've never seen an army advance in such a manner."

"It's no army, unless it's one that includes dogs, llamas, women, and children."

"Then what is it?"

Gabriel stood shoulder to shoulder with Pizarro.

"It's something astonishing, Don Francisco."

The two men fell silent once more, before Pizarro said in a low voice:

"You have found the right word for it, my boy. And that you should hide something from me, that too is something astonishing."

TWENTY-FIVE

Cuzco, December 25, 1533

The deep bellow of trumpets filled the entire valley. No one could tell if the sound was produced by horns answering one another from opposing slopes, or if it was the result of a natural echo. With each sustained note Anamaya, rolling gently with the movement of her porters, felt the joyful and grave anticipation of the forthcoming celebration grow within her.

At their departure from Coricancha, Villa Oma had been visibly delighted when Manco had ordered him to take the place of honor immediately behind him and right beside the palanquin bearing the mummified body of Huayna Capac.

That morning, Anamaya had suggested to Manco that the presence of both his father and of the great Sage Villa Oma, Atahualpa's most faithful servant, would show that the coronation of the thirteenth Inca was not a celebration of one clan over another.

And now, in her palanquin, Anamaya was bemused by the memory of the way Villa Oma's face had lit up when she had proposed this idea. For the space of a wing beat, the Sage's face had almost given way to rage: how dare she, once again, speak as though she were the authority running the Empire. But then he had realized what her words meant, and his eyes had looked into hers with an irritated respect. "The *Coya Camaquen* is right," he had admitted, conceding once again—once too many times—that although he was, in name, the second most powerful man in the Empire, this strange young woman held far greater sway over the Emperor's decision making than he.

Anamaya also ensured that the spot next to her in the procession would remain empty. The Sacred Double should have been there, but, faced with the Strangers' avidity, their lack of scruples, the tradition would have to be broken. They were capable, as soon as the procession was finished, of getting hold of the Sacred Brother and sending it to the smelting pot in the Governor's palace.

Anamaya's heart constricted at the mere thought of this and, more than ever, she found serenity in the acceptance of her destiny.

During the slow climb from Coricancha to the Aucaypata, the crowd thickened, and the pace of the procession slowed significantly. Anamaya heard singing but, above all, she heard the crowd's increasingly loud clamoring as they laid eyes on the Inca. But which one, Manco or his father? Anamaya felt a certain pride—a guileless pride, devoid of vanity—that for the first time in many moons the energy of almost all the Indian tribes was united by a common purpose.

The war that Quizquiz and Guaypar persisted in fighting in the North of the Empire seemed to belong to another time, another world, one that gradually grew smaller and smaller. Oddly, she often saw Guaypar's face in her dreams, and in them he was always staring at her with his severe and impassive face, with an air of threat and of defiance, and with that fury that burned eternally in his eyes. But with time his features grew increasingly indistinct, sometimes disappearing entirely, just as water erases any signs drawn in sand.

Anamaya felt the rhythmic caress of the drums pass through her body, and she watched as the cadence rolled through the crowd like a wave passing over the entire valley.

Then her face clouded over, and she had to close her eyes to support the distress now echoing through her mind.

Gabriel.

She no longer found anything beautiful or serene in the rich, colorful tapestries protecting her, or in the down pillows, or the seashell that was her palanquin, a shell floating on an ocean of men. All hope drained out of her, and she was left with only a feverish restlessness.

Gabriel.

She murmured his name, then repeated it, louder and louder.

And just as the procession came out onto the Aucaypata, amidst a cacophony of indistinguishable cries, chants, drums, and trumpets, she shouted out his name at the top of her lungs.

*   *   *

Gabriel hadn't taken his eyes off Bartholomew once throughout the Mass. The monk was officiating alongside Bishop Valverde. Whether he was holding open the Holy Book for Valverde, or solemnly handing him the chalice, Bartholomew's humility and discretion were so complete that one couldn't help but be impressed by his natural authority evident both in the calm precision of his actions and in the soft glow of his gray eyes.

There was an odd mood of both reverence and excitement in the great hall of La Cassana, temporarily converted into the nave of a church. Gabriel had watched some soldiers bring in two gold llamas during the preparations for Mass. A plank had been set atop them, and then a modest white sheet, and they now served as the legs of an adequate altar. But the freethinking university graduate couldn't help but ponder, grinning as he did so, the golden calf's now being idolized here at the edge of the world.

All the Spaniards were there, as were a large number of Indians, including those who had already converted to Christianity either through fear or opportunism, and those who had come out of curiosity to see from which gods the Strangers drew their strength.

The first doors and the first locks ever to be made in Cuzco had been installed at the far end of this great hall. They had been made to guard treasure, and behind them lay piles of gold and silver. Dozens of torches had been fixed to the walls, giving the hall a slight resemblance to the lighting of a Spanish cathedral. A picture of the Virgin, painted on wood, sat on the right side of the altar. It was the one that Pizarro took with him everywhere, and it was the only religious image in the place.

All the men's eyes were gleaming. They were happy to sing psalms, or at least to murmur them as best they could, for they didn't understand a word of them. And they fervently prayed that God grant them a moderate, even a great, part of the treasure that had been eluding them for so many days, the distribution of which the Governor—may God bless him—had repeatedly promised would take place "tomorrow, tomorrow." But now tomorrow was today.

Alonso told himself that he deserved more than Diego, and Cristobal, the cavalryman, felt that he should receive at least double the share allotted to Pedro, the foot soldier. And yet, despite their avarice, which lit their faces as much as the torchlight, Gabriel looked at them and understood what the Governor had meant when he had said that he admired them. Certainly they were brutal and coarse, but still they were courageous, untiring, and driven by childlike faith.

As Valverde gave the final blessing, Gabriel looked at Pizarro. The entire congregation was looking at the bishop, but Don Francisco was staring at the Virgin. Gabriel knew that he was privately praying to her once again.

Gabriel then caught Bartholomew's gray eyes looking directly at him, which made him distinctly uncomfortable, as though he had been caught committing some sin, and he was grateful to be carried along by the crowd of his companions as they streamed out of Mass.

With Pizarro at their head, they came out of the palace as a happy, disordered jumble, Spaniards with Indians, hidalgos and yanaconas, rich and poor. They made their way to the center of the square through the crowd come for Manco's coronation, a crowd a hundred times bigger than the one that had come to meet him on his arrival. Gabriel found himself a few paces behind Don Francisco and flanked by Candia and Sebastian.

The sun shone brilliantly in the pure blue sky.

Manco, in his Inca tunic, was sitting on his *tiana* awaiting the Governor as a king awaits a vassal. All the mummies had been gathered and placed on their gold pedestals. The priest Villa Oma stood nearby, his tall and hostile silhouette visible to all. Smoke rose from the braziers amid the jars of *chicha*.

Gabriel saw all of this, but his attention was distracted by the flight of a white butterfly, a butterfly that had lost its way and now fluttered above the heads of the Elders before disappearing into a volute of smoke.

Gabriel looked for Anamaya, but in vain.

"Do you remember, Your Grace?"

He didn't need to turn around to identify the speaker. And he didn't need to reply to prompt the memories to come flooding back. He could taste on his lips the bitter and delicious flavor of a bowl of cheap wine, he could see the shop sign "The Bottomless Jug" in his mind's eye, and he could see the two giants sitting at a table, dreaming of the adventure that then awaited them, and that was now a reality, indeed a reality far beyond the limits of what they had imagined back then.

He felt a powerful hand take hold of his. He tried to catch Sebastian's gaze, but the African giant was staring directly ahead at the group of Inca noblemen. All that Gabriel managed to obtain was a sly smile, and the warm, amicable grip of his old friend's hand.

Bartholomew took in the entire scene of the gathering of Inca noblemen. He saw Manco, of course, on his gold *tiana,* resting on some cushions with his feet spread out on finely woven blankets. He saw the long-faced priest sitting on a silver bench. He saw all the caciques, sitting on lower and lower levels according to rank, on tin chairs, then on wood, then on bamboo, and finally, the lowest, on straw.

He could not help but be impressed by the beauty and order of this civilization. He drank in the harmony of color and of precious metals, and the dignity and pride of the noblemen's faces.

Pizarro stood directly in front of him, dressed in his silk velvet attire, his ceremonial sword on his hip, and he appeared to Bartholomew not unlike a petty provincial official. He was cramped into clothes too small for him, and the white lace ruff around his neck did little to hide its thinness.

But there wasn't a trace of self-doubt in his voice when he addressed Manco.

"Noble Lord, we came to you as friends, guided by the One True God..."

As Felipillo translated, Bartholomew looked through the Indian faces for that of his new friend. He couldn't see him, however, and his absence caused the monk a disagreeable sensation in his stomach.

"...and you shall now hear the *requerimiento,* as our law dictates. We ask that you state that you have understood it and that you accept it, both on your own account and on behalf of your Council of Elders. After that, we shall be friends forever, and we shall undertake to protect you against all your enemies."

Manco gave a very slight nod to indicate that he had understood, and Pizarro signaled to Pedro Sancho de la Hoz.

Pedro's grating, lackluster voice was infamous amid the Spaniards. But he was the Governor's secretary, and the only one in a position to read such a significant proclamation. His voice was duller than usual on this momentous occasion, perhaps to ensure that his words weren't heard, or that the Indians fled before the end of the reading.

The words themselves were like heavy, majestic boulders, but the voice reading them rendered them more like pathetic pebbles.

"On behalf of the Emperor and King Don Carlos, and of Doña Juana, his mother, Sovereign of Castile, of León, of Aragon, of the two Sicilies, of Jerusalem, of Navarre, of Granada, of Toledo, of Valencia, of Galicia, of Majorca . . ."

Pedro tried, in vain, to inflate his voice with each enunciation, to accord every province and every country an equal solemnity.

". . . Count of Roussillon and of Cerdagne, Marquis of Oristan and Gothie, Archduke of Austria, Duke of Bourgogne and of Brabant, and Count of Flanders and of the Tyrol. To the Rightful Sovereign of the Barbarian Peoples of Peru, and to your Subjects, we profess to you and testify to our utmost ability that the One True and Eternal God created Heaven and Earth."

Pedro's voice had even less solemnity than Felipillo's disagreeable squawk.

Bartholomew had great trouble suppressing an almost irresistible urge to laugh.

"Because of the great multitudes of generations that have proliferated in the five thousand years since the world was created, it has been made necessary that some men go one way and others the other and that they divide themselves into a great many separate Kingdoms and Dominions. Our Lord God chose one man amidst all of these to be Sovereign over all of the men of the world, a man called Saint Peter . . ."

When Bartholomew at last found Katari, he remarked that the Indian had been watching him closely for some time now, wearing a smile on his lips. It was not a mocking smile, but rather a questioning one, as though he was saying, "You'll explain the meaning of these strange words to me, won't you."

". . . As a consequence of this, we beseech you and call upon you to understand clearly what we have just told you . . ."

Thus continued the interminable *requerimiento*, and words like "Catholic Faith," and "malicious prevarications," and "Their Majesties," and the promise of God's blessing echoed against the walls of the palaces and mingled with the water flowing from the fountain.

Bartholomew broke eye contact with Katari a number of times, as though embarrassed. But whenever he looked back again, the Indian was still staring at him, his eyes friendly but full of questions.

"... *But if you refuse to do so, we testify to you that we will use all our power to make war with you, with God's help. We will place you under the yoke, and extract your obedience to the Church and to Their Majesties. We will make slaves of you, your wives, and your sons. We will sell them as slaves. We will take your goods and chattel and we will bring upon you as much harm as is right to bring upon disobedient vassals who deny and resist their Lord. We strongly declare to you that the death and damage that would result would be your fault and not Their Majesties', nor ours, nor that of the knights accompanying us here.*"

Bartholomew watched Katari's face cloud over and his entire expression change as the translation continued, and the Indian now bore a look of extreme incredulity. When the monk tried to give him some signal indicating his friendship, some sign to mitigate the extreme violence of the words being spoken, he could no longer catch his friend's eye.

Pizarro approached Manco and bent toward him as though to kiss him, but the Inca didn't budge from his bench.

Trumpets sounded as the standard bearer stretched the royal banner.

Only then did Manco rise.

"She's not here."

Gabriel had felt at a loss throughout the ceremony on the great square, a stranger to his own people, and a stranger amid the Indians' inscrutable faces. All he could hear was the horrid buzzing sound of the *requerimiento*.

She wasn't there, and that was the only fact he could think about, the only thing he could feel, see, or hear.

Their last embrace lingered on his body like a burn that wouldn't fade, a wound that wouldn't heal, a desire that made him regret not having been even more violent, more violent than she had asked him to be, more violent than his fear had allowed. Violent? He wondered at himself, and pulled himself up. Not more violent, but more gentle, infinitely gentle, caressing her entire body while whispering those little words that had no meaning in themselves yet were the very currency of love.

Occasionally a breeze rose up and lifted the hems of the Indians' tunics, their splendid feathered costumes, and their broad fans.

Occasionally a trumpet echoed across the valley.

Occasionally a beam of light would illuminate the idol of the Sun God that had been uncovered near the Sage Villa Oma in the center of the square, just beside the fountain.

Occasionally he imagined he detected one of the mummies moving slightly, the mummies that had arrived one by one on the square, each one majestically seated on a gold throne, surrounded by the crowd and by wealth, and that represented the past reigning over the present.

But Gabriel knew only one thing for sure: that his beloved wasn't there, that his loneliness was excruciating, and that his blood boiled with rage at his lack of power. He stared at Manco with a cold hatred, privately cursing him, secretly challenging him to bloodthirsty duels. But Manco didn't look at him once, no more than he looked at Pedro Sancho de la Hoz during his proclamation, or at Felipillo as he translated it. His eyes never wavered from Pizarro.

When Manco stood and Anamaya at last appeared behind him, Gabriel's mouth opened to cry out to her, and he had to bite his lip to stop himself.

Pizarro embraced each of the Inca noblemen and a clamor of shouts and song rose from the crowd overflowing from the square into the surrounding alleys and palaces, a rumbling noise rising from the entire valley, the mountains, and perhaps even from beyond.

Perhaps it was joy, some absurd joy, some hope for something undefined, but whatever it was rose up in Gabriel as well, and his body began to tremble with joy and hope, despite the jealousy still poisoning his blood.

The entire world seemed to be celebrating, to be preparing itself for a celebration that was to last for days and days, a celebration that would blot out all fear and the memory of war.

Who was being crowned? Whose victory was this?

What did it matter?

Everyone began to dance.

But Gabriel and Anamaya alone remained still, facing one another from a distance, together yet each one alone. They could see nothing but their love.

TWENTY-SIX

Cuzco, January 1534

Each night was indistinguishable from the one preceding it. They were filled with shouting and singing, drinking and feasts. On the Aucaypata, as on all the city's other squares, in the palaces and in the most distant *canchas*, the jars of *chicha* were repeatedly emptied and refilled, and the braziers burned endlessly, feeding both the living and the dead. And after watching the mummies come out of the temples and palaces and take their places on their golden thrones, surrounded and served by people, one ended up actually hearing the murmur of their voices, the echo of their ancient power.

Even Gabriel heard them.

The mummies spoke of the Empire's legends, of fierce battles, of gods revealing themselves, of vanquished enemies. They spoke of the Sun God and of the Lightning God, and of the solitude to be found in the mountains, where the air was thin and the condor ruled.

Gabriel hadn't seen Anamaya again since the day of the coronation, and he trailed about the endless festivities intensely frustrated and bilious.

At La Cassana, the councils between the Governor, his brothers, Soto, and Almagro polluted the air night and day. But it mattered little, because Gabriel was no longer welcome to join them. Don Francisco himself had gone out of his way to avoid him ever since the affair of the missing statue. And so Gabriel's "treason" made of him a grateful pariah. He had no desire whatsoever to participate in these ridiculous festivities. Still, he had to find something to do with his days, lest the depression caused by Anamaya's absence engulf him. So he wandered about the strange city, smiling only at children and old women, and was a stranger even to his friends.

"Gabriel!"

The hail startled him, and he reached instinctively for his sword.

"Hola!"

"Whoa, my friend, I know that you're well versed in the art of fencing because I taught you all you know, and I don't want to be at the wrong end of your blade."

The two threatening silhouettes emerged into the friendly forms of his colossal companions Pedro and Sebastian.

"Forgive me, my friends, I was looking . . ."

". . . to avoid us, by the Virgin! As you have been doing these past days."

The Greek grinned amicably as he said this, but his smile and goodwill did little to relieve Gabriel of his dejection.

"We've been looking for a remedy for your languor," said Sebastian, "and we think we might have found something."

Gabriel couldn't help but be curious, despite his ill humor.

"And what might this powerful antidote be, I wonder? Condor sperm? Llama shit?"

"Better! Come, stop your grumbling and follow us."

Gabriel hesitated for a moment, then followed them.

The long shadows of afternoon loomed over the *cancha*, and Gabriel could hear women's voices rising from it like birdsong.

He shrank back from the building, but both his friends urged him on, and he allowed himself to be led.

They entered a cheerful room. Like all Inca interiors, it had no furniture to speak of, but it was rich with tapestries, bed mats, wool blankets, and resplendent feathers. Three young girls stopped their talk as the Strangers entered, but their beaming smiles showed that they were already well acquainted with Gabriel's two companions, and that they were evidently looking forward to becoming so with him.

Colorful tunics covered the alluring shapes of their bodies. Their legs were bare below the knee and Gabriel could see the honeyed color of their flesh that so pleased the Spaniards.

"We have been campaigning," began Sebastian with feigned solemnity, "against the barbarity that drives the ignoble among us to force themselves on young ladies. Once we had learned that the *requerimiento* had been accepted by the Inca and his council, we took it upon ourselves to teach the true chivalry of the *caballero* to the local population."

Gabriel couldn't help but smile. The girls' zeal to please made it clear that his companions' lessons had borne precocious fruit. He felt soft hands touch his shoulder, urging him to sit with his friends on a pile of mats covered in blankets, a pile that promised a delicious indolence.

"I don't . . ." he began, rather weakly.

"You don't say a word, and you follow our lead," said Pedro.

And in fact, Gabriel found it pleasurable to do so. Why exhaust oneself struggling in vain against ill fortune? The young girls busied themselves around him in some graceful ballet, bringing him drink in gold goblets and murmuring to him, in their language, that they found the Strangers handsome and strong. They giggled as they looked at one another, like all young girls in the world do, and they spoke with an astonishing liberty.

"I don't care to be impious," said Candia, crossing himself, "and may the Reverend Valverde forgive me, but I find that paganism has a lot to offer."

"My friend, I've known that since birth," replied Sebastian.

"Yes, but what with having spent years among us, in Don Diego de Almagro's service, and with having been baptized, and having been awarded your sword, well, all that's enough to change a man. But look at these girls. The merest misreading of the Holy Book would corrupt them, and they would resist us."

"Yes. And I would add that they seem to have read some other types of books, in which it is written that it was their destiny to become better acquainted with us."

Gabriel grinned as he listened to their banter. Fatigue, disappointment, and a slight inebriety took their toll on him, and were gradually leading him into a world where letting oneself go in the arms of an agreeable young woman was the only philosophy, the only thing of any value.

The women's deft hands had already undone his friends' jerkins and shirts, and they now sat there bare-chested. He caught a glimpse of Sebastian's powerful torso, and also of Pedro de Candia's, slighter but still impressive. Then he caught a pair of dark eyes staring at him, two young, innocent, and questioning eyes promising him pleasure.

"You're very pretty," he said in Quechua.

The young woman showed no surprise when he spoke her language to her. Her gaze became even more intense, more velvety, and her slightly parted lips revealed two rows of delicately chiseled white teeth, teeth that could nibble as much as they could bite. She squatted down beside him on the mat, close enough to touch him, to kiss him, but she didn't go so far as to touch him. He breathed in her scent of trees and flowers, and he closed his eyes to better savor this perfume, allowing it to flood over him.

He heard a piece of wood crackle in the fire, a muffled laugh, and now there was only the silence of pleasure, a silence loaded with harmony and abandon. The young girl put her hand on his forehead, ran her fingers down his nose, rested them for a moment on the crack in its middle, a relic from a fistfight long ago, then lingered on his lips. He remained still, his eyes closed, and despite the desire rising up inside him, he didn't kiss her fingertips. His breath grew shorter, and he felt his entire body swell when she undid his shirt and placed her hands on his burning flesh. *By God, how I want her,* he said to himself.

But a troubling thought slipped in amid all these sensations, amid his instinctive urge to abandon himself to those fingers. He tried to shoo away the thought as though it were a fly, but it had irreversibly taken root in his mind. *Anamaya, Anamaya, you run away from me yet you seek me out, you elude me now, but you won't forever.* The girl slipped his shirt off his shoulders, and Gabriel felt his manhood harden with desire. He opened his eyes.

He looked around the room, and saw his two friends lost in a sea of caresses. And now he saw the young girl looking at him, her eyes half-shut, as though looking at him through louvers. She let him take her wrists in his hands, ending her caresses. Still she showed no surprise, only willingness to give him anything he wanted. Her ease and power made him smile.

He lifted her up from the mat and stood her before him. He ran his hands through her hair and she purred like a cat and closed her eyes. He stood up, put his shirt back on, and allowed her to lean against him.

He was in the balance.

He was dancing to a silent tune that led him gently from the urgency of desire to tenderness, and he didn't rush her any more than she had rushed him. "I want you," he murmured, as much to himself as to her, "but I want to wait for her more than I want you. How much suffering there is in waiting. But thanks to you I now know that there is nothing more tender than that wait."

Her body slowly relaxed, and she smiled at him when he separated himself.

"You're very pretty," he repeated, "but . . ."

He blew her a kiss and left the room, crossed the *cancha*'s courtyard, and came out onto the street. He inhaled in great gulps the clear air of the Andes.

A moment later, he was hit by the first punch.

For a moment, his body clung to the warmth of the room he had just left, to its caresses, to the intense desire he had felt there, and to the wonderful lightness that had entered his spirit. But the rain of punches eventually shattered this image, and he felt a rage rise up inside of him as he stood there helplessly being beaten.

There were four of them—the two who had grabbed him from behind and who were now holding him despite his furious efforts to break free, and the two who were punching and kicking him methodically.

None of them said a word, and he could hear only their exhalations and grunts and another odd sound that he couldn't identify for a moment, until he realized that it was his own furious cry, a cry that carried in it all his rage at his own weakness, and at his own futile efforts to escape or dodge the beating he was receiving.

Night veiled his assailants' faces, and in any case they had gone to the trouble to wear bandanas across them. He could see only their black eyes flash before him.

Then a red fog passed before his eyes, and he felt increasingly weary. Warm blood was flowing from a head wound, bothering his vision, mixing with his tears, his sweat, and his snot. Some vital instinct in his gut urged him not to faint, to fight on. To fight on? He could manage a few ungainly movements, about as useful as those of a frog. But his resistance urged his attackers to further violence.

Shreds of thoughts passed through his mind: *If they wanted to kill me . . .* If they had wanted to kill him, he would already have been dead.

And so, resisting vainly to the last, he fainted. He had a vision of

Gonzalo's curly brown locks, of his smiling, charming face, floating above him like some fallen angel.

Had he seen this before passing out? Or else was it the first image of a nightmare?

He writhed on the ground in the middle of the alley like some drunkard.

Blood flowed from his mouth into the gutter.

TWENTY-SEVEN

Cuzco, January 1534

"My poor friend."

Pizarro looked upon him with a mixture of irony and regret, of disdain and of pity. Gabriel felt as though not a single part of his body had been spared, and he still hadn't had the courage, since he had dragged himself to La Cassana Palace, to look at himself in the mirror.

"Have you seen Juan de Balboa yet?"

"Don't concern yourself for me, Don Francisco, I need no surgeon."

"I don't know what it is that you need, my boy. Words of advice, perhaps? You would do well to heed a few."

The Governor had always ensured that his quarters were set exactly the same way no matter where he was, whether in a tent or a palace. He had a narrow bed, a table with two chairs, and a painting of his beloved Sacred Virgin. He motioned to Gabriel to sit, but the young man preferred to remain standing, broken as he was.

"Well, as you won't listen to anyone, then I shall listen to you."

"You haven't even asked how this happened to me, Don Francisco."

"Do I need to?"

An even smile flashed across the Governor's thin face.

"You have no need to ask me for one reason only: because you already know very well what happened."

"Do you accuse me?"

"Accuse you, Don Francisco? By the faith, I don't know what to call what I blame you for."

"Tell me anyway. That way you won't have to give it a name."

"Your brothers, Don Francisco, your brothers," said Gabriel, growing pale merely mentioning them, "your fucking brothers, their souls to hell."

"What about my brothers?" asked Pizarro quietly, pretending not to notice Gabriel's rage.

"Not content with being thieves and of having less dignity than swine, Don Francisco, not satisfied with heaping dishonor on your name by their cowardice, their greed, their hypocrisy . . ."

Gabriel began choking on his litany of evils, and Pizarro raised his black-gloved hand to interrupt him.

"Enough, young man. Not another word."

The two men defied one another with their eyes. Gabriel was trembling.

"I am happy to forgive you," said Pizarro slowly. "They were very severe on you, and it is your humiliation that speaks now . . ."

"It's my humiliation that drives me to tell you a truth that is on everybody's lips, and that everybody hides from you."

Pizarro burst out laughing.

"Do you imagine that I am unaware of what they are? Do you think that I am blind to the reason why they are with me here, and to what they are after? Do you think that I arrived in Cuzco blinded by blood ties?"

"I haven't known what to think for a long time, Don Francisco," said Gabriel with uncharacteristic bitterness.

"That's right, young man. You no longer know where you are, you have forgotten yourself ever since you laid eyes on that blue-eyed priestess, ever since you carried out I know not what subterfuge with that golden statue. Your sense has given way to your sentiments, and now you insult my brothers."

Gabriel said nothing for a moment, absorbing the shock. Pizarro had broached a subject that Gabriel knew was less than clear. But he also knew from experience that it was at such moments that calm and lucidity returned to him, as they often did during the chaotic height of battle.

"You're right, Don Francisco. But despite that, and even in my confusion, you are still the one at fault."

"Oh? Explain to me how."

"You believe that your brothers are a necessary evil, one that has limits, and that you can control them just as you do Don Diego de Almagro and all the men who follow you. You are superior to these men. You have more stamina, more courage, and you see further than others. You are not blinded by gold as they are. You think things through, and your hand is steady. You are a captain whereas they are dogs. But what you don't see is that these men—your brothers and Don Diego—are ready to turn against you the minute you show the slightest sign of weakness."

"My own brothers?"

"Yes. Oh, they won't fight you directly. But they will do you so much harm that the blows I received from them will be like a woman's caress in comparison."

For once, Pizarro looked slightly astonished. His face wore a perplexed expression that was most unusual for him. The two men stared at one another in the ensuing silence. The sum of their long and strange acquaintance passed between them, as well as their mutual love, one that persisted despite their own wills.

Don Francisco opened his arms.

"You still love me, then."

"Without a doubt, Governor."

"Without a doubt . . . those are truly the words of a schoolboy. Bah, it's not important. I shall help you, my boy."

"Help me?"

"Yes. I might even save your skin."

Gabriel listened to the Governor without interrupting. And as the Governor talked, Gabriel felt himself defeated, more defeated than he had been in the alley.

When he finally staggered out of La Cassana Palace, the light blinded him, and he groped his way along toward the fountain.

It began to rain. He was alone.

The day passed.

He didn't move.

The wet, the cold, and then the heat returned to him, as did all his shifting pains, but nothing affected him as much as the Governor's words still echoing in his head.

Dusk was falling.

His fellow conquistadors passed by and looked upon him with pity or with mocking. He ignored their taunts. He kept his eyes fixed obstinately on the mountains. He watched the shadow of the fortress as it grew longer with the setting sun.

He slipped into the cool of the night.

A torch approached him and lit his face. He raised his hand to protect his eyes from its glare.

"Who wishes me well now?" he sniggered sarcastically.

"Me."

"You too want to save me, then, like him?"

Bartholomew said nothing. He took Gabriel gently by the arm and
pulled him up. Gabriel didn't resist. He had done nothing but resist
since the previous day. He had resisted the girl's dark eyes, he had
resisted against the blows, against the Governor's words. He'd had
enough of fighting against the whole world.

They walked slowly through La Cassana Palace, and Bartholomew
led him to his room.

The pale yellow reflection of a candle flickered across their faces.
Gabriel lay down with infinite care, and stopped himself from groaning
in pain. Bartholomew sat down beside him on the bed and placed his
two joined fingers on his chest. Gabriel didn't resist. Bartholomew didn't
speak until Gabriel's breathing had grown more regular. Then he asked:

"Well?"

Gabriel was suddenly overwhelmed by sorrow. He wanted to speak,
but no words came out of his mouth, and all his impotence, all his loneliness and rage, rose up and choked his heart. He broke down sobbing.

Bartholomew said nothing, letting the tears flow. His curious gray
eyes shone consolingly at Gabriel.

"I'm not much of a warrior," sobbed Gabriel eventually.

"Who told you that warriors don't shed tears?"

"You speak well, my brother."

Bartholomew only smiled.

"He told me that I had to go with him. He told me that he would
soon leave Cuzco to found the capital of the kingdom and that he
needed me with him. He said that if I stayed in Cuzco I would be killed
and that, dead, I would be of no use to anyone. He said that if I stayed
in Cuzco she would die because his brothers would stop at nothing to
satisfy their hatred. He ordered me to go with him. He said that we
would return one day."

"What are you going to do?"

"I'm going to obey him, of course. Because he's right, because what
he said was loathsome but true. He knows that I'm not frightened by his

damned brothers. But he also knows that I fear more for her life than for my own."

"What can I do for you?"

Gabriel looked at Bartholomew, astonished.

"For me? Nothing. What would you want to do for me?"

"Anything you ask."

"Is that all? Brother, the Lord reveals to you his greatest mysteries."

"It goes without saying."

Bartholomew grinned. Gabriel dreamed out loud:

"What I want . . . what I pray for . . ."

"I'll do my best," said Bartholomew.

Gabriel stared at him in surprise.

"How . . ."

"Isn't that what you want? I'll do my best, believe me."

The monk rose and left the room, taking the candle with him, before Gabriel had a chance to say another word.

TWENTY-EIGHT

Kenko, January 1534

Gabriel had no idea how long he had been following the dwarf.

Sometimes he felt as though he was sleepwalking, and he couldn't tell whether he was walking or whether the path was sliding backward under him, like some giant ribbon, and he was actually remaining in the same place, held there by some invisible hand.

For a while he considered a few possibilities of where he might be. The fortress at Colcampata? But soon there were no more houses to be seen, they encountered fewer walls, and they had left the towers of Sacsayhuaman behind them. He had taken note that they had set out to the northeast, but now that knowledge helped him little. He advanced with his hands stretched out before him, and he had the odd notion that he was swimming among the stars. It was a grand, infinite night, one that swallowed up the earth.

His injuries bothered him less now, although he still felt somewhat numb. What a strange thing is man, he thought philosophically as he limped along. A man might be overcome by despair in the morning, and then lighthearted, almost carefree as soon as night, with all its promises, had fallen.

Even the fact that he would be leaving tomorrow, perhaps later, no longer seemed so cruel. Truth was hidden somewhere in this night sky, not in the Governor's words.

He didn't know where he was but he had the impression of having left Cuzco below for a higher world. The air was thinner here, there were no trees, and the stony scree surrounded him in the liquid night. He was a traveler through time and space, and he felt as though he could feel the presence of the gods.

The dwarf had remained dumb throughout their journey. Perhaps he was the first citizen of this higher world in which Gabriel was now arriving.

When the dwarf suddenly veered away from the path, Gabriel didn't hesitate to follow him toward a rocky outcrop, the breadth of which he didn't see until the very last moment. It was, in fact, a large, natural amphitheater with niches carved into a surrounding wall, niches not unlike those he had seen in the city's temples and palaces. When he had turned around again, the dwarf had disappeared.

He walked to the center of the amphitheater and stopped before a boulder there. He didn't know what it was meant to represent, but he could feel its power.

"The hand of man worked on this stone. But a god was born of it."

"I thought I would never see you again," said Gabriel. He was answered with a giggle.

"And you still don't see me. Follow me."

And in fact, no matter where he looked, Gabriel saw only a fleeting shadow. He followed it down a gentle slope to a cave carved out of the cliff face.

"Anamaya . . ."

He hesitated at the top of the broad stone steps leading into the cave.

He walked down a few steps, then stopped, surrounded by a blackness blacker than the night outside. His hands searched for a wall, for something solid, but they met with only the cool, moist air rising from the ground. He smelled the odor of herbs burning, a sickly sweet odor that both lured and repelled him.

He took a few more steps, tripped, and fell heavily to the ground. His cry echoed throughout the cave.

"Anamaya!"

But he had no reply other than his own dull voice echoing back at him.

"ANAMAYA!"

"Come . . ."

Her whisper came from close by, and as she guided him to her, his fear evaporated. He made his way to her step by step, until he could see her eyes smiling in the night. She took his wrists and put his hands on a stone table, a sort of altar.

"I told you that I would be here."

"It was so long ago."

"I told you to trust me."

Anamaya's hands passed over his own, then moved up his arms, over his shoulders, around his neck—he was bruised and injured everywhere, yet she didn't hurt him at all. Still, he stiffened somewhat.

"Don't be frightened."

He closed his eyes and let her explore his body with her hands, soothing him like a flowing brook or gentle breeze. He felt a splendid warmth spread through him, and he let himself slip into it. His breathing slowed, his body relaxed.

"Your gray-eyed friend found Katari and told him that you needed me."

"Bartholomew?"

"I don't know his name. Katari and he often meet and exchange knowledge with one another."

Gabriel sighed in frustration and said:

"I've been ordered to leave, Anamaya."

"I know."

Gabriel was astonished by how calm Anamaya's voice was. He looked into her eyes as she said:

"You are in too great a danger here. You must leave. . . ."

"Manco?"

"I told you that Manco would do you no harm. I'm talking about your own people."

"Are there other dangers of which I'm unaware?"

"There are always dangers of which one is unaware," said Anamaya, smiling. "He who believes otherwise is a fool."

"Or else very wise."

He could see her smile.

"Or else very wise, yes. But be that as it may, you must leave Cuzco."

Gabriel listened to the silence surrounding them, and inhaled the strange odor in the air.

"Where are we?"

"In a *huaca,* one of our sacred places. There are hundreds around Cuzco, arranged in a circle with the capital at its hub. Some hold treasures that your people will steal soon enough. Others are so secret that you will never find them."

"Do sacrifices take place here?"

He noticed Anamaya hesitate before replying:

"Sometimes, yes."

And suddenly Gabriel realized what the smell was. It was the smell of burned flesh, of boiled blood. An icy shiver ran down his spine.

Anamaya noticed his discomfort and led him away.

"Come, let's leave."

The fresh air outside relieved him somewhat and, after the darkness of the cave, so did the starlight. They climbed a stone staircase to the summit of the *huaca*.

"Difficult times are upon us," she announced.

"And must I disappear during these difficult times?"

"The peace we are living is a lie. It is riddled with lies and deceits."

"Are you talking about Manco? About your people?"

"I'm talking about all of us, Gabriel."

"Is that why I have to disappear? Answer me."

He spoke with almost unwilling stiffness. Anamaya was clearly a little taken aback and answered:

"Of course not. You must go because you must live."

Gabriel immediately calmed down. Still, even the undeniable love of her words didn't relieve him of the black torment at the bottom of his soul.

An odd canal carved into the rock zigzagged across the top of the hill. Figures were also carved into the rock, and two blocks, not unlike mooring posts, rose up in the middle of nowhere.

Gabriel gave Anamaya a questioning look. She said nothing, only smiling and hugging him closer.

They lay down on a rock.

Gabriel could no longer feel his injuries.

"Tell me why . . ." he began.

"Look at the sky," she interrupted. "Look at the stars, and stop asking why."

He dreamed with her.

He forgot all about what he didn't know, all his questions and doubts. He bounded like a puma, flew like a condor, he crossed the sky like a bolt of lightning, all the while holding her hand. Not a word was spoken between them.

She cuddled herself against him.

She let him see her own weakness, her own sadness, and he was moved by her trust in him. Together, and still without a word, they shared the simple, human sadness of their impending separation. When she eventually detached herself from him, she looked at him for a long, long while, and he saw everything he wanted in her eyes: he saw their entire story, he saw all he knew about it, all he sensed unconsciously, and all that she kept hidden at the bottom of her heart.

"Look," she said.

The moonlight outlined a shape between the two monolithic rocks, and the rocks themselves had become two pale eyes shining in the night. The shape was that of a cat, peaceful yet menacing.

The puma.

He asked no more questions.

By the first light of dawn, she was long gone.

The puma's eyes were once again two round rocks atop a boulder.

Gabriel didn't return to the cave.

He headed back down the road to Cuzco, knowing in his heart that the road ahead of him would be much longer than the one he had traveled so far.

PART FOUR

TWENTY-NINE

Cuzco, July 1535

The Governor's brothers reached Emperor Manco's palace so early on that day in July that the sacred cornfields facing the Colcampata were still covered in early-morning fog.

Gonzalo had stuck some splendid blue and yellow feathers into his hatband. As for Juan, he had wound an odd-looking swath of white silk about his own. They were laughing loudly together, and their laughter reverberated between the high walls of the alley, rising above the clumping of their boots and those of the dozen or so henchmen armed with pikes and crossbows following them.

A group of Indian warriors, commanded by a lieutenant whose helmet had been denuded of its gold ensign, made a show of defending the entrance to the royal *cancha*. Gonzalo Pizarro shoved the lieutenant aside. Juan feigned indignation, grabbed his brother by the collar, and said:

"Please, Gonzalo. We come here as friends."

Gonzalo burst out laughing, and his companions followed suit. After this outburst, they readjusted their somewhat worn doublets as the Inca soldiers stared at them, their eyes burning with incensed powerlessness. The Spaniards formed a double column, one neat enough to pass review in an Andalusian palace, and they marched thus through the *cancha*'s outer courtyard into the inner one. All the servants and lords they came across stopped dead in their tracks, astounded at their intrusion.

Don Gonzalo, a radiant smile lighting his perfectly proportioned face, led his men straight to the door of the *cancha*'s biggest building. The young guards guarding it crossed their spears at the Spaniards' approach. One Spaniard bounded ahead of the Governor's brothers. He didn't even need to raise his hand for the Indians, after only the slightest hesitation, to quit their façade of defense.

Gonzalo led them in. Inside, they stopped short, surprised as much as they were amused.

Emperor Manco was standing bare-chested surrounded by his wife and concubines. With his head slightly tilted, his torso bowed forward, and his eyelids lowered languidly, he was examining the range of tunics being offered to him by his women, each one as delicately woven as a feather. One of his concubines noticed the Strangers. She uttered a short, involuntary cry without raising her head. Manco stiffened. A cloud of rage passed over his face, but he immediately suppressed it.

"Greetings, Sapa Inca," opened Gonzalo, bowing.

Manco ignored his hail, turning his attention back to the *unkus*. He deliberately took his time selecting one.

"Let's let him get dressed," suggested Juan, turning away.

"But of course, brother. We're not savages, after all," sniggered Gonzalo, walking into the room.

He walked up so close to one of Manco's wives that the young woman stepped back, looking away. Gonzalo grabbed the tunic from her hands. He waved it at his henchmen, who burst out laughing when he held it up to himself, tilted his face upward, and batted his eyelids like a coquettish girl.

"The King's costume becomes me, no?" he said with cold irony, eliciting a few guffaws from his men.

Manco kept his appearance of indifference, not even glancing at the Spaniards. He pointed at a midnight blue *unku* decorated with crimson geometric patterns. Two trembling women helped him into it despite the Strangers' gibes, while another held out the royal band on a folded *manta*.

A crowd drawn by the scene had gathered in the courtyard. Men and women, servants and lords, all murmured disapprovingly among themselves. In the low-risen morning sun their eyes glowed with terror at the irreverence their Emperor was being subjected to.

"Gonzalo . . ."

Juan stopped short to look at whatever it was that had caused an outcry of laughter around him. Gonzalo had ripped one of the tunics rejected by the Inca from a servant girl's hands.

He approached a concubine and offered her the *unku*, urging her to try it on. More terrified by the profanity than by the Stranger's brutality, she defended herself as best she could.

"She wants to, really," said Gonzalo. "She just needs some encouragement."

"Gonzalo . . ." said Juan, increasingly embarrassed.

The other women had gathered in the corner farthest away from Gonzalo. Manco, his face as impassive as ever, hadn't budged an inch. He seemed to be paying no attention at all to the scene, not even when the young Indian woman fell to her knees to escape Gonzalo's unwelcome advances.

Then a voice known to all cut through the air:

"Gentlemen, the Emperor never receives guests in his chamber. Please go out into the courtyard, where he shall grant you an audience."

The Spaniards, startled, moved aside. Anamaya stood at the threshold, her blue eyes burning with rage. Gonzalo shuddered, then laughed when he caught his brother Juan looking reverently at her.

"To tell the truth, fair lady," he said, "you are well arrived: it is you whom we are after."

Anamaya stared at the two brothers. She gave no sign of the hate, anger, and fear raging inside her. She stood tall and proud, and even Gonzalo had to turn his eyes away, unable to sustain her gaze.

"You lied to us," growled Gonzalo. "You promised us gold. Where is it?"

He waved his arms as he paced about in the sun. Manco remained seated calmly on his *tiana,* not saying a word. Anamaya was standing a little behind him, looking tense and staring at the Spaniards. The Elders, who had rushed to the royal *cancha,* were gathered on the other side of the courtyard, and were keeping a safe distance between themselves and the threatening line of Strangers.

"Three months have passed, Sapa Inca," continued Gonzalo, pointing at Manco, "since the day you promised us more gold. You pledged yourself a friend to our King, who is also yours, and you did so to prove to us that the rumors of an uprising against us were groundless. Time has fled since then, yet all we have received is a few plates and some baubles you stole from your servants."

He stopped, and silence filled the courtyard.

A flight of tweeting birds passed overhead. Their shadows crossed from the Spaniards to the Indian lords as quickly as arrows. Juan Pizarro was persistently trying to catch Anamaya's gaze. But she gave him no more attention than she did any of the others. Finally, Manco smiled wanly and pointed at the palace courtyard, the buildings' walls, and the threshold of his room.

"Do you see any gold here, my friend?" he asked in a disturbingly calm tone. "Winter has visited us twice since you arrived in the Puma's city. Cast your mind back to that day: Wasn't there gold here then? Gold on the walls, gold in every room of my *cancha,* gold in my gardens, gold in the palaces of the noblemen of my court? Didn't my wives and concubines wear gold in their hair then? You amused yourself with one of them a few moments ago. Let me ask you: Was she wearing any gold? Turn around, brother of my friend the Governor. Look at the noblemen in my court. Look at their ears. Do you see any gold ear plugs in them? No. Only wood. Look at their chests and arms. Are they not as bare as those of peasants? They have already given you all the gold they have. Where could I possibly get more gold when you have it all already? Where would I hide it, now that you are masters of this country?"

Gonzalo grinned at him malevolently.

"You're lying to me," he said, emphasizing each word and pointing at him. "I know that there's more gold in this country. A lot more gold."

"Have you seen any, foreign friend? Tell me where so that I may send for it."

Gonzalo hissed maliciously, then padded up to Manco as softly as a cat. He looked as though he was about to spit in his face, but instead he turned his gaze upon Anamaya.

"You know very well what gold we're talking about. Where's the big gold statue that my brother the Governor demanded? He has run out of patience, as have I. You've been telling us tales for months. I want that statue in my house no later than three days from now."

Silence followed. Juan stepped forward.

"That is impossible," said Anamaya in a clear voice.

"Ah? And why is that, milady?" asked Gonzalo in a chillingly courteous tone.

"Because that statue is no longer in this world. It lives now with the Noble Ancestors in the land of the setting sun."

Gonzalo stared at her for a moment in silence. His eyebrow was raised in astonishment, and he looked as though the meaning of her words was slowly dawning on him. He raised his hand as though to strike her, and a shocked murmur rose from the Indians. But instead he set his hand on Manco's shoulder with a measured gentleness.

"Isn't my friend the Inca the Son of the Sun?" he said. "Isn't he sovereign over the dead as he is over the living?"

"You are forbidden to touch the Emperor," said Anamaya dryly.

"Come now, my friend, the Inca will surely not spurn this gesture of intimacy, so natural between friends. With us, you see, amicability is expressed naturally, with smiles and hugs. And with gifts."

Still smiling, Gonzalo let go of Manco as brusquely as he had grabbed him. The Inca tried to recover his dignity as Gonzalo turned to one of his soldiers. He motioned to him to approach. The man was carrying a large leather saddlebag over his shoulder. He opened it and drew a large-linked chain from it, together with irons and a steel padlock. Gonzalo dropped the irons at Manco's feet.

"See, I'm not like you," he said. "I've brought you a splendid gift."

Manco and Anamaya looked at the irons.

"Do you know, my friend Sapa Inca, that this is the very chain with which *your* brother Atahualpa, the late Inca, was protected from the affections of his own people by *my* brother, Governor Don Francisco Pizarro? The thought occurred to me that this device might find a place of eminence among your treasures. Am I right?"

Not a sound rose from the courtyard.

"I hope that, in return, you will present me with the gift I am seeking."

Neither Manco nor Anamaya reacted to the threat. The Elders, meanwhile, along with the palace guards, had closed in on the Spaniards. They slowly formed a defensive line around their sovereign. Juan took his brother by the wrist and smiled at the Indians with a distressed air.

"Wait a moment, brother. Don't you remember that we have another proposition for the Sapa Inca?"

He removed his hat and bowed to Manco, a belated attempt at respect.

"Sapa Inca," began Juan in a conciliatory tone, "it is true that we've been disappointed of seeing this famous statue, which we are told is without rival either in beauty or value. But people do us an injustice when they say that we prefer gold to beauty. What disappoints us, you see, is not the fact that we don't have possession of the statue, but the way your attitude reveals your mistrust of us. Some even believe that it's a sign that you're preparing to go to war with us. We don't agree with them, of course, and that is why I bring this proposition to you, a proposition which, if you accept it, will make it clear to the whole world that we are friends, and shall always be so."

Juan paused to let the weight of his words settle. His calm, conciliatory voice defused the tension. Even Manco relaxed a little. He nodded and stared with a slightly confused air at the hat Juan was waving about.

"Today, Sapa Inca, I have put a white silk ribbon in my hat. In my country, this means that I wish to take a wife."

Juan turned toward Anamaya. He stared at her intensely for a few moments, and then, sticking his chest out a little, declared:

"I have chosen you, fair lady. I was told that you are without a husband, or that your gold statue was, according to your customs, your husband, and that this forbade you any other marriage. Now you tell us that this statue is no longer in this world. This is sad news, but also good news. You are thus free to come to the church and share the benediction with me, a benediction that will bless you forever."

The blood drained from Anamaya's stunned face. Juan took a step toward her and tried to take her hand, but she instinctively held it tightly against her stomach. Meanwhile, Manco had stood up, his face had turned scarlet, and the veins in his neck had swollen with rage.

"The *Coya Camaquen* belongs to my father," he cried, "and none other shall lay a hand upon her!"

"Ha! That's a likely story!" screeched Gonzalo. He looked at Manco defiantly, then said in a muted voice:

"She's as much a virgin as a Panama whore. Everybody knows who she parts her thighs for. . . ."

Manco was now standing in front of Anamaya. He pushed Juan aside so brutally that the Spaniard stumbled and fell to his knees.

The courtyard was in turmoil for a few moments. Gonzalo bounded forward and grabbed Manco's arm, prompting the Indian guards to rush forward to protect their Emperor.

The Spanish henchmen confronted them, and the ensuing scuffle distracted everyone's attention from Anamaya. Women were fleeing from the edges of the courtyard to the outer enclosure, uttering high-pitched cries as Juan tried to get a grip on Manco.

A dark shadow suddenly emerged from nowhere, causing Juan to release Manco immediately, whereas Gonzalo froze with his hand gripped around the Inca's arm.

"Have you all turned mad?"

Anamaya recognized Bartholomew the monk, Gabriel's friend. He was as pale as a sheet. He pointed his joined fingers at Gonzalo and thundered:

"Have you lost your mind, Don Gonzalo? By what right do you brutalize the Indian lord?"

"By my own. This is outside your domain."

"Release him!"

Bartholomew's gray eyes burned with the ferocity of a wolf. But it was the strength of his self-composure that carried the most weight.

A ghost of a smile passed across Gonzalo's lips. He relaxed his vise-like grip a little. Juan took Gonzalo by the arm and led him away from the Inca, but his brother shook him off.

"This savage makes game of us," spat Gonzalo. "We came to take this woman," he said pointing at Anamaya with his chin as though she was an earthenware jug, "as a wife for my brother, then he claims that she's untouchable. Untouchable!"

Bartholomew glanced briefly at Anamaya as though he had just noticed her. He stood between her and Manco and said:

"Sapa Inca Manco is sovereign over the Indians of this nation," he said in a voice loud enough for all to hear, "Emperor Charles V has placed him under your brother the Governor's protection. Have you forgotten this?"

"Spare us the sermon, Brother Bartholomew, it's not Sunday today," clucked Gonzalo. "I'm well aware that my brother is the Governor. I'm also well aware that my brother is far from here, busy founding capitals and building empires. Meanwhile, he has placed us in charge of this city."

"And you shall answer for it to him! Just as you will for the way you have treated this man."

"It is for us to decide who is a man and who isn't," said Gonzalo furiously. "I don't think that my brother Francisco is in any position to teach us a lesson on that."

"The eyes of Spain are upon you!"

"Spain? Where's that?" scoffed Gonzalo. "But enough. Who are you to play the saint? By what authority do you sermon me thus?"

"Gonzalo, please!" burst Juan.

"I have no authority over you, Don Gonzalo," replied Bartholomew calmly.

"Just so," hissed Gonzalo, "so be gone, and go and save some souls. But spare us your lectures."

Gonzalo looked hatefully at the monk before bending over to pick up his hat, knocked off during the fight. Juan looked utterly dejected. Bartholomew smiled modestly and said:

"It is true that I have no authority over any of you, gentlemen. The ultimate judgment belongs to God. He is the God of divine mercy, the God of the humble, and the God of vengeance against the proud."

"Brother . . ." began Juan miserably.

"Shut up!" cried Gonzalo.

Gonzalo gave Bartholomew one last hateful look as he left the courtyard.

Anamaya hadn't stopped trembling throughout the entire scene.

Bartholomew leaned unassumingly against the *cancha*'s wall and watched Anamaya coming and going into the enclosure. He waited until a degree of calm had returned before going to meet her.

He said to her in his somewhat broken Quechua (of which, however, he was very proud):

"I know that it is very difficult to forgive one man for the actions of another, *Coya Camaquen*. Nevertheless, I must ask your forgiveness for the insults that you and Sapa Inca Manco have just endured. If it were in my power to banish such insolence, then it never would have happened. I loathe crudeness, and I'm ashamed of it."

Anamaya looked at him for a moment, then gave a slight wave with her hand and said:

"I know you do. And allow me to thank you for what you did."

"No, please don't thank me. I wish only that you explain to Emperor Manco that he mustn't think that we're all like the Governor's brothers."

Anamaya said nothing for a moment. She returned Bartholomew's gaze, then shook her head gently and said:

"I don't think that there are enough of your kind for Sapa Inca Manco to be at ease."

Bartholomew nodded, a thin, sad smile on his lips. He pulled an envelope from his cowl with his oddly deformed hand. He clicked his tongue as he unfolded the brownish sheets densely covered in a neat hand.

"There are at least two of us, I believe," he murmured. "Don Gabriel asked a favor of me, one that I am glad to do. His letter reached me yesterday. In truth, I came to bring it to you, not to save you from the claws of the Pizarro brothers. But it seems that God, and your Ancestors, had willed things differently."

He laughed quietly.

Indeed, he found it easy to relax in Anamaya's presence, as though her mere beauty was enough to calm and comfort him. He pointed to a patch of shade by a building in which servants, returned from their daily chores, were now preparing the soups and game that constituted Manco's dinner.

"Let us move into the shade, if you will, so that we may be at ease while I read this letter to you."

A few moments later Anamaya, her eyes aglow with a happiness that spread through her like the intoxication caused by *chicha*, found herself listening to Gabriel's voice through Bartholomew's. She listened with the utmost attention, with her eyes closed, and his words became as tangible as caresses.

"City of the Kings, June 18, 1535

"Brother Bartholomew, dear friend Bartholomew,

"I hope that very soon your eyes shall be reading these words that I scribble on this poor-quality paper, paper that is far too humid, but the only to be had here.

"Possibly you will be surprised by this letter. I have frequently told myself that it would do me good to write to you, that it would help me ward off my black moods and melancholia. And then some vile impetus would arise to spoil this pleasure. Days have gone by not in a flash but with an appalling slowness, so great is the hole I feel within. In short, it shall soon be eighteen months since we saw each other last. I

carry a memory of our somewhat curt farewell, one in which I
failed to thank you properly for your friendship and your help
during the difficult times I went through, and that led to the
exile to which I am still kept. The mistrust that I once felt
toward you seems completely foreign to me today, even childish,
and it now feels quite natural that I should confide in you.

"I have often had occasion, during my travels at the
Governor's side, to think of you and to miss both the pacifying
warmth of our conversations and your expert understanding of
human character. I must say that I have missed the first cruelly,
constrained as I am to this solitude that Don Francisco has
imposed upon me in order to appease his brothers; and I have
found myself wanting in the latter on far too many occasions.

"No doubt I can tell you little that you haven't already heard
by one rumor or another: you know as I do that the problem
with rumors is not their untruthfulness but rather that they are
in fact too often true. My friend Soto has sailed for Panama
after having become convinced that the Governor's brothers
will never permit him to become as wealthy and as honored as
his worth and his actions lead him to deserve. His absence is a
great loss for me, for we were well together despite the fact that
everything was done to separate us, and I hope to keep many
good memories of him.

"Your bishop, Fray Vicente Valverde, has also sailed, he for
Spain with Don Francisco's fulsome blessings. The Governor is
increasingly becoming the avuncular sage, with his white beard
and twinkling eye. It is a role that suits him well, I believe.
There is a virtuous core beneath the shell of madness that lured
him to this land. The more I watch him grow old, never overly
susceptible but seeking peace and quiet far more often than he
used to, getting his wife with child—who is one of the late Inca
Atahualpa's sisters (the Governor's way of honoring his promise
to watch over his family for him)—and behaving with true
kindness, the more I tell myself that there are two Pizarros. I
loathe the first, the one capable of anything in his single-
minded pursuit of his goals: of violence, of lying, of an
abominable toadying that taints his otherwise limitless valor.

That man is not far separated from a mere beast. He has
strength and will the likes of which the world has rarely seen.
Then there's the other man, the attentive, intelligent one, the
one with great political acumen. A man who has but one
extraordinary objective: to found a nation, no less. The truth is
that gold interests him no more than it does me, except that he
needs it to establish his power. I believe that he is capable of
sharing it with the Inca lords in Cuzco. At least, I hope he is.

"I'm never quite sure which of these two men is the one
who calls me 'son.' Please don't laugh, Brother Bartholomew. I
haven't been deceived by the charm that he intends by this. But
I have, nonetheless, felt the sincerity of it. He chose me over
his brother Hernando, over the vile Gonzalo, and over the
wretched Juan. He chose me even though others foisted
themselves upon him and would have been rid of me—you
witnessed it for yourself—by whatever means possible. I sense
that he has a real affection for me, an affection that is evident
even in his iniquity toward me, an affection that might be
described as fatherly. You know my story, Brother
Bartholomew. It was what landed me in the jails of Seville
where we first met. You know, then, what significance it has for
me, and why I live in his shadow a little.

"In order not to dwell on the time I am spending away from
her, I keep myself busy each day with tasks great and small.

"One of the more important of these, as you may well be
aware, was to find a site on which to found the capital of Peru.
I must admit that this was one of the most beautiful moments I
have lived during these long, long months that I have been
gone from Cuzco.

"Not a day had passed since last autumn when Don
Francisco hadn't searched for a site worthy of his grand project.
He was of the opinion, and we were all of the same mind, that
the ideal spot would have to be on the coast of the South Sea so
that a port might be built, which would facilitate communication
with Panama and Spain. So we surveyed hundreds of leagues of
desert before finally reaching, one day in early January, around
midday, a true Garden of Eden. Imagine a valley so rich and

bountiful that one might ride through it for three hours under branches bowed with fruit without once having to squint against the sun. Imagine an orchard dotted with fields of corn, sweet potato, and with houses made of mud or cane with beautifully kept little gardens in which guavas, avocados, and tomatoes grow like flowers, the whole place kept irrigated with a brilliant system of canals that never run dry. From a distance, it reminds one of the subtlest Toledo marquetry.

"We reached a shallow river in the center of this enchanted valley. Near its bank, we came across a barrow common to Indian temples set in a glade surrounded by flowering bushes and shrubs with purple or yellow leaves.

"We entered the glade at a trot, as though fearful that such a magical place might evaporate before our very eyes. The Governor gave me one of those looks, you know the one that he usually gives only to his blessed portrait of the Sacred Virgin during moments of great victorious excitement. 'It shall be here,' he said, and removed his hat.

"As it was the day of the Epiphany, he added: 'The capital shall be called *La Ciudad de los Reyes.*'

"It only took a few days for the wish to become reality. On the 18th of January of this year 1535, the foundations of the capital were laid in this place, which the locals call *Lima.* Pegs were placed to mark out the royal square, the future cathedral, the future market and, of course, the future palaces of the Governor and the municipality. A cleric fresh off the boat from Panama blessed these imaginary places. The poor fellow was not yet used to the way things are done here, and he trembled horribly. He was persuaded that the Indians watching him were surely going to roast and eat him at the first opportunity.

"I must admit that the moment moved me more than I had expected it to. To say to oneself 'We have arrived in a country and today we are founding a city' was more stirring than I had imagined it would be. To imagine that tomorrow there would be carriages moving noisily down streets between buildings and shops, that there would be monks and—forgive me—thieves, life in all its seething chaos, in a word, on the very spot where today there were but a few freshly whitewashed lines on the green grass moved me to my very soul. Yes, I can promise you that I felt something then that tied knots in my guts tighter than any battle. I can at last believe—hope—that we have come to this strange and marvelous country for reasons other than looting it of its gold. I can believe at last that we are here to build something that is, if not exactly God's work, then at least that of men of dignity.

"At least that is how I wanted to see things during that arousing moment.

"Brother Bartholomew, my friend, I imagine your thin smile as you read these lines, wondering why I have sent you this detailed description.

"The truth is that I wanted to find some good news for you. As you are no doubt aware, things are going badly between the Governor and Don Diego de Almagro. After a hundred disagreements, reconciliations, and even outright threats of war, a solution had to be found to separate them, so volatile was their antagonism.

"The news reached me the day before yesterday. As you doubtlessly already know, it has been decided that Don Diego de Almagro will set off to conquer the south of Peru. The region is said to be richer with gold than anything we have seen until now, and this somewhat appeased Almagro's noxious voracity for the stuff. However, it seems to me that that rumor should be taken with a grain of salt.

"Don Francisco asked me to join Don Diego's expedition and, to be frank, to be his spy.

"It is a task that I cannot love, and I loathe especially what it entails: another year of traveling, perhaps longer. And what a journey it shall be, when every day I shall be burdened by the thought of what I have left behind.

"Dear friend, permit me to write her name: Anamaya.

"Not one morning, not one evening, not one quiet moment, passes without which I think of her. Not a day passes when I do not see her face, as I do whenever I close my eyes, so clearly it's as though she has been branded into my mind with a white-hot iron. Dear friend, my love for her boils within me, and I tremble with anxiety for not knowing what to do about it. I grow anxious whenever I imagine the thousand caresses of love we are missing, caresses that never end. I tremble for the fear of ever forgetting her voice, her lips, or the scent of her skin.

"I shudder, and then I tell myself that it's over. We have been apart too long now. And I fear that this latest departure of mine will sunder us forever.

"I shiver with fear whenever I think how vulnerable she is, and I grow furious for not being able to protect her. I know what the Governor's brothers are capable of.

"I know that I have good reason to be anxious.

"Dear Brother Bartholomew, forgive me for confiding in you, a man of God, these feelings that I myself cannot separate from the heat of desire, its frustration, and that rapture that makes us human. Yes, truly human, because one loves with all one's being. Knowing that another human being exists who is so different from me, so foreign to me, and yet from whom I cannot cleave myself without finding in her place a bottomless void, gives me a taste of the infinite happiness that fulfills me as a man.

"But in these circumstances, you are the only person who can help me. Could you let Anamaya know that I am leaving? Could you let her know that I go against my own will? Above all, could you offer her some protection? Could you consider her a friend and warn her of Gonzalo and Juan's ill-intentioned frenzies? They are bound to return to their old villainies once Almagro has left Cuzco. They will be masters of the city, but not of their own folly.

"Will you have her leave Cuzco, if necessary? I will let you be the judge of whether it is necessary or not.

"As you can see, I am in great need of paper. I must end here. I deliver myself to you as a drowning man surrenders himself to the will of God.

"Sebastian will privately bring you this letter. You can trust him and ask him for help or even for gold. He has just pulled off a great stroke at Jauja. Having become an expert at dice, he relieved Mancio Sierra de Leguizamon of his wealth in only one day and one night. Sierra looted the great temple in Cuzco of all its gold two years ago. So now Sebastian is Don Sebastian. His skin is still black, but he is rich and free. Your God sometimes shows himself capable of the greatest irony.

"I say *your* God. Today, I wish I could sincerely pray that he is also mine. Adieu, dear friend Bartholomew. Take the greatest care of her, I beg you. I love her more than I do my own life, and I will not forget her, even in the hell to which I am heading.

"Yours, and hers,
"Gabriel."

Bartholomew looked up from the letter to see, for the first time, the *Coya Camaquen* crying. She had tilted her face upward and was gazing at the magnificent mountains far beyond the *cancha*'s walls. She didn't bother to wipe away the tears glistening on her cheeks.

Slightly embarrassed, Bartholomew threw up his hands in a little fatalist gesture. He said gently:

"I am considered, in my country, a man close to God, just as here you are admired for being close to invisible presences. That should make us incomprehensible to one another, for God knows no invisible presence other than himself. Yet, each time I see you, I feel that this draws us closer together."

Anamaya knitted her eyebrows, as though expunging the thoughts tormenting her.

"I know that you find it difficult to understand us. Even he does," she said, pointing at the letter as though it was Gabriel himself, "even he finds it difficult. But I thank you for trying anyway."

"I'll be there for you whenever you need me," said Bartholomew. "Gabriel is in the right of it. You are indeed in grave danger here. You must be very cautious."

"I know what that word means, but it plays no part in my life. I do what I must do, with or without caution."

A flash of a smile lit up her still wet blue eyes as she stared at Bartholomew, who couldn't help but be disturbed by the depth and intensity of her gaze.

"Perhaps," she said gently, "you are the one who needs to be cautious?"

THIRTY

Tiahuanaku, August 1535

He had been on the road for two weeks now trying to catch up with Almagro's column. He had followed the coast along the South Sea for some time before an Indian had guided him inland into the valleys and hills.

For two days he had been on his own again, and as far as he knew he was completely lost in the barren wilderness. For two days he had seen nothing other than the void, and had fed more on the dust and wind than on the victuals that still filled his saddlebags.

He occasionally had the impression of being on the roof of the world. The insects here didn't flee at his bay's step, which was absorbed by the dry, yielding earth. The vast plateau extended smoothly unto the horizon, with patches of *ichu,* that short, thick grass, scattered here and there. It was alternatively whipped by squalls and burnt bone-dry by the sun. The sun was setting now, and the entire earth turned a rusty color beneath the somber blue of dusk.

Gabriel had covered his face with his kerchief, to protect himself from the dust. He felt as though he had gone blind, so long had he been staring at the same, unchanging landscape. Suddenly he heard a cry, or at least some kind of sound, shiver through the air. He stared for a while before making out, due west in the gathering shadows, tall shapes rising from the flat horizon. Perhaps he was finally getting somewhere!

He wet his kerchief with water from his gourd and wiped his face with it. Then he gently urged his horse into a trot. It would take him another half hour at least to reach the strange objects.

They turned out to be enormous, angular statues rising from the barren ground, two or three times bigger than a human. He could make out, in their dark stone, faces, hands, and limbs, and they looked like giant, crude dolls. The ground a little beyond them was strewn with massive, polished boulders, half-buried in the dusty earth, as though a monster from the core of the earth had tried to swallow them.

Some looked like giant doors, with their strap hinges and lintels carved from a single boulder. How was such a thing possible? How could these prodigious objects, over thirty feet long and fifteen wide, have been worked, sculpted, polished, and transported here, where there was nothing but sky, wind, and dust? With what instruments, what tools, what craftsmanship had they been chiseled from boulders that could only have been even larger in their original states?

A man stirred about before these immense monoliths, twirling about as though dancing with them. He was slightly shorter than Gabriel, but of far greater bulk. A mosaic of wrinkles covered his broad face from his forehead to his neck, and he looked out from slanting eyes set above a flattened nose. His only remaining teeth were two skewed black stumps through which he flicked his nimble tongue. His clothes were mere rags, and his legs were bare despite the freezing wind blowing across the highland. He wore a square, brightly colored embroidered cap, a very strange headpiece indeed, with each corner of its square angled upward like a billygoat's horn.

As Gabriel approached, the man stared emphatically at his horse. But he didn't show the slightest trace of fear, as Indians usually did upon seeing the animal for the first time. He said nothing in reply to Gabriel's greeting or question: whether he had seen a long column heading south.

"A column of strangers dressed like me and with beasts such as this one," continued Gabriel, smacking his horse's flank.

The man screwed up his eyes, but said nothing. Gabriel told himself that he hadn't made himself understood. He had discovered, ever since he had left the coast for the interior, how many different tribes of Indians there were, and how many different languages were spoken in this country.

The old man suddenly started windmilling his arms. He exclaimed in passable Quechua:

"*Taypikala, Taypikala!* This place is the *Taypikala!* You are in the center of the universe, Stranger. What you see here are the humans of the past, who were human before we were. They're made of stone, but they can see you. And they can see me. That's why I come here every day to salute them. Every day that the sun is over my head. Yes, yes, yes! You should salute them too, Stranger. Do as I do."

The old man rolled his eyes into his head, bent his knees, and raised his arms to the sky. He muttered incomprehensibly in his high-pitched voice in a language unknown to Gabriel.

Gabriel stood there looking vaguely amused, the bridle of his horse flung lazily over his shoulder. He watched the man raise his arms to the sky and shake his torso back and forth while making a cluck-clucking sound like a chicken. When he noticed that Gabriel had remained standing motionless by his horse, the man stopped short and eyeballed him furiously.

"Why do you not salute the Men of Stone?" he reprimanded in his broken Quechua. "They can see you, you know, and they shall certainly become very angry with you. Salute them as I do, or else you'll regret it."

The man spoke with such earnest conviction that Gabriel almost believed him. The place, one of the most extraordinary he had ever seen, also contributed to his disposition to believe.

As though he had read his thoughts, the man approached Gabriel. He grabbed Gabriel's shirt with his long nails, as black as claws. His breath carried the stench of the starving. He muttered:

"A long time ago, Stranger, Viracocha, the Maker of the Beginning and the End, wished to put humans on the earth. But the beings that he originally created didn't walk upright. Or else they behaved like animals. They killed, grunted, and ate one another like animals. They copulated like animals, and their offspring did the same. There was no difference then between humans and animals, Stranger. So Viracocha destroyed them. He turned them into stone. You see them before you now. Viracocha said to himself, 'I'm going to create perfect men, human beings that are strong, wise, and beautiful. I shall give them a perfect city to live in. They shall educate themselves, the ones that aren't perfect, that aren't yet complete human beings.' And then he created the Inca clans and Cuzco, the city of the Puma. There, everything is perfect, Stranger."

The old man fell silent. He winked at Gabriel, clicked his tongue, and released the Spaniard's shirt. He turned toward the immense sculptures, now bathed in the golden glow of dusk, again raised his arms to the sky, and said:

"Such was Viracocha's work, Stranger. He went on to create all the nations loyal to Cuzco. He sculpted what you see here, he modeled from giant stones men old and young, women, and children, one for each nation. He accorded each one a headpiece particular to them, a particular color for weaving, and *quipus* without a single knot in them. He built them a *cancha* here with enormous doors so that they might learn to live both in and out of doors. Then he gave them the country around Cuzco's sacred mountains."

The old man clicked his tongue harder with each successive sentence. His eyes bulging, he shouted as though he was worried that the icy wind would whisk away his words as soon as they had left his mouth.

"Viracocha said to them, 'Humans, here are your nations: here is the nation of the Canchis, there that of the Kollas, here the Yungas. And you shall all serve the Noble Lords, the Sons of the Sun, the Cuzco clans. They will teach you how to cultivate land and build roads. They will teach you how to be wise, as humans should be.' Then Viracocha had guides brought for each nation. He ordered them, 'Submerge yourselves into the earth with the Men of Stone and come out only onto the land of the nations that I have designated,' and this they did. They traveled through the earth, coming out only at springheads, caves, and great, broken rocks. There, Viracocha's guide blew on their massive stone bodies and said, 'Rouse yourselves, humans of *Taypikala!* Come to life! Become human, and go forth and populate this desert land. Propagate yourselves, respect the will of Viracocha and of the Sons of the Sun!'"

The old madman screamed these last words. Gabriel felt a shiver run down his spine. He grabbed his doublet, which he had slung over his saddle, and put it on. The old man turned around. Still completely ignoring the horse, he grinned and clapped his hands. Gabriel smiled back at him, feeling slightly ill at ease. The man nodded and pointed to a point across the plateau.

"The ones you seek are over there, Stranger," he said, his voice now returned to normal. "They are many. There are some Cuzco Lords with them, and other men, Strangers, like you."

"Thank you!" said Gabriel, his voice a little husky from lack of use.

The man laughed through his two black teeth. He said:

"They are over there, Stranger. Viracocha is going to have to start all over again."

He waved his arms as though he wanted to grab the monoliths and fling them off the plateau.

"The *Taypikala* is over," he exclaimed. "Look around you: you will see that everything is disintegrating. Those that you are joining are like animals. They kill, grunt, and fight among themselves like animals. They steal women, without distinguishing between old or young, in order to copulate with them like animals. There is no longer any difference between humans and animals, Stranger. Things have returned to what they were before Viracocha put humans on the earth. It's a new *pachacuti*. The *Taypikala* is over."

Gabriel shivered again, not from the cold wind but from the old madman's sinister laughter. He bid farewell and set off at a trot. He heard the man's laughter diminishing behind him, his cries still echoing through the cold air:

"The *Taypikala* is over! Viracocha must begin again!"

Night had fallen by the time Gabriel crossed the plateau and reached Almagro's column. He could see and hear it from afar, an immense body of men camped in a fold on the plateau lit by a thousand torches. At first it reminded him of the army raised two years previously at Cajamarca. It was as heavily manned as that one, with perhaps ten thousand Indians now following Almagro and his conquistadors.

Gabriel spurred on his bay, and galloped diagonally across the plateau to the head of this giant human herd, where the Spaniards were usually to be found. But there were so many Indians that he reached them before getting to the end of the column. What he saw left him dumbfounded.

He saw men chained together in groups of ten. He saw two dozen others standing almost naked despite the wind and the night, their ankles tied together with leather straps. By moonlight he saw women, both young and old, in the same position, their faces twisted with pain. He couldn't see fires for them to keep warm by or tents to take cover in anywhere. They were all terrified, they all avoided his gaze, and they remained mute to all his questions.

The old madman's cry returned to the front of his mind: *"There is no longer any difference between humans and animals, Stranger."*

With his heart in his mouth, Gabriel rode for an hour amid the horror, and when he at last reached Don Diego's camp, lit by a row of torches mounted on halberds, the screams and laughter rising from it warned him of what he would find there.

He lifted the tent flap and was assailed by the cacophony, the brightness of the lamps, and the heat from within. It was a bigger space than he had imagined it would be. The pallid, bilious, one-eyed man sat dozing in an armchair at the end of a long table on which sat the remains of roasts. Two dozen drunken Spaniards sat around with goblets of beer in their hands, shouting, guffawing, and tormenting a number of half-naked young Indian women. Indeed, some women were already completely naked, their eyes wide with terror, or else they too were drunk and laughing and crying at the same time.

Don Diego de Almagro emerged from his daze and was the first to notice Gabriel enter the tent. His only eye came alive, mocking and agleam. He cried out, bringing silence to the room, and everyone turned toward Gabriel who, looking at each person, realized that he knew almost none of them.

"Why, Don Gabriel," exclaimed Almagro, "what a surprise!" He jumped up out of his chair. He brought both his palms slamming down onto the table, startling the women and causing the men to laugh.

"Gentlemen, allow me to present to you Don Gabriel Montelucar y Flores, a very dear, very close friend to my friend Don Francisco."

The evident venom in Don Diego's voice was enough to sharpen the drunkards' attention toward Gabriel. They clearly shared Don Diego's hatred of the Governor. Gabriel refused to be baited, however.

"Don Francisco sent me to assure you of his support. He bid me to tell you that his support extends beyond the merely financial, and that should you require something of him, you need only send him word and he would be honored to send you whatever you need."

Almagro began laughing again.

"I am most grateful for his generous attentions. Don Francisco's pockets overflow with gold. At this very moment he sleeps in a bed of down, whereas we continue to march along roads, finding nothing but dust and more dust. But he has a pair of eyes whereas I have but one. And before you, gentlemen, you have his second pair."

"Don Diego," interrupted Gabriel, "save your fatuities for the rest of the trip. I have just spent an hour riding through the hell that is your column. You treat these people like animals. Do you hope to have the entire country rise up against us?"

A silence as cold as the wind outside ensued. Almagro replied icily: "Do you dare to lecture me, Don Gabriel?"

Gabriel hadn't time to reply. A man rose from the table. He grabbed one of the young women nearby. He drew his dagger, and cut her entire tunic away from her.

She touched her bare breasts and then looked at the blood on her fingers with an expression of terrified bewilderment.

"Here," bellowed the man as the woman tried desperately to escape his grasp, "we do as we please. Here, our Governor is Don Diego."

Gabriel had already drawn his sword. But he was met with the sound of twenty others being unsheathed. A line of steel blades bristled at him.

Almagro's thin, pockmarked cheeks started quivering uncontrollably.

"You see how generous my men are, Don Gabriel. You see how naturally they call me by the title that was refused me. And that's not all: you see how far they're willing to go for me. Come now, I know you're a brave man, but there are five hundred of us, whereas there's one of you. I fear that the odds are too great, even for you. As Don Cristóbal de Narvaez has just explained to you, I am the ultimate authority here. And I march as I see fit. If my ways displease you, then run back to Don Francisco and clean his boots for him."

Gabriel slowly sheathed his sword. His limbs were heavy with fatigue after his long trip, and he had a bitter taste in his mouth.

He heard them sniggering as he turned on his heel and left. The old madman's words reverberated sadly in his head:

"*The* Taypikala *is over! Viracocha must begin again!*"

THIRTY-ONE

Cuzco, August 1535

"Help, milord!"

"I'm going to pierce right through you!"

"Ouch, *caballero!*"

"Titu! Lloque! Be careful with those sticks or you'll hurt yourselves."

The two boys, five or six years old at the most, paused for a moment and looked at the sticks in their hands that had become swords in their imagination. Then they looked at their mother. She was busy, along with the other servants, cleaning the great common hall, shaking out the beds' *mantas*. She turned away as soon as she had finished reprimanding her offspring, and the two children burst out laughing as she did so. They bounded about like puma cubs, continuing their game, their splendid, new game: sword fighting, just like the Strangers did, and with the same weapons they used.

Anamaya sat perfectly still in the shade, watching them. She was smiling, but it was a grave, melancholic smile, one that lent no light to her eyes.

"What are you dreaming about, *Coya Camaquen?*" murmured a soft voice nearby.

"Inguill!"

Anamaya, surprised, turned around to look at her young friend's tender face.

"I didn't hear you arrive. You always move about as quietly as a current of air," she said warmly.

"Not so. I've been standing here behind you for some time now, but I didn't dare interrupt your thoughts. You seemed so fascinated by those little ones. I told myself . . ."

Inguill hesitated and nibbled on her lips before whispering:

"You were thinking of him as you watched them, weren't you?"

Anamaya simply nodded, and looked again at the children. They were running now, chasing one another from one end of the courtyard to the other, running themselves out of breath, laughing and yelling out in Spanish the few words that they had picked up from the Strangers.

"You're missing him," said Inguill, "yet so many moons have passed since you saw him last, you could almost forget his face. Not like me; I don't have your strength, and I would have died long ago from crying."

Anamaya repressed her desire to check the young girl. Inguill's affection was sincere, and she wasn't aware of the hidden cruelty of her words. What's more, she was right: Anamaya had had to keep her love for Gabriel stifled for a very long time now, and she confided her pain and her loneliness only to the darkness of night and the silent, looming mountains.

"Sometimes things happen that way," she said in a low voice, "sometimes I manage to forget about him for an entire day. Sometimes I sleep through an entire night without waking up with him on my mind. Sometimes I'm frightened that I'm forgetting his face, as you say, forgetting what he looks like, the shape of his mouth, the gentleness of his touch. But then I remember without knowing why. Nothing is ever forgotten. Walking across the courtyard earlier, I saw these boys playing. And suddenly there he was, before my mind's eye."

"But why do you go on thinking about him even though you're not sure he'll come back to you? Worse yet, you know that he can never be your husband, not in the proper way. You suffer in vain, *Coya Camaquen*."

Anamaya could tell from the smarting in her eyes that she was about to cry, and she batted her eyelids to block the tears. She let out a little laugh, her eyes shining. Inguill held out her hand, and she took it in her own.

"No doubt you are right. But that is how it is. What can I do about it? I think about him because he's in my heart. I think about him because he's in my soul, and maybe also in the soul that waits for me in the Other World. I think about him because my body yearns for his caresses, his and nobody else's."

"It must be terrible for you."

"No, not always."

They fell silent again as the boys' mother called out to them for a second time. This time she confiscated their sword sticks, triggering an outburst of tears.

"Gabriel isn't here, and yet I feel him so close to me, so close that I keep a space for him between my breath and my skin," murmured Anamaya as she watched the scene between the mother and sons. "On certain days I feel him so strongly, so violently, that it's as if he has only just left Cuzco. On those days, I imagine that if I were to turn around he would be there, and I could touch his face, and he would take me in his arms. But you are right: the rest of the time, I know the truth. He is far away, so far that I have no way of knowing if he still lives in this world."

A single tear rolled down from Anamaya's eye. She furtively wiped it away. Laughing, self-mocking almost, she grabbed hold of Inguill's arm and led her to the *cancha*'s door, saying in a firm voice:

"But come now, let's stop our prattling. Come with me to the great square at Aucaypata. The mummies of the Ancestors of Manco's clan were brought this morning. I want to pay my respects to them."

Inguill, looking pensive and blushing with emotion, nodded and followed Anamaya.

A trumpet blew a brief report as they approached the *cancha*'s surrounding wall. Six guards, armed with spears decorated with feathers in Emperor Manco's colors, appeared to escort the *Coya Camaquen* without an order having been given.

As they set off down the steep road toward Aucaypata, Inguill suddenly asked in a low voice:

"Anamaya, is it possible to love a Stranger in the same way as a man from our own race?"

Anamaya, surprised, slowed down. She glanced at the guards escorting them before answering to make sure that they couldn't hear.

"Gabriel isn't a Stranger like the others. It's difficult to explain. He has a strength that makes him stand out from other men, whether they're from here or from his own country."

Inguill shook her head and smiled an impish and embarrassed smile. She asked again, in a whisper so low as to be practically inaudible:

"What I mean is, do they make love like men from here do? I've heard women say that they attach a greater importance to it than our own men, that they like doing it more than our own men, and that for us, for women, I mean, well . . ."

Inguill didn't dare finish her sentence. Anamaya came to a standstill. They could see the great ceremonial square from where they were, with the mummies lined up to the left, each with a brazier burning before it maintained by a priest.

"Why are you asking, Inguill?"

"I want to help Manco. I might be able to if you help me, Anamaya. I know that the Strangers came yesterday to torment him, demanding that he give them your husband, the Sacred Double made of gold. They shouted at him, even threatened him. I couldn't sleep at all last night, so much did the thought of what they asked of him torment me."

Anamaya knew too well what Inguill was referring to. The memory of Governor Pizarro's two brothers Juan's and Gonzalo's threats still lingered unhappily in her mind. What's more, those two devils were the reason why Gabriel was so far from her now.

Manco had once again bravely refused to give them the gold statue. Once again they had insulted him, insulted the Inca, the Son of the Sun, as though he was nothing but a mongrel dog. Then they had made a vile proposition to him: that the *Coya,* his own wife, leave his bed for Juan's.

"I'll never allow it, never!" growled Anamaya furiously.

The men of the escort looked at them curiously. Anamaya set off toward the square again, with Inguill at her side. Anamaya said, in a low but still furious tone:

"Manco must no longer accept that they treat him with such disrespect. He cannot give them the *Coya* any more than he can give them me. Curi Ocllo is Queen. The Sun and the Moon have blessed her womb so that the Emperor may seed his lineage in it. She is even more sacred than I am. What an infamy it would be were a Stranger to take her. The Elders would lose all their trust in Manco. His authority would evaporate."

"Anamaya, he has no choice," protested Inguill with a resigned look on her face. "Manco cannot refuse them again. The Strangers will certainly put him in chains. O may Viracocha help us."

Anamaya sternly waved the escort away from them as they reached the last paved steps before the square. There weren't very many people on it, just a few Inca noblemen, some priests, and a gaggle of boys around the mummies. A small group of Spaniards stood a little way back, looking on with a bored curiosity. They had stopped being fascinated by the ceremony long ago.

"No, Inguill," continued Anamaya sharply, turning to face the young girl, "don't let fear overwhelm you, for fear is always the worst of counselors. We must leave Cuzco. It's for the best. It's no longer possible to share this city with the Strangers."

"Anamaya! That would be madness! It would mean war!"

"It's a necessary risk," replied Anamaya calmly. "Did you see the children earlier? They were pretending to be Strangers and they spoke words that they had learned from them. Their sticks weren't clubs or spears or bows used by Inca warriors, but the weapons of the Strangers. What will become of them growing up if we leave things as they are? They'll stop loving Inti and Mama Quilla. They'll no longer be the children of the human beings to whom Viracocha gave the Empire of the Four Cardinal Directions. They'll be nothing but slaves to the Strangers, despising all our Ancestors and calling our nation 'Peru.' You know very well, Inguill, that I did all I could to prevent war breaking out when Chalkuchimac wanted only that. I had to do it so that Manco could be crowned Emperor. But today, Emperor Manco must be prepared to make war."

"But he can't!" cried Inguill. "Forgive me for interfering in matters that are beyond what an ignorant girl like me can understand, *Coya Camaquen*. But everyone says, in the *acllahuasi* as elsewhere, that we aren't strong enough, that we don't even have enough warriors to fight the Strangers."

"Circumstances will be different a few moons from now."

"A few moons from now, Manco will have chains around his feet and neck, just like Emperor Atahualpa!" cried Inguill. "The Strangers are coming for the *Coya* in just three days!"

Anamaya turned away with an exasperated sigh. She concentrated on the priests for a moment in order to calm herself and avoid speaking harshly to Inguill. They wore long, fringed tunics and were offering oblations to the mummies, throwing corn kernels and strips of meat into the braziers with precise, composed movements. Then they raised the jars of *chicha* to the preserved bodies, as though inviting them to drink.

Without looking at her and without being able to withhold her sarcasm, Anamaya asked Inguill:

"Very well. You seem to have worked everything out. Can you offer a better solution?"

"Yes! Please don't be angry with me, Anamaya. I only want to help you and Manco."

"How do you hope to do that?"

The young girl stiffened before gushing:

"The Strangers can have me."

"You?! Inguill, don't talk nonsense. You're not the *Coya*."

"I know that, but they don't. And everyone says how much I look like Curi Ocllo."

Anamaya, flabbergasted, stared at Inguill's tender, innocent face for a few moments, at her broad and high cheekbones, at her small but well-defined lips, and at her slightly hooked nose. It was true that she looked like Manco's wife. Anamaya, moved, shook her head nonetheless.

"No, Inguill. It would be madness. You don't know what you're saying."

"Anamaya, listen to me. You know that I love Manco more than anyone in the world. I love him as much as you love your Stranger. I owe him my life, remember. So now, even though he doesn't want me in his bed, I want to show him how much I love him."

"By becoming a Stranger's wife?"

"By helping him avoid a war for which he isn't yet prepared."

Anamaya was shaken, and stared at her friend.

"But do you understand what would happen to you?"

"I've thought about it for a long time," said Inguill with a wan smile. "That's why I asked you earlier how the Strangers made love. I would be wife to the oldest, the one called Juan. I've been watching him, and I don't think he's as cruel as his brother."

Anamaya shook her head again, incredulous. Tears rose to Inguill's eyes as she laughed and said:

"At least I'll get to be Queen for a short while! Help me, *Coya Camaquen*. Take me to Manco so that I can tell him my plan."

Hidden behind the *manta* hanging over the doorway, Anamaya watched the festivities going on in the courtyard. Manco had done things well. The Strangers looked gratified for once.

There were only a dozen or so Inca guards and Spanish soldiers in the courtyard. A number of pretty young women came and went, all wearing brightly colored ceremonial tunics and garlands of red *cantutas* on their heads. They set dish after dish before the Emperor and his guests, platters laden with sweet-smelling delicacies such as roast vicuña stuffed with prunes, roast turtledoves and partridges served with tiny potatoes, and a purée of *quinua* and peanuts.

Juan Pizarro was wearing a new coat with voluminous sleeves and a lace ruff as broad as a hand around his neck that hid his beauty spot. He held his gloves in one hand and a white cattleya orchid in the other, and he brought this to his nose every now and then, making a great show of inhaling its scent while batting his eyelids. Gonzalo, standing beside him, received the fruits and honey-laden corn cakes proffered to him with such grace that no one who saw him then would have believed him to be a blackguard. Both brothers sat on a bench made more comfortable with fine woolen blankets. Manco sat before them on the three-legged seat reserved for Emperors.

"Everything's going well," said Anamaya in a low voice, "the Strangers are pleased. Manco is playing the happy host. But they're bound to ask for the *Coya* soon."

Inguill murmured from behind her. The girl was squatting in the shadows, and only the glint of her gold headpiece could be seen.

And indeed, as the servant girls, their necks bowed and eyes turned downward, brought forth the jars of *chicha*, Juan Pizarro declared:

"Sapa Inca, your table is delicious, and your hospitality generous, but I don't want you to forget why we are here."

Manco, saying nothing, held up his right hand. The servant girls immediately stopped their activities and formed two lines up to the door to the outer courtyard.

The first of Manco's concubines appeared. She advanced slowly, gracefully, preceded by two young girls dressed in white tunics. The two Spaniards examined her broad face, her small waist, and her well-defined lips as she slowly made her way through the two ranks of servant girls. She was perhaps more robust than she was beautiful, but she was clearly a sensual woman. She went straight to the Emperor and prostrated herself before him, not even glancing at the Strangers.

But before Manco had even ordered her to her feet, Gonzalo had a derisive look on his face.

"Why, Sapa Inca," he carped, "would you have us believe that this woman is your wife?"

"Certainly she is," replied Manco, grinning.

"Of course she isn't. You're trying to deceive us. She doesn't look any-thing like the *Coya*," groused Juan, piqued. "Look, Gonzalo, she's older than I am."

"Sapa Inca," sighed Gonzalo, rising to his feet, "surely we're not going to quarrel once again. My brother needs the most beautiful of your women. Your favorite wife, in fact."

Anamaya saw the restrained anger in the Spaniard's smile. Manco must have noticed it too, because he laughed quietly and said:

"Well done! You're absolutely right, dear Governor's brother. You spotted it right away. But this woman is indeed one of mine. She is the one who, a long time ago now, taught me how a man is to behave between his wife's thighs."

The two brothers burst into laughter as Manco continued:

"It would displease me to give my most beautiful woman to a man who doesn't recognize beauty. I am happy to learn that your taste is as exacting as mine."

He clapped his hands. Twenty young women emerged from the great communal hall opposite his private chamber. The Spaniards, turn-ing around to look at them, stared wide-eyed and openmouthed.

"My dear friends," began Manco in a friendly tone, "here are my most beautiful women. I cannot do better than to let you choose."

From her inconspicuous position in the shadows, Anamaya watched the flabbergasted expressions on the Strangers' faces as the young women, looking fearful but resigned, approached them. They were all wearing the same light blue *añaco* and white cape brightened with only a few colorful patterns on their hems.

"It's begun," murmured Anamaya, "the concubines are here."

Inguill, nervous and tense, had drawn so close to Anamaya's shoul-der that she could smell the heavy scent of oil musk that the young girl had covered herself with.

"Look."

Anamaya pushed the *manta* very slightly aside so that Inguill could watch the scene.

Under the sun beating down on the courtyard, the Governor's brothers inspected the concubines. They would lift one by her chin, take another's hand, stroke another's shoulder, have one, then another turn around. Gonzalo's gestures and giggles became increasingly peremptory.

Now he would feel a breast, a belly, and would stroke them so immodestly that Anamaya shivered with disgust.

"Inguill, are you sure about . . ."

"Yes! Absolutely," interrupted Inguill, "my only fear is that they choose a concubine before even seeing me."

But that didn't happen, and everything went as planned. Gonzalo frowned and drew his brother aside, even though Juan seemed completely enchanted by the women, and was endlessly saluting them with a flourish of his hat. The two brothers spoke privately together for a few moments. Then Gonzalo turned to Manco. Now his eyes were glowing with rage, and he walked right up to the Emperor.

"Sapa Inca, by the blood of Christ. When will you understand that you must not lie to us?"

His loud words echoed across the courtyard, causing the servant girls and concubines to freeze.

"You must never lie to us again!"

Inguill instinctively gripped Anamaya's arm as though she was frightened that the Spaniard's mere anger would break her.

Manco, meanwhile, reacted with disarming calm. Ignoring Gonzalo's cries, he asked Juan, his voice quite unfazed:

"Do none of these women please you then, dear Governor's brother?"

"Why, it's not that they aren't pretty, Sapa Inca," said Juan, embarrassed. "They're pleasant enough to gaze upon, it must be said, and they're young and shapely."

"But none of them is the *Coya!*" interrupted Gonzalo angrily. "And you know very well that . . ."

"Dear friends," sighed Manco, "you are indeed very exacting."

"No more games, Sapa Inca. I am growing impatient. We want to see the queen this very instant."

Manco's face suddenly clouded over. He stared dead ahead of him, as though his heart was shattering into pieces. Anamaya had goose pimples, and she drew Inguill closer to herself.

"He's about to send for you," she whispered. "Look after yourself, my friend."

She noticed that Inguill's cheeks were wet with tears. The young girl muttered, as she kissed Anamaya's hand, and against all evidence to the contrary:

"I'm not frightened! I'm not frightened!"

Anamaya pressed her face against hers. They heard Manco calling out:

"Curi Ocllo! Fetch me the *Coya,* Curi Ocllo."

"Don't forget that I love you always!" whispered Anamaya urgently, "and promise me that you'll run away if he hurts you."

Now the servant girls had lifted the *manta* aside and were prostrating themselves on the threshold of the room. Anamaya retreated farther into the shadows as Inguill stepped forth into the light.

The Spaniards' expressions immediately grew more relaxed and self-satisfied. Inguill had never looked so beautiful, and the Strangers' faces seemed to reflect her beauty. She was wrapped in an ocean-green *añaco,* one so finely woven that it was impossible to make out its stitches, and which accentuated her swanlike figure. A violet *lliclla* floated as lissomely as smoke from her shoulders to the ground and was embroidered with ingenious geometric designs that matched those on her belt. A number of gold gilt seashells were strewn through her hair. Her face was immaculately made up, with her eyelashes curled as though by an artist's paintbrush. The fact that her eyelids and lips were trembling and that she was on the verge of tears only accentuated her beauty.

"Aaah," cried Gonzalo, "here she is at last, my brother. Here is the *Coya.* I recognize her."

Juan seemed to be greatly troubled by the vision of beauty before him. Anamaya saw that his discomfiture was more genuine than she had thought him capable of. He stared at Inguill as he approached her hesitantly. He offered her a courteous salute, bending at the waist, and when he righted himself again, his expression still full of awe, it was clear that there was true respect in his joy.

"Yes, yes, this one!" Juan stammered to Manco. "That's her, Sapa Inca, I recognize her, she's the *Coya.* I must have her right now."

As he reached out to take Inguill's hand she began screaming, as had been arranged. She turned away from him, cried out, covered her face with her hands, trembled, and cried out that she didn't want to leave her master and husband the Emperor, and that these people frightened her. The faces of all the concubines and servant girls still present reflected Inguill's fear and pain, some of whom began murmuring and even crying. A wave of apprehension filled the room.

"*Hola,*" laughed Gonzalo. "Calm down, Lady *Coya*. What kind of welcome is this for your new husband?"

As Juan looked on with consternation, Inguill threw herself at Manco's feet, ruffling her beautiful clothes. She made one think of a luxurious flower suddenly unfurling its petals all at once. She cried: "My Lord Emperor, don't forsake me. My Lord, I love only you. Emperor, my heart beats only for you and for the Ancestors in the Other World. My Lord, split open my chest and tear out my heart, but don't give me to the Strangers."

Despite the fact that she had rehearsed these lines with Inguill previously, Anamaya couldn't help but shudder at the sincerity with which the girl delivered them. Anamaya saw that everyone, including the Strangers, was sincerely disconcerted and shaken.

"Rise, woman," said Manco gravely. "Go with my friend, the Stranger Lord. Don't concern yourself that he's a Stranger. You may serve me by becoming his faithful wife. Such is my will."

"O Lord Emperor, have pity on me! Please kill me, for I have no reason to live if you leave me in the hands of another man."

Anamaya winced once again. Inguill's words were like arrows. At that moment Manco, who was meant to cruelly ignore her tears, instead leaned forward toward the young girl. He took her by her arm and lifted her to her feet. He pulled her brusquely to him and kissed her on the mouth. It wasn't a long embrace, but the silence that accompanied it filled the courtyard for what felt like an eternity.

Anamaya caught a fleeting glimpse of Inguill's face as Manco pushed her away. Her face and eyes were lit by a marvelous smile that lingered even when Juan roughly snatched her up, and even as Spanish soldiers dragged her away toward the courtyard's gate.

In less time than it took to say it, the Governor's brothers had disappeared with their catch. Anamaya came out onto the threshold of the room, her gut pinched with shame, anger, and hurt. The faces of those gathered in the courtyard seemed more like masks than faces, all with the same fixed, wretched expression.

Manco stood up and went to her. He cast aside the concubines and servant girls who rushed up to him. His gait was that of a heavy-hearted man. He wore a tense smile on his face, or at least an attempt at a smile that was in fact no more than a strained, joyless grimace.

Beneath the deep blue sky, Anamaya raised her eyes and looked at the walls of the Sacsayhuaman Fortress with its three seemingly indestructible towers.

"We did it," said Manco earnestly.

Anamaya looked at him and nodded. She sensed the sadness and bitterness now taking root in the depths of his soul.

"That's what remains of your power," she said, pointing at the walls of the fortress on the mountainside. "The façade of power beneath the sun. The memory of power . . ."

"*Coya Camaquen,* please don't."

"A power that reduces us to sacrificing a pure-hearted young girl to satiate those monsters' hunger . . ."

Manco's face turned white, and he clenched his fists as he said:

"Don't think that I don't know it. Don't think that her suffering doesn't tear at me like the claws of a puma."

Anamaya said nothing. The word "puma" had startled her. Her puma was strong, but so far away.

"Come back," she murmured to herself. "Please, come back and help me."

TIIIRTY-TWO

A gentle rain was falling. Anamaya listened to it pattering across the roof above her. The rainwater was soft. It streamed down gently from her hair, across her forehead, and wet her *añaco*.

Anamaya listened to it slap into the mud puddles outside in the courtyard. She felt an urge to leave her bed, to go outside and watch the rain falling gently through the night. She saw herself wake and get up. At that moment she realized things weren't as they should be.

How could her hair and forehead be wet with rain if there was a roof above sheltering her? What's more, the *cancha*'s courtyard was paved with flagstones. How could mud puddles form there?

She got up and went to the door. Yes, she had been mistaken. She wasn't in the *cancha* but in a hut in the jungle village of her childhood, the one where she was born. Now the rain grew heavier, as it did on that night so long ago, that last night before the beginning of everything.

Before she had become the *Coya Camaquen*.

Anamaya quickly told herself that she was still asleep, that she was dreaming. Perhaps she should wake up and end the dream. But she couldn't help but be fascinated by the village, with the four great communal huts surrounding the central courtyard. It was exactly as it was then, except that the huts were totally empty. She had a presentiment of danger, and was frightened that Emperor Manco's warriors were about to attack.

She was frightened, and she knew that she should try to wake up.

But the silvery flash and gentle patter of the rain falling through the night were so mesmerizing that she couldn't break away. It was extraordinary to be back in the village where she had been a little girl. And if she mustered up all her courage, she might perhaps see her mother's face.

She was grateful to her husband, the Sacred Double, for having accorded her this dream. She would go and thank him after she woke up. She felt both lighthearted and frightened.

A sudden sound made her jump, a scurrying sound, like that of an animal. Another followed it. She thought she could make out the growl and silhouette of a light-coated beast bounding toward the outer fence.

But no, she was mistaken. What she heard was the sound of steps on the wet ground. It was a particular step, one that she instantly recognized: the sound of a Stranger's boots.

Her heart ignited the moment he walked into the hut. Gabriel took off his hat, and his face shone in the night as luminously as if it were day. He was dry despite the rain. His golden hair was dry. He smiled. He spread his arms toward Anamaya, whose belly and chest quivered with happiness. She had waited for him for so long. At last, he was back, as alive and as handsome as he was the first day they had laid eyes on one another.

A marvelous happiness surged through Anamaya when he embraced her. She could feel the heat of his body through his shirt, and she listened to his breathing quicken as he kissed her and began undoing her *añaco*. She laughed at his eagerness. He lifted her as though she were a feather and carried her to her bed. She wanted to see his face, his eyes. She had missed his face for so long now, his soft lips, his straight aquiline nose, and his bright cheeks. But he was impatient, so impatient that he became violent. As she tried to shove him away, she realized that a beard covered his mouth and chin. His face had changed.

She screamed.

Now she was awake, wide-eyed. The man sprawled out on top of her wasn't Gabriel. His fingers were frantically grasping for her breasts, and he was violently trying to strip her clothes off. She realized that he was trying to rape her, and screamed again.

This time her aggressor retreated, his eyes full of hate. He swore in Spanish, slapped one hand over her mouth, and reached for her throat with the other.

"Don't resist me, bitch!"

She didn't understand the words coming from that mouth foaming with desire and hatred, but she recognized the voice: the Governor's brother.

Anamaya's fear gave way to rage. She tried to roll away but the man held her in place. She struggled and shook her head violently from side to side, trying to get free. The Spaniard's fingers slipped into her mouth, and she bit down on them as hard as she could. She tasted blood on her tongue and heard the man scream out in agony.

"Spread your legs, damned Indian whore!"

She took advantage of his shock to fold her knees back over her chest. Gonzalo moaned with pain. He had trouble holding her with his injured hand. He fell on top of her, trying to hold her in place. But Anamaya managed to slip the balls of her feet against his gut, and she used all her strength to kick him off. He stumbled back and slammed into the wall, but not without first ripping her *añaco* from her and scratching one of her breasts with his nails.

Anamaya jumped to her feet and cried out for the servants to come to her aid. She realized that it really was raining and that Gonzalo's breeches were soaked. Even his shirt, under his unbuttoned doublet, was wet. His hair was plastered against his demented face. He was grimacing and sniggering as though it were all a game. He groped around for his sword, which he had taken off and placed near the bed. He found it and stood up.

"Shut up, slut!"

But before he had had a chance to unsheathe it, Anamaya had kicked him with a strength that she hadn't known herself capable of until then. Gonzalo tried to dodge her foot, but in vain. Anamaya's whole body was concentrated on killing him. She felt her heel slam into the Stranger's face, slip up his cheekbone, and burrow into his eye cavity. She fell back down onto her bed. Gonzalo's head bounced off the stone wall like a rag ball.

"Coya Camaquen! Coya Camaquen!"

The servant girls rushed in screaming and surrounded her. Then the guards arrived with torches, spears, and clubs. Everyone stared at the scratches on her face and at the bloodstains on her torn tunic. They all began speaking at once, but she silenced them with a wave of the hand. She gathered her breath as best she could.

"I'm all right," she said, speaking to herself as much as to them, "I'm all right. He didn't do anything to me. . . ."

The Governor's brother still lay unmoving at her feet. Blood flowed from his temple and zigzagged in a thin stream down his neck to his shirt.

Anamaya wrapped a cape, offered to her by a servant girl, around her shoulders and asked:

"Is he alive?"

A guard leaned over the Spaniard and put first his hand on Gonzalo's chest, then his cheek by his mouth. He smiled and nodded.

"He's only knocked out, *Coya Camaquen*. But I can kill him for good if you want."

She closed her eyes and took a few deep breaths to suppress the desire to give the order.

"No," she whispered. "No, let him live. Simply call the Emperor."

When Gonzalo came to, he was still leaning against the wall in the room, and his left eye was swollen crimson. He felt it with his fingertips, moaned, and shoved away the servant girls trying to set a plaster on his temple. He was stupefied to discover that there were two dozen spearheads pointed at him.

The Emperor's guards stood to each side of Manco and Anamaya. A few noblemen from the court were also present. The dancing light from the torches lit their impassive faces and accentuated their severe expressions.

The Governor's brother tried to laugh, but the effort made him grimace in pain. His face no longer had anything angelic about it, and instead made one think of a cruel and wounded beast. He looked at Anamaya through his uninjured eye with such ferocity that she felt a chill run down her spine.

"What I promised you earlier is mild compared to what I'm going to do to you," he murmured savagely.

He gave her an obscene smile, and Anamaya felt a terrible fear spread through her body.

Gonzalo swayed unsteadily as he tried to rise to his feet. But his pride drove him on and, his face twisted with pain, he managed to stand up and lean against the stone wall. Then Manco said in an even voice:

"Governor's brother, I should kill you for what you did. I'll repeat what I told you already: no one is to lay hands on the *Coya Camaquen*."

Gonzalo stared at him with a surprised look on his face before uttering a dreadful little laugh that twisted his face further.

"It is our law," continued Manco, "to hang a man guilty of raping a woman by his hair in the jungle and leave him there until the beasts have eaten all of him but his bones."

"Well then, try it. Kill me!"

Gonzalo took a couple of unsteady steps. The circle of bristling spearheads tightened around his chest, forcing him to stop. He eyeballed Manco and Anamaya with his good eye. Then, recovering his arrogance, he growled:

"You think that you scare me! You're nothing but a coward, Sapa Inca. You're not a man. You don't have what it takes to kill me right here, right now, even with two dozen warriors to do it for you. And I'll tell you why . . ."

He spat and cleared his throat. He broadened his wicked smile.

"Because you know that my death means your own, and you love your own life above all else. More than your gold, more than your women, and more than your honor . . ."

He stared at Manco with utter hatred, and spat insults at him as though he was striking him with a sword:

"See what we've made of you, O Son of the Sun, O divine Sapa Inca! A mere puppet, a bawling, gesticulating doll. The sounds that come out of your mouth have no more meaning than the wails of an infant. . . ."

Gonzalo went on and on as the warriors pushed their spears toward him. The bronze spearheads were touching his dirty shirt now. He brushed a few of them violently aside, but the effort made him dizzy. He stumbled backward like a drunkard and leaned against the wall before continuing:

"O great King of Kings! You think that you can dupe me? Me?" he sniggered again and spat blood onto the flagstones.

"Your *Coya* is nothing but a servant girl. That poor fool Juan thinks he's fucking your Queen, but in fact he has nothing but some virago in his bed. And you thought that I didn't notice!"

Manco signaled to the warriors to step away from the Spaniard. He held Gonzalo's sword in his hand and, pointing it at his gut, he came up so close to him that only the bare blade separated them. The Spaniard's good eye hazed over with fear.

Anamaya also stepped forward. She made as though to hold Manco back. But the Emperor, moving so quickly that the guards jumped back, raised both the sword and his knee. He slammed the blade down, snapping it in two with a high-pitched sound.

"We're the ones," spewed Gonzalo, "who decide who lives or dies! We're the ones with the power over life or death!"

Manco, his eyes bulging with rage, grabbed a club off a guard and swung it above his head.

"No!" cried Anamaya. "Emperor, no! Don't do it, not yet!"

Everything was suspended for a moment. All eyes were on Manco's fist. The whites of his eyes were now as red as Atahualpa's used to be.

The only sound was the Spaniard's raucous, wheezing breath.

"Let him go, my Lord," continued Anamaya gently. "There is truth in his lies. He will do you more harm dead than alive."

Manco let his arm fall, then flung the club at Gonzalo's feet.

"Get out of here, Stranger," he growled. "Leave this *cancha* immediately."

Gonzalo grinned. He shook himself free of the warriors holding him and ran his hand over his cheek, which was bleeding again.

"Yes, listen to your untouchable whore, whom I'll be touching soon enough. It's best for you that I stay alive."

The servant girls and guards moved aside to let him pass. He turned around in the doorway, spat on the ground again, pointed a bloody finger at Manco, and said:

"Give up your high and mighty airs, Sapa Inca. You're nothing here, nothing more than mule shit. From now on, I am Cuzco's true ruler."

As Anamaya watched the guards reluctantly move their spears and clubs to let Gonzalo leave, she thought about his parting words.

They were horrible, grotesque, contemptible.

And they were true.

"We must leave tonight, Emperor," said Anamaya as soon as the guards and servant girls had withdrawn. "You must go as far as possible from Cuzco."

"You shouldn't have prevented me from killing him earlier," growled Manco, not listening.

"His brother would have come to kill you tomorrow. You must harness your rage and not allow it to rule you."

Manco cried out in anger and threw his fists up at the night, as though he was trying to expel all the violence stifled within him. The rain had at last stopped.

"You should have let me kill him! He sullied you with his hands, yet you spared him! Where is your pride, *Coya Camaquen*?"

Anamaya met his gaze directly with her own cold, stony stare.

"Killing him would have started a war. War would have broken out tomorrow! You aren't ready to go to war with the Strangers, Emperor. First you must leave Cuzco and gather your troops. You know as well as I do that we haven't enough warriors at the moment. The Strangers are still stronger than us."

Manco stared at her.

"Do you believe that the time for war is upon us?"

"The time to prepare for it is upon us. We must leave Cuzco this very night. You can no longer remain in this palace."

Manco continued staring at her, as though the meaning of her words was slowly dawning on him.

"Prepare for war . . . but how? Villa Oma and my brother Paullu are with Almagro, on their way to the southern provinces. We have split our forces in order to force the Strangers to split theirs, as they are divided among themselves. Villa Oma and Paullu must be at least two moons away from Cuzco now. I have only five thousand men left in the mountains around the Sacred Valley. If I flee Cuzco without a real army under my command, the Empire of the Four Cardinal Directions is doomed. Who will believe me strong enough to want to join me?"

"If you are placed in chains, if you become the Strangers' prisoner, then your people will certainly shed their tears, but they won't rise up, Emperor. We will be like a body without a head. But if you go into the mountains, then your Ancestors will surely help you. Most of the *chaskis* are still loyal to you. You only have to say the word and they will mobilize all the provinces. We'll form the army you need. Villa Oma and Paullu are ready to come to you with thousands of troops the moment you send for them. Everyone will help you, because everyone will be proud of you."

"Did my father tell you all this?"

There was a trace of sarcasm in Manco's voice that disturbed Ana-maya. But she maintained his gaze and said in a low voice:

"Manco, you know very well that your father, Huayna Capac, hasn't visited me for a long time now. But I'm just like you: not a day passes when I don't yearn to hear his voice. Tonight I had a dream and I thought . . . I thought that he would come to me."

She fell silent for a moment and tears welled up in her eyes. The memory of Gonzalo's assault passed before her mind's eye and mingled with her memory of Gabriel, unnerving her.

She felt the weight of Manco's gaze and continued in a stronger tone:

"Trust me, Manco. I know what the Strangers are made of. What happened just now clearly shows that nothing will stop them. As the Governor's brother said to you, he'll do everything to humiliate you. We must flee now, tonight, without losing another moment. We must leave before it's too late for you to call the people of the Son of the Sun to arms. I beg of you, Manco, please listen to me. Dawn brings with it many dangers."

But Manco still hesitated. He ran his fingers along the edge of Ana-maya's torn *añaco* beneath her cape, and he brushed his hand along her cheek scratched by the Spaniard. Then he gave a resigned nod and said:

"Yes, I trust you, *Coya Camaquen*. Have the necessary arrangements made. We shall leave Cuzco by the secret staircase in the Tower of the Sun."

The light of dawn was already visible over the mountains to the east by the time they were at last coming out of the vast secret labyrinth that linked the terraces of Colcampata to the high Tower of the Sun of Sac-sayhuaman. The fortress's enormous walls overlooking Cuzco looked like the head of a giant sleeping monster by the early morning light.

There were about thirty of them. Manco wanted only a few of his favorite wives and servants and five or six noblemen from his court. The rest were ordered to remain in the royal *cancha* and to go about their business in a normal way, so that the Strangers didn't discover Manco's escape for as long as possible.

Breathing heavily, their chests burning from the effort of the climb, the escapees spread out on the terrace at the base of the tower. A film of sweat covered Anamaya's forehead, and her thighs were tight from their quick ascent up the stairs. She watched the dwarf jump with surprising agility about the low walls that led to a terrace overlooking the city. Then his small form stood still and became obscured in the lingering darkness.

She heard the porters setting down the palanquins, then saw the dwarf returning.

"All's well," he announced with a grin. "Not a sound to be heard. The Strangers are all dreaming of gold. We aren't going to wake them."

He lost his smile when he saw Anamaya.

"Are you all right?" he asked, taking her by the hand.

"I'm fine," she said hoarsely, "just tired from the climb."

But in truth, the memory of her dream of Gabriel and the horrible vision of Gonzalo tearing at her clothes hounded her in waves, utterly draining her. She had already vomited twice, and her nausea had only increased as they had climbed to Sacsayhuaman.

"Come," said the dwarf, leading her to the palanquins, "you must at least rest for a little while. Try to eat something. I brought these for you."

As she lay down in her palanquin, he pulled out a fire-roasted corncob and a mango from a little woven bag he wore slung across his shoulder.

Anamaya, touched, smiled. She stroked the dwarf's hand as she took the fruit and the corn from him, but she placed them at her side rather than eat them.

"I can't possibly eat anything now. But I'll keep them for later."

Manco, standing nearby, surprised them both when he said loudly:

"Eat. The dwarf is right. You must eat and recuperate. We have a long day ahead, and I'm going to need you."

She tried to smile, but she felt almost too weary to do so. She was there—she was always there—to help Manco when he needed her. But who was there for her when she needed help?

Loneliness, her old, familiar, terrible loneliness, invaded her like a shadow.

They skirted around to the east of the town in almost complete silence. They walked quickly, but without running. The cortege made its way along the outer walls of the noblemen's *canchas* before heading down an alleyway into the goldsmiths' section of town. In the square surrounded by adobe houses, they saw the red glow of furnaces still burning. Then they crossed the part of town adjoining the plain where those not born in Cuzco lived. The houses were spaced farther apart here, and were set in well-kept gardens, but were without any protective outer walls. A man or woman occasionally appeared, arms laden with firewood. They would stop dead in their tracks and, astonished, would watch the column slowly disappear into the darkness.

The escapees passed the city's great storehouses before heading south on the well-paved Royal Road. They marched in total silence for over an hour, hearing only the sound of their own sandals shuffling along the flagstones and the noise of birds greeting dawn, as the sky above them slowly turned the color of vanilla.

Anamaya had made space beside her for the dwarf so that he wouldn't exhaust himself running on his short legs. She hadn't left the *cancha* for months, and she was surprised to find how beautiful the fields and mountains behind them were. The previous night's rain had sharpened the reds and ochers of the shimmering terrace plots stepped one above the other, and the mountain looked as though it had been covered in some giant, finely-woven, ceremonial *unku*. Banks of fog, buoyant and ephemeral, slid down from the peaks into the folds of the valleys. The sight of Mother Earth's beauty all around her somewhat eased Anamaya's anxiety. She dared to hope that this serene beauty was in fact a sign from the Ancestors, happy to see them leave the city now sullied by the Strangers, as Anamaya herself had almost been.

But her hope faded quickly.

As the first rays of the sun reached the peaks, a soldier ran along the cortege until he reached the litters, his eyes bulging with panic:

"Emperor! Emperor!"

Manco pushed aside the curtain and ordered the young man to speak.

"My Lord, a *chaski* has just caught up with us. The Strangers have discovered your escape. They know that you've left your *cancha*. They have destroyed it, and . . ."

"Oh no, they're already on our heels!" cried the dwarf, looking at Anamaya.

"They'll catch up with us in no time with their horses," cried an old Lord, fidgeting with his gilded wooden ear plugs. "May Viracocha help us!"

"Now isn't the time to panic," interrupted Manco harshly.

He ordered, in as few words as possible, the noblemen, women, and servants to continue south along the Royal Road.

"There's no point hurrying. If they catch up with you, tell them that I ordered you to join my brother Paullu and their friend Almagro. I'm going to disappear into the valleys to the east. The *Coya Camaquen* is coming with me."

"Me too, Emperor, please!" cried the dwarf, prostrating himself.

"Let him come," said Anamaya, seeing Manco frown. "You know that he'll give his life for you if necessary."

"Even better," muttered the dwarf, "I shall persevere living so that you may remain free."

Manco shrugged, then ordered the porters to set off, which they did at a run, despite the weight of their load. They were no longer on the Royal Road, and the unpaved paths they were now negotiating were littered with slippery stones and mud puddles, but they ran as though they had claws on their feet. They reached the edge of the valley in very little time. Day was now well established. One of the porters suddenly cried out and pointed with his arm. The dwarf, who had been watching the horizon, cried out at exactly the same moment:

"There they are!"

Manco and Anamaya saw the troop of Strangers appear beyond the gray-green *quinua* fields. They looked like giant black-shelled insects skimming with supernatural speed along the top of the plants. And their horses did more than just allow them to travel quickly: from their elevated positions, they were able to see farther across the plain.

"They're on the Royal Road," said Manco hopefully. "They're chasing the women. They won't see us."

Anamaya shook her head.

"I'm afraid they will. The palanquins are clearly visible above the fields."

"She's right, Emperor," agreed the dwarf, abandoning all proper etiquette due a monarch. "If we can see them, then they can see us."

They remained frozen in indecision for a moment and watched the troop of Spaniards galloping on. The wind carried to them cries like those of animals hunting across the plain. Then the dwarf suddenly clapped his hands and jumped down to the ground.

"Emperor, there is a marsh over there," he shouted, pointing at a clump of bushes at the edge of the plain. "The Strangers avoid them because they're no good for their horses. Let the porters continue with the palanquins up the mountain path while we hide there."

Manco assented.

The dwarf was right. The clump of bushes a few leagues beyond the terraces marked the beginning of a bulrush-covered marsh.

The dwarf snapped off a number of reeds and mixed them with others, either dry or rotten, with astonishing speed. He gathered a pile of deadwood and mud, and with them made a great heap of brushwood that looked as though it had been lying there for ages. But when he invited Manco to hide within it, the Emperor hissed disdainfully between his teeth.

"Do you take me for a guinea pig?"

"Emperor . . ."

"No!" shouted Manco angrily, "the Son of the Sun will not hide under a pile of rotten twigs! What would my father say?"

"Manco, it's only for a little while, to get away from the Strangers," said Anamaya gently.

Manco gave her a furious look.

"*Coya Camaquen!* Do you think that I'm going to begin my war against the Strangers by hiding like a coward? Do you want Illapa and Inti to see me huddled up like a child beneath this stinking pile of bushes? Do you want to lend truth to the Governor's brother's words that I'm nothing but a coward?"

"I just don't want you to get caught," replied Anamaya, but in vain. Manco had turned around and now haughtily declared:

"It is for my father and for Viracocha to decide, and I shall remain standing for as long as it takes them to do so."

And with that, he marched off to hide amid the bulrushes, ankle-deep in water.

Anamaya couldn't think of a way to explain to him that he wasn't talking to Gonzalo now, and that he would do better to use crafty military tactics rather than proud, useless speeches to recover his dignity.

They stayed like that for a long time, with Anamaya and the dwarf packed together beneath the pile of branches and Manco waiting only partly hidden amid the bulrushes. But the wet and the cold very soon chilled them to the bone, and Anamaya had to clench her fists to prevent herself from trembling.

For a while, however, Anamaya told herself that they had succeeded. The Strangers' shouting remained distant, and occasionally even seemed to fade farther away. Then, suddenly, she felt the dwarf's fingers tighten around her shoulder.

The first thing she noticed was the thudding of hooves on the earth. Then she heard shouting close enough for her to make out what they were saying.

"Over there, Beltran. Go have a closer look at those bushes."

"They're coming," whispered Anamaya.

The dwarf replied by tightening his grip.

They watched, through the crisscross of branches, two riders approaching side by side. They were moving slowly, looking around carefully. They were coming toward the hideout. One of them slid down the side of his saddle and peered more closely into the bushes. Anamaya closed her eyes. She listened to the hooves thudding past them. Past their hideout. The Strangers hadn't seen them. They were continuing along the swamp.

At that moment, they heard cries echoing from the direction of the mountain.

"By the damned spit of the llama," cursed the dwarf, "they've caught the porters. Now they'll see that the litters are empty."

They heard more shouting. They stared at the rushes in which Manco was hiding. They heard the sound of a horse walking through water, and then a cry, in Spanish:

"Ho, Don Pedro! Have you found him?"

There was no reply, and the two cavalrymen came back along their tracks, passing the hideout once again. At that moment, a very large Stranger emerged from the other side of the marsh. His horse, foaming at the mouth, splashed water in every direction as it turned around in circles.

"We've found their palanquins," he cried. "He can't be far."

As the man's sweating horse reared up, Anamaya recognized him as one of Gabriel's few friends.

"*Hola!* I've found him! Here he is, friends!"

"No!" murmured Anamaya. "No!"

"Shhh . . . keep quiet," whispered the dwarf hoarsely.

The horses splashed through the mud as their riders pushed aside the reeds. Manco was revealed, standing proud and tall. His calves were covered in black mud. He looked as though he was wearing Spanish boots.

"Don't move," said the dwarf again, gripping Anamaya's arm tightly. They listened as the big Stranger gave his orders.

"Beltran! Go and inform Don Gonzalo that we've found him. And have the Sapa Inca's palanquin sent here."

For a fleeting moment, Anamaya thought that Manco was looking into her eyes through the pile of deadwood. She had stopped breathing and if it weren't for the dwarf she would have immediately come out of hiding.

Now Manco turned away, his face utterly expressionless, as though this was no greater nuisance than having to get out of his bath. His porters arrived running. The Greek smiled and respectfully invited Manco to get into his litter. Manco pushed aside the curtain and climbed in.

"I must go with him," whispered Anamaya.

"Are you mad?"

"We can't let him go by himself."

"And what exactly will you do to help him, once the Strangers have their hands on you?"

"I must go . . ."

The dwarf slapped his tiny hand across her mouth.

"Please, say nothing more! Have you already forgotten what happened last night? What do you think the Spaniard is going to do with you now?"

At that moment, as though emerging from the dwarf's nightmare, Gonzalo appeared galloping at full tilt on the edge of the swamp, accompanied by three other horsemen. He rode right up to the palanquin, so close that one of its porters was struck by a hoof and fell to the ground with a cry of pain.

The Governor's brother yanked back on his reins and turned his horse about, splashing stagnant water on everyone around him. He wore a scarlet kerchief around his head, hiding his wounded eye.

"Well, I must say that I'm very happy to see my beloved King, my soaking wet Sapa Inca, once again."

His voice was calm and spat venomous irony. He rode up as close as he could to the litter, leaned forward brusquely in his saddle, grabbed Manco by the hair, and dragged him out off his seat.

"Manco . . ." breathed Anamaya.

"Shut up! Don't watch!" hissed the dwarf.

"Don Gonzalo," reprimanded Candia, "you cannot treat him like that."

Gonzalo ignored him. He pulled Manco out of his palanquin.

"Don Gonzalo!"

"Enough from you, Candia the Greek! Why don't you go check if your mother doesn't need her ass wiped!" shouted Gonzalo, dropping Manco to the ground. "Have the chains fetched here, and shackle this monkey king."

Anamaya couldn't watch anymore. She felt as though her heart would stop beating. She heard the clanking of the chains, the shouts and insults, and she felt the light extinguish in her soul. The dwarf was hugging her as though he wanted to squeeze the breath out of her.

"O Lords of the Other World, O Viracocha! Why have you abandoned us so?"

"Shut up," whispered the dwarf. "Please, shut up."

The Spaniards made away with their prisoner, and silence returned to the marsh.

When there was no other noise but the whisper of the breeze and the lapping water, the dwarf hugged her with unbelievable strength.

"Now there's only you, Princess, there's only you. Don't let them catch you, you hear me? Never let them catch you."

THIRTY-THREE

Tupiza–Grand Salar, November/December 1535

There were hundreds of them, both young and old, and shackled in groups of ten or twenty. Each one had the same type of grimy iron collar clapped around his neck. Their shoulders were all grazed and bruised from the swinging of the chain linking them together. They all had the same hollow look brought on by hunger and fatigue. And they all had the same vacant stare in their eyes, eyes that could no longer tell the difference between the blinding brightness of day and the dark of night.

They had been marching together for days now. They had crossed mountains and traversed bare plains, and they strained their emaciated muscles to carry baskets that weighed as much as they did, baskets laden with clothes, food, pewter plates and goblets, in short all the supplies needed by the Spaniards.

Around midday, under a sun beating straight down, one of them stumbled. He righted himself for a moment. Then his knees gave way and he passed out. A whip cracked in the air above him, but he didn't wake up. The chain linking him to other men tightened. It cut into the other men's necks, half-strangling them. But no one complained about this now familiar event.

Oddly, the basketful of goblets and platters on the man's shoulders remained in place. But he was dead. His muscles had contracted in spasms, and his arms now seemed to be fused to his burden while the rest of his body had surrendered.

At last the basket tipped over, and all its contents tumbled to the ground with a loud chinking sound. The men chained together came to a standstill. A low murmur rose from those men immediately around the dead man. His head was gruesomely held upright by the chain, his body hanging limply beneath it.

Gabriel, riding fifty paces away, turned around in his saddle when he heard the metallic sound. What he saw chilled him to the core and made him feel as though his own body was nothing more than a pile of bones.

A horseman wearing a broad hat was standing before the dead man suspended from the chain between two other Indians. The Spaniard passed his whip nonchalantly from his right hand to his left and drew his sword from its scabbard. Gabriel realized what he was planning to do only when the blade was glinting high in the sunlight.

He circled his horse around and violently spurred it on, shouting at the top of his lungs:

"No! No!"

But the blade was already flying through the air. The Spaniard leaned forward in his saddle and, extending his arm as though sweeping a scythe through wheat, he sliced off the dead man's head. It rolled away between the clumps of *ichu* grass as the headless body collapsed in a heap, under the frantic gazes of his companions.

Gabriel only caught a glimpse of the body collapsing as he galloped along. He drew his sword on the run, provoking a cry from the mass of porters watching him approach. The Spaniard turned around in his saddle, looking bewildered beneath the broad brim of his hat. He hadn't time to cry out or even defend himself. With his fist clenched within the shell of his sword, Gabriel struck him in the chest with incredible force.

A sound like dry wood cracking cut through the air as the man flew out of his saddle. He tumbled over the rear of his horse and fell with a thud on the ground. He tried to stand, wide-eyed with incomprehension, blood streaming from his mouth. He was eye level with Gabriel's boots, and when he looked up he saw a man with a demented look to him, as though ready to destroy the entire world. Now Gabriel pressed his blade against the man's glottis, blocking his air passage and cutting off the air to his brain, so that he barely heard Gabriel cry:

"I'm going to cut your swine head from your body, you whoreson cur!"

The man felt the steel dig into his flesh. He grabbed Gabriel's sword with both his hands and was about to push him away when a voice thundered through the air:

"I wouldn't, if I were you, Don Gabriel. Make a move and your brains will be lying splattered on the ground."

Gabriel turned his head slightly and saw a crossbow pointed at him not five paces away.

For half a second he felt the urge to go ahead and kill the man on the ground. He felt as though hearing the crack of the crossbow releasing its quarrel at him would at last put an end to the shame that had been wasting him for days.

"Move back slowly, or else I'll order him to shoot!" cried Almagro again, sensing Gabriel's hesitation.

Don Diego sat on his horse behind the crossbowman, pointing at Gabriel. The familiar ugliness of his face was heightened by his crimson rage. His lips had turned violet and his cheeks, already severely pockmarked by his many erstwhile battles with syphilis, seemed about to explode like balloons. His body, inordinately thin, looked ridiculous beneath his cratered, puffed-up face.

The man at Gabriel's feet crawled away, moaning. Gabriel let him go. The column had come to a complete standstill, and hundreds of Indians were watching this scene with fearful and remote expressions on their faces. Not one of them had done anything about the headless body from which a steady stream of dark blood continued to flow.

Almagro cracked his reins on his horse and rode up to Gabriel.

"By the blood of Christ," he growled, "what's come over you?"

"You're a dangerous lunatic, Almagro. Look around. Not one man here walks free. Every single one is in chains. They're dying like flies from hunger and thirst, yet you never relieve them of their burdens. You even have them carry your foals on palanquins. And by night, you hobble them together like animals, without shelter, even if it rains or hails. The children are the lucky ones; at least they die within a week. As for the women, they're raped by dozens of your men until blood flows freely down their thighs. If villagers try to flee your cruelty, you burn their villages, or else you remove the roofs from their huts so that you can cook your meals in them. And now your vile henchmen have taken to decapitating corpses so as to save themselves the bother of having to actually unlock the irons. You are the scum of the earth, Almagro, it's written on your face. You leave your foul stench lingering behind you with every step you take."

Gabriel fell silent, trembling with anger. Almagro's laughter had grown with each declaration Gabriel had made, and now it erupted into a frank guffaw, the captain's entire emaciated body shaking with mirth. He had two dozen Spaniards now gathered around him, both cavalrymen and foot soldiers, and they laughed with him.

"Poor soul! Poor delicate little bird!" chuckled Almagro, eliciting more chortling from his men. "D'you hear, gentlemen? This fop presumes to teach us our duty! Well, I suppose there's an explanation for it. Having licked Don Francisco's butt one too many times, his Eminence Don Gabriel has become accustomed to the scent of roses!"

Gabriel stepped forward and rigidly pointed the tip of his sword at Almagro's rakish form. The laughter instantly stopped. The Indians, who had been watching wearily, now stared with disbelief. A group of cavalrymen surrounded Gabriel and drew their stiletto daggers. Almagro, smiling contemptuously, raised his hand to stop them.

"In all his time here, the Governor has never allowed the people of Peru to be treated with such brutality," shouted Gabriel for the benefit of all. "Almagro! When you arrived at Cajamarca, you brought with you shame and disgrace. You have spread nothing but terror around you. Atahualpa died because you lied and hoodwinked good people. You are nothing but a stain on the honor of the conquest. I pray that there is such a place as hell. It cannot be different from the one that you have created here. And if God exists, then I'm sure he'll welcome you there."

Gabriel, beside himself, almost thrust his blade home, but his bitter diatribe had opened the floodgates of bile within him. He suddenly felt nauseous. He broke out in a cold sweat, and was obliged to set one knee on the ground. He leaned against the hilt of his sword as though it were a walking cane. He felt all his strength drain from him, his eyes welled with tears, and he bent double as he vomited out his guts.

Laughter broke out again from all around him.

Don Diego spurred his horse closer, and set his heel on Gabriel's bowed neck.

"*Gabrielito,*" he warbled, "I feel that this journey is bad for your health. Your poor little heart is so fragile, as is your soul. The way you're going, I fear that this journey might be your last. Take my advice: leave us to continue on our road to hell and return to your lovely Garden of Eden."

Gabriel said nothing in reply. He heard the jeers and laughter all around him. He felt a new emotion rise up inside him, a bitter brew that he was forced, despite himself, to drink to the last drop.

He was forced to listen to every jeer, to every snigger, and to look at those faces twisted by the free reign of man's most ignoble instincts. He forced himself to get up and swallow the bile gathered at the back of his throat, swallow it as though it were nectar. In his humiliation he found the fountainhead of his strength.

Gabriel, a bitter taste still lingering in his mouth, galloped along the length of the entire column until he reached the palanquins of the Inca grandees. Their leaders, in theory at least, were the Sage Villa Oma and Paullu, Sapa Inca Manco's favorite brother. They were, also in theory, meant to be leading the column itself.

There were no chains or starved faces here. A few guards, dressed in tunics as clean as they had been on the great square in Cuzco, tried to bar Gabriel with their spears. An order thundered out from behind them. The guards uncrossed their spears and now escorted Gabriel to Villa Oma's litter. The hanging enclosing it opened, as did the one of the neighboring palanquin. Gabriel recognized Paullu's noble and wily face.

The two Inca lords looked at him with a degree of incredulity. Gabriel made a deliberate effort to slow his racing mind and get hold of himself, and he made sure to salute them appropriately before saying:

"Sage Villa Oma, in the name of the Governor Don Francisco Pizarro, I have come to ask you to put an end to the appalling suffering being endured by your people in this column. It is not possible to continue south in such a manner. Your people will all be dead before we arrive. I can promise you that Don Francisco would never allow such unspeakable horror. It is a clear violation of his orders."

Young Paullu gave Gabriel a furtive look of fury before turning away. The Sage, however, remained impassive. He went on passing his ball of coca leaves from one cheek to the other, offering Gabriel no sign of a reply.

"You must know what I'm talking about," insisted Gabriel. "You must intercede; you must go to Don Diego. You must insist that the porters be freed of their chains. You must demand that the women and children be allowed to leave the column. In the name of Emperor Manco . . ."

Now the Sage's black eyes weighed on Gabriel so heavily that he fell silent. All around him, there was nothing but silence.

His bay, ill at ease and stamping at the ground, snorted loudly. Gabriel was obliged to turn around before continuing:

"Sage Villa Oma! I know who you are, and you know me. I was at Cuzco when Emperor Manco placed the royal *mascapaicha* on his head. I know that he designated you as second in command of the Empire of the Four Cardinal Directions. And I am a . . . a friend of the *Coya Camaquen*. I beg of you, listen to me: it is not Governor Pizarro's wish that your people be abused so. Lord Paullu, Sage Villa Oma, how can you stand by and watch?"

Despite his fury and his frustration, Gabriel could tell that the silence greeting his words was like a bottomless well. All the noblemen and all their porters and guards were looking at him now, their faces utterly indecipherable. And together they presented him with a wall of silence.

Then the sage spat a thick green line of coca juice to the ground between Gabriel's horse's hooves. He clicked his tongue, ordered the porters on, and let the curtain fall back across his litter.

He had a long, cold, sleepless night.

He sat with his back against a boulder on the edge of a talus that partly sheltered him from the wind less than a quarter of a league from the immense column. For hours he watched the torches glowing red in Almagro's camp. At the other end of the column he could see the torches burning in front of the Inca lords' tents. Between these two beacons was darkness, a darkness that hid suffering and shame.

And at the blackest moment of the night, when the moon had gone and the sky above was empty, apart from a few stars low to the south, Gabriel let his anger and impotence overwhelm him. He clenched his scabbard between his teeth so that his howls wouldn't carry too far, and he cursed God, mankind, the earth, and life itself.

And then he saw Anamaya's face in his mind's eye, and the mere thought of her was like a breath of purified air. He was trembling again, but this time not from the choler of being human in this godforsaken place at this godforsaken time. For a moment, his entire body grew light. For a moment, he imagined extending his arm and touching the warm and reassuring flesh of his beloved.

Dawn approached. It rolled, like some pallid, celestial wave, over the mountains rising majestically to the east. Gabriel was still wide-awake. He shivered every now and then, his blanket heavy with dew. The fire he had built the night before was now nothing but embers. He knew he had to make a decision soon. He had to decide which was the lesser of two evils. He could either continue on the road to hell with Almagro and his henchmen and thereby suffer their jeers and taunts, or he could return to Don Francisco in Lima, his "Garden of Eden," as the vile Almagro had put it. Either way, he would need both his shoulders to carry his shame.

His bay stood a few paces away from him, half-asleep. It opened its eyes every now and then and gave him an anxious look, pricked up its ears, snorted, and shook its mane from side to side, before coming over and nuzzling him with its nose.

Suddenly the horse stiffened, bristled its spine, and turned around on itself. Gabriel heard stones crunching beneath someone's step—a light step, like someone treading softly to avoid being heard. He quickly drew his dagger beneath his blanket. He looked to the right, expecting the intruder to come from there, so he was surprised when he heard someone whispering to him from the left.

"Don't be frightened, my Lord. Don't be frightened."

But Gabriel was already on his feet, dagger in hand.

He saw an old, dried-up hand with deformed fingers emerge from beneath a dark red cape. The hood of the cape fell back and revealed a face so wrinkled and so old that at first Gabriel couldn't tell whether it belonged to a man or a woman. The face gave him a toothless smile and its pale gray eyes, the color of melting snow, shone brilliantly.

"Don't be frightened, my Lord."

The visitor offered Gabriel a cloth package, its four corners tied together.

"Here is some food that I put aside for you."

Astonished, Gabriel took the package and began untying it. Inside was a handful of corn and a few shriveled and blackened potatoes, potatoes that had been frozen in the ground for a long time before being cooked.

"Thanks," he murmured, then: "Why have you done this?"

The visitor uttered an elfin laugh, revealing herself to be a woman.

"Because of your courage and decency yesterday, Stranger. We saw your fire burning by itself out in the night, and we wanted to thank you."

"We?"

The old woman pointed at the column with her buckled hand and said:

"All of us. Everyone knows what you did. People talked about your rage throughout the night, and of how you went to the Sage and told him to rise up against your own people."

"Oh yes? Then perhaps you can explain to me why Sage Villa Oma didn't even answer me."

The matriarch hesitated for a moment. She stared intensely at Gabriel, making him ill at ease.

"Because he had already made up his mind. He left last night to free Emperor Manco and prepare for war with the Strangers in Cuzco."

Gabriel's hairs stood on end beneath his doublet.

"What are you saying?"

"Emperor Manco is held captive in Cuzco. The *chaski* brought us the news two days ago. The Strangers there are of the same mold as the ones here. They placed a chain around the Emperor's neck."

"O sweet Jesus!"

At first, Gabriel didn't dare ask the question burning on his lips. But he stared at the ancient face before him and finally asked:

"And the *Coya Camaquen*? Do you know if she's being held captive too?"

The old woman shook her head slightly and curled her lips.

"Who is the *Coya Camaquen*?"

Gabriel said nothing. He had a nightmare vision of Gonzalo and Juan mauling Anamaya. He saw Anamaya with a chain around her neck. Anamaya . . .

He had to stop his imagination. The road to Cuzco was too long—he would go mad before getting there.

He stood up, folded his blanket, and picked up his saddle. His horse snorted and came up to him as though it had been waiting for this.

"Which way did the Sage go?" asked Gabriel as he saddled the horse.

The old face smiled at him.

"He took the discreet paths through the mountains, but you'll catch up with him quickly if you follow the guide who brought us here. You should take water and more food with you. I'll help you find some."

Gabriel slipped the saddle strap through its buckle, then turned around with a frown and asked:

"Why do you want so much to help me?"

"Because I like you."

"Well, I like you too, Grandma. You're cute."

"Cute, ha, ha, ha!"

The old woman laughed as daintily as a girl.

He heard her laughing still as she headed back to the column and he finished saddling his horse.

For the first time in a long while, his soul was at peace. A glimmer of life had appeared before him, a crack in the wall of wickedness.

Now he had only one task ahead of him.

And that reassured him, even if it was the height of recklessness.

THIRTY-FOUR

Huchuy Qosqo, December 1535

It was a cool evening. Anamaya stretched out her hands toward the fire that the dwarf had lit. A soup boiled slowly in a terra-cotta pot, releasing the sour odor of wild onions and tomatoes into the moist air.

Anamaya glanced surreptitiously at her loyal friend. She hadn't recognized him when he had arrived in the village a little earlier, shivering after having walked through the rain for two days, and his face still showed signs of his ordeal.

The high red walls of the *canchas* of Huchuy Qosqo loomed above them in the gathering dusk. The walls glowed carmine in contrast to the sharp greens of the corn and potato fields that covered the plateau right up to the edge of the cliff overlooking the valley. In more peaceful times, Anamaya had enjoyed the pleasing symmetry of this city suspended between sky and earth. But now it seemed as though Pacha Mama, the beloved Mother Earth, was suffering the same agony as the dwarf.

That morning a terrible storm had lashed the Valley of the Royal Cities.

While the sky directly above them had been covered only by a thin mist, a thick bank of clouds as black as smoke had gathered at the edge of the plateau.

A short while after, the entire valley had turned into a cauldron spewing steam from the Underworld. The terraces of corn and *quinua*, spread like butterfly wings on the banks of the River Willkamayo, had disappeared, as had the slopes and the steep road leading to Huchuy Qosqo.

And then a wave of liquid silver had billowed across that sea of clouds and everyone heard Illapa growl, although the thunder rolled from the valley rather than from the sky.

The peasants had begun murmuring among themselves. The women had brought their children indoors. The Elders and priests of Huchuy Qosqo had gathered at the wall at the edge of the plateau. They had all had the same thought: the world was being turned upside down.

The fields and alleyways of Huchuy Qosqo had been bathed in Inti's light winnowed by the mist. Over in the distance, beyond the Valley of the Royal Cities, the eastern mountains were glowing beneath Inti's glare. But the sea of clouds had continued to seethe between the two, forks of silver light occasionally ripping through it.

And then it had ended. The clouds had spiraled upward into whorls that had been quickly torn apart by the wind. A lukewarm fog had rolled in over the fields, had combined with the light rain, and had left a lacquer of moisture on the *canchas'* mud walls. The sky had darkened. It had rained nonstop until late in the afternoon.

That's when the dwarf had arrived, filthy and exhausted after having trekked along the arduous mountain paths.

The sky was cloudless now. The only turmoil was on the dwarf's face. Anamaya filled a big terra-cotta bowl with steaming soup.

"Eat," she ordered him gently. "Eat. You're trembling from hunger as much as from cold. You can tell me your news after."

The dwarf held out his hands like a child and took the bowl. He stared at the rich reddish stew for a moment, then shook his head and looked up at Anamaya from under his thick eyelids.

"No," he said, "I can't eat. First I must tell you . . ."

But he fell silent. His eyes burned feverishly and stared at Anamaya. She reached out and caressed his temple lightly with her fingertips. He set the bowl down on a stone next to the fire, took hold of her hand, and pressed his forehead into it as though he might draw from it all the strength that he lacked.

"First of all," he murmured, "they dragged him across the lower city. They led our Emperor, Emperor Manco, before the Coricancha with chains around his neck. Then they kept him on Colcampata Square for three days, their chains around his neck and ankles."

The dwarf paused, as though expelling the poison that these words were contaminating him with. He pushed away Anamaya's hand and curled up on himself.

"They left our Emperor there, outside, and in chains. His *unku* was torn and filthy. He wore the same one for three days. Three days, Anamaya! The Son of the Sun appeared thus before the mummies of his Ancestors, before the eyes of the people of Cuzco. And the Strangers came to taunt him from dusk till dawn."

The dwarf fell silent again. Anamaya couldn't bear to even look at him. She kept her gaze fixed on the distant peaks. She looked at the snow-capped mountains rising in the night, and she felt as though their snow was chilling her to the bone.

"When they at last took him from Colcampata, the entire City of the Puma wept for him," continued the dwarf. "They took him to the house in which the foreign devil tried to rape you. The Emperor's servant girls wailed with grief when they saw how he was being treated. Some ran away, others used the Strangers' weapons to slit their own throats or cut open their own bellies. All the concubines went to the Strangers and begged them to treat the Emperor with more respect. The Strangers laughed at them. They locked the concubines in the courtyard, brought Manco to them, bound in chains, and tore his women's clothes from them before his very eyes. Then they raped them throughout the night, forcing him to watch. Many were dead by the next morning. Their lives drained out of them from between their legs."

The dwarf was having trouble breathing. He was trembling so much that he had to lean against the mat to prevent himself from toppling over. He didn't dare look at Anamaya. She was sitting extremely still, and her stillness belied a tension that seemed on the point of exploding.

Suddenly the dwarf let out a sob and swiped his fist through the air, knocking over and breaking the pot of soup. The fire went out in a hiss of steam.

"They threw him in a pit and pissed on him by the dozen," he said.

"That's enough," said Anamaya, rising to her feet.

Her face looked as though it had been carved from a block of chalk.

For Anamaya, war had always been something remote, the sound of fighting in the distance, the always baffling sight of thousands of warriors facing one another across a battlefield.

Now, she felt the spirit of war burning within her.

The Sacred Double glimmered by torchlight.

The statue so coveted by the Strangers was set on a cotton-filled woven cushion on a large polished stone, in a small temple. Coca leaves were burning in a brazier at his feet, their heady odor filling the room.

Anamaya entered to find two young women sprinkling *cantuta* petals on the ground. They had just presented the Sacred Double with his meal. Anamaya waved them away.

Her face was empty and expressionless. Two silver strings held a long woolen cape around her shoulders, but still she shivered with such violence that her teeth chattered.

She filled a ceremonial goblet of painted wood with *chicha* from a jug. She raised it above her head. She stared into the Sacred Double's golden face. He was as impassive as she was.

But instead of saluting her husband from the Other World, she let her arms fall back down to her sides. She didn't pour the *chicha* on the ground as an offering. She held the goblet tight against her chest and closed her eyes. She barely opened her mouth as she whispered:

"Why do I offer food and drink to you day after day, O Sacred Husband? Why do I pray to you and tell you of my suffering if you cannot hear, Emperor Huayna Capac? What have we done, that you should remain silent for so long? What have we done to deserve the shame that we are suffering here in this world?"

She fell silent. She was swaying from side to side, perhaps unwittingly.

She frowned and drew her lips tight. Then she cried out so violently that the torches flickered and almost went out:

"Why have you abandoned us?"

Anamaya stepped forward without opening her eyes and stretched out her arms. She let fall the goblet of *chicha* to the ground, and she sobbed as she hugged the golden statue.

"Are you there, Noble Lords of the Other World? Can you not feel our love for you, or hear our cries? Do you not see our suffering? O Noble Lords of the Other World, not a day passes that we do not obey your will in everything. You are on our minds from the moment we wake until we lie down to sleep at night. We watch the flight of birds and the patterns of clouds to better understand your will. We grow the finest ears of corn for you, we offer you the blood of our best llamas to please you, and so that you will be proud of us. We weave tapestries of the finest colors to honor you in this world as in the other. We obey all your laws. But still you give us only this silence. Are you frightened of the Strangers' gods? Have you become as weak as us?"

All Anamaya's muscles seized up with pain and anger, and she felt as though she were being torn apart. She shook the Sacred Double on its cushion, unable to help herself, and shouted:

"Are you there? Didn't you hear what the dwarf said? Didn't you see your son Manco being pissed on by our enemies?"

Her words tore through the still and empty night.

"O Emperor Huayna Capac! You, who held my hand before you joined Inti and when I was still just a girl, don't forsake me! Don't turn your back on me. Don't let me think that we are all alone, like children lost in the mountains. Would you let us be destroyed in war as you let us be in peace? Don't abandon our people's fate to the Strangers. If I, the *Coya Camaquen,* have offended you, then I am ready to be burned to ashes."

But her implorings were met only with silence.

The villagers of Huchuy Qosqo had gathered outside the little temple to listen to the *Coya Camaquen*'s despair. Now they trembled with her, and they bit their lips as she did. They hoped, as she did, that the silence would give way to something greater.

But the only sound was the regular drip-drip of rainwater streaming off the *ichu* roofs onto the flagstones.

It was almost dawn when she finally decided to leave the temple.

The torches had gone out, and no one had dared relight them.

Although the night was still dark, when Anamaya came out of the temple she had to blink to adjust to the light.

It happened in a flash.

The plateau, the Sacred Valley, and the eastern mountains were illuminated in a light as bright and as harsh as the sun's. The plain looked as though it had been covered in an even, chalky blanket of salt. The entire world seemed to have suddenly turned into a desert. The earth's surface was nothing but an old, cracked layer of dead skin. There were no more shadows, no more trees or bushes, not a single sign of life. Not even an insect.

Anamaya felt her knees collapse beneath her. She didn't notice the

A . B . D A N I E L

dwarf's small but strong hand reach for her. She didn't hear the murmurs as she fainted. All she saw was what the world of man would look like when it was finally and irreversibly dead.

And then she saw him. Gabriel.

She saw his blackened skin and his clothes torn to rags. First he appeared far away on the endless plain, then right up close, so close that she could hear his labored breathing and see his swollen lips and his cheeks cracked like old leather. She saw his pupils burned by the white death. Sweat dripped from his eyelashes, which the sun had turned into minuscule salt crystals. She saw his hands and fingers covered in clotted blood. He was swaying like a man on the edge of death. Like a man who had nothing left but his own shadow. His gaze was empty, absent.

Each time he took another step forward through the white desert, his heel kicked up a little cloud of dust that immediately settled and covered his tracks. He wasn't even leaving a trail behind him. Suddenly, he stumbled and fell.

Anamaya cried out.

She had understood two things at once: that Gabriel was dying somewhere at that very moment, and that the Lords of the Other World had heard her cries after all.

THIRTY-FIVE

The Grand Salar Desert, December 1535

As far as he could see, everything was white.

They had just reached the top of the last hill. The path ahead of them twisted back and forth down a steep slope, then came out onto a broad desert valley, a sea of salt stretching beyond the horizon and flanked by steep mountains. It looked white, hard, and devastating, like a door opening into the void.

"*Lloc!*" said a raspy voice. "Now is the wrong time to cross."

The owner of the voice was the embodiment of the landscape that Gabriel had been traveling through these last few days. He was short, very dirty, and very tanned. His long, filthy hair fell in matted knots from under a bonnet of faded colors. His only clothing was a threadbare, stained tunic and a long llama leather cord around his waist. The muscles of his thighs and calves were so well defined that they gave the appearance of being raw and without a cushioning layer of skin. But his feet were the most remarkable part of him. They seemed to have been molded to the shapes of all the stones and paths that he had walked across. They looked more like animal paws than human feet. The toes were no longer really distinguishable, and the toenails had been overgrown by a skin so thick that it didn't bleed when it cracked open.

Gabriel had met him the previous night. After having vainly tried to catch up with the Sage Villa Oma, he had had to admit to himself that he was well and truly lost.

Ever since he had left Tupiza, the Sage's slender lead had incomprehensibly grown. Yet Gabriel had continued on, resting his horse only when it was absolutely necessary. In the villages where he stopped for a little food, he learned that the Sage had been recruiting men wherever he passed. All had been ordered to the north. He thus had an innumerable supply of porters, and he was traveling day and night, both eating and sleeping in his palanquin.

Gabriel's first thought had been that the Sage's haste was an indication of the gravity of the situation in Cuzco. And if the Sage was mobilizing every man he came across, then war was certainly imminent.

His second thought had been one of despair. He knew that there was no longer any way he could catch up with Villa Oma and cross the Empire safely with him. In other words, he wouldn't get to Anamaya as quickly as he could have. Instead, he would have to make his own way, and that meant getting lost, taking the wrong turns, turning back, and generally advancing at a snail's pace while the Pizarro brothers would certainly be submitting Anamaya to the worst atrocities. What he had just witnessed among Almagro's thugs left him without a trace of hope. Now, not a day passed without the most appalling visions assailing his peace of mind.

He reproached himself both for his rashness and for his misguided devotion to Don Francisco. The Governor had once again drawn him too far away from his reason for living. From her.

He fantasized about how he would go about ridding the earth of Gonzalo. He dreamed of metamorphosing into a bird and soaring away from the excruciating slowness that pinned him to the ground and left him unable to do a thing to help her. He dreamed of meeting her, of finding himself once more in her arms, of rediscovering the tenderness of her breasts, of finding her as beautiful and as unharmed as the day they had parted.

He had pushed his bay harder than was sensible, forcing it to carry on into the night. And in doing so, he had gotten lost.

He had wandered about in frustration until this ageless man, like some demon emerged from his cave, appeared before him as he was traversing a scree.

The man was now looking at him through eyes as black as night. He warned Gabriel once again in his poor Quechua, repeatedly clicking his tongue:

"*Lloc!* If you cross now, then you'll either arrive quickly or die quickly."

One only had to look at the great emptiness of the salt pan before them to believe him. The sun was rising behind the mountains and their inordinately long shadows stretched across the wan desert. The pallid northern horizon, covered in morning fog, was as curved as the sphere of an ocean.

"Three days, you say?" asked Gabriel for the tenth time.

"Three days, if you make it. Three days, if the sun doesn't consume you first."

"Perhaps we could travel by night instead of day."

"You'll get lost by night! The clouds will hide the peaks of the Apus from you, and they are your guides. You'll die. And if the clouds are absent for too long during the day, you'll also die. Inti will devour you."

Gabriel gave his horse a reassuring slap. The animal had grown skittish, as though it had understood the Indian's words.

"Three days," repeated Gabriel. "Whereas if I go through the mountains, you say that it'll take me six or seven."

"*Lloc!* Yes. Seven or more, because it's the rainy season, when all the paths turn into rivers. Seven or more. But you won't be dead."

"What good will it do me not to be dead if *she* is? Come, no more talk, we're wasting time. Will you guide me?"

Gabriel asked the question without much hope. So he was surprised when the man nodded.

"You're even crazier than I am," he said.

They entered the desert.

As Gabriel entered the Grand Salar, what he saw astounded him. He had expected to find nothing but salt but instead found nothing but water. The sun was veiled behind a light haze that obscured the horizon. The sky and water blended together into the same washed-out color. Gabriel felt as though he were traveling into an untouched canvas. Both men shielded their eyes, as though to avoid glimpsing evil spirits that might inhabit this strange world.

The Indian showed him how. First he soaked his bonnet with water from one of the four jugs solidly attached to the horse, and then he pulled it low over his forehead, covering his eyes.

"You do the same for yourself and your horse," he decreed raucously. "Otherwise the glare of the salt will burn through your eye sockets and set your head on fire."

Gabriel pulled his last shirt from his saddlebags and ripped it to shreds, then wet them from the jug. His bay didn't complain when he tied a dripping shred around its eyes. But the horse looked so comical in its makeshift eyeshade that Gabriel grinned at it. He wrapped his own head in a piece of cloth like a Moor, leaving only a small slit through which to see ahead of him.

He set off in silence with his horse's bridle over his shoulder. He followed the Indian into the wan waste ahead of them. The Indian's silhouette seemed to float on the void.

The water had disappeared within an hour. It gave way to a world so still that it seemed as though nothing in it would ever move again. It was a harsh world, one that crunched beneath their feet. Its earth was cracked into thousands of salt plates as hard as rock and that extended as far as the eye could see.

The haze had also evaporated, revealing a sky so deeply blue that it unnerved Gabriel. His step fell into time with the familiar rhythm of his horse's hooves.

The mountains' long shadows had long since retreated. The air was still. The Indian looked dead ahead as he trekked on, not once turning his head to look to the right or left. They walked for a while with a patch of rocky scree to their left. It was scattered with cacti so big that to Gabriel they looked like warriors come from another world. The spaces between the mountains at the edge of the sea of salt gradually grew larger, and the peaks themselves appeared and disappeared on the horizon, tremulous in the shimmer of the rising heat.

The sun became a giant burning orb long before it had reached its height. Gabriel felt his skin burning on his unshaved chin and cheeks, burning as though a naked flame was being held to the parts of his flesh not protected by the piece of cloth. It was very tempting to drink some water from one of the jugs. But he managed to resist.

Suddenly the Indian stopped dead in his tracks without saying a word. He stopped so suddenly that Gabriel almost walked right into him.

The man turned around slowly, checking the sight lines on the horizon. Then he looked at Gabriel. He tilted his hat up and shook his head.

"What is it?" asked Gabriel, his mouth dry. "Are we going the wrong way?"

The man pointed at the sky and said:

"*Lloc!* Too much sun."

"What do you mean, too much sun?" asked Gabriel, widening the eyehole in his head wrap.

"Not enough clouds. The sun is going to eat us."

Gabriel didn't seem to understand, so the man waved his black swarthy hand at the expanse of desert and again at the crystal blue of the sky.

"There's too much sun today, as there will be tomorrow and the day after. We will not cross the desert. The sun will eat us. We can make it back to the hills by nightfall."

"No!" protested Gabriel. "That's out of the question. I won't turn back."

The man took a couple of steps back and shrugged.

"Your animal will also die," he said quietly. "No one can cross the sea of salt without clouds above them."

"You're just frightened, that's all. I will cross."

The man looked at him for a moment, then murmured:

"Sometimes it's good to be frightened."

He pulled his hat back down over his eyes and said:

"Tomorrow, if Inti wills it, he will show you a mountain shaped like two hands holding one another by the fingers. He's called Apu Thunupa. Before becoming a mountain, he was a human being, a noble-man like those of Cuzco. He marks the end of the sea of salt. But you must still have eyes to see him."

And with that, the man headed back toward the hills to the east without so much as a good-bye to Gabriel.

Gabriel hesitated. He knew that the Indian was right. He knew that being alone would make crossing the sea of salt even more difficult. But he urged himself on by telling himself the only truth that mattered: What good would being alive be if she wasn't?

He watched the man heading back toward the hills, and noticed that his shadow was very short. He wondered how the Indian managed walking barefoot over the vast cracked salt bed when his own feet felt as though they were boiling in their boots.

When the Indian had walked about a hundred paces without looking back, Gabriel turned away and stroked his horse's mane.

"Come, old buddy, come. We'll do fine on our own."

And he set off before he had time to doubt his own words.

They set off into the desert again before dawn, the sea of white gleaming beneath the night sky. Gabriel found comfort in the myriad of stars
twinkling overhead. It even stayed cool enough, for a few hours at least,
for him to ride his horse instead of leading it by its reins. He used the
Southern Cross as his guide. Then a fog rose. Gabriel told himself that
the Indian had been wrong, that the sun wouldn't eat them after all. It
appeared intermittently through the clouds, a white orb hanging over a
white sea.

All seemed well. The heat wasn't such an ordeal, and the sun's rays
weren't so deadly. Gabriel dismounted and began to walk, leading his
horse. He maintained a brisk pace for almost half a day.

He began to feel the fatigue that had been rising imperceptibly in his
thighs only when the sun was already low in the west. At first it was only
a dull, faint pain. But soon it felt as though a thousand needles were
piercing into his muscles. He took a break for the first time that day and
lay down for a while before setting off again, his bay looking at him with
concern.

Then, less than a league farther on, he had to stop once more. The
pain had become unbearable. He felt as though all the muscles in his
thighs had been twisted hopelessly into knots.

He stopped and started so many times that the horse began to put
his big head in the small of Gabriel's back and push him forward.

Suddenly Gabriel heard a horrid cracking sound as the bay neighed.
The horse's head smacked violently into Gabriel's back, sending him
tumbling over. The horse itself collapsed to the ground with another terrible neigh.

Gabriel, dazed, was too tired to get up off his knees. His worst
nightmare had become reality.

His blinded horse's right hind leg had fallen into a hole the size of a
hand in the thick crust of salt. And it had snapped clean.

"The bay," murmured Gabriel, pulling off his head wrap. "The bay."

The horse pulled back its lips and revealed its yellow teeth. It extended its neck and whinnied plaintively, its nostrils quivering. It made a desperate effort to get up. But its legs just waved helplessly in the air, and Gabriel could tell that its terrified round eyes were glimpsing its own death. It fell back down onto its side with a thud and neighed again.

Gabriel at last emerged from his daze and crawled to his horse. He grabbed its head and felt a terrible shiver run through his faithful companion. The bay was now breathing fast and hard. Its barrel shook as it breathed laboriously. Blood flowed from its belly and stained the salt beneath it.

Only then did Gabriel realize that the horse had collapsed onto the jugs of brackish water and that a shard had pierced into it like a dagger and perforated one of its lungs. Blood was already trickling from its mouth.

"The bay," whispered Gabriel, holding its head against him. "The bay. I never gave you a name, and now it's too late."

The horse fluttered its eyelids over its glassy eyes.

Gabriel made one last, futile effort, ignoring the pain in his thighs. He removed the horse's curb chain, bit, and harness. But the horse looked at him as though asking him only to stroke it. It shuddered again from pain or fever, its whole body trembling.

Gabriel lay the horse's head down on his thighs again. He stroked it for a long time, scratching its ears, caressing its nose.

He knew what he had to do. But he couldn't steel himself to the task.

He pulled his dagger from his belt and set it on the ground at his side.

He told himself that he still had some time, although he could feel the bay's breathing becoming increasingly labored as its lung became painfully flooded.

He cried salty tears. His chest shuddered with fear and a terrible sadness.

And then he did it without thinking about it. His fist closed around the dagger's handle and plunged it into the softest part of the animal's throat.

At the moment of dying, the bay shoved its head so strongly against Gabriel's chest that he fell backward, covered in his horse's blood.

*   *   *

Another night passed. Gabriel no longer knew how long he had been walking.

He was still covered in horse blood. It had coagulated into a crust that protected him from the sun. The sun had returned, and wanted to devour him. Gabriel knew that his time had come.

His lips were so cracked that he had trouble breathing. He thought that if Anamaya were to see him in this horrible condition, she would turn away from him in disgust.

But he forced himself on. He could no longer feel the pain in his legs. He walked as though walking was the only thing his body could do. His hands dangled at his sides, as swollen as balloons, and burning as though they had been baked in an oven.

He raised an eyelid every now and then and pushed back his head wrap with his knuckle. He thought he saw Thunupa's jagged peak, the mountain that had once been a human being. But he knew that he would never reach it. The soles of his leather boots had split, and his feet were becoming like those of the Indian who had been wise enough not to accompany him on the road to death.

"You're even crazier than I am," he repeated over and over, not sure of whom he was talking.

He pictured Anamaya before him, and he walked toward her. He smiled at her, and she at him. He told her:

"I can't join you now, but I'll wait for you. Never forget that I love you."

She nodded and told him that she was all right, that he mustn't worry about her. She said to him:

"Never forget that you are the Puma."

He laughed. He had a vision of her standing in the rich green mountain grass on Thunupa's slope. She was far away now, and he couldn't make out her eyes. She was standing before a little cottage made of red earth with her arms open toward him. She cried to him again:

"Don't forget that you are the Puma, and that you can always find freedom!"

He told himself that he had lost his mind, and that he should pray to God to save him and her as well. He told himself that he still had time to say a prayer, and that he shouldn't offend God.

Once again he heard Anamaya call to him, much closer this time, no more than fifty paces away. He knew that he shouldn't believe it. But he did.

His heartbeat slowed suddenly, and he felt a sense of peace come over him.

At last his long, futile journey was coming to an end. He stopped walking. He raised his bandana with his monstrously swollen hands.

He didn't see the green slopes of Thunupa, but the same infinite white desert of the sea of salt. But he was astonished to see a long train of silhouettes shimmering through the heat in the distance. They seemed to be heading toward him. The silhouettes were dancing, singing, spinning around on themselves.

He smiled as he realized who they were. Angels.

He felt Anamaya's breath on his cheek, he felt her kiss, and he knew, as he collapsed to the ground, that she would be waiting for him in paradise.

THIRTY-SIX

Huchuy Qosqo, February 1536

At dawn, hundreds of them came pouring over the peaks overlooking Huchuy Qosqo. With their shields on their shoulders and their studded clubs in their hands, they streamed through the potato terraces and reached the red walls of the *canchas*. Hundreds of llama-leather sandals shuffled along the flagstones like some obstreperous murmur rising from the bowels of the earth. Everyone, noblemen and commoners, young and old, came out to admire the warriors, some of whom wore tunics from the north, others from the south, and still others from the distant provinces on the coast.

The warriors gathered in an orderly fashion on the great ceremonial terrace overlooking the valley. Most wore grave looks on their faces, but some were smiling happily. Some wore the ensigns and carried the spears that marked them out as generals, while others were but junior officers. Most were officers who had fought under Atahualpa's or Huascar's commanders. But today, this long-awaited day, all old quarrels were forgotten.

Inti himself was happy to see them. The rain had stopped, the weather was clement, and only the lightest clouds were scattered like feathers through the sky. The smoke from coca leaves burning on the braziers rose straight up in the still air. The sun, the Emperor's beloved father, rose above the peaks.

Young virgins served jugs of fresh water and fermented llama milk to the warriors as they arrived, and offered them fruit and corn bread. Priests stood at the four corners of the terrace and around the Sacred Stone to which Inti hitched himself every day. They ceremoniously poured sacred beer onto the dark earth. A drumroll announced the arrival of the Sage Villa Oma and the *Coya Camaquen*.

The Sage carried a heavy gold spear, the symbol of the army's supreme commander. He wore a green and crimson *unku* decorated with geometric patterns that only he was permitted to wear. His leather helmet, covered in gold and with a crescent of blue and yellow feathers rising from it, shone like another sun throwing its light into the Empire's four directions.

A few of the younger warriors murmured with proud approval as they watched Villa Oma approach the *Intihuatana,* the Sun's hitching post, in the center of the *ushnu.* The gold disks set in the Sage's earlobes were bigger and finer than any they had ever seen.

The *Coya Camaquen,* walking at Villa Oma's side, was also wearing magnificent jewels that everyone had thought had disappeared into the Strangers' coffers long ago. She wore a white tunic and had a heavy gold disk, the disk of Inti, hanging from her finely woven sash. Gold adornments shaped like the snake Amaru were coiled through her hair. Amaru, like the *Coya Camaquen,* was known for traveling between the visible and the invisible worlds.

A conch shell sounded loudly as Anamaya and Villa Oma came to a halt facing the mass of armed men. Its deep tone reverberated through the mountains, echoing back at them from farther and farther away, breaking apart and multiplying as it streaked across the Valley of the Royal Cities like a falcon. The warriors gathered on the square and bowed to the two most powerful people in the Empire of the Four Cardinal Directions other than the Emperor.

Anamaya advanced toward the bowing warriors and took hold of the gold disk hanging on her chest. She raised it up above her head and in a strong voice she chanted:

> *O Viracocha, O Inti,*
> *Great Fathers of the Universe,*
> *Beloved Fathers of all that will be,*
> *Hear our supplication!*
> *O Viracocha,*
> *You reign in the sky above!*
> *O Inti,*
> *You reign in the sky below!*
> *O Viracocha, O Inti,*
> *Beloved Fathers of the origin of the World,*

Cast your eyes upon us!
Exalt us with your strength!
O Viracocha, O Inti,
We want nothing more than to experience your Being
In the Day that follows Night.

A brief silence ensued as the warriors straightened. They fixed their fiery gazes on Anamaya's pale eyes as she said in a loud voice:

"Noble Captains of the armies of Tahuantinsuyu. I am overjoyed that you have answered my call. I wanted to tell you the news directly: Emperor Manco will soon be free. The chains that the Strangers had shackled around his neck and ankles are already broken, and soon he will suffer their ignominies no more. Two moons from now, his father Inti will cast his shadow over the Sacred Valley, where the Emperor will join us."

The murmur that had been rumbling through the crowd now exploded into a roar, a raucous, violent outcry that whipped through the crisp morning air like a thousand slingshots being swung.

Villa Oma smiled a brief, bitter smile, revealing his green-stained teeth. He approached Anamaya as the roar diminished, and motioned to four soldiers standing at the edge of the terrace. The men brought him a large basket. They opened it and tipped its contents onto the ground so that all the warriors could see.

A torn doublet, black with coagulated blood, a pair of boots, and a sword snapped in two tumbled out onto the grass. Then another thing fell out of the basket, an odd, round, dark object, both hard and soft. Villa Oma stuck his spear into it.

His face impassive, he slowly raised the bundle of flesh into the air. It was the white skin of a Stranger who had obviously been flayed alive.

The older, more experienced officers didn't bat an eyelid. But a shocked murmur rose from the younger ones. Anamaya looked away. She did her best to suppress the nausea rising up inside her. Villa Oma thundered:

"The man who used to wear this skin had his dogs devour our children. He was the first of the Strangers to have sullied the Coricancha. His name was Moguer. His agonized cries were music to my ears, because they blocked out the sound of those laughing and humiliating our Emperor Manco. This is our answer to the Strangers."

Villa Oma's face was as hard as a bronze axe as he carried the trophy past the warriors on the point of his spear, making sure that everyone saw it. He continued in the same stentorian tone:

"While I was away the *Coya Camaquen* obtained the support of the Elders of the Other World. The Sacred Double of our beloved Huayna Capac proposed to come and free his son, Emperor Manco, himself! We must all be grateful to her. Even though she's only a woman, she behaves like a warrior. But tomorrow, when the Emperor joins us here in this valley, free at last and with the light of Inti upon him, we must provide him with the force necessary to punish those who laid their hands on him."

Villa Oma flicked his spear through the air, and Moguer's hide flopped down in front of the younger officers.

"I, Villa Oma, second in command of the Empire of Tahuantinsuyu, declare that, before the month of Aucaycusqui, we will retake the City of the Puma from the Strangers, and we will celebrate the great Festival of the Sun within its walls. We shall purify Cuzco with a great battle so that our Emperor may return to his rightful throne in his *cancha* and our Ancestors' mummies may once again enjoy peace in the great temple of the Coricancha. From today onward, each of you must begin recruiting men and gathering weapons. I want enough men to cover the peaks of all the hills surrounding Cuzco. On the day of battle, I want Emperor Manco's warriors to form a noose around the city as strong as a belt made of llama leather. And then we will tighten it around the Strangers' throats so that not one of them remains alive."

Villa Oma mimed strangling the enemy with his hands. But the shiver that ran up the warriors' spines wasn't caused by this gesture.

A rain shower had been moving from one mountain to another as the Sage had been speaking. When he fell silent, the seven-colored Arc of Cuychu suddenly appeared. Its curve rose high into the sky and its ends disappeared into the steep slopes falling away at the end of the Huchuy Qosqo plateau. It shone clearly and splendidly for all the warriors to see.

Anamaya, Villa Oma, the residents of Huchuy Qosqo, the warriors, everyone raised their palms up toward the rainbow, the messenger from the Gods of War, and chanted:

"We see you, Cuychu, we see you clearly. Welcome here among us, you who bring us the strength and joy of battle."

*   *   *

In the small temple's gentle half light, the beams of sunshine that filtered through from the exterior drew a smile on the Sacred Double's face. Villa Oma considered the statue for a long time before glancing at Anamaya, who had the offerings ready.

"*Coya Camaquen,* I'm happy that we find ourselves together once again for this momentous occasion," he said, "and I'm very proud of you. What you've done for Manco is invaluable."

Anamaya shook her head unceremoniously and said:

"It's only the beginning of something that I'm longing to see the end of. The Governor's older brother has returned from his country. He now commands the Strangers in Cuzco. He is vain and proud, and he takes advice from no one. He smiles at the Emperor and pretends to be his friend only because he wants more gold. We managed to get some vases and plates to Manco. He gave them to the Governor's older brother, and his chains were removed. Then the priests agreed to sacrifice a statue of Viracocha, and we sent that too. It's as big as my husband the Sacred Double, but it's hollow. Manco presented it to the Strangers and they were so gratified that he is now allowed to come and go as he pleases. Soon he will suggest to the Governor's brother that he go and fetch the Sacred Double. All the Strangers talk about it, about how heavy it is, and how it's made of solid gold. Then Manco will leave Cuzco, and will only return with our armies."

There was real joy in her smile.

"I am only putting into practice what you taught me, Villa Oma," she added.

The Sage's laughter sounded like sand crunching beneath someone's step. He nervously stroked Anamaya's wrist.

"Oh, I might have taught a few of the more elementary things to a strange child called Anamaya. But the *Coya Camaquen* is no longer that child, and hasn't been for a long time."

Anamaya blinked and lowered her eyes. Villa Oma's compliment confused her.

"May I ask you something, Sage?"

Villa Oma screwed up his eyes, and she felt herself blush under his sharp gaze.

"Ask whatever you want, *Coya Camaquen*. There is nothing I know that you cannot know too."

She almost reneged the opportunity, but her desire to know was too strong. She had spent too many sleepless nights worrying recently, and it had become unbearable.

"Have you seen him?" she whispered.

Villa Oma stiffened like a bowstring. His mouth became tight and his eyes burned with anger.

"Who are you talking about, *Coya Camaquen?*"

"You know. You were with him on the road to the south, and . . ."

"How dare you?"

"Villa Oma!"

"How dare you! You, of all people! And today of all days, when we have just decided to go to war with the Strangers."

"Villa Oma, Gabriel isn't like the rest of them. He's the Puma."

"Shut up! Do not pronounce his name in this place. Do not dishonor the temple. All the Strangers are the same, *Coya Camaquen*, d'you hear? All of them without exception. I watched them for days and days destroying everything in their path. Men, women, children, houses and animals, temples, everything! They spread destruction day and night. They are demons, *Coya Camaquen*, and he is one of them."

"No he isn't! He's the one that Emperor Huayna Capac sent to me."

"You're mistaken."

"In that case, Sage Villa Oma, I must have been mistaken about everything else. I must have been mistaken about the comet that designated Atahualpa as Emperor. I must have been mistaken when the Sacred Double designated Manco as our Inca to me. If I'm wrong about Gabriel, Villa Oma, if he isn't the Puma who is meant to guide me, then I've been wrong ever since that first night when Emperor Huayna Capac held my hand."

The Sage spat a long stream of green coca juice onto the temple's threshold.

"Believe what you want, *Coya Camaquen*. But I am the supreme commander of the Inca's armies, and I warn you: you will not save this Stranger from the fate that awaits him. I will personally make sure that he is one of the first to die. And think about this as well, if you can: if you betray your husband, the Sacred Double, with this man, then you are putting all of us in danger. If you behave like an adulterous young girl yearning for caresses, then you are going to destroy Manco and the entire Empire of the Four Cardinal Directions, Anamaya. And if you do that, I will kill you myself."

Anamaya watched him storm away. He seemed absolutely certain of himself.

Trust the Puma.

For the first time, she wondered if she hadn't made a mistake.

THIRTY-SEVEN

Lake Titicaca, February 1536

He heard the sound of glass breaking, of crystal tinkling, of shouts and laughter. Then an icy chill came over his body. Everything went red. The pain was excruciating, as though he had been caught in a workman's vise. He wanted to cry out, but his voice produced no sound.

Night returned, bringing relief with it.

Again, everything was red, as if he were swimming in a sea of his own blood. Perhaps he was in the process of being born: he felt as though he were being carried in a liquid, enveloped in its protective bubble. The red grew deeper, more intense. He heard the laughter and the crystal again. He felt a bitter cold bite into his head, and he opened his eyes.

His teeth were chattering and he felt like he couldn't breathe. But he managed to draw in a long breath, and after that he calmed down a little. His vision cleared, and what he saw was wonderful, almost too good to be true.

He was surrounded by blue. What he had taken for crystal was in fact diaphanous water. He was submerged in a vast, icy sea, one surrounded by mountains so high that he couldn't see their peaks.

Gabriel took another breath, shivered, and discovered twenty faces staring at him intensely, including those of women and children. They looked deeply amused and heartily satisfied. Some were in the water with him, others were standing on the shore nearby. They came up to him and stretched out their hands toward him. He worried that he had landed in some supernatural world, and he wanted to get up and run.

His feet struck sand and stones at the bottom of the icy water, and he managed to stand. The children's laughter grew more intense, as though this feat of his gratified them amazingly. Gabriel turned around. He saw the peaceful half-moon of a sandy beach by a creek. A few houses stood next to it. He saw trees that looked like pines, and others that could have been olives. For a moment he thought that he must have been dreaming of his native land in Spain. His heart beat joyously. He wanted to run to the shore, but his muscles wouldn't carry him. He collapsed with a splash after only three steps, causing another outburst of laughter.

He gathered his strength, got on his hands and knees, and crawled forward through the shallow water, his beard trailing in it. But soon he felt hands reaching for him and supporting him. They belonged to perfumed young women with long, oiled hair. He found them to be real, very real, and very beautiful, and he found that he was as naked as the day he was born. He shook himself free and tried to cover up his nakedness, causing another hearty outburst of laughter. Eventually they managed to carry him up onto the beach.

A small, stocky man sat there observing him. He looked friendly and serene. His long hair hung loosely over his shoulders. His hands were disproportionately big and strong. He greeted Gabriel with a nod as the young women lay him down on the sand. Only then did Gabriel realize who the man was.

"Katari!" he cried, then immediately stopped. He didn't recognize his own voice.

"Greetings to you, friend of the *Coya Camaquen*," replied Katari quietly.

"Please, tell me which world we're in."

In reply, Katari silently opened his right hand and revealed a small black stone in his palm. He flicked his wrist and launched the stone into the air. It hung in the air for a few seconds, defying gravity for an unnaturally long moment before falling back into his palm.

Gabriel watched this, then gazed about at the surrounding landscape.

It was a place both of this world and of another, set in the present moment and in its parallel in time. Katari grinned at him and said gently:

"Welcome to the world."

Gabriel was lying on a pile of finely woven *mantas*. A woman was patiently smearing a balm over his body. The unguent warmed him and loosened up his muscles, which felt as though they had melted like snow in the sun.

They were outdoors, just above the beach where he had regained consciousness. The bay before him could easily have been taken for a Mediterranean one were it not for the dozens of agricultural terraces lining it, and the similarity moved him deeply.

A number of boats of a design completely unfamiliar to him lay sheltered from the wind in the bay. Some were small, others large enough to carry twenty passengers, and all of them were designed as rafts rather than as hulls. Fishermen came and went from them as though they were walking on water, which was the vision Gabriel had had in his unconsciousness. What most surprised him, though, were the materials with which they were built. Their bodies were not made of wood or their sails of canvas, but of a clever assembly of yellow reeds.

What Gabriel had taken to be a sea was in fact a lake. But it was a lake of such vast proportions that its farthest shore could not be seen. The horizon to the north disappeared into a thick bank of fog. To the east, the sparkling slopes of the highest mountains Gabriel had ever seen stood beyond a steep and arid shore, and he could see their snowy peaks reflected in the calm water below them. To the west and south, the slopes were covered in agricultural terraces as far as the eye could see. These rose high onto the peaks without a break between one and the next, and they formed a giant tapestry of rich, velvety green, the folds of which, supple and silky, fell gently down the mountainsides into the blue abyss of the lake. It was as though the mountains were created not by some divine will but by vast numbers of men, who had raised them terrace by terrace and wall by wall until they soared into the sky.

The sheer grandeur and beauty of the landscape completely absorbed Gabriel, and as he contemplated it, uncertain whether he was truly awake or not, he became oblivious to the caresses that were bringing his body back to life.

"This lake is called *Titicaca*," explained Katari, squatting a few paces away, "and it's here that the world envisioned by Viracocha was born. Those mountains that you see, the strongest and the biggest, those are called Apu Ancohuma and Apu Illampu, and they were the first beings to be born here. The Lord Mountains saw you come back to life today, and they're rejoicing."

Gabriel looked at Katari to make sure that he wasn't making game of him. But the Inca Master of Stones was contemplating the snow-

capped peaks with an earnest expression on his face. He was fiddling
with the black stone that stayed with him always.

"You are on an island," he continued. "The very island where Inti, on
the day he was born, emerged from the sacred rock before rising into the
sky. There's another island over there, behind that hill. It's a smaller
island than this one, and that is where our Mother the Moon rested the
day she was born. Just as you are doing here today."

Now Gabriel sensed a slight degree of irony in Katari's tone and in
his expression. The young woman nursing him, clearly unencumbered
by any Spanish sense of modesty, was now massaging the cheeks of his
buttocks so firmly that Gabriel felt like a mollycoddled baby.

"Must she really palpate me thus?" he asked.

"It's for the best," said Katari, amused. "You spent many moons completely immobile. If you want to be able to stand without feeling great
pain, then you need to be massaged a lot. But don't worry about your
modesty. This girl is familiar with your nakedness."

Gabriel ignored the girl's smile, and pushed away her hand when she
tried to add substance to Katari's words.

"Katari, I must return to Cuzco as soon as possible!"

The Master of Stones uttered a little laugh.

"You won't be able to for at least another moon. You no longer have
a horse to carry you. You'll have to walk. You'll need all your strength."

"That's no good. I must leave sooner."

"If you're worried about the *Coya Camaquen*'s safety, then you
needn't," said Katari gently. "She's fine. She's living in a city in the mountains that the Strangers in Cuzco don't know about."

Gabriel propped himself up to look at Katari. The girl paused her
massage.

"You said 'Strangers in Cuzco,' Katari. Is that because you don't want
to hurt my feelings or offend my pride? No one knows better than I do
how evil those people are. A terrible madness now plagues those whom
Governor Pizarro brought here. Blood and gold are their only goals, the
only things they think about, and their very reasons for being. They can
no longer tell good from evil. They can no longer tell what is human
from what is base. Their madness terrifies me and, I can promise you, it
isn't mine."

"I have observed them," said Katari gravely. "They are worse than animals because animals are never cruel for no reason, and animals have no knowledge of slavery, and animals kill only to feed themselves. But it's true that you aren't like them. If you were, then I doubt the *Coya Camaquen* would hold you in such high regard."

"Thank you."

"I can tell good from evil in this world, in my world."

"There's going to be a war, isn't there?"

"No doubt."

"Anamaya must get away from Cuzco," murmured Gabriel.

Katari shook his head and said:

"No, the *Coya Camaquen* cannot go far from Emperor Manco's side. She is going to free him, then help him run the war. Anamaya is the Son of the Sun's only source of direction. She's the only one left who can hear the Ancestors speaking to us. Villa Oma, whom you were pursuing, is no longer a real sage. He has become a mere warrior bent on vengeance."

Gabriel said nothing for a moment, absorbing everything that the Master of Stones had said. Two things, at least, relieved his anxiety: Anamaya was alive, and far from the Governor's brothers.

"How did you come to save me?" he asked suddenly. "How did you find me in that hell, that sea of salt?"

Katari's laugh was almost tender.

"As for that, you must thank Anamaya, not me. She had a vision, and in it she saw you dying in the salt desert. A *chaski* told me of it, and I set out to find you. You were almost in the Other World when I did. We had to look after you here for many moons to make sure that your soul didn't leave your body."

"I've been asleep for many moons?" murmured Gabriel, greatly surprised. "But I feel like I've been asleep since only yesterday! I remember when I fell. I remember my horse dying, and I remember watching my own shadow refuse to go on. I remember my thirst as well, and the burns on my skin. But . . ."

He looked at his hands and arms. He felt his shoulders, glistening with oil and still being massaged by the servant girl.

"My skin has recovered!" he said a little nervously. "I am intact. It's as though I dreamed the whole thing and that I never crossed that hellish sea of salt."

Katari's dark pupils glowed with bemusement. He launched his black stone into the air once again. And once again Gabriel thought he saw it hang a moment too long at the top of its curve before falling back into the Master of Stones's palm.

"You slept for many moons," he confirmed, "and it was necessary for you to do so because the salt had started desiccating you from the inside and you were turning into a mummy. Had you woken up, the pain would have been so unbearable that you would have died straightaway. So I made you drink herbs that kept you asleep. Slowly, very slowly, we put the water back into your body. Right up to the day when you woke up and crawled out of the water!"

Katari laughed with pride at having saved a life. He motioned to the servant girl, who finally finished her massage and handed Gabriel a yellow *unku*. He slipped it on. He had trouble getting his beard through the neck hole, and the young woman helped him with particular gentleness.

"I need a shave," grumbled Gabriel, embarrassed. "I hate wearing a beard."

"You'll upset all the women on the island if you do," joked Katari. "They're very partial to the gold hairs on your face. They think that you're a gift from the Mountains, and that soon all men will look like you. If you lose your hair, I'll have to cure them from a malady far more serious than yours!"

At last, Gabriel smiled. He extended his hand toward the Master of Stones and said:

"I owe you a lot, Katari, my friend. I don't know how I'm going to be able to repay you."

Katari took his hand firmly in his own.

"There's nothing to repay in this world or the next. We have what we have to give it away, my friend, and to give it away again."

Katari was right about everything.

When Gabriel shaved off his beard, all the women on the island cried for a week and hid their faces in their hands whenever they crossed his path. As for being able to walk, at first all he could manage was ten paces, and he had to labor every day until he got to twenty, then fifty. He was as worn out and exhausted as if he had just climbed the highest Apu in the mountains.

But after only about ten days, he was able to walk slowly along the lakeshore for an hour with not too much trouble. Soon his walks led him farther and farther astray, and he discovered all the island's wonderful sights, including the vast esplanade overlooking the beach of his "rebirth." Trees broke the sharpness of its edge, and herds of llamas grazed on it in utter peace.

He gradually came to experience for himself the almost supernatural power of the high mountains to the east. Their deep valleys and huge peaks surged from the stillness of the sleepy lake. But they also seemed to contain a latent threat, as though in some great, prodigious movement, they might drag the entire earth into the abyss of nothingness.

After two weeks, Gabriel managed to climb the highest hill on the island, and from there he was afforded a staggering view of its western aspect. There wasn't a llama or a single corn or potato terrace to be seen. What little vegetation that survived there was dismal and almost doleful in appearance. The wind tore away at the bushes, whipped the grass, and polished the stones until they shone.

From time to time, Gabriel examined the great Sacred Rock and Inti's temple on the other side of the island, although he was careful never to get too close, for fear of arousing suspicion. The inhabitants of the lakeshore all congregated there on sacred days.

His walks grew longer with each passing day, and Anamaya occupied his entire mind. His need to be with her became increasingly urgent. With his eyes fixed on the lake's horizon, he tried to conjure up each part of her body and to remember the details of every moment that they had spent together. He half-hoped that the wind out of the west would carry her scent to him, that he would hear her words transported on its airs. He looked at no other woman on the island, instead living only with the image he carried of his beloved.

At night she came to him in his dreams, and when he woke with a start, his arms grasping at the emptiness beside him, her absence became even more brutal and unbearable.

The island itself seemed to have a quality that protected his love for her, a love that at times cut his legs out from under him far more effectively than the fatigue he was recovering from. He saw himself living out the rest of his days with Anamaya here, living in one of the houses by the beach, at last fulfilling the destiny that binds a man and a woman together in love.

He made something of a ritual of it. Every evening, at sunset, he sat on the same rock facing vast Titicaca and daydreamed about what their life would be like in this wonderful and tranquil place.

One night he caught a glimpse of a bright green flash on the horizon. A fearful shiver ran down his spine. But he couldn't deny what he had seen. The sun had just disappeared behind the western peaks, and a crimson bank of clouds was suspended above them. He saw long green trails streaked through the darkening sky. He sat up, expecting to see some sign that the world was about to change irrevocably. He jumped with surprise when he heard a voice behind him hum:

> *The Sun,*
> *The Moon,*
> *Day and night,*
> *Spring and winter,*
> *Stones and mountains,*
> *Corn and* cantutas.
> *Nothing exists without a reason, O Viracocha.*
> *The shores of Titicaca are the source of everything.*
> *It was here, O Viracocha, that you held the rod of origin,*
> *And it is here in the Titicaca that I am with my soul mate,*
> *The soul from above and from below.*
> *O Viracocha, it is your will*
> *That he who leaves Titicaca*
> *Is already on the road home.*

It was the girl who had looked after him so well over the past few weeks. She smiled at him, but her eyes were sad. She pointed at the sky where the green streaks, now gone, had been.

"When the sky becomes green," she said, "it means that Viracocha is bestowing peace upon the human race. Viracocha is telling you that he loves you."

She took Gabriel's hand and squeezed it tenderly.

"It is time for you to go, Stranger. The lake has begun showing you that which your eyes do not see. One day you will wish to return here because although your skin is white and your hair gold, Viracocha has recognized you. You come from his rod of origin, and a soul from below waits for you here."

After having spoken these strange words to an astonished Gabriel she squeezed his hand again and hummed:

> *The Sun,*
> *The Moon,*
> *Day and night,*
> *Spring and winter,*
> *Stones and mountains,*
> *Corn and* cantutas.
> *O Viracocha, it is your will*
> *That he who leaves Titicaca*
> *Is already on the road home.*

THIRTY-EIGHT

Calca, April 1536

In Calca's temples, the priests and soothsayers had been pressing the oracles for answers for two days now. Quantities of coca leaves had been burned, and the hearts of both black and white llamas had been closely examined. In the stone tower outside the *huaca*, those who counted time endlessly went over their calculations, and in the warehouses, the *quipu* knotters attentively manipulated their bundles of knots. The generals appointed by Villa Oma took stock of the number of weapons and supplies amassed in the secret *tambos*, and tallied the number of warriors recruited.

The royal *cancha* had been a hive of activity for the past two days. The servants prepared a hundred different dishes, the virgins wove piles of fabulous tunics, ready for the Inca to wear, and his wives and concubines spent hours grooming themselves.

For two days the men, women, and children of Calca had been fasting and drinking only water, no matter what physical condition they were in.

All this because two days previously, Emperor Manco had been freed. And that morning, in the burgeoning dawn, trumpets had sounded throughout the valley. From the slopes surrounding Calca, everyone could see the cortege forming around the Emperor's palanquin. They could see a hundred virgins sweeping away the dust ahead of him and they could hear a hundred others singing and drums rolling. They could see a thousand warriors wearing immaculate tunics and carrying bows or clubs following him.

In the royal *cancha*, Anamaya ordered the Sacred Double to be placed in the center of the courtyard. Offerings of coca, food, and *chicha* were spread out all around him.

Then the heads of the Cuzco clans and some provincial ones as well came to pay their respects to the golden Sacred Double before taking their places at the edges of the courtyard, each one standing behind a heavy rectangular stone. The wives and concubines followed and stood in a row a few paces back from the royal stool, which was set on a long *cumbi* woven from bat hair.

Everyone knew his place, and their faces revealed their pride. Not since Manco had been crowned with the *mascapaicha* had so much pomp and ceremony been witnessed. It seemed to everyone present that the glory of the Empire of the Four Cardinal Directions was at last restored, and that it was as intact as if the Strangers had never set foot on the land created by Viracocha.

Anamaya's face was radiant, and her every movement was suffused with a dignity that inspired the warriors watching her.

But she had to hide the lake of melancholy and waiting in which her heart was drowning.

Before the sun had reached its zenith, the sound of trumpets and drums echoed from between Calca's walls. The wives and concubines prostrated themselves in the royal courtyard. Then the Lords and generals picked up the heavy stones at their feet. Each man placed one on his shoulders and, bowed under the weight of the stones, waited for Emperor Manco to arrive.

The hundred virgins stopped singing. The trumpets and drums let out a final flourish.

Now complete silence prevailed over the city as each person held his or her breath.

Indeed, the silence was so complete that everyone heard the rustling of Manco's very fine *cumbi* as he stepped out of his litter, and even the swish of the feathers with which the virgins swept the flagstones before him.

And everyone heard him clearly when he touched Anamaya's shoulder and said:

"You may stand up, *Coya Camaquen*. Stand and look at me."

Anamaya stood. She had to hold back her tears when she saw Manco, saw with her own eyes that he was truly alive and free. He seemed as radiant as the sun itself, and the gold on his helmet and tunic was as resplendent as the Sacred Double's.

"I am overjoyed to see you, Emperor," Anamaya burst out. "I've missed you terribly. We've all missed you."

Manco smiled faintly before turning away from her to look at the Lords bent under their stones. Only then was Anamaya shocked by his appearance.

Now he seemed as dark and as hollow as night. He was terribly thin. His cheeks were hollow and his lips were slighter than before. He now had crow's feet around his eyes. And his eyes themselves looked like they belonged to a man whose spirit had retreated so deep within himself that life barely showed in his pupils.

Everything that was young, mettlesome, and alive had been wiped off Manco's face. It was hard to believe that this was the same man who, as a boy, won the great race at the *huarachiku.*

The Strangers had left the terrible scar of their torments on his face, and it had been frozen into place by the icy breath of hatred.

He raised his hand and touched Anamaya's cheek with his fingertips. She shuddered as he touched her, and she had to suppress an urge to shrink away.

"I too am happy to see you again, sister Anamaya. I know that I owe you much."

His words were warm, but they were spoken in a cold and distant tone. Anamaya could feel Villa Oma's burning gaze from behind Manco.

Manco drew his hand away and whispered:

"You find me changed, don't you?"

Anamaya hesitated before replying:

"No, my Lord. You just need rest, good food, and a little peace."

Manco smiled a cruel smile.

"No, *Coya Camaquen,* you're wrong. I just need to go to war."

"The war is waiting only for you, Emperor."

She smiled at him. She felt more alone than ever before.

"Anamaya!"

Anamaya didn't hear the dwarf's call the first time.

The moon was high in the night sky. The festive noise of celebrating rose up from the royal *cancha.* The Lords were drinking heavily, both to steel themselves for the battle and to mock their enemies. They shouted more than they spoke, especially when they told the stories of past battles and of the Ancestors' glorious victories.

Anamaya, standing alone outside the courtyard, watched them from afar. Their faces looked both childish and terrifying in the torchlight.

"Anamaya!"

This time she turned around and saw the dwarf's diminutive profile against the corner of the building. He motioned to her to come closer.

"Why are you hiding?" she asked him.

"So no one sees me," the dwarf whispered hoarsely, grabbing hold of her cape. "Bend down so you can hear me."

"Why all this subterfuge?"

"Bend down!"

She complied, sighing wearily. When her face was level with the dwarf's, he whispered:

"He's here."

Anamaya twitched. She reprimanded herself for the thought that crossed her mind. She forced herself to frown as she asked him:

"Who are you talking about?"

"About him. He's here."

The dwarf laughed mischievously, but when it became clear that Anamaya refused to understand, he grumbled:

"Don't play the fool. *He's* here. The Puma."

She gripped the dwarf's hand as though her legs were about to give way. She closed her eyes and tried to gather herself before asking:

"Where?"

"I put him in a wool warehouse. It's the safest place. I'll take you there."

The dwarf indicated a basket beside him.

"I've brought you a black cape. You'll be less visible leaving the *cancha*."

Anamaya held his arm.

"Chimbu . . ."

"Why, Princess, it must be serious for you to call me by my real name!"

"I'm frightened."

*   *   *

For a moment she doubted that it was really him.

He was wearing a yellow tunic, peasant's trousers, and a four-cornered bonnet, like those commonly worn around Titicaca, covered his shorn blond hair.

He stood a few paces away from her, took off his hat, and laughed nervously.

"I know I must look strange in these clothes," he murmured, "but they allowed me to get here unnoticed. The hardest part was getting the dwarf's attention."

But Anamaya wasn't listening: his laugh was still echoing inside her, fanning a flame of happiness. She took a few more steps, and now all the stiff self-restraint appropriate to a *Coya Camaquen* disappeared in a flash.

He was still laughing when he wrapped his arms around her. She extinguished his laugh with her lips and melted into his warmth.

Then she brusquely broke the embrace and stared at him by the poor light of an oil lamp. Now she was the one to laugh uncontrollably, and she caressed him and danced around him as she said over and over:

"You're alive! You're alive!"

He caught her and started kissing her neck almost violently before moving down to her breasts and kissing those as though he wanted to feast on her skin and her scent. Between kisses he whispered:

"Yes, I'm alive, but only because of you! I was already dead!"

They ran their hands over each other's faces as though their long, long separation had made them blind. Their desire, frustrated for too long, and for too long existing only in their imaginations, now fired their loins so much that their caresses became almost brutal. Anamaya pulled Gabriel's tunic off and ran her fingers over the birthmark on his shoulder.

"Puma," she moaned, "my puma."

He took her up in his arms and carried her to a pile of raw wool. There he went over and over her body as though discovering it for the first time. They lost themselves in one another, fusing together, flesh to flesh, belly to belly, breath to breath.

Far away by a mountain lake, Katari threw his black stone into the air for them. It stayed suspended in the air, stopping time so that their love could find a moment of refuge amid the chaos.

*   *   *

Afterward, the timidity common to young lovers arose between them. They helped each other find words between caresses, telling one another the experiences that each had suffered during the months apart. The gravity of their situation slowly dawned upon them, and they were eager to sustain the lightness of their happiness.

Eventually Gabriel declared:

"The dwarf told me about everything that happened in Cuzco to Manco and you. . . ."

She didn't reply but closed her eyes, entwining her fingers in his. She surrendered herself to his caresses once again, giving him her breasts, her belly, and her thighs.

Gabriel continued stroking her for a while. But then he closed his hand around hers and whispered:

"I know about Gonzalo. I know what he tried to do. I promise you that I'll kill him for it."

"It's already disappeared from my soul," she replied. "It's as forgotten as though it never happened."

But the tears pearling up beneath her eyelids belied her words. Gabriel drank them with little kisses.

"I think I know who the Puma is," he said, deeply moved. "I saw him . . ."

Anamaya said nothing.

"I saw him in the shadows and by the light of the sun, in the night and in the stones. I saw him in your lake of origin where I was reborn. On my way to you, I realized that the Puma was within me, that I am the Puma. And my fear left me."

Anamaya remained silent. Nothing she could say could bring anything more to the universe. And yet none of what he had said had truly relieved her of the loneliness that was within her, and that had always been there.

"We're leaving," he said, his eyes shining. "I came here to get you, to take you with me, away from this chaos. We're going to live on the island in Titicaca, where we'll find peace and where no one will be able to destroy our happiness, no one, not the Pizarros, and not Manco. . . ."

She stiffened and glanced away from him. She heard an odd sound rise out of her throat, almost a sob. Wordlessly, she took Gabriel's face in her hands and kissed him for as long as it took for desire to return to her.

She gave herself to him more slowly this time, as though she were trying to banish the reality of the visible world, and to become a lake of promises.

It was a long night. But day follows night, and soon the light of dawn would rise over the distant hills.

It was a night that they wished would never end. But its end was near.

They were lying side by side and cheek to cheek, naked and perfect.

"I must stay with Manco," said Anamaya finally.

"No!"

The cry had burst involuntarily from his mouth, and she placed her hand over it tenderly.

"Gabriel, we're going to war. We *must* go to war, otherwise there will be no more Sons of the Sun."

Gabriel looked away from her.

"You can't stay here," she continued. "You can't stay with me. Villa Oma wants you dead."

Gabriel nodded, a look of cruel irony on his face as his eyes welled up with tears.

"I came to you with love, and you turn me away! I travel all this way, and you turn me away! I tell you the things that I feel in the depths of my heart, but they mean nothing to you. You talk to me about your war . . . your people respond to the madness of mine with their own!"

She hesitated. She pulled her black cape up over her shoulders.

"You are the Puma, and you are the only man who can reach me in this world or the other."

"But you'd rather I left for the other!"

"Please, stop it!"

Gabriel began trembling uncontrollably, and his movements were those of an inconsolable child. She tried to hold him to her, but he pushed her away angrily. When she turned away, he took her by the throat, he scratched her, he held her tight, he caressed her . . . and then he pushed her away again even more brutally, as though he needed to be violent to release the words burning in his mind.

"You cannot win this war. You're weak, and your world is collapsing.

Our conquest is unjust, I know. It has been accomplished with crimes of which I'm deeply ashamed. But you will lose just as you did at Cajamarca and everywhere else. Don't you see?"

"We must have this war because the mountains and our Ancestors need us to fight, otherwise they will disappear into the void. And I must be at Manco's side. That is my proper place."

Gabriel stood and uttered a cry of rage. He pushed aside the hanging over the warehouse's door. The cold outside made him shiver.

"In that case, we're going to fight against one another."

"You don't have to," she murmured.

"If your proper place is at Manco's side and not at mine," said Gabriel with icy calm, "then it's because you think I'm a 'Stranger' like the others. Well then, my proper place is with the Strangers."

They stared at one another for a long time, both searching for some sign of hope in the other's eyes.

"I must fight this war," murmured Anamaya at last. "I must, don't you see? Otherwise Emperor Huayna Capac might as well have never held my hand!"

A terrible calm filled Gabriel, as though all his rage had disappeared like a receding tide.

"Very well. I understand. I don't know what it means, but I understand it to the very depths of my soul. And I accept it."

His calm rattled Anamaya more than his cries, more than his words of outrage. Now he really was the Puma, the one she had been waiting for. And at this moment of their separation, they were as close as two beings who had once been only one in the lake of origins could be, like twin souls reunited after having crossed an ocean of stars.

"I hope . . ." he began. "I hope against hope, I hope against this war. It's so difficult, so very difficult . . ."

His voice broke, and he cleared his throat before continuing:

". . . It's so difficult to leave you after everything I have gone through to reach you. . . ."

"I love you."

Gabriel nodded. Tears blurred his vision. He approached her and this time it was he who took her head in his hands and kissed her on the mouth.

Later, during the time of darkness, in the din of battle, amid the shriek of sling stones and arrows, when he would lose all sense of the meaning of life, he would use, as a defense against loneliness and despair, the memory of how soft her lips had been when he had kissed her after she had pronounced those last words to him—and they would provide him with the utterly illogical certainty that in every death there is always another birth.

GLOSSARY

Acllahuasi—House of the Chosen Women (*acllas*).

Añaco—A long, straight tunic reaching the ankles worn by women.

Apu—Quechua word meaning "Lord" or "Governor"; also used as a title preceding the names of mountain divinities.

Ayllos—A throwing weapon similar to a bola; it consists of three leather strips ballasted with rocks, designed to entangle the legs of a running quarry.

Balsa—A wooden raft made of balsa wood.

Borla (Spanish) or *mascapaicha* (Quechua)—Along with the *llautu* and the feathered *curiguingue,* this woolen fringe makes up the royal headpiece of the Sapa Inca.

Cancha—An open inner courtyard; also a collection of three or four buildings around such a courtyard, forming a single living area.

Chaco—A large hunt in which hundreds of beaters flush out game.

Chaquiras—Small pearls from pink shells (*mullus*) that are made into necklaces or woven into ceremonial costumes.

Chaski—Runners who carry messages by relay.

Chicha—A ceremonial beverage; also a fermented beer, usually made from maize.

Chuño—Naturally dehydrated potatoes that keep for months.

Chuspa—Small woven pouch decorated with religious motifs and used to carry coca leaves.

Collcas—Circular or rectangular buildings made up of a single room and used as warehouses to store foodstuffs, weavings, weapons, and luxuries.

Coya—Title accorded to the Inca's principal wife.

Cumbi—The finest quality of woven cloth, usually made from vicuña wool.

Curaca—A local chief or official.

Curiguingue—A small falcon; its black-and-white feathers were used to decorate the Sapa Inca's headpiece.

Gacha—Soup or stew made from a base of cereal or starch; one of the mainstays of the medieval diet.

Hatunruna—Quechua word meaning "peasant."

Huaca—Quechua word meaning "sacred." By extension, any location or sanctuary in which a divinity is kept.

Huara—Shorts. Boys were given a pair of these during the initiation rite called the *huarachiku.*

Ichu—A type of wild grass that grows at high altitudes and is used mainly to thatch roofs.

Inti Raymi—One of the major festivals of the Inca calendar; occurs during the winter solstice.

Kallanka—A long building with doors that usually open onto the square of an administrative center.

Kapak—Chief.

Llautu—Long, woolen plaits wrapped several times around the wearer's head to form a headpiece.

Manta—Spanish word meaning "blanket," but used to denote the cape worn by Inca men (*llacolla*) and women (*lliclla*).

Mascapaicha—See *Borla.*

Mullus—Shells from the Pacific Coast, usually of a red or pink color. They were widely used during Inca religious rites, either in their natural state or after having been worked.

Pachacuti—A great upheaval signaling the beginning of a new era.

Panaca—Lineage from an Inca sovereign.

Plateros—Spanish word denoting those metalworkers who specialized in precious metals.

Quinua—An Andean cereal rich in protein.

Quipu—A device of colored strings in which knots were tied. The knots served as a mnemonic system for keeping records.

Sapa Inca—Literally "Unique Lord." The title of the Inca sovereign.

Tambos—Inns set at regular intervals along the Empire's roads. In such places the traveler could find food and shelter, as well as fresh clothes, all provided by the state.

Tiana—A small bench or stool reserved exclusively for the Inca and for *curacas,* which was a symbol of power.

Tocacho—A tree, fifteen to twenty-five feet high, that resists the cold.

Tocapu—A geometric motif with symbolic meanings used to decorate Inca weavings.

Tumi—A ceremonial knife, the bronze blade of which is set at a ninety-degree angle to the handle.

Tupu—A long needle made of gold, silver, bronze, or copper, used to clasp a cape, or *manta*, together.

Unku—A sleeveless, knee-length tunic worn by men.

Ushnu—A small pyramid set on the square of an Inca settlement and reserved for the use of those in power.

Viscacha—A rodent of the genus *Marmota*, with a tail similar to a squirrel's, which lives in scree.

Look for the compelling conclusion to
the *Incas* trilogy, *The Light of Machu Picchu*,
available in March 2003.

And also look for Book 1 of this
captivating trilogy, *The Puma's Shadow*.

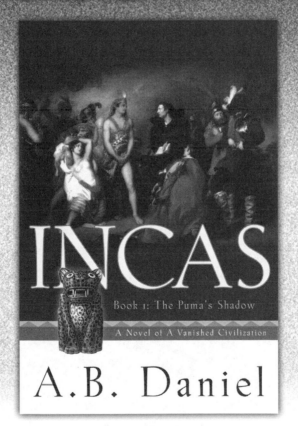

0-7434-3274-6 • $14.00

SCRIBNER
PAPERBACK
FICTION
A Division of Simon & Schuster
A VIACOM COMPANY